Guilty
Tiger

Chris Brown

Published in 2012 by FeedARead.com Publishing –
Arts Council funded.

A CIP catalogue record for this title is available from
the British Library.

Designed and artworked by Chris Brown and
Gary Mattock. Cover image courtesy of iStock.

Dedicated to my parents – Hilda Joan and Frederick Charles Brown. RIP.

As Fred always used to say: *'You're not a bad 'un. You're not a good 'un either, but you're not a bad 'un.'*

I always took that as a compliment, thanks Dad.

Acknowledgements

After much thought and deep deliberation I've decided not to acknowledge anyone for the idea, concept or ultimate writing and delivery of *Guilty Tiger* – it was all down to me... and a little help from Gary Mattock, Tom Henry and my old mate Dave Ward – oh and Keith Richards – to you four, many thanks.

CHAPTER ONE

S ITTING in trap three, trying to put off the meeting for as long as possible, Steve Allen feigned disinterest as he read the article in the *Daily Mail* – 'Ten tell-tale signs that you're going through a mid-life crisis':

1. No longer 'knowing' the person staring back at you in the mirror.

This is a pretty sure sign that somewhere along the line you have lost connection with the essence of who you are. Getting back into alignment with your true, authentic self requires some honest soul searching, to find the answers to fundamental questions about what is important to you and what really matters.

2. Worrying about where your life is going.

You may well feel you're in no-man's land – you realise there is definitely no going back but there is no clear way forward. If you don't know where you're headed, any road will take you there – so, consult your inner map and make decisions about where you WANT to go. That way, you'll arrive at your destination of choice, rather than simply ending up 'somewhere'.

3. Feeling frustrated with just about everything.

When that nagging voice of dissatisfaction simply refuses to be silenced, then maybe it's time to listen to it! Don't just hope it will eventually go away, but ask yourself instead, 'What am I NOT doing that is causing this frustration?'

4. Experiencing feelings of regret.

Dwelling on what can't be undone keeps you locked into the past rather than focusing on the future. Learning from painful regrets and using them as a catalyst for change will help you move on and put the past where it belongs – behind you.

5. Focussing on what you are losing.

It feels as though you are standing on shifting sands, that your best years are behind you and that everything is changing – but not for the better. Things are changing certainly, but not ending. Remind yourself of what you have now and be open to all possibilities in readiness for the next new chapter in your life.

6. Feeling almost 'invisible'.

You may feel stripped of your identity and purpose and find it increasingly difficult to be 'seen' when you no longer attract instant admiration. Finding a new identity and a new visibility comes through learning what YOU value in yourself, what you have to offer others and feeling comfortable with the person underneath the facade.

7. Thinking that time is running out.

Midlife is that time when you metaphorically turn a corner and see the finishing post for the first time! Use your new awareness of time as a precious and limited commodity, to bring a sense of urgency to your dreams and provide the impetus to make them happen.

8. Questioning the meaning of life.

Midlife has been defined as the time when you reach the top of the ladder only to find it's leaning against the wrong wall. If you keep asking yourself 'Is this it?', then chances are your ladder is indeed against the wrong wall. Finding the right wall comes through redefining success in your own terms, so you make choices that activate and focus your life force.

9. Feeling trapped.

Somewhere along the way, various dreams and goals may have been silently shelved and before you know it, you feel hemmed in by thoughts of what life 'could have been'. What's the first thing we do when we feel trapped? We look for ways to escape! If you feel the urge to do a 'Reggie Perrin' or a 'Shirley Valentine' remember, Reggie and Shirley ultimately realised that what they were looking for wasn't escape – it was change.

10. Wanting to make some changes but not know where to begin.

Feeling overwhelmed saps your power and keeps you stuck, helpless and fearful of making the 'wrong' choices. The way to move out of the paralysis is to stop 'getting ready' and start 'doing'. Take responsibility for making change happen, no matter how small and remind yourself how good it feels to be in control.'

'What a load of old bollocks,' he said out loud, startling the occupant of trap two. He then flushed, folded the paper and unbolted the door, time to face the music...

Normally he quite liked Fridays – end of the working week and all that. 'Dress down Fridays' meant one thing – the fragrant young fillies in the office would dispense with their austere power suits in favour of sexy little outfits and tight, figure hugging T-shirts. Flitting around the office like skittish butterflies on a warm summer's afternoon they succeeded in making him very happy indeed. He himself had also reluctantly participated in the ritual, but he never felt right, night quite able to carry off the T-shirt and grubby trainer look – he left that to the young bucks with their spiky gelled hair and those horrendous diarrhoea coloured skinny jeans that they all seemed to wear. Steve had standards, high standards.

He'd tried the casual look and received a few wry smiles from those in the know with his *Stax* and *Clash* tees, but he decided to call it a day after wearing his favourite *Trojan* emblazoned sweatshirt – tiring of having to explain to the uninitiated that it was a record label and not a brand of American prophylactics.

But this Friday he had a knot in his stomach due to the 'two o'clock' teleconference booked in to 'firm up' the latest campaign, a campaign that made him feel distinctly uncomfortable.

The shape of the bird was obvious enough – there was even a grimace on its face impregnated on the glass. He could make out the wings and the tail feathers very clearly and yes, there it was – a definite trace of greasy kebab with jalapeno pepper and maybe even a hint of chilli sauce. No doubt the bird had evacuated its arse when it impacted the fourth floor window.

'So are you *comfortable* with this or not Steve?'

Steve struggled to respond. It was overly warm in the office and mid Friday afternoon was never conducive to meetings – he mumbled an apology of sorts.

'I was saying are you comfortable with this iteration or do you want to push back – we can touch base later if you like?'

Laura Essex – efficient, gorgeous, brain-dead Laura – looked at him questioningly. She was the latest in a long line of eager, ambitious and ever-so-fuckable campaign managers that Steve had to deal with, thankfully Laura did

4

not disappoint on the 'Dress down Friday' look, he was not only distracted by the plight of the deceased seabird but he found himself addressing her superb chest as it exploded out of a cute low-cut Hollister top.

'Comfortable? Um yeah I guess so,' he shifted position and gathered his thoughts, 'but do we really need to discuss once more if we need three people in the canoe? You – sorry we – are trying to flog a loan that these poor saps can't afford to repay... so no, I don't feel entirely *comfortable* with it, since you ask.'

Fiona Mason, a hundred or so miles east along the M4 butted in. She leant into the screen to make her point...

'Well we know it's *facilitating* a loan Steve,' she said, finger jabbing, 'but it's whether you want to challenge it or not? What's the Target Audience Profile? What were the results of the focus group again?' She asked of no one in particular as she leant back into her black leather chair in her office in the Square Mile.

'Look I'm sorry but it's imperative we get sign off today,' she added impatiently. 'I'm only running this up the flag-pole but I'm wondering if the couple should be BEM? Or perhaps have an infant?'

BEM? WTF? Steve flipped through the list of PC-approved abbreviations and acronyms glossary that he kept in his head, BEM – Black and Ethnic Minority. Then there was the sign off, someone would have to sign off the sign off – or it wouldn't get signed off. His head was spinning, his thoughts elsewhere.

'Yeah sure and why not make the kid a spas... sorry paraplegic while you're at it.' He regretted it as soon as he'd said it, the room went quiet. There was a distinct and *un-comfortable* silence.

'Can I have a word offline Steve?' said Fiona from across the ether, 'after this telecon.'

'Sure.' He felt himself redden. Sometimes Skype could mangle conversations – although obviously not this time.

Laura and her colleague 'Teflon' Tom Richards – all *Build a rocket boys* T-shirt and those diarrhoea-coloured jeans, left the room, leaving him alone to ponder the bird's and his own fate, once more.

'What the fuck was that all about?' The echoey, disembodied voice filled the room again.

'Sorry Fiona, it's been a long week. I just get frustrated with all this "pushing back" and "challenging" all the time. Why can't they speak fucking English – and I've touched base more times than Babe *fucking* Ruth.'

'Same old belligerent, tell it like it is Steve Allen eh? Look I know where you're coming from but there's no need for that kind of derogatory language – not this day and age. Times have changed Steve, we both know that.'

He knew Fiona was right. She was not much younger than him but she seemed to have grown up in a different era – being able to pick low hanging fruit while taking a helicopter view like the best of the Suits. She'd found it easier to cope with the transition, it was patently obvious that Steve had not.

'I know, I know,' he protested, 'like I said I'm sorry, it won't happen again.'

'It had better not,' said Fiona 'or those *fuckwits* in HR will get to know about it and it will be on your record.'

Steve wasn't shocked with Fiona's language, she could swear like an Irish priest – and drink like one when the occasion arose.

'So fucking sack me,' he mumbled under his breath.

'What was that?' asked Fiona.

'Nothing, nothing. Someone's at the door that's all... What's that?' He queried with his imaginary interlopers. 'You've got a three o'clock booked?'

'Okay Steve. Tell you what, why don't you have an early one, I know you've worked your balls off with this latest campaign, it's nearly all delivered so get off early – surprise Debbie for a change.'

'You sure?'

Not that he needed anyone to give him permission to leave work early. If he wanted to he would, he just never did – just his awkward, truculent way.

'Okay, thanks Fi. Say hi to Barry from me – tell him I hope the Hoops pull it off.'

'I will. Have a great weekend.'

As he exited the lift Laura and Teflon waited for him anxiously. Teflon tentatively took a step forward.

'Hey Steve. Everything er, cool? Wonder if we could firm up the outcome... mate.'

'Outcome?' Steve replied mockingly. 'Here's the thing Tom – I'm fucking off early.' He stared at Tom's T-shirt and tried to make sense of the blue squiggle and the message – he shook his head then glanced at his watch.

'It's way past beer o'clock and I've got an urgent meeting with Mr Wetherspoon. I'm gonna firm up with a few beers – care to join me?' He asked, knowing full well what the answer would be.

'Um, er – no I'll take a raincheck. Perhaps some other time,' replied Teflon nervously.

'Cool,' said Steve with just a hint of sarcasm.

'Totally, absolutely... cool.'

Steve somehow managed to avert his gaze from Laura's impressive breasts that were only just managing to stay in her top. He caught her eye with a pleading look.

'Laura?'

'No, no that's alright Steve. Sorry I'm, I'm meeting um... Katie and Jo in The Front Room later.'

'Shame.'

He genuinely meant it. He realised there was a definite *frisson* between them – he knew, just knew if he pursued it, laid on the charm he could... *one day*, he thought.

Laura blew Steve an exaggerated kiss – secretly she enjoyed his attention. 'In your dreams,' she mouthed as she sashayed away.

As he exited the building he looked up at the office he'd just been in, then back down to the ground where he spotted the crumpled body of the deceased bird with its broken neck. What he saw surprised him – it was no flying rat, no itinerant seagull that rummaged through litter bins after losing its instinct to hunt at sea.

Steve knew his birds – not that he would describe himself as a 'twitcher' – it was just a bit of a hobby he kept secret from his mates, like a lot of things. This was a rare visitor to these shores – a beautiful, black-capped Petrel. How it came to die of a broken neck while choking on a discarded doner kebab in the centre of Bristol he could only guess.

TFIF – Thank Fuck It's Friday – another week over, another week closer to retirement. Was that what it had all come down to? Counting down the days to retirement? He should be counting his blessings – he hasn't a penny of debt to his name so he should be laughing, but he's not – at times he's crying, crying from sheer exhaustion, worry and frustration. To forget his problems Steve binge drinks and snorts cocaine, not a lot, just something for the weekend – it gives him a lift, a kick, a thrill. He's not addicted – yet – but his cravings increase and he gets more agitated as each weekend approaches. His other 'pleasure', although he continually has to remind himself that it is still that, is football. Back in the 1970s he and the rest of his mates, 'The Big Five', battled and consequently made their names on the terraces – they were respected, revered even – but no longer. He would now often go to games on his own, drink on his own and stand on his own, his only excitement now being the half-time Chicken Balti pie. There was no longer a Big Five, it was now a Small One – him.

As well as the drinking and the recreational drugs – which he keeps assuring himself he can give up at any time – he's also addicted to online porn sites. Apart from the cocaine it's the only thing that now delivers the thrill since the buzz of casual Saturday afternoon violence had disappeared from his life.

Steve loves music. But like his football he lives and longs for the past – sounds from his youth and his troubled teenage years: ska, reggae, soul and punk. The rest leaves him cold. He knows his stuff, some might say he's anal, an anorak even. He doesn't care – music soothes his soul and lifts his spirits. Music helped him come to terms with a dark period of his youth when he somehow got involved in rightwing politics – it seemed the done thing at the time, but he quickly regretted it. Music cured him of his phobias, his anxieties and his hatred. At every opportunity he tries to prove the new Steve Allen is not the same as the old Steve Allen, his bigotry has long gone, replaced with a less narrow, less prejudiced mind – on his bad days he still hates, but it's more selective now, he thought it a good compromise, a happy medium, but for all that Steve has a very dark side. Truth be told it's a side he rather likes.

He's just celebrated his fifty-sixth birthday, although celebrate was hardly the appropriate word. At one time his life could be described by those subtitles that accompany feature films being advertised on TV – *contains frequent strong language, scenes of a sexual nature and gratuitous violence.* Now, only the strong language remained.

The job that he hates so much though finances his lifestyle. A top of the range Audi sits gleaming on the driveway of his four-bedroom detached house, he and his adoring wife Debbie enjoy all inclusive adult-only holidays while trendy, designer-labelled clothing adorn their walk-in wardrobes. He's got lucky with investments and timed his dealings to perfection – selling his shares to the greedy and buying from the scared. His two grown-up sons have flown the nest increasing his disposable income, the eldest boy, Sam, is a heating engineer who migrated to Australia with his nurse girlfriend two years previously. The youngest, Harry, has problems though – he's unemployed and lives in a squat on Stokes Croft, somewhere the press dubbed 'Telepathic Heights'.

Harry has served time for petty drug dealing and street crime, but that should be the only blot on Steve's perfect landscape – to the outside world and to his mates in particular he was a top man, he had it all, had it made – Steve Allen was living very nicely on easy street.

But the hard reality of his life won't go away – he suffers from high blood pressure, high cholesterol and a low sex drive. He takes Citalopram to combat his depression, Privastatin to lower his cholesterol and Angiotensin-Converting Enzyme inhibitors to lower his blood pressure – as well as Viagra to combat his 'erectile dysfunction', although he's convinced he's the only man in the country in possession of a packet of the little blue tablets that have gone past their best by date.

For all his health problems he tries to keep himself fit with regular work outs at the gym where he fantasises about having sex with the young black girls who train there. He's self-assured, vain and aware he appeals to younger women – so he thinks – but despite many offers and being tempted on more than one occasion, he's never strayed or been unfaithful to Debbie.

No matter what he thinks or what he keeps telling himself, whether he cares to admit it or not, Steve Allen is in the eye of a storm – a storm of a mid-life crisis.

CHAPTER TWO

H E toyed with going straight to the Moon under Water and meeting the rest of The Big Five, the mates he'd known since his schooldays. He could be there at five, same time as they usually got started, instead of his usual seven when he would be greeted with the inevitable abuse and ritualistic insults.

Only George was another late starter for the 'sesh'. Come hell or high water Gerwazy 'George' Smolinski would have a two-hour workout in the gym before he got to the pub – even then he struggled to drink his orange juice. George Smolinski was known to all and sundry as a bit of a tart.

He decided to take Fiona's advice, be a good boy, get home early and surprise Debbie. She would like that – and the bunch of flowers he bought at Morrisons on the way. *Brownie points – in the fucking bag*. The Big Five could wait, as they always did. He eased the Audi 7 onto the driveway

11

while Marvin Gaye effortlessly sung about the plight of the world on the CD player...

'Picket lines and picket signs.

Don't punish me, with brutality.'

'Forty years on Mr Gaye and fuck all has changed... Twat!' he shouted out loud as he spotted the white van blocking his way.

He then remembered Debbie telling him that 'Brad the Blindman' was fitting the shutters on the French doors leading into the conservatory. He clutched the bunch of tulips, lightly whistled along to *What's going on?* and pushed the door open. Looking into the lounge he noticed the shutters were up.

'Looking good,' he said, 'nice choice Mr A, nice choice.'

He peeked into the kitchen. There was no one around, the house was quiet. He looked through the window into the back garden and glimpsed his two Jack Russell's 'Prince' and 'Buster' sniffing round for squirrels. One day they would catch one – it would serve the little bastards right for digging up his lawn and vandalising his loft. *Nothing but rats in cute little Armani suits*, thought Steve.

He heard a giggle from upstairs and had a sudden vision of those TV programmes that Debbie liked watching so much, where the husband came home early and caught his wife having the living daylights banged out of her by his best friend, he smirked to himself and dismissed the thought immediately...

She giggled again, louder this time. He paused for a second and pondered... *not my Debbie, surely?*... His heart sunk then thumped, he felt sick, dropped the tulips and went through the kitchen to the hallway. He stopped and listened intently, knowing full well what he would find as he ascended the stairs. 'No not my Debbie,' he whispered to himself.

Silently he crept across the landing. *In my own fucking bed, not my Debbie in my own fucking bed...*

He could hear the unmistakable sounds of sex coming from their bedroom, the door was slightly open... *I'll kill the bastard, I'll kill the bitch, after all these years, after all I've done, the fucking, dirty bitch.* He stopped, the animal sounds grew louder, he heard her squeal like he never had before, his heart was in his throat, he was sweating profusely... to his surprise he was also getting aroused.

Sneaking a look through the gap in the door, no more than two inches, he could see the top of both of their heads. She was jerking and arching upwards, she clung on to the headboard making low noises, then whelps, 'Eugh, eugh, eugh' moaned Brad the Blindman.

'Come in me, come in me now, now, now, now!' screamed Debbie.

He could see her full breasts, bigger now than they had ever been in the thirty odd years that he'd known her. They were heaving and bouncing, Brad sucked them, she screamed louder.

'Come on, come on fuck me harder,' she begged him.
'Not yet,' gasped Brad, 'there's more.'

Brad's head disappeared down the bed. Steve edged the door open a little more so he could take in the full scene. The two of them were oblivious in their own world of lust and lechery. Brad's tongue went to work on Debbie, she moaned even lower. *Bitch*, she wouldn't let Steve do that. *'Disgusting,'* she'd said. Brad carried on drinking in her juices, he grunted and slurped, she whined and whimpered – he was big, maybe forty, fit, full head of hair, tribal tattoos across his shoulder and forearms. He obviously worked out, Steve wondered if George knew him from the gym. He looked back at his wife's face, lost in a world of pleasure that she hadn't enjoyed for a long time, perhaps ever before... Steve slipped his right hand down the waistband of his trousers and grasped his erect penis, he rubbed it up and down like he'd done hundreds of times before, *fucking wanker* – his breathing got faster and lower, he tugged harder and quickly found his rhythm, he pulled and pushed, he was expert at it. Brad's head then came back into view – he moved up the bed and pulled Debbie upright. Steve could see what she was focussing on. Brad's erect penis came into view, still wet and moist from where it had been exploring Debbie's vagina moments earlier.

'Now it's your turn,' said Brad the Blindman.

Steve closed his eyes and stopped masturbating as Debbie took Brad's penis in her expectant mouth. She sucked and groaned while he grabbed the back of her head forcing it backwards and forwards. She wasn't reluctant, unlike with Steve. Once, twice, three times at the most she'd performed fellatio on him and had never enjoyed the experience. It was under protest, like everything. Every time they had sex it was under protest, even when she'd performed with her mouth she would never let him come, not a spit, not a swallow – never, and there she was, not three feet away from him sucking and licking like some celluloid surgically enhanced whore. He fumbled in his pocket, pulled out his iPhone, pressed the video button and filmed this whore, this slag, this bitch... his wife, sucking off another man in his bed.

He stepped away and eased back down the stairs, his erection rapidly subsiding. Tears pricked his eyes as he picked up his car keys and walked out. He stopped, remembered the flowers, walked back and picked them up just as Brad exploded in her mouth. She didn't gag, she didn't complain, she wasn't sick, she didn't spit – she swallowed and licked his throbbing cock until it was dry – and she enjoyed every bit of it.

Steve got in his car and drove. Where he was going he wasn't sure. His first thought was to go to the Moon under

Water, get the boys, go back and give the both of them a kicking, but he thought better of it. It wasn't exactly something he wanted to announce to the world.

He headed out on the ring road where the traffic was now beginning to build up. Within an hour Bristol would be at a standstill as everyone tried in vain to get home to enjoy the start of the weekend. He turned off and headed out towards the countryside.

Arriving at Tog Hill with no thoughts or intentions of what to do, he parked up, got out and looked north-west out over the city. The sun was beginning to set and the lights were coming on over the urban sprawl. He could clearly see the BT tower on Purdown. Forty years ago from this spot the floodlight pylons at Eastville would have been visible, on a big cup night you would even have been able to hear the crowd. Those days had long gone... *'The flowers are dead and gone behind the Eastville goals.'*

He turned up the collar of his jacket, got back in the car and fumbled in his glove compartment for some music – Marvin, Curtis and the Reverend Al all seemed an ir- relevance – he needed something to suit his fucked up head, a Faithless CD appeared.

He wrenched the disc out of the case, slammed it in the slot and forwarded to track eight, *Salva Mea – 'Save me, save me.'*

'Fuck off Dido gimme Maxi Jazz' – *'Save me, save me...'* *I could murder a fucking line.* He took out his iPhone and texted Gary 'Bulldog' Rattigan, small time drug dealer, his small time drug dealer – his Candyman.

'Bulldog – you about 2nite? I'll be in the moon c u l8r'. He toyed with the phone then played the video. The bitch – look at her fucking enjoying it. He closed his eyes and leant back, he couldn't get the vision out of his head – he watched stuff like this on Redtube, *Save me, save me.* He unzipped his flies, got his cock out and finished off what he'd started not half

an hour previously while Maxi Jazz got off his tits. He came surprisingly quickly, didn't attempt to hold it back or conceal it, he groaned, realising he'd spunked up over his strides. 'Fucking-bollocks-arseholes!' He reached back in the glove compartment for a cloth, looked to his left and spotted a face peering through the misted up window.

'What the fuck! Fuck off you dirty cunt!'

The dogger nonchalantly walked away, limping as he stroked his own erection through his pocket. Steve shook his head, breathed in, turned off the CD and gathered his thoughts.

'What am I doing? What the fuck am I doing here?' he said out loud.

He switched on the ignition and roared out of the car park, dispersing the doggers and rent boys in a shower of gravel and dirt. He drove home, breathing deep breaths, trying not to let the usual arseholes on the road annoy him. *I could do a line right now.* He got home just after six, still early for a Friday night. He picked up the flowers from the back seat, inserted the key in the door and walked in.

'Alright love, home early?' shouted Debbie from the kitchen, he could smell fish – they always had fish on Fridays. At least he thought it was fish.

'Yep, sneaked off early,' he replied, still not sure where this was going.

'Good for you. Cup of tea?'

'Please.'

He took his coat and shoes off while the dogs wagged their arses off around his feet.

'How's my boys?' He greeted them with a smile. At least someone was genuinely pleased to see him.

'Are those for me?' Debbie asked. 'What have you done wrong then?'

'Me? Nothing, nothing, I just thought...' *It's you, you bitch. You're the one who's done something wrong.*

16

'Only kidding hun, they're lovely.' She took them and kissed his cheek.

'The shutters are up. They look great – go and have a look.'

Steve walked into the lounge and took in the shutters once more. Even he had to admit Brad the Blindman had done a good job.

'Nice.'

'Yep, he was brilliant, had it all done by twelve,' said Debbie as she entered the lounge, the flowers now in a vase in her hand. There wasn't a hint of emotion or guilt in her voice. She was a brilliant liar as well as a good cock-sucker, he would give her that. He wondered if she'd been at it before.

He drunk his tea and ate his dinner – pan fried sea bass. They didn't say much, they never did, they watched the news – job cuts, factory closures, council cutbacks – *picket lines and picket signs* – pensioner attacked in her own home – *don't punish me with brutality* – big drug bust in Easton. Cameron's Britain, *fuck me*, he thought, *it's the eighties all over again.*

'Out tonight love? JB phoned earlier – they're down the Moon,' said Debbie, not taking her eyes off the screen.

'Spose, nothing on the telly I guess.' *I could do a line right now.* This was the usual Friday evening ritual, she knew he would go down the pub, he knew she would cosy up in front of the telly with a bottle of wine. Normally he felt knackered after work on Friday, sometimes he even looked for an excuse not to go out, he looked at her, thought about punching her in the mouth, right then, right now, thought about getting a knife from the kitchen and slitting the bitch's throat.

'Go on, do you good,' she said.

What, so you can have Brad the Blindman around again giving you another good fucking?

17

'Okay, I'll just get changed.' *I could do a line right now.*

Entering the bedroom he realised she'd changed the sheets. He opened the airing cupboard and threw the lid off the laundry basket, he pulled out the pillow cases and sniffed – *fucking Lynx, fucking cheap bastard.* He sniffed again – there was also the smell of sex, unmistakable and musky – *the sweaty, fucking cheap bastard.*

Shit, showered and shaved, in that order, he was ready to face the world. He put on a clean white 'wife beater' T-shirt and thought of the irony, then slipped on his new Smedley sweater that Debbie had bought him for Christmas. He put his Breitling Aviator Colt on his wrist, belted up his freshly washed and ironed Diesel jeans and put on his Ox blood Loake loafers. He then dabbed his smooth face with Hugo Boss, his teenage penchant for Brut had long gone – thankfully. He remembered that combination of Clearasil and Brut – the whole of the country smelt of it in 1971 – he smiled. He was going to get through this. *I could do a line right now.*

Steve's iPhone danced in his pocket. The Maytals' *Pressure Drop* heralded a joke from Pete McNulty *'A Muslim tourist was shot dead by Metropolitan police on suspicion of being a terrorist. When asked why he had 68 wounds, a spokesman replied "that's all we had".'* Steve smirked and thought about forwarding it to Fiona, then thought better of it. His phone buzzed again, it was John Burston: *'Where the fuck r u wanker?'* read the message.

Steve texted back, *'5 mins – cunt.'*

'See you later love.' He said as he kissed Debbie on the forehead.

'Yep, have a good time,' she replied, transfixed to *Emmerdale.*

He got in his car and drove, he would leave it at the pub – he fancied a sesh. 'I could really do with that fucking line now!'

He parked up and walked towards the pub, there were a couple of lads he knew vaguely outside smoking. 'Alright' he nodded in greeting.

'Alright' they nodded back.

As he walked through the cloud of second-hand smoke he let out a feint but discernible cough, although he'd never smoked himself, in all honesty he hankered after the smokey, atmospheric pubs of the past.

The boozer was packed with the usual mix of Friday night revellers plus the obligatory scaffolders, builders and roofers, all scruffy dirty fuckers with soiled clothing and filthy hands – some still wearing their work hats – Steve's nemesis. Pubs were desperate these days – they would let any arseholes in. Steve loathed them – he had more class in his little finger than that lot. They were pissed already, getting steadily wankered since late afternoon – lairy fuckers. Some cheap tarts with council estate facelifts hung on their every word, bottles of super strength lager clutched in their nicotined-stained fingers.

'Scuse mate' said Steve as he worked his way to the far end of the bar where he could see John and the rest of the boys. One of the scaffolders turned and sneered. He still wore his soiled overall with *Hook & Eye Scaffolding – the lads with the scaff* emblazoned across the back.

'You smell nice darling,' he said, the stale odour of sweat and cheap cider emanating from every pore of his body.

'Thanks,' replied Steve as he stopped and stared at him coldly. It was the look he reserved for pieces of shit like this, he'd used it many times over the years – usually to good effect. His balls shrunk as his muscles tightened, he was unflinching and kept his stare, firmly fixed on the scaffolder's bleary pupils.

'What's it called?' said the scaffolder after finally plucking up courage to take it further. Steve held his stare.

'Boss,' replied Steve without blinking.

The moment passed, he'd gained the upper hand. He was sober, calm and collected, with a rage in his belly after today's events, not to mention years of experienced street fighting under his belt. He gave off an air of confidence which was enough to make the scaffolder bottle it, he blinked and looked away. Steve walked towards his mates, the best mates any man could have...

John Burston – 'JB' was a year older than Steve. If this diamond was any rougher he would be a lump of anthracite. He had a permanently red bull neck and a head so large and wide he was known as 'Widehead' by friends and enemies alike, although not to his face. His arms were muscular and adorned with various tattoos that he'd garnered over the years: 'Mum and Dad', wives' and children's names, hearts, swallows, daggers and leaping leopards – no tribal markings and no Latin inscriptions, like his tattoos John Burston was old school and proud of it. He was expelled from school at fifteen and eventually joined the Army, serving in the Marines and fighting in the Falklands as well as mean streets of Northern Ireland. Before joining the forces JB went to Detention Centre in his teens – some fracas on the terrace or on the dancefloor that had long been forgotten. His time inside and in the Army had given him the edge on the others, honed his fighting skills and according to him, made him the man he was today.

His first marriage had ended in a bitter divorce and he was now married to a younger but equally demanding temptress named Sharon who was not only statuesque and fit but also a raging nymphomaniac – which explained the broad smile that JB usually had across his face. The two of them had a young, precocious daughter, Chelsea, who didn't get on very well with her extended family of step brothers and sisters, but as she was away at private boarding school most of the time it didn't particularly bother them.

JB owns his own building company, which is now in serious financial difficulties due to the bank calling in his business loan. To add to his woe the CSA are on his back for more money for his kids from his first marriage. He was about to lay off staff and was staring down the barrel of bankruptcy. He lived in a five-bedroom Moorish style house which he'd built himself, it had a nameplate beside the front door – 'Llamedos'. He drove a beast of a motor – a 4.2 V8 Supercharged Vogue with 'JB 555' personalised plates, which he couldn't even afford to put petrol in these days. He gambles and drinks excessively – and swears like the trooper he once was. JB made a good friend and an even worse enemy.

Gerwazy 'George' Smolinski at 56 was the same age as Steve and they'd been classmates since infant school. Son of a Polish Second World War fighter pilot, George was born and bred in Bristol and fiercely nationalistic towards England, especially at football – except when they played Poland. He'd worked as an engineer at Aeroengine International since leaving school, it was a steady job with good pay and plenty of overtime, but no prospects due to him being an argumentative, truculent, hot head. George was an obsessive fitness fanatic, working out at the gym every other day. When he walked it was like he had two basketballs under his arms. He didn't drink or socialise with others apart from his four best mates and he could start a fight in a phone box, even if he was the only one in it. He took vitamins, protein drinks, Creatine and steroids, and was often bad tempered, pugnacious, pumped up and angry – am Eastern European volcano waiting to erupt. George was married with kids who lived in fear of him, while he lived in fear of dying of the same prostrate cancer which killed his beloved father.

Pete 'Mac' McNulty at nearly 58 was the eldest of Steve's friends, but perhaps not the wisest. A one-time top man on the terrace – but sadly no longer. He was at least three stone overweight and had gone to seed, finding it difficult to walk without breaking into a sweat. He inherited money when his parents died and consequently paid off his mortgage and bought a villa near Malaga. He was a qualified electrician but now only did occasional odd jobs for mates, never charging them the going rate. He's semi-retired and spends his days in the pub or watching daytime TV, he especially likes *Countdown* but that's mainly because of the easy-on-the-eye assistant. Everyone loves Pete – he's happy go lucky, full of jokes, with not a care in the world, but inside Pete and his partner Sue have real problems. Their daughter, Natasha, was raped by a paedophile when she was eight and understandably had never been the same since. She was now in her twenties but still suffered from nightmares and needed regular psychiatric treatment and medical care. Pete was diabetic with severe liver and heart problems and he often cried himself to sleep, but his wife was unaware of this as they slept in separate bedrooms.

Mike Cribb was 55 and the youngest of The Big Five. Apprenticed in the print trade after leaving school he had been successful and was now a director of a major print company – 'GlobePrint'. Mike told everyone his great, great, great grandfather was Tom Cribb, the famous West Country bare knuckle fighter, but no-one believed him. No one believed Mike about anything – he would've given Walter Mitty a run for his money. Mike was always going to buy a new house, buy a new car, go on a world cruise, sort out his noisy neighbour – but he never did, instead he lived in the shadow of the other four and their reputation.

He was smaller and slighter than the others – 'wirey' he liked to describe himself as. He had a shock of thick blond, but now graying, hair perched nestlike on his narrow head, a sort of scruffy 'wedge' which although common and trendy in the eighties appeared at odds and out of place, especially when compared with the others and their regulation shaved heads. For all that Mike was a game fucker and rarely let them down in a fight, he would eagerly get the beers in and generally do as much as he could to endear himself to his mates. He'd get a bit carried away when they talked about the state of the country, advocating petrol bombing mosques and castrating kiddy fiddlers – but knowing what he was like the others just ignored him.

For all his warped views Mike was articulate and well educated and he should have gone to University, but council house kids didn't do that back in the seventies. He's been married for twenty odd years but has no children – he's impotent and like Pete McNulty he doesn't sleep in the same bed as his wife. She – Karen – drinks a bottle of wine every afternoon and has numerous affairs – at the moment with George Smolinski.

They'd been known as 'The Big Five' since their youth, they'd made their name on the Holt End at Villa Park back in 1971 when together with a handful of other Rovers' lads they attempted to take the cavernous and fearsome end. They succeeded – for a while, only to eventually find themselves surrounded by Villa's finest who, despite numerous attempts, failed to evict the Bristolian boot boys from their terrace.

They weren't a 'firm' as such, just a bunch of mates who always stuck up for each other and would always stand their ground, whether on the Tote End fighting the usurpers of the day or on the streets of Bristol city centre on a drunken Friday night. They didn't go looking for trouble, but some-how it did seem to follow them around, like a bad smell.

Steve slapped JB on the back.

'Alright John?'

'Right Steve, what kept you?' The others broke off from their conversations. 'Right Steve,' they all said in unison.

'Right Mr Allen – what was that, bit of trouble?' asked Mike Cribb, nodding in the direction of the scaffolders.

'Nah, nothing lads, don't worry about it.' They all nodded back in simple recognition.

They were no Mockney lads, there was no *'Oi, oi, saveloy'* from Danny Dyer's TV world – no back slapping, no dodgy handshakes, no hugs, no false camaraderie – they had nothing to prove to each other, they were mates – nothing more, nothing less.

'Get them in you cunt – you got some catching up to do,' said JB.

'Let me get 'em.' Offered Mike Cribb, but Steve had already worked his way to the bar – he had his cloak of invisibility on again and was getting wound up.

'For fuck's sake love, how about a bit of service?' he shouted, waving a twenty pound note.

'In a fucking minute,' she mouthed above the din – smiling sweetly.

She was in her late thirties and a new face behind the bar. She wore a tiny mini skirt which showed off her long slim legs – she was well fit. He forgave her.

'Pint of Guinness, two pints of Pride, pint of Fosters and an orange juice.' George wasn't drinking again, it would interfere with his training – and fuck up his Creatine intake.

She pulled the drinks and gave him his change, just a handful of shrapnel from the fresh note – he had a wallet full of them, just in case. *I could do a line right now.* Steve studied the change, shook his head and dumped it in his pocket. She smiled again. She was gorgeous. He noticed the name badge 'Chantelle'. Soft cunt, he was. He checked his phone for any messages and wandered back to his mates, laden with the drinks.

Steve sunk over half a pint of Fuller's finest in one go.

'Looks like you needed that?' asked Pete who was known as 'Super Mac' in his youth but now it was the moniker of 'Big Mac' that seemed more appropriate.

'Too fucking right,' answered Steve. He still didn't know if he was going to tell them the events of earlier in the day or not. Inside he was cracking up, wanting to get off his tits that was for sure, maybe later – maybe six or seven pints later – at least. He looked around again and checked his iPhone once more.

'Nice jumper Steve – Matalan?'

JB smirked. It was a running joke that Steve spent a small fortune on clothes. He stared back dismissively at his mates in their 'George at Asda' tops and 'Next' shirts – *fucking losers.*

'John Smedley actually, not that any of you cunts would have heard of him – fucking Primark more your dap off.'

They all giggled, schoolboy giggles. They knew they had touched a nerve. Steve sunk the remainder of his pint.

'Come on, whose round is it?'

'Got a thirst on?' Pete asked.

'Nope just want to get out of it, that's all – anything wrong with that?'

'Whoa! Okay chill mate – no nothing wrong with that at all. Work problems is it?'

Steve didn't answer. They all knew his problems at work. That is, he worked too fucking hard, they all did apart from Pete. But Steve, he lived to work – whereas they all worked to live.

'No not this time. To be honest I don't want to talk about it.'

He looked around again then studied his iPhone.

'Who you looking for Stevie?' asked George – 'you've been twitchy since you come in.'

'No one, alright, just leave it,' he snapped.

25

He couldn't talk about it, not with his mates anyway. They were good mates, close mates, but they never talked about personal things, they couldn't discuss their problems, their fears, their worries – they all had them, some more than others, but it just didn't happen, it wasn't right, they would just take the piss, they always did, it was what real mates did, take the piss, it was what made them what they were.

Mike broke the silence. 'Did I see you pulling out of Tog Hill car park earlier – bout half five? Thought you said you was working late?'

Steve felt himself reddening again, 'I uh, I had to meet a client ... from work, they had some proofs to sign off.'

'What in "Dog" Hill car park?'

'Yeah yeah, they uh, came back from London, they live near Bath – made sense, didn't want to come back into town to meet me, so thought we'd meet up there.'

The rest of The Big Five looked at each other and laughed.

'Fuck off, you was up there importuning for young boys, you fucking nonce!' JB shouted out, barely containing himself.

'Always thought you were suspect Allen, what was you doing up there – doggin?'

'Straight up, straight up – business, honest.'

They quietened down for a bit, winking and nudging each other – it would be a story resurrected over the years, he knew that, they wouldn't let it go, they never did.

Two underdressed teenage girls – jailbait – squeezed past them, more flesh on show than an Old Market lap dancing club. The boys turned as one and leered, the girls acknowledged their stares with shy, embarrassed giggles before responding with a 'fuck off you dirty old cunts.' Steve sighed with relief that the subject had changed – for now.

The night progressed and the usual subjects were religiously ticked off – overrated and overpaid Premiership footballers, women, immigration, women, Europe, women, Human Rights, women, Asian gangs kidnapping white girls in the Midlands, women, Rovers chances of avoiding relegation, women, Cameron being a cunt, Brown being a cunt, Blair being a bigger cunt, Thatcher being the biggest cunt of all, they all agreed on that – except John Burston.

Steve felt disappointed there was no Charlie to be had, not tonight anyway. Bulldog obviously wasn't showing – the fat, fucking bastard.

They stayed put in the Moon, getting drunker and louder as the night wore on. There were a few odd scuffles – the scaffolders were pissing everyone off now, a few crying girls – bad jokes, good jokes, 'remember when' stories, references to doggin' surfaced at regular intervals, abuse, name calling. Mostly though there was hate – hate for everything around them, hate for the state of the country, hate for hoodies, hate for politicians, hate for bankers, hate for footballers, hate for illegal immigrants – same as every other Friday night – *hate, hate, hate.*

Closing time came round all too soon, they staggered out of the pub.

'Wanna lift Steve?' George was driving again, no-one else ever volunteered – something else to piss him off.

'Nah, that's alright mate – I could do with the walk, honest.'

'You sure?' There was a moment's uneasy silence. 'You alright mate? You seem a bit... vacant, got something on your mind?'

For a moment Steve thought about unburdening all his problems, telling them all about what he'd witnessed Debbie doing earlier on in the day, plus his problems at work and the worry over his health...

'No honest, sound as a pound mate, just a bit tired that's all. Thanks, thanks for asking ... see you next week same time – unless you're up the Rovers tomorrow?'

'Are you fucking joking? They bastards didn't come and see me when I was bad, huh, huh, huh – laters,' bawled an inebriated Mac McNulty.

'Yeah okay, laters.'

'Yep, fuck off Allen and get walking you fat bastard!' JB always had to have the last word.

He staggered to his car, fumbled for his keys and for a brief, irrational moment considered driving.

'Driving – in your state?'

Steve turned and refocused his eyes in the dark, Chantelle stood in the doorway lighting up. He blinked hard, needing to confirm he wasn't wearing his beer goggles.

'Eh? No, no chance, just checking it was locked that's all,' he said, sucking in air in a desperate attempt to sober up.

'Pity, nice motor – you could've given me a lift.'

'Chantelle isn't it?' He queried as she mooched over to him. It was now her turn to be caught out.

'Yeah, how do you ... oh, the name badge, right?'

'I did notice – not deliberate like, wasn't looking or any-thing, just...'

'Noticed you too. Nice clothes, love that watch, girls notice things like that – you're not bad for an old 'un.'

It wasn't the first time that he'd heard that.

What Steve had learnt about younger women these days was that they weren't backward at coming forward. She flicked her cigarette into the dark, put her hand on the back of his head, pulled him forward, pressed her lips against his and licked and sucked the living daylights out of his mouth. He'd loved that taste of fresh cigarette smoke and alcohol since his teenage days – he had missed it. Steve responded, both tongues explored each other, darting in and out. Fumbling in his pocket he pulled out his car keys, not once breaking the rhythm of their locked mouths. He pushed her against the car, opened the back door and they both fell in, her tight skirt was already riding up, he glanced down and got a glimpse of her pink panties, almost glowing in the dark.

Pushing his right hand up under her sweater, he felt the lace of her Wonderbra, he manoeuvred his hand over the cup and eased out her nipple. Easing up the sweater further, he looked down – the expression chapel hat peg came to mind. He took her erect nipple in his mouth while her hands moved down and started pulling at his belt and flies, fumbling more than he did.

'Let me, let me,' he pushed her hand away, semi stood up, undid his belt and unzipped his flies – his erection pushed against his Calvin Klein's, he pulled them down deftly and his erect penis was revealed in all its glory – he was thankful he'd shaved his bollocks and shaft earlier, he'd heard the young ones liked it that way, Chantelle certainly looked impressed.

She pulled her knickers down and off from around her shoes, tugging them off the ridiculously high heel – there was nothing to them, just a tiny bit of pink, silky delicious material. She opened her legs revealing her bare vagina, not a hair to be seen and as smooth as his recently shaved chin. He loved that, made a change from what he had to witness at home – a badly packed kebab that fucking scared the living daylights out of him.

In his youth he had to worry about coming too soon. Many a time he'd soiled his Sta-Prest as he fumbled on the settee with his sort of the day. Now it was the opposite, especially after a few pints – it was already crossing his mind and once he started thinking of the inevitable he knew it was only a matter of time...

'Come on, what are you waiting for? I need fucking,' she said with pleading eyes.

Chantelle was begging him, he hadn't had it offered on a plate like this for a long time – he should have been in heaven. She was ridiculously attractive, it certainly wasn't the beer goggles deceiving him, her dark hair was cut fashionably short and neat, she had beautiful dark brown eyes and an incredible body – and she was young, well young compared to him – but most importantly she was willing. Going down on his knees he starting fingering her, one finger, two fingers, three fingers, she was dripping already. It felt wonderful, tight and firm, he guessed it hadn't had a baby through it yet. He thrust his fingers in and out, then found and expertly rubbed her clitoris, causing her to wail like a banshee...

'No more,' she said, 'I want your cock – now!'

Almost meekly he attempted to enter her, it was like trying to shove a piece of limp spaghetti through the eye of a needle, he pushed and wriggled, she squirmed – it was going nowhere.

'For fuck's sake!' she snapped, looking at him with real anger in her eyes. Pushing him away she moved her own right hand downwards – she closed her eyes, leant back, went to work and quickly resumed her moaning. Her fingers moved quicker and quicker, intermittently a single digit would delve inside, the rest of the time she adroitly rubbed her clitoris.

Fuck, this was good. He could feel the blood returning to his penis and momentarily considered getting his iPhone out again, but then thought better of it. He tried once more, he pushed her hand away and attempted to insert his erect penis in once again – just as she reached orgasm.

'Nuh, nuh, nuh... nuuuuuhhhh – no not now, fuck off, get it out. Get it fucking out!'

He fell back, baffled by the turn of events – she just lay there moaning, slated and satisfied. He resorted to what he did best, he rubbed his penis, then pulled and pulled – it didn't take long, he orgasmed and spurted all over her – onto her bare legs and her exposed midriff. He could see it splat on to her Wonderbra and more hit her face – she twitched in disgust.

'You dirty fucker, you dirty fucking wanker – is that all you can do. Fucking wanker!'

It caught him out, he opened the door and tumbled to the tarmac, jeans awkwardly around his ankles and Calvin Klein's around his knees, he quickly pulled them up and tucked himself in, breathing heavily as he did so. This wasn't quite how he had imagined his first sexual encounter outside of marriage.

Chantelle opened the door on the opposite side – she pulled her skirt and sweater down and patted them back into place then wriggled back into her knickers. She walked off not saying a word and without looking back.

'Chantelle! Wait, wait. Sorry I've, I've been drinking – it's normally, I'm normally... better than that!' He squirmed at his own pitiful pleading.

She carried on walking, failing to respond – instead she raised a solitary one-fingered salute.

'And it's not even Chantelle you wanker. It's, it's ... oh what the fuck, it's Gill, boring, boring Gill.'

He let out a sigh and contemplated getting back into his car, just as a lone police car slowly drove past, he reconsidered and instead walked off in the opposite direction. It began to rain, his John Smedley would get ruined, he now wished he'd worn his Baracuta jacket – *can today get any fucking worse.*

'Oi boss.'

Yes it can. The voice came from a doorway he'd just walked past – he'd semi expected it.

Some while later he opened his eyes. He was out for maybe a couple of minutes, he came to and found himself lying on the pavement in a puddle of blood and muddy water. Cars drove past, slowed down and took in the scene, but none stopped. He felt the back of his neck and was thankful he hadn't copped it across his head – it might have killed him. The bastard had used a scaffolding spanner, poleaxed him in one and gave him a couple of kicks to the ribs. He'd had worse in the past – a lot, lot worse. He dragged himself to his feet and shook his head, feeling like he'd been hit by an express train.

He staggered home, beaten and soaked through. In the kitchen he took his Statin and his ACE tablet, then topped them up with a couple of Neurofen. He dragged himself up the stairs and looked in on Debbie. She was snoring, low and deep – a contented snore, no doubt dreaming of Brad the Blindman. The spare room door was ajar, a sure sign she didn't want him in the marital bed – she always made him sleep in there when he'd been drinking as his snoring kept her awake. He almost laughed out loud at the irony – instead he slipped into the cold, empty bed and cried like a lost child.

CHAPTER THREE

STEVE woke on the Saturday morning with a headache of epic proportions. He tried to get up but his back was stiffer than a wanker's handkerchief. As he lay in bed he thought of the previous day's events. He felt nauseated and violated – but unnervingly parts of it had excited him.

He remembered once, after a drunken barbecue when the lads and their partners came round, Debbie had been flirting outrageously with JB and George. He later mentioned it to her, told her it excited him – there was talk of threesomes, her and one of his mates, or her and one of her mates, he wouldn't mind – he would just watch. She was horrified but it planted a seed of thought in her head – he was giving her tacit approval to take on a lover, or lovers – well that was how she saw it. That was how she justified it.

She wasn't bad for a bird in her mid-fifties, not quite Cougartown but she scrubbed up well. Like Steve she'd started going to the gym and got herself fit, she needed something to occupy her now that the boys had gone. She tried not to dwell on the boys – but she missed them so much. They'd bought the Jacks as a replacement for them, but it wasn't the same, they were Steve's dogs anyway – they didn't take a blind bit of notice of her. She tried to keep in touch with both boys, Skype was a godsend with Sam and Natalie in Melbourne, in fact she felt like he was still home at times, but with Harry, well, he could be the one on the other side of the planet for all she knew. She phoned him when she could but he changed his mobile number so often he was hard to track down. Last time she saw him he was hanging around Turbo Island on Stokes Croft, drinking White Lightning and flogging the *Big Issue* – it broke her and Steve's heart.

It was 6.30. It didn't matter how exhausted he was, how late he got to bed, he still woke at the same time. Desperate to get some heat on his neck and back he headed for the shower – hoping to ease the pain from the beating the night before but it didn't work. He got out of the shower and went into the darkened bedroom where Debbie was still snoring lightly. He looked at her and thought about punching her in the face or even smothering her with a pillow... he shook his head. Instead he got a clean pair of jeans out of the wardrobe – his Levis this time, together with his black and gold trimmed Fred Perry. He went back into the spare bedroom and got dressed, dumping his still damp jumper and jeans into the laundry basket where they nestled alongside the spunk-stained sheets from the day before.

He went downstairs and opened the kitchen door – Prince and Buster greeted him as only devoted dogs could. They let out low gentle, muffled barks as he leant down and fussed over them.

'Shush, shush boys, stop it.'

Not wanting to wake Debbie, he let them out of the back door where they set off in another fruitless pursuit of elusive squirrels. He put down clean food for them – he loved his boys, all four of them.

Kitchen appliances shone at him, Gaggia coffee maker, Alessi toaster, kettle and fruit basket – Debbie liked Allesi.

After his Jordans' organic porridge with skimmed milk he swallowed a Citalopram, an ACE tablet, a glucosamine tablet and a cod liver oil capsule, he flushed them all down with a cholesterol-busting Benecol drink. He scrambled around in the cupboard and found some Dichlofenac and swallowed one with a couple of Neurofen, he then wandered into the lounge and contemplated his iPad2, his iPhone4 and his MacBook Pro – he decided on the latter. As he sat down on his leather settee he swore he could hear himself rattle.

He visited *The Guardian* site and took in the news, same old, same old – riots in the Middle East, unrest on the streets of London, economy in meltdown, unemployment heading for new highs. He yawned and clicked on his Facebook page – an invitation to 'Skinhead uprising' in Cardiff in May, *I'll give that a miss* – not his favourite place Cardiff. A few of his mates have poked him, he can't be arsed to poke them back, there's a message and photos from Sam and Natalie lounging on a beach looking ridiculously fit and happy, *that's nice.* He thought about uploading the video he had of Debbie and Brad the Blindman, but no, revenge is a dish best served cold – this would have to be defrosted by the time he worked out what he was going to do with it.

There's a joke on Pete's wall that he forgot to tell last night. *'My mate drinks brake fluid, I think he's addicted but he says he can stop any time.'* For the first time in a while Steve laughed out loud.

He started typing on his status *'came home early yesterday and found Debbie giving a blow job to Brad the Blindman'*, his finger hovered over the post button. He held it there, twitching... then he deleted it.

Debbie came down the stairs and entered the lounge.

'Alright love, you're up early – have a good night?' She stifled a yawn.

Steve logged off and closed the lid. 'Yeah, yeah – it was okay, usual bollocks.'

'Where did you go?'

'Just stayed in the Moon – you know, couple of beers, bit of a chat. Left the car there and walked home.'

'Good, good, anything going on?'

'Nope, the boys all alright – they all say hi.'

'Ahhh, that's nice – cup of tea?'

'Please.'

Saturdays meant football. He didn't bother with away matches much these days – none of them did. Come to think of it not many of them bothered with home games either. Rovers were now down to a desperate 5 to 6,000 diehards – the 'blue few' as the red half of the city called them. Steve wondered where the other 30,000 had gone that had cheered them to promotion at Wembley a few seasons earlier – *glory hunting bastards.*

He didn't know why he bothered, he was sick to death of football in general not just with Rovers. It was no longer the game he loved as a youngster – it was now full of Johnny foreigners, greedy owners and even greedier players and agents. The prawn sandwich brigade had taken over – Steve recalled a rant on a QPR forum that Fiona's husband, Barry had sent him. It was a lengthy diatribe berating modern day football. He found it hard to disagree with any of it – he printed out one particular statement and it stuck on his wall at work:

'I hate the Prem and the myth that it is exciting this year. Man City breaking into the top four isn't exciting. They spent loads of money. It's no more exciting than that Nameless Cunt getting to number 1 in the charts after winning the X-Factor.'

He received complaints, especially from born-again Manchester City fans, but fuck 'em – it was staying.

Steve watched his team out of nothing more than a sense of misguided loyalty and pity. He drank a can of Natch in the Victoria on the Gloucester Road – there were a few old faces, a few old gnarled wise boys who had fought alongside him and The Big Five back in the 'glory' days of the seventies and eighties. They'd been there, done that, got the T-shirt – literally, a couple of them were wearing *'100% genuine Tote End boot boy'* shirts, he smiled knowingly.

As he entered the ground he nodded to some old mates but chose to ignore others for no other reason than he couldn't be bothered. Some of the youngsters, the 'yoof', went out of their way to greet him.

'Alright Steve, how's it going?'

He didn't know their names and he didn't want to learn them. He returned their greetings with a nod of acknowledgement, knowing they would appreciate it and boast to their mates that they 'knew' Steve Allen. Some of them were probably the ones who kept requesting him to be a friend on Facebook – he just ignored them, much to their disgust.

He stood on his own, clapped the quarters as they came on the pitch – and didn't clap again for the entire 90 minutes, it ended in a 1-0 defeat. Some fans booed, he didn't blame them, it was painful and pitiful – shit ground, no atmosphere, no future. He didn't even get to eat his pie as they had all sold out – this weekend was really not going at all well.

There was no trouble, there was rarely any trouble – unlike the old days he thought. He got in his car and drove home, switched on the radio and heard that City had won away. *Somebody up there doesn't like me.*

Steve's iPhone rang as he drove home: *'The flowers are dead and gone behind the Eastville goals...'* sang Ben Gunstone. Steve answered, it was Debbie.

'Get a couple of curries love, usual for me – how was the game?'

'Crap.'

'No change there then. See you later – I got a bottle of wine in the fridge.'

Deep joy. What had happened to the riotous Saturday nights he used to enjoy as a teenager? A curry, a bottle of Sainsbury's Pinot Grigiot and *Strictly come dancing* on the telly – 'Happy days,' he said sarcastically.

The Chicken Pathia made his nose run and the Pino Grigiot revived his headache. He picked up his iBook and powered up again. He went on the football forums, a state of apathy prevailed in North Bristol: 'Sack the manager', 'Sack the board', 'Tea hut runs out of pies – again.' Usual messages – he couldn't be bothered to read them.

The Guardian news: riots escalating in the Middle East, ex pats flown home. *Wish some fucker would fly me out of here* he thought. Next stop Facebook – three friend requests: Danny Bainbridge and some joker who thinks it clever to go under the pseudonym of 'Tyler Durden'. Wannabe football hoolies by the look of 'em. Fake Stone Island sweaters and those crappy quilted jackets – usual pram-faced delinquents from the sink estates who he had no desire to know or class as a 'friend'. Finally some woman called Kirsty Clifton...

He didn't recognise the name. *Kirsty Clifton*? She sounded like an online hooker, her photo made her look like one as well. *Not bad for an old 'un, though, a real MILF without a doubt.* He was just about to press 'ignore' but the name Kirsty rang a bell, he looked at her profile photo again – *Is it? It can't be?* There was also a message, a message which made his stomach churn and his heart leap out of his throat. *'Hi Steve, remember me, your Guilty Tiger?'*

He could find no other info about Kirsty – just the one photo and the rest was set to private. He couldn't click 'accept invitation' quick enough. He waited – waited through *Strictly come dancing*, waited through *Harry Hill's TV Burp*, he couldn't be arsed to wait through *Match of the Day* – Alan Hansen's glib and facile opinions gave him heartburn.

The Pinot Grigio had gone to work on Debbie – she'd dozed off with an empty wine glass at her feet. He thought of Kirsty – all those years ago, Kirsty Donohue then, his first love – maybe his only love. Finally he gave up waiting, he powered off and angrily slammed the lid down waking Debbie. 'Come on,' he said 'bed.'

Steve and Debbie had sex for the first time in a while, he came quickly. It was exactly seventy-three days since the last time they had made love – Debbie had been counting.

He didn't sleep well. His body was still aching from the kicking the night before and his head was a maelstrom of thoughts and memories and right in the middle of that whirling brain of his was Kirsty. They had started 'courting' when they were only kids – she was fourteen, he was fifteen. She'd been expelled from her previous school and removed from her foster parents' house to be incarcerated in the local 'naughty girls home'. She had a history of drug abuse, mainly Mandrax and Dexidrene, shoplifting and self harm. She was a troubled girl – she needed help.

Her first day at school had ended in a near riot. She had naturally blonde hair styled in a fashionable feather cut and wore a bottle green Trevira suit with a skirt way above her knees exposing long slim legs that went on forever. A yellow check Ben Sherman shirt with a matching silk handkerchief in the breast pocket held in by a tie tack and a cute little pair of tasselled loafers completed the ensemble. She was a vision, everything a young skinhead male could want – and more.

Why she chose Steve he never knew. She could've had the pick of the school, including John 'JB' Burston who was the year above and the 'David Watts' of the fourth year. But she chose Steve – he thought Christmas had come early. The early seventies were wonderful, *Wonderful world, beautiful people* as Jimmy Cliff had sung. They were two young skinheads in love, she was his first love – he lost his virginity to her, sadly the reverse wasn't true, even at that tender age. They made love in parks and bus shelters, that furtive, hurried, squelchy love of teenagers, no guile, even less prowess, all function no finesse. He bought her a record from RCA in Picton Street, *Guilty* by Tiger on the Camel label, she thought it was called *Guilty Tiger* – they laughed, it was their song, *Guilty Tiger*.

They were inseparable, his mates disapproved. Not of Kirsty but of the lack of time he spent with them. The fledgling 'Big Five' had only just started, they had their lives ahead of them and Kirsty was in their way. But they got around it, she tagged along and went to football with them, went to the youth club, went to the Locarno on a Monday night where they sneaked her a Port and Lemon in the Bali Hai. She turned heads wherever she went causing numerous fights which Steve secretly enjoyed. Steve cared for her, loved her and kept her in check – they made each other complete.

Steve's parents hated her. She had no parents to disapprove of Steve – she and her brother had been abandoned when they were young. But he didn't care – he would look after her forever. She was his girl, his sort, he was proud of her. When he walked down the street with his boots on his feet and her on his arm, he was Mr Big Stuff, The Boss. She was good for him too, got him to think of the future – she kept him out of trouble, mostly.

He left school at 16. While his mates got labouring jobs or apprenticeships Steve went to college and studied art and design. His mates called him a ponce and worse – a hippy. For a while they nicknamed him 'Warhol', thankfully it was shortlived. They got engaged and they collected for their bottom drawer. She left the following year and got a job in the typing pool at the *Bristol Evening Post* – life was good, mostly.

She'd been hurt a lot in the past. She had deep, dark periods where she stood at an abyss looking in. Insecure and psychotic, she couldn't bear Steve to leave her. She threatened suicide, slashed her arms, carving his name with a Stanley knife on her upper arm – at times she frightened him. They got through it – she moved out of the home and got a flat. He stayed there most nights but they couldn't afford to move in together.

At 17 their skinhead days were long behind them. They stayed in and watched the telly, thought of names for their kids – Cherry for the girl, Winston for the boy. He wasn't keen on Winston, but she convinced him it was after Churchill, nothing else, no-one from her past – he had his doubts.

They grew their hair and changed their clothes. Velvet jackets, flares, cheesecloth shirts, clogs and love beads – not quite hippy, more fledgling soul boy and soul girl. They listened to George McRae and the Hues Corporation – she fancied John Shaft, he discovered Maceo Parker. They went to discos and danced the Hustle. He landed a job at an advertising agency and they moved in together – life could not be better.

He still saw the rest of The Big Five but she resented it. The terraces were exploding into violence, Steve was part of it – she resented it. Rovers got promoted – she resented it. By 1976 oppressive dog day afternoons prevailed, the heat wound them up. They argued, they fought, she resumed her self harming, she attacked him with a knife – he headbutted her and she ended up in hospital with a broken nose, but she didn't tell the police – nevertheless the clock was ticking.

A year later as Steve was discovering speed and the Sex Pistols she started seeing Ewart Samson behind Steve's back – he treated her right, *ba-aaby*. They could be good together, *ba-aaby*. He gave her money and bought her nice clothes. He gave her a tab – *ba-aaby*.

The summer of punk came and Kirsty moved out. He moved on and took his records with him. He went back to his mum and dad with 'told you so' ringing in his ears. He missed her for a bit but the boys made up for it. *Welcome back Stevie, we missed you.*

He made up for lost time and took his anger out on the terraces. Worse was to follow – fascists strode the streets and recruited on the terraces. It was personal for Steve. His anger, hate and prejudice could not be contained – he wore the badge and boots with pride. He went on marches, sprayed graffiti, abused Asian shopkeepers – *White riot, white riot, white riot, wanna riot of my own.*

Britain was in meltdown – winters of discontent, power cuts – chaos reigned. Thatcher got elected and Kirsty disappeared – off the face of the earth for all he cared.

He heard rumours about Kirsty – nasty, vile rumours that he didn't want to believe. Not his Kirsty, not his *Guilty Tiger*.

CHAPTER FOUR

SUNDAY morning – he woke at his normal time and lay in bed for a while wondering what the future had in store for him. This time yesterday he'd been weighing up what to say to Debbie – thought about confronting her, thought about kicking her out but then reconsidered. They had a good life together, had a great house, enjoyed each other's company – did he really want to lose all this? *What would happen to the dogs?*

How about if he just ignored it? Told her he was cool with it – *as long as he could watch*. Perhaps he could then reciprocate, one of those 'open' marriages that he'd heard about ... maybe try and patch things up with Chantelle or Gill, whatever her name was. Perhaps have a proper crack at Laura, she was definitely keen. But then he had received that message on Facebook...

'Hi Steve, remember me, your Guilty Tiger?' Seven words that were about to turn his world upside down.

He decided to get up, usual routine, usual breakfast. He let the dogs out, watched them and laughed as they chased the squirrels. He picked up his iPhone, checked his messages on Facebook – Kirsty Clifton accepts you as a friend. She was online.

He typed a quick response. *'Hi Kirsty, nice to hear from you – how's things?'*

How's things? How's fucking things? He hadn't seen or heard from Kirsty for over thirty years and he's saying *'How's things?'*

A minute passed with no response, then a message appeared. *'OK, not really used to this facebook lark, don't know what to say.'*

'How about – what's been happening for the last thirty plus years?'

'Thirty three years,' she responded – a bit too quickly, he thought.

'Been counting?' he asked.

'Yes, you?'

'I guess.' He upped the ante. *'What's this all about?'*

There was a longer delay... he hoped he hadn't blown it.

'I've been living in London ever since we split up. I've just retired from my job and decided to move back to Bristol. Thought I'd look up a few old friends.'

She's moved back to Bristol! Fucking, fucking, fucking hell – he'd dreamt of this day.

'Can we meet?' he typed.

Another delay, he began to sweat.

'Yes, I'd like that. Can I ask are you married?'

He thought of lying, hesitated for a second.

'Yes – sort of – is that a problem?' As soon as he pressed return, he thought, *shit, what the fuck does 'sort of' mean?* He knew she would ask.

*'What do you mean *sort of*?'*

'Been married 28 years, you know how it is – not getting on too well at the moment.' He suddenly realised he hadn't asked if she was married.

'No I don't know how it is – I'm not married, never have been.'

He was genuinely shocked. He'd always imagined her married with a half a dozen half ca... mixed-race kids.

'Not to Ewart?' he asked, secretly delighted that this wasn't the case.

'No.'

She couldn't have answered any quicker – he wasn't sure what to ask or mention next. Now it was his turn to be hesitant.

'You still there?' she asked.

'Yes sorry, just don't know where this is going to be honest?'

'Neither am I. But let's have that meet and we can catch up. When can you make it?'

He didn't want to seem too keen, even though he obviously was.

'Any time next week would suit, after work, say 6ish – ok with you? We could meet in town?'

'Sounds good, I've actually got an apartment in town, on the docks, you could always meet me there. I don't know if I recognise much of the city now, it's all changed so much, unless the Guildhall Tavern's still going LOL!''

He was pleased that there was humour in her tone, or was it because she was new to Facebook? He wondered if she meant 'Lots of love' instead of 'Laugh out loud'. He thought he'd best keep it formal when in truth he just wanted to say he hadn't stop thinking about her since they split.

'Ha! No the Tavern went years ago – your place would be fine, I work in town, what's your address?'

'Apartment 24. I'm embarrassed now – it's the Penthouse, Atlantic Apartments. It's those new ones just down from the SS Great Britain – Tuesday evening okay – 6ish?'

'*Sounds good, look forward to it,*' he replied.

'*Me too x.*'

There was a kiss, he was 56 years old, heading for retirement but he felt like a teenager again. He wondered if he should do the same, he hesitated...

'*Bye x.*'

He logged off and smiled. 'Roll on Tuesday,' he said out loud, then as an afterthought, he added 'The Penthouse – sweet.'

CHAPTER FIVE

ONDAY dragged, Tuesday dragged more. He told Debbie he had a business meeting after work and he wasn't sure what time he would get home.

'That's all right love, there's a Catherine Cookson on the telly I want to watch.'

He wore his best Paul Smith suit into work. Debbie didn't notice but Laura did, but it was too late now – *you had your chance love.*

He bought a toothbrush and toothpaste at lunchtime in Boots, wondered about some aftershave but thought better of it. He brushed his teeth before leaving work and looked in the mirror – he wasn't bad for his age he told himself, in a Bruce Willis sort of way. His hair had mostly gone but he shaved it anyway – Debbie said it suited him.

An all year tan thanks to numerous holidays gave him a healthy glow. He sucked in his stomach and patted it, he'd put on a few pounds – okay maybe a few stone since he'd last seen Kirsty but he wore it well. He suddenly wondered what she would look like in the flesh – the photo on Facebook could be years old, *probably a right munter* he thought. No wonder she'd never married – probably a wrinkled up old spinster. 'Bet she's got tits like Spaniels' ears and a face like a bag of spanners' he said to himself, half jokingly. Perhaps this wasn't such a good idea.

He decided to walk to her apartment from work – there wouldn't be anywhere to park and the fresh air would do him good. He knew the apartments, knew of them but hadn't been in them. They had sprung up all over the dockside in the last few years – it had been a long time since the Floating Harbour was a working docks, maybe forty years. There were still a few old cranes and warehouses in place but in the main the old dockside buildings had either been demolished or converted into arts centres or museums. Wine bars and trendy eating houses now prevailed – the old south Bristol dockers wouldn't have recognised their own city.

Walking past the SS Great Britain, the jewel in Bristol's crown, he found the apartments. They had an entryphone system, he found the number – 24, 'the Penthouse'. He could still barely believe it – he looked up and admired the building. It was striking – all steel and glass. This place must have cost a pretty penny he wagered. That's it – she's a high class madam, those rumours about her all those years ago were true. He wondered if she was still at it. He nervously pressed the button.

'Hi Steve come up – it's the sixth floor.'

It was the first time he'd heard her voice in thirty-three years. It didn't sound like her – the harsh Bristolian accent had long gone. He entered the lift and pressed the button for the sixth floor, he could smell fresh paint – the apartments had only just been finished, he wondered how long she'd been planning to move back 'home'.

He exited the lift and saw her door just to the left. The penthouse took up the entire top floor of the building, there were potted plants and muted lighting, this was some gaff he thought – she must have been damn good.

Doubt suddenly overcame him. He stood in front of her door and hesitated, feeling sick with anticipation and trepidation, even though he'd looked forward to this day for so long – in fact he thought this day would never come. He pressed the buzzer, not knowing what would greet him behind the door.

The door opened and she stood in front of him. Not a word was said for a minute or so.

'Come in,' she finally said.

He took a tentative step towards her. She offered her cheek – he kissed it. She did the same to him.

'You'll have to excuse the mess,' she said, 'I've only just moved in.'

Steve couldn't respond – he just nodded.

He was transfixed by Kirsty – she radiated beauty. A few laughter lines maybe and her nose looked different – he wondered if she'd had it fixed. The long slim legs were the same, the cleavage if anything had improved. Her hair was still the colour of summer straw, just a few flex of grey, but it was now piled on top of her head and tucked in place with a butterfly clip – the teenage feather cut had long gone.

She oozed class. She looked and smelt of wealth. This was one successful woman – he knew he'd made a big mistake all those years ago. He wanted, needed her again.

He managed to tear his gaze from her. He looked around – the apartment was prodigiously large. His eyes were drawn to the floor-to-ceiling window at the far end leading out on to a balcony, the murky water of the Floating Harbour lay below. Beyond that the gaily painted houses of Clifton Wood gave a playful touch of the continent to the city. Further on the wealthy streets and cobbled mews of Clifton beckoned to the city's elite and rich newcomers. It was a district he didn't particularly care for. He rarely visited Clifton – it wasn't part of *his city*. It was an interloper, a usurper. Truth-be-told he loathed Clifton and its residents.

He clumsily proffered the cheap bottle of Merlot he'd bought earlier, he felt embarrassed – thinking she would probably have more expensive tastes.

'Thanks,' she said, 'I'll try and find some glasses and a corkscrew.'

'It's a screw top,' he squirmed.

'Just the glasses then,' she said with a smile, trying to make him feel at ease.

'You okay?' she queried.

'I, I just don't know what to say.'

'About what?'

About what? About fucking everything. Where have you been? What have you been doing? Why are you called Clifton and not Donohue – he had a sudden thought about the view. *Why did you contact me? What the fuck is going on?*

'Where do I start – there's so much to talk about. After all these years – why?'

'Why what?'

'Kirsty I've dreamt about this day for so long. I thought it would never happen. I thought I had lost you forever. I prayed for this day – and now it's here and you're acting as if you've just come back from a trip to the shops.'

'You've prayed for this day?'

'Yes. I've been trying to contact you for years. Tried to track you down, contacted your foster parents, searched for you on Facebook and Friends Reunited but realised it was a longshot. I trawled through all the Kirsty Donohues but none of them were you, guessed you had married – even looked for Kirsty...' He hesitated, even after all these years he found it difficult to say the name. 'Even looked for Kirsty Samson. I thought I'd tracked down your brother but it wasn't him. Tried to...'

'It was.' She cut him off.

'It was what?'

'It was my brother – Paul Donohue. I'd already told him that if you tried to find out about me that he had to deny who he was – deny who I was.'

'How come?'

'I had my reasons.'

'So why now?'

'Steve, sit down. Let's open that bottle of wine.'

She disappeared into the kitchen. He could hear her opening and closing cupboards. He took another look around the apartment – there were a few photographs around, many of a striking blonde woman in her thirties. He looked closer, she could have been a young, or an old Kirsty depending on which way he looked at it. Another photo showed two beautiful young children, one boy, one girl – they looked liked twins. Okay she said she'd never married, but she didn't say she didn't have partners.

'Ah, here we go.'

Kirsty reentered the room, picked up the bottle, opened it and poured out two large glasses.

'Cheers.' She said as she raised her glass.

'Cheers,' replied Steve.

'Okay, it goes something like this...'

Kirsty went on to explain how when she and Steve split up she moved in with Samson straight away. The two of them decided to move to London – he had friends there, it made sense. She had too many bad memories of Bristol – it was a big village, everyone knew each other. She knew her and Steve would inevitably bump into each other.

She didn't like Steve and his politics – he tried to interrupt but she stopped him. No, he could have his say later – she wanted to say her piece... So they went to London – Notting Hill, before it became gentrified.

Ewart was good to her, despite what Steve may have heard back in Bristol. Okay, he dealed – he had to to get by.

This was the late seventies – it was tough being a young man in Britain in the seventies, especially if you were black. But then it all started going wrong – she got pregnant.

Steve visibly paled at this revelation, but stayed silent.

Kirsty continued… her and Ewart weren't exactly over the moon but Kirsty was desperate to keep the baby, they could manage.

Ewart got a proper job – nothing special, working on the Underground. But what with that and the 'extra' money coming in from his street deals they would survive. The baby, a girl she called Cherry, was born in the first week of May 1979 – a child of Thatcher's Britain, a white child of Thatcher's Britain.

'You mean…?' Steve tried to interrupt again.

'Please Steve, just listen.'

Ewart moved out – after giving Kirsty a couple of black eyes to remember him by. She was destitute – she had nothing. She thought about moving back to Bristol, moving back to Steve, but she'd heard bad things about him. She didn't like his politics – didn't like what he'd become.

She stayed put in London. Some of her neighbours helped her out and got her back on her feet. They offered to babysit if she needed to get out and earn some money – after all she was young, pretty and blonde, she could earn good money – any money was good money.

There was no way that she would give up her baby, not after what she'd been through as a kid. Steve tried to interrupt once more – she put her hand up, reminding him how forceful she could be.

She admitted it – she didn't walk the streets, but she'd worked for an escort agency. Nothing sleazy, mostly businessmen and foreign diplomats – she earned good money but decided that she couldn't keep up the lifestyle. She went to night school, got some qualifications and landed a good job with the GLC. She stayed with them for over thirty years until now. Government cut backs she said – she took voluntary redundancy and a gold-plated pension.

No she had never married. Oh she had plenty of offers, came close a couple of times but her career just got in the way of relationships. No Steve, she assured him, she was not saving herself for him, it just never happened. She was now sitting pretty. That's it, that's all there was to it – she decided to move back to Bristol and here she was – sitting here, drinking a glass of Sainsbury's Merlot opposite Steve Allen.

'This daughter you had... is she, is she mine?' he finally stammered.

'Sorry Steve – I don't know how to say this, you *had* a daughter. Cherry sadly died last year. You do have two beautiful grandchildren though.'

He glanced over at the photos. If his world was upside down before he met up with Kirsty, it had now turned inside out and self imploded. He gathered his thoughts.

'Sorry, in the last ten minutes you've told me I had a daughter and now you've told me I've lost a daughter?'

'Uh, it's not exactly easy for me Steve. It was me who brought her up – I've lost *my* daughter. You, you never had one...'

'And whose fucking fault is that!' Steve exploded.

He stood up and strode around the room, rubbing his face in disbelief.

'Jeez, I don't know what to say, what, how... how did she die?'

'Car crash,' replied Kirsty matter-of-factly.

'Car crash? Is that it?'

'Yes. I don't want to talk about it, like I said it was only a year or so ago.'

Steve walked over to the photo he'd spotted earlier. 'I guess this is her?'

'Yes,' she hesitated 'and the photo next to it – they're *ou*r grandchildren, Oscar and Olivia – they're twins.'

He picked up the photo of Cherry, ran his finger across it and looked at her. She was beautiful, she was his daughter, their daughter – he could tell. He sat back down.

'I'm sorry.'

'So am I, I wished I'd told you before.'

'What, that I had a daughter or that she was dead?

'I wish I'd told you that you had a daughter. I should've told you years ago – you had a right to know.'

'Too fucking right I had a right to know.'

He sipped on his wine, contemplating what to say next.

'A daughter,' he said to himself, 'a dead daughter.'

He was too numb to cry, but he felt like it. The room fell awkwardly silent – he needed to change the mood.

'What's with the name change?'

'Oh, yeah – it's been so long. I changed it by deed poll when I started... when I started at the escort agency. In one way I wanted to forget my past, but I thought Clifton was a nice reminder of my home city. I remember my foster parents taking me to the zoo and the Suspension Bridge when I was a kid. We took a walk around Clifton and I remember looking at all the expensive houses, the fancy restaurants and all the posh people in their nice clothes. I thought one day this'll be me, I'm going to live in Clifton with all the posh people – some dream eh?'

He looked around the apartment once again.

'I don't know,' replied Steve, 'this place doesn't look too shabby.'

'This? Yeah I did alright selling my place in London – got a small fortune for it compared to what I paid. I carried on living in Notting Hill – it rapidly went upmarket and I kept trading up. What with the retirement money, yeah, I guess I'm not doing too bad. So how about yourself – looks like life's treating you good?'

'Okay I suppose. Stayed in the graphic design world, I now work at one of the big financial groups, I'm the Art

Director in their in-house studio. Pays well – had a good few bonuses. Yeah life's okay I guess.'

'Looks better than okay. Nice suit and that watch looks like it cost a few bob – nice Audi as well.'

'Oh the watch? Yeah, my dad died a few years ago – he left me a couple of grand, I decided to get something to remind me of him.'

'Sorry, sorry – I didn't realise your dad died.'

'That's alright, but he was only 70. Heart attack finally got him – tough old boy, glad he didn't suffer. I do miss him though.'

'Yeah, yeah, he was okay to me – and your mum. Is she still alive?'

'Yes, like you care though.' Kirsty and Steve's mother hardly saw eye to eye.

'That's not fair Steve. She didn't exactly welcome me into the family home. Is she still in the same house?'

'Yep, still in the same council house in Southmead. I've offered to buy it time and time again, but she would have none of it.'

'Still a dye in the wool socialist then?'

'Oh yes, the red flag still flies high in the Allen household.'

'What, including yours? After what you were like?'

'That was a long time ago. I made a big mistake Cherry, there isn't a day that goes by that I don't have regrets about my past, but things have changed.'

'They sure have,' said Kirsty, 'they sure have.'

They caught each other's eyes for a moment. Hers still had the devil in them. She studied his, deep and dark – just as they always were. Both of them knew then they were still in love with each other.

'Kirsty...'

She interrupted – aware he was going to say something she wasn't ready to hear. Not yet anyway.

'Tell me about this "sort of" marriage you're in – sounds intriguing?'

Steve felt uncomfortable. He squirmed and shifted position.

'Oh that. Yes well, been married for nearly thirty years, got two boys, Sam and Harry, they're great-*ish*. But well, since they moved out, you know things have got a bit... stale, bit boring. You know "ABC sex". So uh, so we're in an "open marriage". We're still friends, but more like brother and sister. You know we sort of do our own thing – she sees other blokes and I uh, I see other women, er...occasionally. Simple as that really.'

'ABC sex?'

'Yeah, yunno – Anniversaries, Birthdays, Christmas.'

She giggled and shook her head – remembering how much he used to make her laugh. Kirsty knew he was lying, she'd heard it all before, he'll be saying *'she doesn't understand me'* next – she didn't believe it from the others and she didn't believe it now from Steve.

Steve thought he'd reinforce his story. He was just about to say 'she doesn't understand me' when Kirsty spoke again.

'Oh, well that's okay then – "sort of" makes us alright then?' She was toying with him.

'Us?' he queried.

'Yes us, thought we could just pick up where we left off – did you? I mean, surely that's why you've been trying to track me down isn't it?'

'Well, yes, I suppose, no, no, not really – I just wanted to know that you were okay that's all. I just wanted to hear that you were happy and that things were ... just okay with you. That's all.'

'What so you could feel less guilty?' She snapped.

'Hold on a minute, it was you who left me. You were the one who fucked off with Ewart *fucking* Samson.'

'Only because of what was happening to us, what was happening to you! You forced me out, what with your mates and your football and your fucking Nazi politics! No wonder I fucking left...'

'Whoa, what came fucking first? You had been sniffing around Samson for ages, couldn't wait to get...'

'He was a friend of a friend Steve. That's all it was, a friendship – at first. You couldn't handle it that I had a black male friend. That's all he was, a friend – if you could have accepted that all those years ago then maybe we would still have been together. Maybe we would have had kids – maybe you would still have had a fucking daughter!'

Kirsty started sobbing uncontrollably. He instinctively got up and put his arms around her.

'Shhhh, shhhh,' he tried to calm her.

He nestled into her hair – she smelt as good now as she did all those years ago. He felt her body against his, she'd put on weight but if anything it was now firmer and more toned. He kissed the top of her head, she brought her head up and their eyes meet – he kissed Kirsty on the lips. She didn't pull away. It was a long hard kiss, the sort they enjoyed as teenagers, the tongues darted in and out – he pulled away.

'Kirsty, I've missed you so much. I'm sorry, so sorry. I can make it up to you. I'll leave Debbie right now. I won't go home tonight, I'll stay with you tonight, tomorrow, forever – I still love you Kirsty. I've never stopped loving you.'

She pushed him away.

'No, no, no – you'd better go. Please go now, this isn't right. I knew this was a bad idea – go, please Steve go.'

She was still sobbing – she broke away from him. 'Go now.... please.'

He stood there, dumbstruck.

'But I, I thought we would...'

'Well, whatever you thought, you thought wrong.'

57

He backed off and opened the door not saying a word. He turned around and gave her a long pleading look.

'Please.' She repeated.

Dejectedly he walked back to his car past Brunel's engineering masterpiece and the overpriced restaurants and bars. He got in his car and drove back home to his wife.

He was baffled by the evening's events. More troubled now than he was before – first he'd found out he had a daughter then found out he had a dead one. But he had grandchildren – *thank heaven for small mercies.*

Did she really think that that would be it? Did she really think that he wouldn't try to contact her again, try to contact his grandchildren? He shook his head – a hundred thoughts ran through his mind. He looked down at the steering wheel and looked at the distinctive four circles of the marque...

'How the fuck does she know I drive an Audi?' he said out loud.

CHAPTER SIX

WEDNESDAY was no different than any other working day for Steve except that he couldn't keep his mind on his work – he was normally so focussed, so conscientious, so proficient – to the point of being pedantic some would say. He knew he was good at his job, that wasn't being arrogant, just a fact. He was skilled in Quark and InDesign, expert at Photoshop and could spot a typo at twenty paces. With the advent of Macs and laptops it meant he could carry out a fair bit of freelance work at home which earned him a nice bit of 'bunce' and paid for the three holidays he and Debbie usually enjoyed each year. He'd been involved in the graphic design business since leaving college, maybe it was too long – perhaps it was time for a major change. Time to get his work/life balance sorted at long last – spend some time with his grandchildren, the grandchildren who until yesterday he never realised he had.

Steve arrived home at 7 and made his usual fuss over the dogs while they reciprocated with childlike whelps and snuffles. He gave Debbie a routine kiss on the cheek and wondered who she'd been shagging that day.

He casually flicked through the day's mail – it was the usual 'shit that folds' trying to flog him insurance for the over fifties – with a free pen, guaranteed investments in foreign properties and loans that he neither wanted nor needed. He discarded them all straight into the bin without even opening.

The next envelope was DL in size, dull brown and officious, he opened it hoping it was a tax rebate from the Inland Revenue. There was a logo in the top right hand corner which he recognised immediately – it was from Avon & Somerset police. He read through it once, broke out in a cold sweat and read it through once again:

Offence committed: Importuning for homosexual activities.

FAO: Mr Steven Allen.

You have been observed committing the offence(s) mentioned above by undercover police officers at Tog Hill car park, South Gloucestershire on Friday 4 March at approx 17.00 hours. This is a written caution of the said offence – we now require you to attend Trinity Road Police Station, on Friday 11 March at 16.00 hours to receive a formal caution.

Failure to do so will result in a visit to your address by police officers to issue the aforementioned caution and/or to arrest said person.

He visibly shook and the colour drained from his face. *Fuck, fuck, fuckity fuck.*

'You alright love?' asked Debbie.

'Yeah, yeah, nothing – caught using the bloody bus lane again. Another thirty quid I'll have to cough up.'

'You don't learn do you? That's about the third one isn't it?'

'Yeah, I'll uh, I'll take more care next time.'

Bollocks, bollocks, bollocks. That's all I fucking need.

He shoved the letter in his pocket and cursed coming home early the week before. If he hadn't he would've been blissfully unaware of Debbie and her sexual exploits and perhaps more importantly, not facing a charge of importuning.

He picked up his iPad, logged onto Facebook and checked for messages, there was nothing from Kirsty – she wasn't online either. He had to contact her again – he sent her a message: '*Hi Kirsty, despite everything it was great to see you last night, we can't let this finish before it's even started, please drop me a line – I need to see you again, there's a lot of questions I still need to ask. Steve X*'

He originally *put 'Love Steve'*, but thought it best not to, an '*X*' would suffice.

He powered off his iPad and kept an occasional eye on his iPhone, he had a few messages – mostly jokes from Pete. Some made him snigger, others made him want to gag but he did laugh at '*Couldn't find my scraper for the ice on my windscreen this morning, had to use my Homebase discount card, trouble is only got 10% off.*'

Finally there was a message from Kirsty: '*OK call me.*' She gave her mobile number.

'Just got to phone someone about work love,' he said to Debbie as he wandered into the conservatory. She nodded in response as he phoned Kirsty – she answered immediately.

'Hi Steve – you okay?'

'No, not really – last night, bit of a shock to be honest. Lots to take in... there's also a couple of things that are baffling me. I just don't get it. I really need to see you again.'

There was a silence.

'Kirsty? You still there?'

'Yes, still here.' Silence again.

'Okay, okay – I admit I haven't been totally honest with you. How about tomorrow? But not at my apartment this time, it might be best if we're in a more public place.'

Steve didn't know what she meant by this but went along with it all the same.

'Yeah, suits me – how about...' he paused for a moment, 'can you remember The Shakespeare in Prince Street, it's not far from your apartment, 6.30ish?'

'Yep I know it – always a bit of an old duffer's pub wasn't it? How about the Garrick's Head?'

'Garrick's Head? Christ they pulled that down years back. Sorry, if you fancy one of the wine bars, think there's a place called The Front Room. I've heard that's quite...cool.'

She could hear the disappointment in his voice.

'Cool? No, The Shakespeare's fine, see you tomorrow.'

'Great, yep – look forward to it.'

Kirsty didn't answer, she hung up. Steve bit his tongue for using the word 'cool'.

Steve liked the Shakespeare. It was one of the few old pubs still left in the city centre – they had an open fire and they let dogs in, Prince and Buster always got a warm welcome. It had no obtrusive music and they served decent ale and pickled eggs. Yes Kirsty was right – it was an old duffer's pub.

He'd told Debbie he was going to the gym after work, then probably have a few beers with a couple of his gym buddies. 'Don't wait up', he said, 'I'll grab a kebab on the way home.'

He ordered a pint of Butcombe, took a long hard swig and looked around, there was no Kirsty. He grabbed a table by the fire, pissing off a couple of students who were about to pounce.

'Fuck off back up Park Street to your student bars,' he grumbled. He could be a miserable bastard when he wanted to. He sat alone for ten minutes, looked at his watch every two minutes and studied the door. *She's not coming, she's bottled it and she's going to cut me out of her life – again.*

The door opened and in she walked wearing a long Burberry raincoat wrapped up tight to keep out the cold evening air, the belt knotted around her waist only served to accentuate her figure. Every male in the bar turned to look at her – she wasn't the usual sight for the Shakespeare on a cold, drizzly night. He thought how unreasonable he'd been – perhaps a wine bar would have been more suitable. Steve stood up to greet her, they kissed on the cheeks – she looked around and took in the environs.

'Sorry – if you'd rather go elsewhere?' Steve asked with a hint of embarrassment in his voice.

'No, it's fine – honest. Just get me a large red okay?'

It was more of an instruction than a request. She was obviously used to giving orders and getting her own way, she was far removed from the insecure teenage skinhead girl he knew all those years ago.

They both sat down, clinked glasses and took long gulps.

'How do you know I drive an Audi?' He asked bluntly, he could be just as forceful.

'What? I um, when did I say that?' stammered Kirsty.

'On Tuesday. You commented on my suit, my watch and my Audi, but I didn't mention my car. So how come you know I drive an Audi?'

'I, er, saw you driving it.'

'You're fucking lying Kirsty, you're good at that. I didn't drive to your place, I walked. I'll ask again... how come you know I drive an Audi? What else are you lying about?' He hesitated for a second then continued.

'Please tell me Cherry is still alive?'

'No, sorry, Cherry is dead. But okay, I haven't been totally truthful with you... I um, look... I didn't work for the GLC.'

Here she goes, she's now going to come clean about her life of prostitution and being a high class madam.

'I worked for the police... the Met.'

'Now I know you're fucking lying.'

'I'm not. What I told you the other night was true – everything up to working for the GLC. I did work for an escort agency – for a while. I did go to evening classes, I got qualifications then got a job at Paddington Green police station, just filing and clerical work. I wasn't a copper at that stage, but they recognised my ability and suggested I joined the force.'

She inhaled, picked up her glass and took a long swig before continuing.

'It wasn't easy. I had to fight against prejudice and misogeny. Talk about "Life on Mars" – met more than my fair share of Gene Hunts, but there were a few in the Met fighting my corner. This was the eighties, the Met really needed to improve their image – I was fast tracked, but it was all on merit. Ended up as a Chief Inspector and yes I have just retired and yes I really did want to move back to Bristol – so here I am.'

Steve stared into space wondering if 'Gene Hunt' was a new bit of Cockney rhyming slang she'd picked up. He finally thought of something to say...

'You got to be fucking joking.'

'Nope that's exactly how it is, honest.'

Steve suddenly remembered his original question...

'But that still doesn't explain how you know about me driving an Audi.'

'Ah, yes, the Audi. Now that is a long story... can you remember getting nicked at Paddington Station in the early eighties – 1982 I think?'

'Like it was yesterday,' he replied, 'but how do you know?'

'Well, I was working that day. I hadn't been there long, still only doing the filing, but it was kicking off everywhere that Saturday. They asked me to come in and help out doing the paperwork. Well I always needed the money so I left

Cherry with a neighbour and went in. Rovers had been playing somewhere in London if I recall and it kicked off on the platform. You lot brawled with some Cardiff fans who'd also been visiting London – good planning by the FA on that one. You and the rest of 'The Big Five' got pulled in, remember it?'

'It was Millwall,' recalled Steve, 'we decided to have a bit of a jolly in the smoke cos JB was on leave from the Army, he was off to the Falklands the following week.' He motioned for her to continue.

'I saw your name and date of birth on the charge sheet – it jumped out like a swear word in the Bible. I knew it was you straight away – I've never forgotten your birthday, often thought about sending a card, but well... Anyway, then the other names cropped up – John Burston, Pete McNulty, obvious they would be there – and the rest of 'em.

'Of course it was still paper records back then – nothing computerised. It was down to me where I filed the papers, the charge sheets, the statements, your pathetic calling cards. I had all the evidence in my hands of Steve Allen and his mates – some nasty weapons you had on board if I recall, talk of Stanley knives and knuckle dusters being used. You should all have gone down for a few years.'

Steve's mind was spinning. He'd always wondered why the case was suddenly dropped, one minute they were look-ing at serving at least two years, the next thing fuck all – all charges dropped. They thought they were the luckiest bastards alive – if they would have gone inside then their whole lives would have changed, JB would have been slung out of the Army and they'd probably be in and out of nick for the rest of their lives.

He was embarrassed she thought their '*You have been visited by The Big Five – BRFC*' calling cards were pathetic though, he thought he'd come up with a nice design and Mike had done a decent job on the print, laminated as well, not like the tat the Soul Crew had. If the Old Bill had done their job properly they would also have found traces of amphetamines on the cards – that laminating came in handy, pre credit cards.

'So I thought Steve Allen's still involved with the aggro is he? He always promised me he would give it up, but I thought I would do you and your mates one last favour. Some of them treated me good, better than you at times to be honest.'

He wasn't sure what she meant by that... he nodded for her to continue.

'Well I had the lot all in front of me. All the files, the statements, charge sheets, mugshots – everything. Nice pic by the way Steve – quality 'tache and wedge haircut, and what the fuck were you wearing? I thought they had nicked Ronnie Corbett.'

Steve recalled his Casual phase – Lyle & Scott roll neck and a Pringle sweater. Not his finest sartorial moment, he had to admit.

'I even sneaked a look at you in your cell. I thought about asking the Sergeant if he could let you out so we could have a chat but thought better of it. Big Steve Allen, king of the Tote End all alone in a police cell, you looked ... so pathetic, so sad. I thought you were going to start crying.

'So what was I to do? Well I'll tell you – I binned the fucking lot. Took all the paperwork home and binned it. Well not the mugshot – still got that somewhere, but the rest I just chucked. I just told them I'd lost it in the station what with all the mayhem going on. They turned the place upside down, but of course they couldn't find anything. Sure they went apeshit – they were in the middle of all those operations against the Headhunters, the ICF and the like but it would've been worse if the papers got to know that they'd lost vital evidence against another mob of football hooligans. So they just brushed it under the carpet. Anyway they had bigger fish to fry than rounding up a few worzels from the West Country.

'They forgave me. I turned on my usual charm, wore an even shorter skirt into work the next day, unbuttoned my blouse, flashed a bit of tit and the lecherous tossers just told me to be more careful next time *'darlin'*. You blokes, you're all the same – and you call us the weaker sex?'

'So if it wasn't for me Steve Allen, who knows what sort of life you would be living now? All of you – I saved you all. By the looks of you and that motor, you haven't done too bad for yourself, and it's all down to me Steve – your life would have changed forever – for the worse, if it hadn't been for me.'

He sat in silence for a while – he was speechless. For one he would never have married Debbie, they'd only been together for a year or so and she warned him, any more trouble and that was it, they were finished. He wouldn't have had his two boys. He wouldn't have kept his job – he wouldn't now be working for Pinnacle. He wouldn't have had the holidays, the clothes, the nice house... he would have lost the whole fucking lot – and it was all down to Kirsty.

'Lost for words Steve? That's a first.'

'I don't know what to say. Thanks ... I guess. But it still doesn't explain the car?' He was now feeling exasperated.

'Get me another drink and I'll finish the story.'

He quickly did as he was told and returned with two fresh glasses.

'I've been watching you Steve, watching you for years. Since that day I've been keeping tabs on you and your mates. It's all on record, right up to the present day. You enjoyed a ruck, got nicked a few times, but by and large you kept your noses clean. You and all your mates, none of you were stupid, well not all of you. Funny though, up until 1982 it was quite regular wasn't it Steve? Little skirmishes here and there, especially when you got involved with the far right but then that was it. You all cleaned up your acts didn't you – why was that Steve?'

She didn't wait for an answer...

'That's right – because of that scare in West London. Well that would have been more than a scare, that would have been banged to rights, that would have been time in Wormwood Scrub with all those real Cockney villains, but it wasn't was it? Because of me, you and your mates kept your liberty. You have got a bloody lot to thank me for Steve, you have got your whole bloody, cosy life to thank me for – so less of the "hard done by looks" please.'

Steve visibly squirmed, eventually finding something of interest at the bottom of his beer glass.

'Don't get me wrong,' she continued, 'it's not as if I've been stalking you, or being your guardian angel or anything. Just every now and then I'd check up and see what was happening. As technology progressed I was able to set up tags so that it flagged up anytime you or your mates' names got logged on the PNC – the Police National Computer – anywhere in the country, I'd know about it.'

He shook his head once more.

'This is... this is incredible. I had no idea... is this legal?'

'Course it is, we're the police,' she corrected herself. 'I *was* the police – here to protect and serve!' She was dangling him on a string – there was laughter in her voice at last.

'Where was I? Oh yes, kept your noses clean – mostly.' She looked at him coquettishly and tapped the side of her nose.

What was she getting at? She fucking knows something.

'Let's see, what were you thinking of getting nicked, what just ten years ago in Cardiff – in the car park wasn't it? Before the game – what is it with you and Cardiff?'

'Like oil and water, Cardiff and Bristol – just don't mix. Anyway, I only got cautioned... was that anything to do with you?'

'No Steve, I wasn't doing this to stop you lot getting charged – that would be illegal. Like I said I was just observing, there was no hidden agenda, nothing. Just self interest I guess.'

'Sure you don't mean self gratification?'

'No. But I suppose I felt vindicated, I still do – like I said you weren't bad lads... men.'

'So apart from that little tug in Cardiff Mr Allen, you've stayed on the straight and narrow haven't you?'

'Go on. You've obviously got something on me, come on – out with it. You've been toying with me all evening, and I've got some idea this is something to do with my car. But I can't believe you've been studying footage of me driving in bus lanes?'

Kirsty hesitated and gathered her thoughts once more.

'Gary "Bulldog" Rattigan – friend of yours is he?'

'I, I know of Gary Rattigan yes. What of it?'

'Well if you know him, you'll know he's a low life drug dealer – cocaine mostly, plus he's got convictions for ABH, assault, possession of offensive weapons – all round bad lad to be honest.'

Steve didn't answer.

'It's no use stalling Steve. We know... I know you know him – not that we were particularly interested in low lifes like Rattigan. He's just a small piece of shit on a very big wheel, but we watched him, or at least my colleagues in the A&S police watched him. Watched him doing his grubby little deals on the street, in the pubs, outside schools, youth clubs – anywhere he could make a bit of cash.

'There's no way they would nick him – and as for locking him up. If we did that to every little two-bit dealer the prisons would be full to bursting, well even more bursting than they are now. No, we're interested in the bigger pieces of shit on that wheel Steve – the suppliers, the Mr Bigs of the world. So guess what? When you pulled up in your flash Audi 7 while we were watching Rattigan, alarm bells sounded. Nice big motor like that, tinted windows and to top it all a Jamaican flag sticker in one corner of the back window and a 'Black Power' badge in the other – well you might as well have had a sign with *"I'm a major coke supplier"* lit up on the roof – the drug squad couldn't believe their luck.'

Steve furrowed his brow before answering.

'That badge... that's not Black Power it's "Keep the Faith" – y'unno Northern Soul, and as for the Jamaican flag sticker – it's The Skatalites – my favourite band.' He sounded and felt pathetic.

'Uh, I vaguely remember them – *Guns of Navarone* wasn't it?'

He nodded, feeling sheepish, then thought about her and the police's generalisation about blacks – so what if it had been a Black Power or a Jamaican flag sticker, that would have made him a drug suspect would it? And she was the one criticising him for being too judgmental – talk about double standards.

'Oh don't worry, you checked out. It soon became obvious you weren't the Big Shit they were looking for. But they had your card marked so be careful – cocaine is a nasty, grubby little habit all the same Steve, and at your age for fuck's sake. Rest of the boys at it as well?'

He could hardly deny it. Banged to rights he guessed. 'No just me. None of them do it or know about me doing it.'

Steve was telling the truth – his mates abhorred drugs, many a Friday night rant revolved around drug dealers and hanging the bastards.

'I, I just got into it through work – fuck me, the British media and creative industries wouldn't function without cocaine. Everyone's at it – we work hard and play harder. I'm not an addict or anything, just a bit of a livener at the weekend – recreational that's all.'

'Oh Steve, don't try and justify it. You haven't got to preach to me about drug use and the middle classes. Every dinner party in Hampstead finishes with a silver salver of Charlie these days. Frank Bough has got a lot to answer for that's for sure – but for every middle-class professional like you who can handle and afford it, there's a hundred who can't and who have to rob, steal and sleep around to get their fix. And any way if you knew what was in it you wouldn't be so keen to shove it up your nose.'

Steve looked at her quizzically.

'Let's put it this way – the price of a gram has barely changed for the last twenty years, yet a kilo of the stuff was about thirty nine grand three years ago. Now with the choirboys – sorry Customs, and SOCA being so successful that wholesale price has gone up to £45,000. Just allowing for inflation from 1990 that gram ought to be costing you over £90, yet you're still paying £40 – what, you think the drug barons are being charitable and doing all you mugs a favour?'

He shook his head and shrugged, even though he knew what she was getting at.

'No chance. What they're doing is cutting it even more. So your gram of coke is in fact mostly benzocaine, phenacetin and caffeine with less than ten per cent being actual cocaine hydrochloride – no wonder they call it Charlie. But don't kid yourself, it's still a Class A drug Steve, it's illegal – it causes misery. Grow up for fuck's sake!'

He felt like a chided schoolboy – and mortally offended that she referred to him as middle class.

'Okay, okay, quit the sermon – I guess that explains the car then – anything else?'

'Anything else? How long have you got?'

71

* * *

Just over a mile away, in a shabby office at the back of Stokes Croft, Leon Campbell was working late yet again. Drowning in a sea of files, reports and new directives, he was exhausted and dispirited. His email inbox as ever was full – he still had 18 emails to get through before he could clock off. He was sure this wasn't the reason he packed in a perfectly good and well paid job at the engineering company some nine years back. He was now 59 but felt like he was 79. He told Margaret, his long-suffering wife, that he wanted to do something more worthwhile – he wanted to put something back into the community, help the youngsters get out of the rut of long-term unemployment and the inevitable problems that went with it. Right now he was sure ruing the day he became a social worker.

He looked at his screen as another email popped in. Fucking BlackBerries – okay for those lightweights sat at home, feet up, watching the telly while making out they're working from home.

'I'm at the fucking coal face 'ere. I've actually got to do the fucking work!' he screamed at the screen.

'Ya bloodclot,' he slammed his fist on his desk and shouted out 'me going home!'

He grabbed his coat, switched off the lights, locked up and got on his bike – *fucking rain, just what me need, this won't help me cough.*

* * *

Kirsty was now in full flow, she knew about Harry – Steve's youngest son – his drug problem and his subsequent stay in prison. She even knew about the trouble his mother had – vandalism on her house back on the council estate, windows smashed by some little toerag hoodies.

'How come you clocked that one?' queried Steve.

'Well, I initially still had your parents' address logged, so it just stayed there. Your mum called the local PCSO, for all the good that would do. I didn't notice it at first but it escalated because her neighbour's house, Mr and Mrs Singh's also got attacked. That showed up as a racist incident which caught my eye.'

'Why did it catch your eye? You mean, you thought it might be something to do with me? For fuck's sake!'

'No Steve, I didn't – I was just taking an interest that's all, like I said it just...' she trailed off.

'It's just what? You thought after all these years I wonder if Steve Allen's still a racist? Well I'm not, so get that nasty little idea out of your head. Of all the things I have regrets about, all those things I did back then, my flirt with fascism is the thing I regret the most, alright? I didn't join the NF, those bastards joined us, geddit? They deliberately targeted us disillusioned, disgruntled boot boys and before I know it I'm branded a racist for the rest of my life. Give it a fucking rest eh? And you're forgetting something – it also all got a bit personal for me, thanks to you.'

'Sorry Steve, I really am – sorry, you're right. We all made mistakes back then – the thought shouldn't even have crossed my mind.'

Kirsty could see he was genuinely hurt and upset, she leant across and kissed him on the cheek, 'forgive me' she whispered in his ear.

'Okay, you're forgiven,' he finally said. 'Am I?'

'Yes,' replied Kirsty. This time she leant forward and kissed him on the lips. He tasted her lipstick, he felt he was back with Kirsty – for good. Another thought crossed his mind.

'Are you still monitoring me by any chance?'

'I might be, why?'

Steve was thinking of the letter he'd received from Avon and Somerset police the previous morning.

'Nothing just wondered that's all.'

'No, only kidding – not since I left the force. That was last year, I've still got friends in it though, so I'm sure I could have a little sniff around if you want me to?'

'No that's alright, it was nothing.' *Thank fuck for that.*

'You mentioned you had been keeping an eye on not just me, but the rest of the boys – got anything on them?' He asked, half jokingly.

She didn't answer, by that he knew there was something.

'There is isn't there? Go on tell me.'

It was his turn to be playful. He just thought it might come in handy some time if he had a bit of dirt on his mates.

'It's nothing much, I'm sure you know already.'

He thought for a moment, but then realised just how secretive they all were about their private lives. He thought he knew them inside out but then again he knew nothing about their fears, their problems – their little dark secrets.

'Well JB has been reported to the local plod for assaulting his wife on a couple of occasions.' She stopped abruptly.

'I really shouldn't be saying this.' The two large glasses of red were loosening her tongue.

'Go on, you know you want to,' Steve coaxed her along, 'another drink?'

He returned with a pint of Butcombe and a large Pinot Noir.

'You were saying – JB and Sharon?'

'Yes well, he'd been reported a couple of times but every time we, sorry they, turned up she would have a change of heart and withdraw the complaint. They said if she did it again they would charge her with wasting police time.'

'Is that it?' said Steve, thinking it was going to be a lot more than JB giving his missus a few slaps.

'Isn't that bad enough? A bloke should never raise his hand to a woman – never.'

He knew what she was getting at, that was another one of his regrets from his youth – he felt suitably admonished.

'Okay, sorry. You're right – it's bang out of order, bang out of order,' he repeated.

'Anything else?'

'Pete McNulty has been done for kerb crawling.'

Steve spat out his beer...

'No fucking way! You are shitting me!'

'Nope – just been cautioned. Been done a couple of times though.'

'Can't fucking wait to see him about that,' said Steve barely containing his glee.

'Don't you dare, this is in strictest confidence Steve. I knew I shouldn't have told you – I knew it was a bad idea.'

'You're right. I won't say a word, especially after what he and Sue have been through – I presume you know about their daughter?'

'Sadly yes, awful – how is she? Natasha isn't it?'

'Yeah, lovely girl. Not good, like a bloody cabbage – and to think the bastard who did it is now out of nick, living a normal life with an identity change. Your fucking justice sucks Kirsty.'

'It's not my justice Steve, that's what...'

'That's what *what*?'

'Nothing, forget it.'

Steve was beginning to think there really was a hidden agenda going on. Something still wasn't quite right, she was still being economical with the truth – and what did she mean 'it was a bad idea'?

'Is that it, surely the other two got something on them?' He thought he would go along with the game for a bit.

'George Smolinski deals in illegal steroids.'

'Now that doesn't surprise me. I knew he was up to something. He's always edgy, always aggressive. I suppose he deals down the gym?'

She nodded. 'He's actually been nicked and charged, appeared in court and got a fine. I don't know how it didn't appear in the papers – guess you lot never found out?'

'Nope, never knew that. But like I said, it doesn't surprise me at all.' He shook his head and muttered 'George you muppet' under his breath.

'So that just leaves Cribby. But I'm telling you now he's always been a bullshitter. So if he's owned up to anything, I wouldn't believe a bloody word of it.'

Kirsty was quiet for a while, she was mulling something over, she finally spoke...

'Shall we go back to my place?'

They walked back to Kirsty's apartment arm in arm. There was something false about the situation, he pointed out the sights of the revamped City Docks while she feigned interest. He wondered why Kirsty went quiet when he asked about Mike Cribb. Despite his pleas, she wouldn't divulge anything about him – she said there was nothing to be told. Not for the first time he disbelieved her.

They reached her apartment with Steve not entirely sure of what was in store for the rest of the evening – he quickly found out. As he closed the door behind him he turned to see Kirsty undoing the belt and buttons of her coat, she took it off and let it drop to the floor exposing her totally naked body. She purposely strode towards him, put her arms around his neck and kissed him hard, Steve responded with equal fervour. They found themselves heading for the bedroom, which like the rest of the apartment was copiously large – an elegant, impressive king size bed with slightly tacky gold coloured satin sheets dominated the room. They fell onto it as one whilst Kirsty tore at Steve's clothing.

There was to be no repeat of Steve's previous disastrous sexual encounter with 'Chantelle' – this was tender and loving, something he'd missed for a number of years. Kirsty's body belied her age, she'd kept in shape – the two of them had. He was surprisingly relaxed, the last time they'd made love was over thirty years ago, he remembered the date, 30 August 1978, the result had been a beautiful daughter – that thought suddenly entered his head and it saddened him, he wondered what might have been. But those frantic, sordid teenage experiences were now way behind them – they made love expertly and joyously, often catching each other's eye, a smile never far from his or her lips. They climaxed together and held each other like their lives depended on it.

Kirsty finally spoke – she was lying on top of Steve running her fingers over the tattoo on his left shoulder. *'Big Five'* – the design based on the Prince Buster label that released the iconic record. She leant down and kissed it.

'I remember the day you and your mates got them done – you were in agony.'

Steve looked at it as if he'd never seen it before.

'Not one of Skuse's finest I guess,' replied Steve, referring to the tattooist Les Skuse and his dingy parlour in St Werburghs. 'You can barely make it out now. It's nearly forty years old.'

'How about this?'

She ran her palm over the large leaping tiger that adorned his right shoulder.

'Looks more recent?'

'Oh that... '

'It's beautiful,' she said, 'is it anything to do with...'

He finished her sentence for her. 'Us? No, no, just fancied having something colourful – had it done on my fiftieth birthday,' he lied.

She knew he wasn't being truthful but decided not to pursue it – inside she glowed with love and pride for him.

'Mid-life crisis eh Steve? You'll be getting a Harley next.'

He made a mental note to himself – must get rid of those motorcycle brochures from Fowlers when I get home.

'Don't start,' he replied gruffly.

'Don't start what?' She sensed there was a storm brewing.

'All that "mid-life crisis" crap that women refer to with a knowing smirk.'

She realised she'd touched a nerve, she had a feeling he was about to explode – the way she'd seen him do so many times in the past, only this time she hadn't expected it, not now. Not while they were lying naked together in each other's arms.

'Sorry what do you mean?'

'You.'

'Me? What do you mean – what have I done?'

'Sorry I don't mean you *per se*. I mean women. All women think it's some sort of joke. They think it's not real, just something us blokes make up – like how you refer to us getting "man flu". Well for a lot of us it's not a joke, it's real, very real, a real crisis that can't be resolved by... I don't know, having an affair with a young bit of stuff, or getting a tattoo done. Or, or getting a Harley Davidson.'

Kirsty could see he was hurting, hurting deep inside, she hadn't expected it, she thought she'd let him continue – continue to wallow in his self pity...

'Just about every bloke I know has gone through it, and some I know have been near suicidal, yet all you do is make fun of us and nudge and wink at your mates. For fuck's sake "Loose women" have made a career out of taking the piss out of men having mid-life crises. Imagine if we, blokes did that about women eh? Imagine a programme called... I don't know "Fucked off blokes" and all we did was slag off women. Can you see that being shown on daytime TV?'

Kirsty made a pathetic attempt to shake her head, suppressing a smile as she envisioned the title sequence.

'No, apart from the title being a bit of a problem it wouldn't be on during the daytime would it? And why's that? Because the target audience – us middle-aged blokes would be too busy working our balls off like we've been doing for the majority of our lives. Working to put food on the table, working to put a roof over our family's heads, working to pay for the holidays – you name it, we pay for it.'

'Steve that's not fair...'

He put his hand up to stop her from continuing.

'Oh don't get me wrong, I'm not saying women don't do their bit, course they do, especially women like you. But for us blokes it just seems so... so relentless, so expected. Women get to fifty and they seem to be content with their lives, content with their nice house, they're happy as long as they can go out and buy new cushions or scented candles or a new handbag, to a bloke well, that's just all, just all garnish, frivolous stuff that doesn't count for anything. We, well we're supposed to be content with all that as well I guess, but there's something missing. We've delivered, done our bit, our job's done – we're redundant, served our purpose but we're still expected to be the man of the house, make the decisions, do the DIY... cut the grass.'

He was clutching at straws – and losing the argument.

'In reality our dreams have gone and our lives are still unfulfilled. It's like we've accomplished everything, reached our career goals and yet, yet we're still... bored and fed up with the same old routine.'

'So that's it is it? You're bored? Is that what you're saying? All male mid-life crises are due to men being bored?'

It was now Steve's turn to feel uncomfortable.

'Yes I guess, but it's not only that – it's like we haven't got a voice. No one listens to us – we're the silent majority, silent majority in our own country.'

'We? You mean men – you're sounding like a bitter and twisted right-wing misogynist Steve Allen.'

'I rest my case,' he replied matter-of-factly.

'What do you mean?'

'Exactly that. I express an opinion, express my grievances, express my fears and concerns and I get branded a right-wing misogynist who's having a mid-life crisis – that's exactly my point.' He thumped his hand on the bed to emphasise his point.

A silence fell over the two of them. He'd said his piece but she didn't want to pursue it any more, she sensed he had more to say on the subject, but now was not the time to delve into his head – she was content just to be with him. They were lying there like they had known each other all their lives, Steve wished they had, wished he could have turned the clock back so that the last three decades of his life had included Kirsty rather than being devoid of her.

'Where's all this going Kirsty?' he finally asked.

'I don't know Steve. Why, does this not fit in with your "open marriage"?'

'No, it's not that – it's just that there's so much going on, so many complications – so much to think through,' he hesitated before continuing.

'I still don't think you're being a hundred percent truthful with me though. You're holding back on something, I know you are – I've got a feeling it's something to do with Cherry – am I right?'

She rolled off of him exposing her entire body. Her breasts were not what they were but they were still firm and impressive – he felt embarrassed as she caught him looking at them.

'Sorry, I, I...' he stammered.

'That's okay.' She was relieved that his mind had wandered from his questioning of her.

'You missed this.' She turned to expose her bare back, on her left shoulder was a small, very fresh, small blood red heart with elegant script wording reading 'Cherry oh baby' below it in a scroll.

He could see the hurt in her eyes.

'Tell me Kirsty. Tell me the truth about our daughter. I need to know.'

She lay back on his chest and took a deep breath.

'Kirsty did die last year, but not in a car crash. She died of a heart attack brought on by snorting cocaine – that's all you need to know.'

Steve looked in to her eyes, her eyes that were beginning to fill with tears.

'How?' he finally said. 'How, why – was she an addict? I've seen the photo – she looks, looked so healthy, so gorgeous.'

'Oh she was. She was perfect, perfect in every way. She just got in with the wrong people.'

'Like who?' said Steve, suddenly seeing an image of Ewart Samson in his mind's eye.

'Okay, okay, I'll tell you the full story,' she rolled off him. The two of them lay back on the bed.

'Cherry was not only beautiful, she was bright, intelligent. She went to Edinburgh University and got a degree in Higher Mathematics. When she came back to London she landed a job at Stuveysant Wilson, the investment bankers in the City. It looked like she was going to have a great career in front of her, but then she met Toby Ashurst – he was a hedge fund manager there. She fell for him. He seemed a nice guy, a real charmer – and rich, super rich. His parents are Lord and Lady Ashurst, they have a huge country house in Buckinghamshire – old money and shed loads of it.'

She hesitated. Steve leant over and kissed her shoulder. 'Go on.'

'Well, they married – there was something about him that I didn't quite like, I'm sure it was his background, me being the working class snob that I am. But I couldn't deny he was good looking and Cherry seemed happy enough so I suppose I was happy for her. I mean her life was going to be so different from mine, good luck to her.

'She fell pregnant straight away... the twins were born and they all moved to a fabulous house in the country, plus they still had their apartment in the City – life couldn't be better for them. They regularly had their photos in *Hello* and *Country Life*, it was all so perfect. Or so it seemed.

'I had no idea about the drug use. When I, when I got the phone call from Toby, he just said Cherry was in hospital with a suspected heart attack. She was in St Barts but by the time I got there, she was, she'd died – they'd been having a party at their apartment.'

'Where were the twins?' queried Steve.

'Oh, I had them over at my place, I loved looking after them, they were, sorry are, a delight. Initially I was told her death was a heart attack, which it was – but after the autopsy it emerged that it was due to her taking cocaine, but not any cocaine – Merck cocaine...'

She trailed off, the tears welled up – Steve hugged her and she composed herself.

'Anyway, her death then became a police matter. Of course I wanted to get involved but I had left the Met and I was working for SOCA then, mainly with big time fraud and money laundering but I'd worked in the Drug Squad pre- viously so I had a lot of contacts – I pulled a few strings, called in some favours, got to see the reports. I knew what was going on, like I said it was Merck cocaine.'

Steve looked at her quizzically, he'd never heard of it.

'It's pharmaceutical cocaine, made in illicit laboratories in the old Eastern Germany. This drug hadn't been seen in this country for years, it was the drug of choice for the rock stars and intelligentsia back in the sixties and seventies but for whatever reason it went out of fashion and virtually disappeared. The Drug Squad hadn't come across it for years, well not on the streets anyway – so guess where they found out she got it from?'

Steve shrugged and motioned to Kirsty to continue.

'Turns out it was Ashurst himself – him and his mates in that sordid square mile were all at it. We're pretty certain it was the first time Cherry had taken it, in fact talking to her friends since it seems it was the first time she'd taken any drugs of any sort. She is ... she *was* a good girl, perfect, just perfect in every way.'

'So this Ashurst, he's been arrested I presume and banged up for a long time?'

'No he's still free. He was never arrested or charged – nothing. He still works in the City. He's a free man, free after what he's done to our daughter.'

'But how come – you said the Drugs Squad knew it was him, so why wasn't he charged?'

'Oh they had the proof alright, the apartment was searched – traces of drugs were found all over it. They questioned his friends and the weasels wouldn't even give him an alibi, they couldn't wait to expose him for what he was, but that was just to save their own skins, some friends eh? So yeah, they had forensic evidence, statements, the lot – should have gone inside for at least ten years, but...'

'But what – what happened?'

'A general election Steve, a general election happened and we got a new government.'

'What's that got to do with anything?'

'I wasn't the only one who was calling in favours. Let's just say a change of government brought in a change of friends, friends of Ashurst. You know old school network – Eton and the like.'

'What are you getting at? I don't follow?'

'There were people in the Home Office, people close to the powers that be, people that were even closer to Ashurst – funny handshakes and all that. Just when all the evidence was coming together and he was about to be charged things took an unexpected turn, a nasty vicious unexpected turn.'

'Like what?'

'People started querying my involvement in the case. Okay I should have left the Drug Squad to do their job. They had been meticulous in their investigation. They would have got him without me getting involved, but suddenly stories were uncovered – accusations were made about me.'

'But how, how were you involved in all this?'

'I wasn't. But after all these years stories came out about my past – my past in Bristol, my murky past, my working as an escort. My so-say involvement with drugs.'

'How the fuck did they find out about that ... and what drugs?' queried Steve, 'a few uppers when you were a kid?'

'No not that. They raided my house in Notting Hill – guess what they found? That's right Merck cocaine, the very same cocaine that Cherry had died from using. They stitched me up and hung me out to dry.'

'Who's they – the police, your colleagues? What do you mean?'

'No, not my colleagues, not the police – well yes, but they were just following orders. The drugs had been planted, probably by Ashurst's cronies – with a little help from those friends in high places. I was fucked, and they knew it.'

'So what did you do?'

'Nothing I or my colleagues could do – the case was dropped against Ashurst and they cut me a deal. Go quietly, go quickly and go with my pension. Keep schtum and just forget the case.'

'And have you?'

She went quiet, unsure of how to continue.

'No, that's why I'm back in Bristol – that's why I need you. That's why I need Steve Allen and the rest of The Big Five.'

He sat up on the bed and propped himself up on his elbows. She did the same – he found himself admiring her breasts once more. She didn't mind – in fact she was flattered.

'Payback time eh? What exactly have you got in mind for us?'

She opened a drawer of her bedside cabinet, took out a folder and passed it to Steve without comment.

Steve studied the contents of the dossier for ten minutes without saying a word. It didn't start and finish with Ashurst. She'd been meticulous in her research and investigations – she had reports, statements, photographs and evidence – real evidence against the drug dealers, pimps and gang members who, for whatever reason had escaped being prosecuted – the sort who were running rings around the British judicial system. He stopped at one page abruptly and froze as an alias he knew from his past leapt off the page and seized him by the throat – *so that's who the fucker is.*

Her return to Bristol was nothing to do with retirement – it was all about revenge for the death of her daughter. It was all about getting Steve to do something the Government were incapable of doing, ridding the country of some of the vermin that filled the streets. He closed the folder and handed it back to Kirsty.

'Well?' She queried.

'Well what?' replied Steve, 'all this does is confirm my opinion that the law are a waste of fucking time. If you've got all this,' he made a point of tapping the folder, 'then how come none of these have been banged up eh? Like I said, the law are a fucking joke.'

'No Steve, "the law" as you call them – the police are not a joke, they're doing a great job with limited resources, and when they do make arrests what happens? It's the law of the land that's a joke – it's the courts and the judges in this country that are letting us all down, believe me the police are the good guys Steve. They're just like you and your mates – and no doubt the majority of the law-abiding citizens of this land.'

Steve furrowed his brow – he'd come across some right bastards in uniform over the years. 'Good guys' was hardly the description he would use for some of the shits whose paths he'd crossed.

'Trust me Steve they've had enough of human rights, soft liberal judges and political correctness. We, sorry they are losing the battle on the streets, their hands are tied.'

She changed tack...

'Do you know there are nearly three thousand active street gangs in the UK running everything from flogging fake designer goods to gun-running, not to mention the prostitution and drugs – it's a United Nations of villains out there – every ethnic group that's ever come to this country is at.'

Steve raised his eyebrows and gave Kirsty a smug, *'told you so'* look.

'Oh and don't give me that look – I know what you're thinking. I remember your politics from back then. You're thinking they're all Yardies, Asians, Turks, Albanians, Russian mafia – foreigners the lot of 'em. That's only partly true Steve, but believe me many of the big players are good ole born and bred, red, white and blue British boys – *just like you and your mates* – they just don't get their hands dirty, that's all. They didn't just fade away once the Krays and the Richardsons got banged up. Have you never heard of the Adamses – the Clerkenwell Crime Syndicate?'

Steve had, but thought it facile to mention they were Irish Catholics – and of George's obvious Polish upbringing.

'Okay, okay,' he held his hands up in mock surrender, 'but what the fuck do you expect me to do about it? I'm a nobody in a nobody city.'

'For starters you're not a nobody – you're a good man. I knew that from the moment I met you, you've got standards, morals, a sense of right and wrong...'

Steve look surprised, seeing how much she knew about him.

'You just wandered a bit.' She quickly added. 'And Bristol isn't a nobody city. Okay it's shit at football, but it's got its fair share of premiership villains and wrong 'uns – Kingswood, Southmead, Lawrence Weston, they've all got toerags and as for south of the river, those Knowle Westers are up there with the Peckham boys... It wasn't so long ago there was a turf war in St Pauls and don't forget Stapleton Road got the dubious distinction of being known as one of the most violent streets in Britain.'

Through all this grimness Steve stifled a smirk.

'That was *after* Rovers left Eastville,' she added – knowing exactly what he was thinking.

'I'm not expecting you to declare war on every low life criminal in this country Steve – that would take a fucking army, but there are names in that folder you can make a start on and... and I want you to help me get even – even with the bastards who killed our daughter.'

So there's more to this than just Ashurst's involvement. 'Bastards? As in plural?'

Kirsty nodded while Steve mulled over his response.

'Okay, where do you want me to start?'

'How about a *quid-pro-quo*? You give me Ashurst's head on a plate, metaphorically speaking and I'll give you arsewipes – starting with the little scumbags who've been making your mum's life a misery. And I'll give you someone you've wanted for years... Ewart Samson.'

Steve had wondered about Samson, truth be told he was disappointed not to see his name in her folder.

'What "Shiny" Samson? You said you hadn't heard from him since he left you?'

'No I didn't – you assumed that. He's involved in all this as well. He's as guilty as Ashurst in all of this... but I wish you wouldn't call him "Shiny", that's still overtones of your racist past if you don't mind me saying.'

Steve nodded and mumbled an apology, then glanced at his Breitling.

Kirsty knew what he was thinking. 'Perhaps it's time you made a move,' she said – again it was an instruction not a question.

'Oh and take this,' she said, handing him a Met issue dark blue balaclava before adding 'and I've got another four for you – if you want them.'

He studied it for a second, thought how sinister it looked with its cut out eyes and mouth, then remembered the last time he'd worn one – it was during the bitter winter of 1963, his mum had knitted one for him.

Things had changed in Britain since those innocent schooldays of the sixties, he nodded to himself, knowing full well that those changes were not all for the better, he knew then that The Big Five were back.

CHAPTER SEVEN

A FTER a fitful night's sleep contemplating the events of the previous evening and the knowledge that his daughter had died from drug use, Steve woke on the Friday morning wary of the day ahead of him. He'd left Kirsty's apartment just after 11, not disagreeing with here when she suggested he should leave. Debbie hadn't queried him about coming in late – she was used to it. He made sure he drove home with the car windows opened – not that he reeked of perfume, Kirsty had been discrete in that respect – no doubt she'd been in this position before although he tried not to think about it.

Then there was Kirsty's involvement in his avoidance of prison all those years ago – her ever watchful eye on him and his indiscretions. He and his mates had a lot to thank her for – but he wasn't quite sure how she wanted repaying. She mentioned retribution, but this was much more than just avenging Cherry's tragic death. As well as details on Ashurst the folder also contained names, and one name in particular caught Steve's eye.

* * *

Steve left work early and drove to Trinity Road police station. He'd told them in work he had a dentist's appointment – they all thought that was unusual, Steve usually went to the dentist first thing in the morning – that's two weeks on the trot he'd left early on a Friday. They knew he was up to something, but no-one dared ask.

'Afternoon sir, what can we do for you?' asked the desk sergeant. Steve was taken aback, he seemed genuinely helpful, unlike the Rottweilers in uniform he usually encountered on the terraces.

'Um yes, I've, I've, I received this in the post,' he stammered as he unfolded the letter.

'And what might that be?'

'It's um, it's a caution – for, um importuning. But there's some mistake because I wasn't at all, I mean I wasn't importuning. I was meeting a client, on, um business.'

'Hmmm, what sort of "client" sir?'

'No, no sorry. Not that sort of client. That's not what I meant – look I was in the car park on business, not looking for business, and I guess I was spotted by some sort of undercover operation. I don't know, but either way I got this from you so I'm here to formally receive the caution, and yes I fully accept it. So give me the caution, take some details and I can be on my way – okay?'

'Can I have a look sir?' The good cop held out his hand. Steve handed over the letter, awaiting his fate. The desk sergeant read it through and cleared his throat.

'This is, um, this has not been issued by us sir. Would you care to look at the reference on it – perhaps read it out to me?'

Steve took the letter back, not quite sure of the situation.

'The um, reference, yes the reference is "TO 55 ER",' he said it again to himself. 'TO 55 ER... *TOSSER*.'

'And can you read out the signatory as well please sir?'

'The signatory, yes – I can't say I noticed it before.'

'Can you just read it out please sir?'

The desk sergeant had now been joined by a colleague. Steve wasn't certain but he thought he spotted the sergeant giving him a wink.

'Signature, yes – it's um "Wayne Kerr".' *Wanker*.

There were stifled laughs from the other side of the desk, the sergeant gathered himself.

'Can you tell your friends that impersonating police officers and forging of official police documents is a criminal offence – but I think we'll overlook that in this instance. Good night sir, drive carefully.'

Steve turned and walked off, the sound of laughter ringing in his ears.

'Fucking, fucking, fucking bastards – fucking Cribb, never trust a hairy arsed fucking printer,' said Steve to himself, he didn't know whether to laugh or cry, *fucking bastards*.

It was now five o'clock – there was a message on his phone, it was JB: *'Get your arse down the Moon – Wayne Kerr.'*

Steve responded by sending a group message to all the members of The Big Five: *'I'll be there, we all need to be there – seriously we need to talk.'*

CHAPTER EIGHT

THE others, including George Smolinksi, were already in the Moon. For a change they were sat around a table, all sullen looking.

'Look Steve, sorry mate, we, um probably overstepped the mark, it was just a joke like...' said Mike Cribb offering an apology of sorts.

'Forget it. That's not why I wanted to talk about, there's something else,' said Steve, making light of the earlier event.

'Yeah, yeah, just a bit of a laugh Steve. And we thought it would get you out of work early,' said JB, trying to excuse it.

Steve held up his hands. 'Honest, just forget it. Yeah, ha, ha, okay? Look I'm laughing, alright?'

The others visibly sighed in relief.

'Okay – you're still a wanker though,' said Pete taking a sip of Guinness.

'Yeah, thanks Pete – don't I know it, just for that, get me a pint eh?'

Pete got up as Steve sat down.

'Anyone else?'

They all shouted in their orders. Steve looked around, the Moon was beginning to fill. An hour or so it would be rammed – he would keep an eye out for the scaffolder – and Chantelle. Fair play to Tim Martin, he knew what the British drinking public wanted, cheap beer and cheap food – *fuck the hundreds of years of British pub culture*, thought Steve. Pete brought back the round of drinks.

'Cheers,' they all said in unison.

'What's up then mate?' asked George, 'got to be something important, you realising I'm missing my work...'

'Yes your workout George – sorry, I just wanted to get us all together for a chat that's all,' replied Steve.

'Eh, but we chat all the time?' said JB.

'Yeah, chat bollocks – we don't talk though John. None of us, none of us actually talk to each other.'

The others looked around. JB spoke, 'what you on about, you going all gay or what?'

'Yeah, been watching too much of that *Loose women* – they're always on about us blokes not talking. You getting in touch with your feminine side Mr A?' queried Pete.

'No, no – well dunno, maybe I am. Look, we've known each other, been mates for what, over forty years? But we don't fucking talk. We talk about football, women, the government, immigrants, kids of today, but we don't talk, talk about each other.'

'Huh, we talk behind each other's backs,' admitted George.

'Well yeah, but everyone does that,' said Steve, 'I'm on about talking to each other – about our lives, our problems, our worries, our fears, it's about time we did. It would help us all – we need to talk.'

'It's good to talk? JB queried.

'Yeah, exactly. It's good to talk... right I'll kick off.'

Steve inhaled deeply...

'Okay – I'm stressed, I'm depressed – my job is killing me. I worry about my health. I worry about having a heart attack like my old man. I take anti depressants – see none of you knew that did you? I take Statins to lower my cholesterol, I take ACE tablets to lower my blood pressure. I take anti-inflammatories 'cos my back gives me constant pain. I worry about my boy, my boys, I miss Sam – I'm hardly going to see him for the rest of my life. I miss, I miss Harry – I know you lot think he's a low life piece of shit for what he does, what he's done, but he's still my boy. I lie awake at night worrying about him, thinking I'm going to get a phone call telling me he's dead... I worry about me and Debbie. We, we, fuck it – we rarely have sex these days...'

He hesitated – just long enough for the others to stop sniggering.

'I can't get it up. You all think I've got everything – holidays, car and the like, but it's all fuck all. It's just, it's just dressing, it's fuck all. It don't, it doesn't make me happy – I'm not happy.'

Steve trailed off – to stop himself welling up he picked up his pint and took a long swallow. There was silence.

'Well?' said Steve at last.

Still silence.

'I'm skint,' they turned as one to JB.

'I'm skint,' he repeated. 'I'm in debt up to my eyeballs. The business is going tits up, I can't afford to pay the blokes. Local government cut backs – looks like I'm losing my contract with the council. I'm gonna lose it all, the business, my house, the car – that's a fucking joke, I can't even afford to run it. The ex is giving me grief, the CSA are after me. I'm fucked, oh and I've gambled for years, I'm a gambler.'

'We all knew you liked the gee-gees,' said Pete, trying to console the big fella.

'No, no this is more than a few bob up Bath races lads – I've gambled big time. Sure had a few big wins, had more big losses though – horses, football, casinos, now fucking online gambling. I can't get away from it... I'm fucked.'

Pete put his arm around JB's shoulder – he'd never done that before, he didn't say anything, he didn't need to. It meant a lot to him.

Steve wondered if JB was going to say anything about slapping Sharon around, he thought better of mentioning it himself.

Pete finally went to speak, gave out a little cough. Cleared his throat...

'I hate my life, I hate everything about it. At times I just want it all to end.'

'For fuck's sake Pete, don't get like that mate – you should, should have said.' JB looked at his old friend – they still had their arms around each other. Pete continued...

'I've...me and Sue. We've never got over what happened to Tash – that bastard ruined our lives. Tash will never be the same again, her life is just ruined. She doesn't talk to anyone, doesn't talk to us – never had a boyfriend, she's beautiful, but she doesn't trust anyone, she doesn't even trust me, her dad. She hates me, hates all men, she hates everyone. Dunno, it's like Sue blames me, we never, we never sleep together – got separate bedrooms. When we go to Spain she's at one end of the villa I'm at the other – Tash in the middle. It's crap, fucking crap. I just get out of my face all the time. That's all I got, alcohol – and you lot. That's all I got.'

They all exhaled, this was tough. Steve wondered what sort of can of worms he'd opened.

'And I use prostitutes.' Pete threw in, just casual, just truthful.

'Fucking hell, what's going on here?' asked George. 'I suppose it's my turn?'

'Not if you don't want to George,' said Steve, 'but it just might help.'

'Help who – you? What is all this about Steve, some sort of confessional? What are you trying to prove? I go to church every... well I go to church more than you lot do. I do my confessional, I get my penance. I get absolved by a priest and by God, I don't need you lot to sit in judgement of me.'

'George, George – we're not sitting in judgement of you. This isn't trying to prove anything, it's just something I needed to do, get off my chest if you like. If you've got nothing to say – fine,' said Steve.

George wrung his hands, sipped his orange juice and finally spoke.

'Yeah, yeah. I'm worried, same as you a bit Steve, worried about my health, worried about getting cancer like my dad, he died in agony, I hated that... I try to keep fit, take vitamins, supplements, that sort of stuff... do a few steroids that's all. I think – I dunno, think that's why I get so fucking angry all the time, I can't control my temper, I just want to lash out all the time. I'm just angry – I want to calm down, but I can't. I just want to smash up something – it's driving me fucking mad.'

'You do steroids?' asked JB.

'You don't just "do" steroids though, do you George?' asked Steve. Then he suddenly realised he'd said more than he should've done.

George looked at him questioningly.

'Okay I sell a few, just down the gym, nothing serious – could be worse though eh Steve Allen?'

They all looked at Steve.

'What, what do you mean?' asked Steve indignantly.

'Well, you missed out a bit in your little confessional didn't you? Eh? You and your little habit, you think none of us knew about that? We all know you're a fucking coke-head... and you're asking us to feel sorry for you and your Harry?' The mood was changing – George fixed his stare on Steve.

'Alright, alright leave it, not now boys, not now,' said JB, acting the peacemaker. Steve and George kept eyeballing each other, Steve hadn't expected this, but George was right – Steve felt the guilt flowing through his entire body.

So that was it was it? He wasn't sure himself where all this was going. Wasn't sure why he'd brought it up now. He still had the bombshell of telling them about meeting Kirsty and of how she kept them all out of prison back in 1982, not to mention telling them she wanted to use them – use The Big Five to exact revenge on Ewart Samson and Toby Ashurst for Cherry's death. Where the fuck was all this going?

'Mike?' said JB, 'anything, anything to get off your chest?'

Steve thought for a moment, thought back to what Kirsty had told him last night about his mates, tried to think what she'd said about Mike Cribb – nothing, absolute fuck all, in fact she'd changed the subject.

'Mike – come on, fess up mate. What is it? Like dressing up in Karen's clothes? Got her knickers on tonight have you? Is that it mate?' Pete was trying to lighten the mood, the others forced out false laughs.

'Mike?'

Mike Cribb pushed back his chair, stood up and walked out without saying a word.

'Mike, Mike, come back here, if you got nothing to say, it's not a problem... Mike?'

He walked away swiftly and didn't look back. The others sat in their seats, dumbfounded.

'Nice one Allen. Perhaps some things are best left unsaid – you on some sort of mission to fuck us all up or something?'

George was wound up. He wasn't happy with the events of the last hour, perhaps the fact that he was screwing Mike Cribb's missus was something to do with it. George wondered if Mike Cribb knew. Is that what got up his nose – he actually felt sorry for him.

'No, I'm not trying to fuck anyone up. In fact I think all this might help us. I'll give Cribby a call, it's probably nothing, he'll be okay tomorrow – it'll all be forgotten. The rest of us, well – we can all help each other – JB, for starters I'm going to lend you a few grand just to get things sorted. Then you can get some help, get to your bank, have a chat with gamblers anonymous or whatever. But you're not alone mate. You got us – ain't that right?'

'Steve, I,' JB didn't know what to say. He was lost for words.

'Think nothing of it mate, we're all here to help each other – right?'

They all nodded.

'Same goes for you Pete. You shouldn't be bottling this up, whenever you're down, give one of us a call. Have you been to the doctors?'

'No, you know how it is. Don't like doctors, they might find something wrong with me...'

'That's what they're there for you dozy twat, they can help mate, honest. Get along on Monday eh?'

'Sure, yeah, yeah, I'll go.' They all knew he wouldn't.

'What's this then Steve, new career as an Agony Aunt?' asked George. 'Cos I don't think you can do much for me mate.'

'I think only you can help yourself George. You know that – but a course of anger management wouldn't do any harm would it?'

'And you Steve Allen. Who's going to sort out your life? Who's going to help you out?' queried JB.

Steve hesitated, 'Kirsty, Kirsty Donohue.'

'You're fucking kidding,' said JB, 'Kirsty Donohue – I thought she was dead.'

Maybe you'll all wish she was.

'I'm going for a piss – look someone get the beers in and I'll tell you all about it.'

Well not all. You're not going to hear about Debbie and Brad the Blindman that's for sure. And what was that with Mike Cribb? Something was wrong there, something was going on. He wondered yet again if Kirsty hadn't been telling the full story. He got out his iPhone and gave Kirsty a call.

'Hi Steve. Having a good time with the boys?'

Just hearing Kirsty's voice raised Steve's spirits – he knew he needed to spend more time in her company.

'Well, no not really. Load of brown stuff hitting fans at the moment to be honest – which is why I'm phoning you.'

'Go on, but I've told you just about everything.'

'No, I don't think you have. There's still stuff you're holding back isn't there? Stuff about Ashurst and Samson and...' he hesitated.

'And what?'

'Mike Cribb . You dished the dirt on all of us last night but you didn't mention Mike. And judging by his behaviour tonight, he's not as squeaky clean as you made out. You've got something on him as well haven't you?'

Kirsty was silent for a second.

'For a start I didn't say he was squeaky clean, I just never mentioned him that's all. Okay yes there is something on him, but, but... I can't say, I honestly can't say, that's all.'

'How come? Is it something serious? I need to know Kirsty – so I, so we can help him.'

Kirsty hesitated again.

'Look Steve, it is serious, and no you can't help him – all I can say is there's an ongoing investigation into Mike Cribb, and that's why I can't tell you. He is involved in a serious criminal matter, he is under investigation right now – which he doesn't know about, so you can't say anything to him or any of your mates, do you understand? Not a word Steve or you could jeopardise everything – the case could collapse.'

Now it was Steve's turn to be silent.

'Steve, did you hear me? Not a word to anyone. Steve, are you still there?'

'Yeah, yeah, I'm still here.'

Steve's brain was working overtime. So that was what this was all about, she was fucking lying again. This was why she'd contacted him – she was working on a case, working on a case against Mike Cribb, a mate of his and she was using him to get to Mike Cribb. This was getting more complicated by the day, the hour – he didn't know how to play this with Kirsty. He clearly couldn't trust her – she was just using him, using him and his mates. So what was it with Cherry and Ashurst? There was no way she was making that up – he didn't know what to believe.

Kirsty was still on the phone, she could sense Steve was thinking things through.

'Steve, you have to trust me on this. I'll tell you, I'll tell you at the appropriate time. But not now, he's being investigated...'

'By you!' Steve shouted down the phone.

'By you,' he repeated. 'All this, it's one big charade isn't it? You're here to investigate him and you want me to be part of it. You're fucking using me aren't you, admit it!'

A T-shirted inked up teenager in the urinal stopped mid flow and looked at Steve. In one of the cubicles a thirty-year old factory worker looking for instant gratification from a line of coke came to an abrupt halt, a solitary fart from another cubicle punctuated the silence.

'What? What you fucking looking at?' said Steve to no-one in particular.

'Steve? Steve? You still there? Steve listen to me. Everything I've told you is true – but there's a few things I can't tell you at this stage, but I am not involved in any case of any sort, believe me. I've left the police, do you hear me, I've retired – honest. But I admit, I still know what's going on, I've still got a lot of friends in the force – they're helping me,

100

they, they can help you as well Steve, but they can't help Mike Cribb. Just leave this well alone please. You've got to trust me on this.'

Steve calmed. She sounded concerned – she sounded like she was telling the truth. He didn't like what he was hearing, certainly didn't like what he was hearing about Mike Cribb. If Cribby was guilty of anything it was of being a serial bull-shitter. No, not Cribby – they must have got it wrong.

'Okay, okay, I believe you, but please no more lies, just the truth eh?'

'The truth Steve, honest this is the truth – talking about truth, are you going to mention me to Debbie?'

Steve had pushed all thoughts of his wife out of his mind. He had something on Debbie, something no one else had an inkling about. He would confront her one day, perhaps in the near future, tell her all about Kirsty, tell her he was leaving her for Kirsty. If Kirsty wanted him that was – but for now he'd just let the dust settle. There was no hurry, he would bide his time.

'No, no, well not unless you want me to – do you?' Steve turned the tables.

'Um, I haven't really thought about it. I mean, this time last week you didn't even know if I was alive or dead did you? Let's see how it goes, let's not rush things eh?'

'No, you're right, but I, I...'

'What, what is it?'

He almost said it. His teenage urges overcame him again. He desperately wanted to tell Kirsty he still loved her – wanted to tell her he wanted to be with her for the rest of his life – but he decided not to.

'Nothing, nothing, just don't, just don't leave me ever again – please.' It was near enough to an admission of love he guessed. He hoped she thought the same.

'I won't Steve, I promise. Bye.' She said and hung up.

He pressed the end call button and finally whispered 'I love you.'

He exited the toilet, put his phone in his pocket and looked across the now crowded pub.

'Stevie Allen, Stevie Stevie Allen. Have I got something for you!'

He was engulfed in a bear hug of epic proportions. A rough, stubbled chin rubbed against his own, a flash of cheap gold sparkled from a scarred ear lobe, a worn leather jacket rubbed up against his pristine Harrington – in the words of Paul Weller, *'he smelt of pubs and Wormwood Scrubs and too many right wing meetings.'*

Gary 'Bulldog' Rattigan finally released his vice like grip but he kept his head up against Steve's, he whispered in his ear...

'Like rocket fuel Stevie, like rocket fuel, quality gear – just for my top man.' Steve felt Rattigan's right hand deftly enter his jacket pocket.

'Fifty quid mate, gone up a tenner, but it's worth it. Like I said rocket fuel mate, fucking rocket fuel, come on I'll give you a line now – on the house.'

Rattigan ushered Steve back into the toilet, his thoughts moved on. His love for Kirsty already forgotten, he was within seconds of a line of cocaine. He couldn't get in the cubicle quick enough.

'Good gear yeah Gar?'

'The best my man. The fucking best.'

Rattigan pulled out a small polythene clip bag from his pocket and emptied a fraction of the powder on to the cistern, luckily the Moon hadn't boxed in the cisterns like in many of the other local pubs – or covered them with Vaseline, it didn't matter if they did, the toilet lid sufficed any way. Steve had his platinum card in his hand already.

'Ere you are Gar, use this.'

'Quality Mr A, quality.'

Rattigan chopped the cocaine, divvied it up into four lines, each just over an inch long.

'Quality,' repeated Rattigan. Steve passed him a rolled up twenty, 'come on Ratters, get a wriggle on.'

It was a tight fit in the cubicle. Rattigan was a big unit, he wasn't called 'Bulldog' for nothing – well it wasn't because he shit on the pavement, but then again he had done once or twice, so maybe it was.

Rattigan pulled the flush then sniffed one line up his left nostril, grunted then sniffed up another through his right nostril.

'Shiiiiiit, fucking shiiiiiit. Good gear even if I do say so myself. Here you go Stevie boy.'

Rattigan shoved the note into his back pocket. Steve got out his wallet and counted out another thirty, gave twenty to Rattigan then rolled up the remaining tenner, leant over the cistern and inhaled deeply – first right nostril then left. He raised his head and looked at the ceiling, he then sniffed heavily again, he finally ran his finger over the cistern and rubbed the remaining powder across his gums, he then handed Rattigan the final ten pound note. The deal had been done.

The two turned and exited the cubicle, shifty looks and prying eyes from others heightened Rattigan's and Allen's euphoria. It was all part of the squalid scene, part of the ritual, part of the thrill. They laughed out loud.

As they exited the toilets Steve could see JB, Pete McNulty and George Smolinski watching him across the bar. So fucking what, his dirty little secret was out, not that it was much of a secret any more – they had all known about him and his habit, but for whatever reason nothing had been said. *Fucking wankers* he thought, *that didn't make them any better, in fact it made them worse, his best mates and they didn't have the balls to have it out with him, fuck 'em, fuck 'em* – at least tonight he had his real mate with him, Charlie – the best mate a bloke could have.

'What you lot having? Who's shout is it anyway? Mine – I think it's mine, isn't it? Or no, no, I got the last ones, JB? Johnnie, beer, hmmm? Pete, beer? George – same again, orange juice, OJ, OJ, yeah, anything else? Wonder what was up with Cribby then, eh? What do you reckon? Think you might have been right Pete. Think you might have hit the nail on the fucking head Pete boy. Think he was wearing Karen's knickers – ha! What's reckon eh? What's reckon – look who I just found, Mr Bulldog himself, Gar, Gary – top man, give us a kiss big fella, eh, eh?'

The two of them hugged – Steve could smell Wormwood Scrubs again, he whispered in his ear 'fuck me Gar, this stuff is shit hot.'

'Told you mate. It's very moreish though – like chocolate Minstrels but less calories.' The two roared with laughter.

The others had no time for Rattigan. They all knew him from football, he used to go years back but like them, hadn't been to watch the Rovers for years, well apart from Wembley – like the 30,000 other glory hunters. They knew Steve and Rattigan had been mates, not like them but mates all the same. It went back to the time the two of them had gone to Brentford for a game – it was the same day as the Hillsborough disaster, 1989. They had a row after the game with some Wolves fans on the motorway – started off just as a bit of banter as the two cars sped along side by side on the M4 but it got nasty when a beer glass was thrown at Steve through the open window and it smashed against his forehead. He still had the scar to this day.

Steve had told the tale time and time again – the car carrying the Wolves fans sped off, Steve was off his head, blood dripping in his eyes as he drove. They stopped on the hard shoulder, he wiped the blood away then picked up stones and bottles from the grass verge – eventually they caught up with the Wolves' fans and pulled alongside, Rattigan leant out and smashed the windscreen of the Wolves' fans Sierra causing it to veer off the motorway. Steve and Rattigan watched in the mirror as it smashed into the barrier, at first they worried that they might have killed them, but there was nothing in the papers the next day – they were full of the horrors of Hillsborough – they almost felt disappointed. It was a good tale, at times Steve felt proud of it – at other times the memory sickened him.

'Well seeing as we had a bit of a Road to Damascus moment earlier, then I might as well tell you that I think you're a prick. Worse than that you're a cunt – anyone who sticks that shit up their nose deserves no sympathy at all, you're a fucking prick Allen and you Rattigan are an even bigger cunt for selling that crap. So the two of you can just fuck off alright?'

JB did not hold back. His anger was visible for all to see, it shook Pete and George, but it shook Steve Allen more. Gary Rattigan just stood and sneered, he was good at that – and at shitting on pavements.

'JB, John, John mate, it's not...'

'Don't you mate me – after what you said earlier as well. Thought you was being a top bloke and all that, offering to help me out. You talked a lot of sense, but now – fucking look at you. C'mon boys I suddenly don't like the company.'

The three got up as one, finished their drinks and left Steve and Rattigan – left them in their world of cocaine, shitty toilets, lies and deceit. Rattigan gave out a derisory sneer.

'Fucking wankers – you're better off without them Stevie boy.'

Steve looked at Rattigan, smiled, flexed his right arm and punched Rattigan straight in the mouth

.

* * *

6.30 Saturday morning. Steve woke and got out of the spare bed, his jaw ached from bruxism – the constant jutting and grinding caused by the cocaine use of the night before. He showered, dressed and went downstairs, opened up the back door and let the dogs out causing the squirrels to retreat to the safety of the trees. He nursed his swollen hand, awkwardly ate his Optivita, took his tablets and drunk his Benecol. He toyed with his phone, plucked up courage and eventually phoned JB – who unfortunately for Steve was in an unforgiving mood.

'Do you know what fucking time it is you cunt?'

'John, mate. Sorry and all that – we need to talk.'

'Think we did enough of that last night. Didn't do us much good though did it?'

'No it didn't, well I dunno. I still think it's better out in the open.'

'What's out in the open? Fuck all – you just stirred up a hornet's nest that's all and on top of that, you haven't even confronted your own demons have you? Seems to me you're the one with the biggest problems – sooner you face up to that and get shot of that waster Rattigan as one of your "mates" the sooner you might be a better person.'

Steve wasn't sure how to answer.

'Am I a bad person John? Are any of us?'

'No, no you're not mate. None of us are, but you? You've just wandered off the straight and narrow a bit that's all. Same as we've all done at some stage.'

Steve thought for a second. That was exactly the same as what Kirsty had said, 'wandered' – *it could be worse.*

'Look, about last night, about my... habit – it's just recreational. I'm not an addict okay? It's just a bit of escapism on a weekend.'

'Steve, Steve – listen to yourself? How many junkies have come up with that line over the years eh? Fucking thousands I imagine, and how many of them have ended up on a mortuary slab eh?'

Steve wasn't going to get in to a bad drug, good drug argument, not with JB anyway. He knew he would lose, he knew his mate was right.

'Look John, I'm knocking it all on the head. Won't have another bit of Charlie in my life, honest, fuck all, you're right it's a mug's game. Fucking waste of time, just turns me into an ignorant, arrogant motormouth who wants to take on the world. As from now not another sniff – honest, anyway you should've seen the punch I laid out Rattigan with last night.'

'You're kidding? What in the Moon?'

'Yep, soon as you left. Smacked him one in the mouth, fucker didn't get up.'

'Nice one Stevie. The fat fuck has had that coming for years – so what do we do now? All absolved, all mates again?'

'Hope so, Big Five back on?'

'Not so sure about that. We gotta find out what's up with Cribby first, and another thing, you gotta tell me about Kirsty. Her coming back in your life is big news – how you gonna handle her, she's trouble. Bet you ain't mentioned it to Debbie?'

'No fucking chance. I wanted to tell you last night. You ain't gonna believe the story I got to tell.'

'Try me.'

Steve spent the next ten minutes telling his best friend all about Kirsty coming back into his life. He told him about the daughter he'd gained and the daughter he'd lost – the daughter he never knew. He told him about how Kirsty had just retired from the police force and how she wanted to get even with Ashurst for the death of Cherry – and how that Ewart Samson was somehow involved.

'That bastard,' interrupted JB, 'I wondered when he was going to resurface.'

Steve left the biggest revelation to last, the revelation that Kirsty had been observing them for nearly thirty years and how she knew about the brawl with the Taffies at Paddington station in 1982.

'If it hadn't been for Kirsty's intervention we would've all done time and our lives would've changed – and probably not for the better.'

JB let out a long, long whistle. 'So what does she want from us – what's she trying to do, blackmail us?'

'No, no, nothing like that. She just wants us to return the favour.'

'How?'

'She's given us a chance of getting back at all the scum on the streets – the scum that are fucking up this country.'

'You sound like a *Daily Mail* reader.'

'Hardly, I'm a *Guardian* man.'

'So what are you talking about, some sort of what – vigilantes, is that what she wants us to become, or more like Charlies... Kirsty's Angels.'

'No, think it more of contributing to Cameron's Big Society, but with baseball bats.'

'Ha Ha! I like the sound of that. But how do we know it's not one big set up? How do we know she's not still Old Bill? This might be some sort of scam – just to get her own back, get her own back on you, on us.'

'It's not, trust me. And anyhow, she hasn't got to get her own back on anyone – she left me, remember?'

'Debatable mate. It was you getting in with the far right, you getting personal with Samson. Dark days in the late seventies Steve – for all of us. Seeing as you got her pregnant then – left her in shit street, maybe she's the one after revenge on you?'

Steve would've been lying if he said the thought hadn't crossed his mind.

'No I'm certain she's legit – she's on the level, I just know. She's out to get the bloke, this Toby Ashurst as well as Samson. She wants us to get them, for killing my... our daughter, plus whatever scumbags we can sort out on the way.'

'Okay, but supposing we go along with it all, supposing we strike back and take the law into our own hands. How do we know she's then not going to stitch us up? She could easily set all this up, get us to do her dirty work then hang us out to dry. She'd be off scotch free and we'd be banged up for the rest of our natural...'

'No, that ain't happening – like I said, trust me. I've had to trust her and now you boys have got to trust me, and what's more we owe her – don't forget that.'

JB was deep in thought. It was what they had all banged on about for the last few years – taking the law into their own hands, divine retribution, teaching the scumbags of the country a lesson. Word might spread, others might get involved, seize back the country from the lowlifes that prowled the streets. They might just be able to mend broken Britain. David Cameron's Big Society – he wondered what it was all about, a Big Society with baseball bats – he had to admit it had a certain appeal.

'Okay, so what's she saying? That she's going to give us a free hand to do what we want? How is she going to make sure we don't get nicked? By giving us get out of jail free cards to give to the Old Bill? I don't think so.'

'She doesn't need to. She wasn't just a run of the mill cop John, she told me. She finished up working for SOCA – that's the serious crime lot, the British FBI. Believe it or not she was a whizz with computers, started off with filing and collation, she had a real talent for collecting and gathering information. She also worked for PITO – the Police Information Technology Organisation and she was involved with setting up the Home Office Large Major Enquiry System. How do you think she kept tabs on us over the years? What's more she's still got plenty of friends working for the boys in blue, from the copper on the street to the Chief Inspectors. Believe me – there are plenty of strings she can pull.'

Steve also thought with those legs of hers there would be a few married colleagues of Kirsty's who owed her a few favours.

'Supposing I go along with this, how the fuck do we get started – just go out whacking a few drug dealers and pimps and keeping our fingers crossed we don't get the six o'clock knock?'

'Nothing as random as that John. She's given me a dossier – all the information we need, well to start anyway. She's still working on a few things, but I got photos, names, addresses...'

'And that get out of jail free card with a bit of luck.'

'Not quite. Look the first thing I'm gonna do is pay a little visit to the fuckers who've been making our mum's life a misery – with or without you mate I'm going to knock on a few doors.'

'Okay, okay – I'll help out, what do you want me to do?'

'I've been thinking. Before we do anything, we all need to get back together again, need to check Mike Cribb's alright. Can you do me a favour and phone Pete and George, tell 'em you've patched it up with me – we'll meet in the Moon at 12 alright? Beers on me.'

'Okay I'll sort it. Laters.'

'Laters.'

* * *

JB was as good as his word. They met at 12, the Moon was half full – sort of a half full moon. Cheap food and even cheaper booze got the punters queuing at the door at 7.30, the reality of Blair's cafe society was not quite what had been envisaged – pensioners and chavs cheek by jowel – at least something united them.

'Sorry about last night lads, I was bang out of order – in a lot of ways. One thing I can promise, I'm never putting that shit up my nose again – honest. And as for Rattigan...'

Steve clenched his right fist and showed the battered and cut knuckles, he then held out his palm and offered it to Pete, they shook, long and hard – then the same for George. He reserved a longer, firmer shake for JB, they were mates again.

'Yeah. JB mentioned you gave that toerag a slap – nice one. Now what's this all about?' asked George.

He repeated what he'd told JB earlier, George and Pete listened intently then asked similar questions to the big fella. They were concerned, dumbfounded and baffled – not to mention intrigued and excited. Then they got on to the subject of Mike Cribb...

'Anyone tried phoning him?' asked George warily.

'I've been trying all morning,' said Pete 'but he's on voicemail.'

George was relieved, he was convinced this was some-thing to do with him and his relationship with Karen, maybe Mike had found out about the two of them.

'Probably best leave it for a bit, he'll come round sooner or later.'

'Yeah you're right George,' said Steve, mindful of what Kirsty had told him. This was serious she had said – leave it well alone.

'I'm not so sure,' said JB, 'especially after what we all said last night. Steve was right, we don't talk enough. If the bloke's got problems – like we all have – he needs our help, that's what mates are for. I reckon we ought to get round his gaff, have a word in his shell like. See if we can help him.'

It was rare that John Burston didn't get his way, his physical presence alone usually meant what JB wanted, JB got.

'Come on, drink up – we're going.'

The four got into JB's Range Rover and arrived at Mike Cribb's house ten minutes later. There had been no conversation on the journey – maybe a few expletives mouthed at wayward drivers but not exactly road rage.

Karen opened the door, she'd lost her way a bit over the years – still had a face that brightened a room but the weight had gone on a bit, mostly due to the bottle of Chardonnay she consumed every afternoon. As a teenager she'd been described as 'having more spots than a decorator's radio' by Pete but the acne had long gone, she was still pretty – from the neck up.

'Hello boys, to what do I owe this pleasure?' She threw a puzzled glance at George – he responded with a shrug that was unseen by the others. She tightened her dressing gown around her ample waist.

'Hi Karen, is Mike in?' asked JB.

'Fraid not – in fact he's never in, never shee him – always at work, or down his lock up. Bessht fucking place for him, a fucking lock up,' she laughed. 'And anyway wass all this about, don't tell me...'

She looked at George again, 'don't tell me you've all found out about me and...'

'Quiet Karen, not now – button it alright?' hissed George.

The three others looked at each other, then at George, then back at Karen.

JB finally spoke. 'No – you're fucking kidding?'

'Fuckin 'ell. What's going on George? You two at it?' asked Pete. Thinking his little secret wasn't so bad after all.

'Yep – too right,' answered Karen, proudly.

'Ain't that wass this is all about? You coming round to knock our heads together – ha! Too late, me and George been at it for ages. Down the gym every Friday my arse. He's round here shagging me tits off– and I'll tell you what, don't believe a word what they say about them stair rods... whatever, steroids. He's got a cock like a baby's arm – ain't that right Georgie?'

She lunged, put her arms around him and kissed him on the cheek, her dressing gown flapped open given the boys a flash of her voluminous left breast and dark areola. There was a collective shake of heads, George pushed Karen away...

'You dozy cow. No one knew about this – no one knew about us. What did you have to open your big fat mouth for?'

'Georgie, Georgie, come on baby. It's best it's out in the open. Come on, come in now baby,' she tried to pull George into the house.

George grimaced. 'Just fuck off you pisshead.'

He turned and walked back to the car, the other followed leaving Karen sobbing on the doorstep.

'George, George – please!' She pleaded.

JB stopped, turned and walked back down the path to Karen.

'Where's his lock up?' he asked.

They all got back in the Range Rover. Words were at a premium.

'Well that was a turn up for the books.' Pete finally said. 'Good shag?' He actually giggled, the other two just smirked – George stared out of the window at nothing in particular. JB floored the motor, the V8 engine announcing its departure to the quiet cul-de-sac.

'Where too now?' asked Steve nervously – still wary of Kirsty's warning to him.

'St Werburghs – Cribby's lock up,' replied JB.

'I dunno mate, is that wise?' There was almost a plea in George's voice.

'Too right it is. I ain't gonna say anything about you and Karen if that's what you're worried about, that's between you and her to sort out. But there's something up with Cribby and I want to find out what it is. He's gonna get help whether he wants it or not.'

Steve gathered his thoughts and finally spoke out.

'Look I don't know how to say this but I haven't been totally truthful.'

'Fucking great, not more bullshit,' said George.

'I haven't been bullshitting about anything,' snapped Steve.

'I just haven't told you the whole story that's all. Look, I told you all that Kirsty had been keeping tabs on us – she knows what we've been up to over the years, she told me, told me about our brushes with the law.'

'So that's what that was all about last night eh? You was trying to get us to 'fess up – wash our dirty laundry in public. But you knew about us all along, fucking hell Allen, this is just getting better and better! What other shit you got lined up for us?' George was beginning to lose patience with Steve – the air was tense. Kick off time was just around the corner.

'Leave it,' said JB, 'just calm down... but George's got a point, you knew all about us,' he thought for a second, 'so what do you know about Mike?'

'Fuck all. But I do know he's in deep shit – that's all Kirsty would tell me. He is involved in something serious. She, the Old Bill, are in the middle of an investigation right now, but I don't know about what, she wouldn't tell me. In fact she didn't tell me anything about Cribby – it was only last night when he shot off that I phoned her. She then told me what I've just told you, nothing more.'

'Well, I'm not leaving it at that,' said JB, 'if he's in trouble with the law, we're gonna help him – within reason,' he added.

114

They drove to St Werburghs and quickly spotted Mike Cribb's BMW, its glistening paintwork at odds with the surrounding area. There were a dozen or so double doors – who knew what was behind each one? Moody motors, knock offs and bent gear mostly. They easily located Mike Cribb's premises – they could hear the unmistakable sound of a printing press in motion emanating from inside. JB tried the door but it was locked – they knocked several times but there was no answer. Pete tried phoning again but there was still no response.

JB had had enough, he gave the door an almighty kick.

'Mike – you in there?'

The Heidelberg finally fell silent. They could hear movement behind the door.

'Who is it?' asked Mike Cribb from behind the still-locked door.

'Mike, it's JB – and I got the others with me. You okay? We were worried about you after last night, just came to see that you're alright that's all.'

'Yeah, I'm fine. Just a... just a little busy.'

'Er okay, just checking like... How about opening the door so we can have a catch up? Never knew you had this place – kept it quiet eh?'

'Yeah, yeah. I just do a few foreigners on the side like – bit of beer money that's all.'

'Right – no problem in that mate. Like I said, just concerned about you. Come on open up, put the kettle on eh?'

'Look John... boys – I got a bit on. Bit to do, deadlines and all that. I need to deliver a rush job this afternoon – how about if we meet up later yeah?'

'Sure, sure – but how about just opening up for five minutes?' JB was getting impatient – he was used to getting his own way.

Steve sensed something was wrong – he wished they had taken Kirsty's advice...

'C'mon JB – he obviously don't want to see us. Let's shoot off, we'll catch up later.'

George felt the same...

'Yeah let's leave it eh JB? We'll see him later – watch the late kick off down the pub, meet up then alright?'

JB thought differently, he was there to help his mate out. If he was in trouble with the law, or his missus, he would help him. That's what they were there for, or – or was there something else. He changed his tone.

'Mike, just open up. I'm not asking, I'm telling. Open this fucking door.'

When JB told people to do something they generally obeyed. They could hear heavy bolts moving, then a key being turned. The door opened a fraction – Mike Cribb's face appeared.

'Alright boys,' he squinted against the sunlight, 'see I'm fine, nothing wrong at all.'

'That's all right then. So you can let us in, have a nose – or have you got something to hide?' asked JB.

Steve felt uneasy. He knew that what was behind these doors was what Kirsty had warned him about. Printers could be dodgy fuckers – counterfeit money, tax disks, government bonds – it had to be something like that.

'Okay let's go then JB. Mike's all right, catch up later eh mate?'

JB hesitated... 'Yeah, okay – suppose. See you later then eh Mike?'

Steve sighed – just as JB kicked the door in.

'If I say open up, I mean fucking open up!' He pushed past Mike Cribb and entered the lock up.

'What have you got to hide in here then Cribby? Something we should be...' JB fell silent.

'What the fuck? What the fucking hell is this?'

The others followed – all five were now in the lock up. Mike Cribb was wedged between John Burston and Pete McNulty.

'Cribb – what are you fucking up to in here?'

JB leant over a pile of printed sheets. He twisted his head and leant in closer...

'For fuck's sake, what the fucking hell is this shit?'

He picked up one of the sheets for a closer look and promptly dropped it as if it was burning his fingers.

'Look, I'm not – I'm not into this myself.' Mike Cribb pleaded. 'Just doing it for someone I know that's all. Just a bit of money on the side – you know it fucking disgusts me as well.'

Pete McNulty pushed through and picked up one of the sheets. He stared in shocked silence for a second.

'It's child porn. It's, it's fucking sick... you're fucking sick. You fucking bastard!'

He flew at Mike Cribb.

'You fucking animal! I'm gonna fucking kill you!'

His right fist smashed into Mike Cribb's left cheek, quickly followed by his left fist which connected to the right side of his mouth. The second punch caused Cribb's lip to split – blood pumped out instantaneously. By the time the third punch connected with his nose, Mike Cribb's knees were buckling and he was falling to the floor. Pete's fists were now pumping – punch after punch connected with the now battered and bloodied face of Mike Cribb. Blood bubbled out of his nose, a tooth had been dislodged and flew across the floor – Steve had seen enough.

'Pete, Pete, fucking leaving it, leave it, he's had enough, leave it for fuck's sake!'

'No he fucking hasn't!' screamed Pete. 'I'm gonna fucking kill him – the fucking bastard.'

The punches rained down on Cribb's face – he was now motionless. His arms were limp at his side, he put up no fight of his own – his system had closed down. Pete then stood upright, pulled back his right leg and kicked Cribb in the side – he finished with a stamp onto Cribb's groin. Mike Cribb finally moved – just a spasmodic motion, his head rolled to the side and he spat out blood. He moaned low and deep.

Steve made a move for Pete, grabbed his arms and held them behind his back.

'Pete – leave it, enough, just leave it. I said we shouldn't have come here.' He looked around at JB questioningly.

'You got a fucking nerve,' said JB, 'if you hadn't started this last night, this would never have happened.'

'Well it's just as well he fucking did then ain't it,' said Pete, 'otherwise we would never have known about this fucking *pae-do.*'

He emphasised the two syllables with another kick to Cribb's prostrate body.

The four looked around the lock up. There was a Mac at a desk together with a scanner and a small desktop printer, there was also various print finishing kit – guillotine, metal rulers, scalpels, tape. In the middle of the lock up a large four-colour press hummed, waiting to be kicked back into motion.

Steve looked at the Mac and pressed the space bar to bring the screen back to life – he regretted it immediately. An image of a young girl, maybe ten or eleven, performing fellatio on a middle-aged man, filled the screen. He could not see the man's face but he could see the distinctive tattoo on his left shoulder – 'Big Five' – it was Mike Cribb.

Steve felt sick – he switched off the screen but not before the others had seen its content. The revulsion was palpable in all of them, they looked at each other then looked back down at Mike Cribb. He was silent apart from bloody, bubbling noises emanating from his pulped face.

Kirsty had told Steve to leave this well alone – how he now wished he had. He realised Cribb was involved in something illegal but not this – not with what had happened to Pete's daughter. He then had an even more disturbing thought – he wondered if Mike Cribb had somehow been involved in that, he tried to get the thought out of his mind.

'What the fuck do we do now?' asked George. It was the first words he'd spoken since they had arrived – a weight had been lifted from his shoulders, only to be replaced with a sickness in his stomach.

'Kill the fucker,' said Pete.

'Don't be fucking stupid,' said Steve.

'I'm not being stupid. I'm going to kill the cunt.' Pete McNulty now seemed in control of his emotions – he was calm and collected. 'I will kill him – you lot can go. Go on, just get out of here – I'm going to kill him.'

'No you're not Pete – come on. I knew this was a bad idea.'

Steve took a hold of Pete's arm and motioned him away.

'I knew we should've left it to the law to sort out. If you, if we do anything else, they're going to know we're involved somehow. Come on, you've given him a kicking, just let the law take over from now and they can finish off their investigation – no-one will be any the wiser.'

'Steve's right. Come on – let's get out of here,' said JB. 'Leave the fucker to drown in his own shit – Steve, how about if you call Kirsty? Tell her what's happened.'

'What tell her that Pete has almost killed Mike Cribb? I don't think so... No let's just leg it, she said they're in the middle of the investigation – let them got on with, he'll get nicked sooner or later and banged up – hopefully with a load of his kiddy-fiddling mates.'

Pete was having none of it... 'I've told you, I'm going to kill him. I'm not letting another sick fuck like him get away with it. I've got nothing to lose – you lot can fuck off and leave it to me. I just wanna kill him.'

JB put his arm around his old mate, whispered something in his ear and Pete nodded. JB turned to George and Steve.

'Okay lads – just give us a bit of time. We'll be out in a few minutes alright?'

George and Steve looked at each other, then back to JB. 'You sure John, what you planning?' asked Steve.

'Nothing, nothing, just get in the car – we'll be out in a minute.'

'John – I'm not happy about this, I think...'

'Just get in the fucking car,' said JB as he fixed a stare on them.

George pulled at Steve's arm and led him to JB's car. 'Come on, leave them to it.'

'What do you reckon they're going to do?' asked George.

'Fuck knows. Just can't believe what's happening – this is a fucking nightmare. How did we get into this fucking mess?'

'Dunno, dunno – Mike Cribb, a fucking paedo. Didn't see that one coming. Fucking hell, no wonder him and Karen...'

George trailed off as the door of the lock up opened.

JB appeared on his own – the two looked at him, he held up in his hand and mouthed 'stay there.'

He took out a cigarette from a packet of Marlboro and lit it with his Zippo. None of the others smoked, Steve hated smokers but he had to admit that it suited JB. Even in this situation he looked cool – the bastard.

The door opened behind him and Pete appeared with something in his hand – it looked like a bloody rag, perhaps a piece of paper, Steve got out of the car.

'What's happening? What you got there?'

He pointed at the red mess in Pete's hand. Pete held out his palm flat, exposing a bloodied piece of skin – a bloodied piece of skin with 'Big Five' tattooed on it. JB patted Pete on the back then tossed the lit cigarette lighter through the door of the lock up – an immediate flash of flame shot out from inside. JB calmly walked to his car and got in – Pete followed and eased himself into the front passenger seat.

'Are you off your fucking trolley!' shouted Steve.

Smoke billowed out as he ran to the door – he rushed in and saw Mike Cribb slumped on the floor – his shirt was off, his upper arm as bloodied as his battered face. Steve managed to grab his legs and drag him out – he got him through the door and pulled him across the cobbled street – dropping his legs he turned to the others who sat motionless in the car.

'You were going to let him die – are you fucking mad?'

'No you are, you cunt – for getting him out!' shouted JB, 'just fucking leave him, get in the car.'

Steve looked down at Mike Cribb's battered and bruised body, he was alive – but only just.

'Will you get in the fucking car!' repeated JB. The engine revved in desperation to leave the scene. Steve got in the back next to George, the big 4x4 finally roared off.

'Fuck, fuck, fuck – what a fucking mess.'

The others said nothing – there was nothing more to be said.

CHAPTER NINE

THE sound of *Pressure Drop* woke Steve from his slumber. It was just after six on the day after he'd witnessed the near death of one of his oldest friends. It was Kirsty – he'd been dreading her contacting him – he knew what was coming.

'What the fuck are you playing at?' read the message starkly. He had no choice, he phoned her back...

'What you on about?'

'Don't fuck with me Steve Allen. You know what I'm on about – I got a call from a mate in Avon and Somerset late last night, asking me if I knew a Mike Cribb, a Mike Cribb who was lying in the BRI on a life support system, the Mike Cribb who I had told you to leave well alone.'

Steve mulled over his response.

'Steve – you still there?'

'Yeah, yeah – you took a risk contacting me didn't you?'

'What do you mean?'

'Well it's just gone six on a Sunday morning. I'm in bed – Debbie might have...'

'You got a fucking nerve!' she shouted, causing Steve to move the phone away from his ear.

'You're involved in an attempted murder and you're now worried you're wife might find out about me and you – have you forgotten you told me you didn't sleep in the same bed as her? ...I don't fucking believe you. You and your mates are in shit street – I fucking told you not to tell anyone!'

'Alright, alright – I'm sorry, it wasn't like that though. I didn't tell them anything – we were, we were just chatting like, usual bollocks on a Friday night and it just came out. You know – problems, worries that sort of stuff. We got round to Mike and he just blanked everyone – we'd obviously touched a nerve and he just walked out on us.

'I told everyone to leave it, but you know John Burston – he's like a dog with a bone, he wouldn't leave it. He insisted on us going to see Mike Cribb – I, they didn't have a clue what he was up to. Well once we found him – in his lock up with all that shit, you can imagine, once we saw what he was up to, it just kicked off... the bastard was lucky to get out alive.'

'You're telling me. Not sure if he's going to survive though – he's in a bad way.'

Steve resisted saying 'Good' but he felt like it, even though Mike Cribb had been a friend of his for over forty years. He thought he would turn the table on Kirsty.

'So what happens now – I mean let's face it Kirsty, this is what you were after wasn't it? Getting me and the boys to rid the streets of vermin like Mike Cribb?'

He had a point and both he and Kirsty knew it.

'But not like this Steve.'

'Then like how Kirsty? Sorry but violence tends to get messy – there's no tactical or strategic way of taking out scum. I might be wrong but I don't think there's a painless way of physically hurting someone, because if there is I'd like to hear about it.'

'Okay, okay point taken. But we were on the case with Mike Cribb – and others. He was involved in a huge paedophile network – this could jeopardise the whole investigation. Others might escape because of what you did to him.'

'What? You mean serve a couple of years in prison and then a whole new life with a new identity? We know what happened to the animal who raped Pete McNulty's daughter – so I'm actually beginning to think we did the right thing – and another thing you're forgetting, what exactly is it you want me to do to Toby Ashurst? Tell him he's been a naughty boy and give him a little slap?'

'You're being ridiculous now.'

'Am I? Okay we'll call the whole thing off. Forget Ashurst, forget Samson, forget, forget Cherry – after all, I never knew her anyway, did I? Thanks to you.'

'Alright, let's just calm down – figure out where we go from here. With a bit of luck nothing will happen about your involvement with Mike Cribb's... accident.'

'Accident?'

'Yes accident. Hopefully he'll pull through, A&S have got enough on him already so they'll probably charge him straight away, just might be a little harder to convict with the loss of evidence.'

'Such as?'

'Well there wasn't much left of his lock up once you lot had finished. The place went up like a missile had hit it, must have been all the chemicals and the like, took out all the rest of the lock ups as well – a right fucking mess down there. But like I said there's probably enough evidence anyhow – let's just hope he doesn't open his mouth and make accusations against you lot.'

'Is that likely and anyway if he does, can't you pull a few strings?'

'This will take more than pulling a few strings Steve. Local plod are asking questions about his injuries, especially that mess on his arm. My gut feeling is he'll pull through though and keep his mouth shut – or at the worse try and do some sort of deal – so you're little vigilante act might then be all in vain.'

Somehow Steve didn't think Pete would see it that way. 'So what now?' he asked.

'Not sure. This wasn't supposed to happen like this – I know I said I wanted you to get even with the scum on the streets but I didn't think it would kick off like this...'

Steve interrupted. 'And I didn't think one of my best friends would turn out to be a paedophile either.'

'Alright, point taken... Look I'm still waiting for some more intel on Ashurst and Samson, when I get it I'll pass it on, but there's a fair bit to be going on with – did you manage to look at the file I gave you?'

'Yeah, sure did. I know who I was planning to visit first, but let's just say events took over. I think I'm going to take a few days off work, what with what happened yesterday I don't think I'll be able to concentrate on work. You okay to meet sometime this week? I just, just want to see more of you – maybe talk about Cherry and the grandchildren I've never met?'

Kirsty hesitated.

She wasn't sure herself where this was going with Steve, her feelings for him had not diminished over the years – she owed him some time. As for the grandchildren – that was another part of her agenda.

'Yes Steve... I'd like that, how's about Tuesday?'

'Tuesday's good, I've got to sort out a few things tomorrow so yep, I'll give you a call then.'

'Okay. Steve...'

'Yeah?'

'Just be careful, no repetition of yesterday's events – promise me?'

'I promise.'

* * *

He switched off his phone, avoided the papers and the internet and somehow nervously got through the Sunday. He took Debbie and the dogs to a garden centre – bought some bedding plants and a couple of pots that would look good on the decking. They had a nice but overpriced lunch and a pint of Bass at a gastropub somewhere near Stroud. When they got back home he pottered around the garden then phoned his mum before catching up with Sam on Skype, Sam wasn't happy – it was the early hours of Monday morning in Melbourne.

In the evening they watched *Waking the Dead* – he connected with Boyd, feeling a real empathy with the unstable detective. He took the dogs out for a final walk, returned and took his tablets before retiring to bed – Debbie was already asleep. He slipped in the cold bed beside her – exhaustion overcame him, he quickly fell into a fitful sleep.

When he woke he decided not to tell Debbie he was taking some time off. He left at 7.30 as normal, switched his iPhone on for the first time in 24 hour – a multitude of missed calls and messages made his phone spring to life. JB, Pete, George and Karen Cribb had all left voicemails. *Fuck knows what Karen was going to make of all this.* Nothing more from Kirsty – he felt relieved.

He drove through the backstreets of the city he knew so well. He avoided the M32, letting the dullards from the sprawling estates of Bradley Stoke and Emersons Green choke on their own fumes. Commuters from further afield fared no better – *tough shit for deserting the city – get back to your smug little villages and commuter towns and fucking stay there.*

Stapleton Road was as grubby and as scary as it had always been. Dark, moody eyes looked in at every junction – it didn't bother him, he felt safer there than driving south of the river that was for sure – there the eyes would be just as moody, just as threatening, just as dead – but a different colour.

He arrived at his gym just before 8.00. He swiped his entry card, changed and entered. He worked out – harder than normal, longer than normal – he had a long session on the punchbag. There were unfamiliar faces – this wasn't his normal time, not his normal mates, not the usual trainers. No Shaneice giggling and telling him he was 'buff for an ole white guy' – that usually made his day. He watched the local news on the screens – there was footage of the fire at the lock ups in St Werburghs but no mention of any casualties. It went on to the football – Rovers had lost again, City had won – *another shit weekend*.

He showered and changed then realised he'd better phone in work – perhaps throw a 'sicky' but it wasn't his way. He phoned and spoke to Fiona Mason in London, his immediate boss. He told her he'd one or two problems, he was going to take a bit of time off – use up his holidays that he was owed.

'Take as long as you need Steve, you deserve it. If I can do anything for you give me a call.'

He might just take her up on that – but he would be talking to her husband Barry not her. Like Kirsty he needed to call in a few favours.

* * *

Leon Campbell arrived in work already feeling weary. His whole weekend had been spent desperately trying to find foster carers for a five year old boy whose parents had both been arrested – heroin didn't do anyone any favours. Like

127

many times in the past he and Maggs had ended up with the damaged goods sleeping in their spare bedroom.

He unlocked the door and wondered what the next week would bring. The phone was already ringing, his email in-box was full to bursting. He was the first one in, as always – the others would be arriving soon, they too would be facing the same Monday morning problems. Some people came to work on Monday mornings and faced challenges, issues, 'push backs' – Leon and his team faced in no particular order child abuse, drink and drug problems and death. Never mind *I don't like Mondays* – Leon fucking dreaded them.

* * *

Steve spent the rest of the day doing nothing in particular. He'd lied when he told Kirsty he had things to sort out, the only thing he had to sort out was his head – he had a full cholesterol laden English breakfast in the Monte Carlo cafe on Stapleton Road then drove into town, parked up and wandered around Cabot Circus – Bristol's latest monument to consumerism. He mooched around a few shops, he was a fifty quid man, fifty quid meant nothing to him, a shirt, CDs, T-shirt whatever. If it was under fifty quid he didn't query it – over he would think about it, but probably still buy it. But nothing caught his eye, he needed a new pair of Loafers but couldn't be arsed with the shoe shops – he would go online and see what J Simons had.

He treated himself to a pub lunch then wandered around the docks. He contemplated calling in on Kirsty but then thought better of it – she had been adamant not to contact him until Tuesday. He wondered what she was up to – he was still convinced she'd been economical with the truth at the very least. He drove around Clifton, mystified as to what the appeal was of the place – overpriced shops and restaurants, nowhere to park and full of Jack Wills' bedecked floppy haired students. Outsiders – full of outsiders, full of falseness and full of bullshit – and what was it with always having their fucking collars turned up, he wondered.

He waited, bided his time – at last it was getting dark. He phoned Debbie, told her he was going to the gym. He then drove to his old stomping ground of Southmead. He found the address – they lived in the next road from his mother's council house. He drove past the scruffy semi – he knew it had to be them.

What had the working class come to? But then he corrected himself – they weren't working class, they were underclass – having no pride or respect for themselves let alone for others. How could they have pride in themselves with tattoos up to their necks and on their faces? They must have been born with ink leeching through their skin and baseball caps melded to their heads. The garden was full of detritus, the fence broken and beyond repair – no pride, no respect, no hope.

He took out his Doc Martens from the boot, sat on the open tailgate and put them on – they felt good and comfortable, they were old friends, good old friends, his nerves subsided. He pulled on the balaclava Kirsty had given him, *'there's four more like this'* she'd said. She wanted them, she needed them to carry out her revenge, needed them to get even for the death of their daughter.

He picked up the baseball bat and considered smashing the windows with a brick first, but he then decided to just go for it. He stood in the garden for a moment, listening to the incessant noise coming from inside the house – the TV blaring, kids bickering, loud drum and bass coming from an upstairs room. A dog barked – shit they had a dog, he got back in his car and pulled off the mask.

'Bollocks,' he mouthed out loud. He hadn't expected a dog. 'C'mon, you can fucking do it, they're scum, not in your league Stevie, do the bastards, just fucking do it.' Then he remembered...

He pulled out the bag of cocaine from his Harrington pocket – it had been there since Friday evening when he scored off Rattigan. He first toyed with the bag, then flicked it to make the contents fall to the bottom. He'd sworn to his mates that he wouldn't do it again, said he wouldn't touch the stuff, 'on his kids' life' – he had lied.

He deftly emptied a small pile of the powder on to the dashboard, then took out a twenty pound note and his Platinum credit card from his wallet. He chopped it and made two lines, sniffing them quickly and excitedly. Tilting his head back he inhaled deeply through his nose and waited. Rattigan had not lied – it was rocket fuel. Bam! Bam! 'Okay Steve Allen – let's fucking do it!!'

The marching powder hit home. Pulling the balaclava back on he picked up the bat and got out of the Audi. He ran towards the house, kicked through the half broken fence and rushed at the downstairs window. He swung the bat and the window smashed with a loud explosion. Turning to the front door he smashed the end of the bat through the two panels of glass – he turned, but didn't run, just casually walked back up the path, through the non-existent gate and waited.

The smashed-in door opened. A large unkempt lump of an oaf appeared wearing a grubby tracksuit top and ill-fitting bottoms – the uniform of those with no pride and no class. He had nothing on his feet, but he still ran towards Steve, 'I'll fucking 'ave you!' he screamed.

Steve held the bat behind him – he stood firm with his legs apart. He braced himself then revealed the bat and smashed it into tracksuited man's legs, causing him to scream and crumple to the ground in a heap. Steve managed to hit him again across his back when two younger versions of tracksuited man emerged, they were fifteen and seventeen years old – he knew that from Kirsty's file, but they could have been older. One in particular was the size of Steve if not larger – he lunged as his father had, Steve side-stepped and evaded him, then quickly turned and smashed the bat onto his back causing him to twist and fall at the same time. Steve went for the legs again, smashing once, twice across his knees. He cried out in pain, his father just six feet away did the same. The youth tried to get to his feet but his kneecaps had been smashed – he rolled back over and moaned loudly.

A dog barked ferociously behind Steve... 'Fuck!'

He turned and faced the animal as it leapt and fixed on to his left arm – its teeth ripped through the sleeve of his Harrington. He tried to shake it off but the terrier's jaws were clamped tight. Steve swung the bat that he still held tight in his right hand – it smashed into the terrier's back making it yelp and fall to the ground, where Steve hit it once again.

Steve felt a punch to the side of his face – it was a good punch delivered by the youngest son but Steve had received and survived better. The dog limped back to the house, yelping in pain with every step.

The youngster now squared up to Steve. He was a game fucker, Steve would give him that – a game fucker who thought it was funny to smash an old woman's windows and push dog faeces through the letterbox of a Sikh's family house. Steve calmly put the bat down and squared up to his young opponent, letting him take a free swing – Steve ducked and simultaneously punched up under the boy's ribcage with his clenched right fist – as the youngster fell Steve grabbed him and gave him a heavy disparaging slap across his face.

Picking up the baseball bat Steve walked over to tracksuit man, stood over him and poked him in the face with the tip of the bat. He was breathing heavily, it was the first proper ruck he'd had in a while – it showed.

'If you can't control your kids, I fucking will – understand? I'm warning you, if they step out of line again, I'll come for you and it'll be more than your fucking legs I break – got it?'

'G-g-gooooot it,' tracksuited man finally spat out. For good measure Steve stamped on his leg as he strode away – another scream pierced the night air.

As he nonchalantly walked past the elder brother he gave him a kick in his stomach without breaking stride. He rested the bat over his shoulder as he walked up the road and got in his car. Steve remembered just how brutal he could be.

* * *

Leon answered the knock on the door, thinking if it's Jehovah's Witnesses they would get a slap.

'Alright Leon, how's it going?'

'Stevie, my man, long time no see you old fucker – come in, come in.'

Leon gave Steve a warm and genuine hug as he crossed the threshold – it was no false greeting. Steve was thankful Leon didn't offer his clenched fist for a Jamaican handshake as he could never get it right – it always caused Leon to laugh out loud *'You white boys just can't touch like us black folk can!'*

'Maggs, look who's here? Put the kettle on love.'

Margaret Campbell came out of the kitchen with a tea towel in her hand. 'Steve – looking good! How's Debs doing – and the boys?'

'Yeah okay Maggs', he leant towards her and gave her a kiss, 'they're all okay… well apart from Harry.'

'Oh right, yeah, yeah. He'll be okay, just give the boy some time eh? Tea?'

132

Steve looked back at Leon wistfully. Leon spotted the tear in his Harrington.

'I think our Steve needs something a big stronger, am I right?'

Steve nodded. 'You're right Leon, you're always right.'

'Come into me den, got some nice Appletons for you.' Leon put his arm on Steve's shoulder, like he had done many times in the past.

'Leon you read my mind.'

'You boys go and have a good ole catch up. I'll bring some patties in shortly.' Margaret Campbell turned and went back to the kitchen.

The two men had met through the Social Services when Harry, Steve's youngest son, had been referred to them when he first got into trouble – he'd been caught smoking weed in school some ten years previously. Initially Steve didn't know what to make of Leon, nor Leon of Steve for that matter. Leon was tall, athletic and as *'black as Newgate's knocker'* as Steve's dad would have once said. He had a trimmed goatee and a head full of silver flecked dreads that finished half way down his back.

For whatever reason though they got on well. Leon, although born in Jamaica had lived in Bristol since the age of five, his accent reflected it – Steve remembered Leon's first words to him... *'Alright me babber?'* Okay it was put on but it made both Steve and Harry laugh out loud and put them at ease.

Leon had been great for Harry – he was a good listener, something that Steve needed right now. But even with all of Leon's help it still wasn't enough. Leon looked out for Harry, gave him advice, kept him on the straight and narrow – for a while. But Harry seemed hell bent on a course of self destruction – he lied, stole and robbed, he would do anything to get money for drugs.

As if cannabis wasn't bad enough he eventually got on to heroin – golden brown, although there was nothing golden about the world of smack. Harry was a smackhead and no matter what Steve, Debbie or Leon did about it, they just couldn't get him off it – he was an addict and it was slowly killing him. Two years ago was the last straw, despite all their help and visits to private clinics Harry was so deep into the world of drugs he mugged an old woman for her pension – he got 18 months in Horfield prison. When he came out he wanted nothing to do with his parents and sadly, they wanted nothing to do with him.

Steve looked around Leon's 'den' – it was just the back room but he'd turned it into a small office with a PC, hi-fi, speakers and shelves full of CDs and vinyl – all alphabetically arranged. On the walls were photographs of Leon in his football kit, posing proudly with his Lebeqs team mates and others of him in his younger days – cool, sharp Leon Campbell, sharkskin suit, porkpie hat – he was a proper rudeboy.

There were others of him with his extended family – both in Bristol and Jamaica. Pride of place were the photos of Leon with various musical heroes, the same pose – Leon grinning inanely with his arm around amongst others Toots Hibbert of the Maytals, Lloyd Brevitt of the Skatalites and his favourite of all, Leon, Steve and Prince Buster taken at the Bierkeller in Bristol some six years previously, Steve had the same photo in his office at his home.

'Bloody hell was that six years ago?' said Steve looked at the date on the Prince Buster photo. 'Sure was a good night eh?'

'One of the best' said Leon 'pity it's all gone a bit quiet now.'

'That's cos they're all bloody dying mate, Gregory Isaacs and Dennis Brown in the last few months, won't be no-one left soon,' said Steve genuinely concerned. Leon handed Steve a glass of Jamaica's finest.

'I still gotta laugh mate,' said Steve, he sipped the rum, 'oooh that's good.'

'At what?' asked Leon, knowing full well what was coming.

'You,' replied Steve, 'that night we met in the Black Swan at Eastville. It was the first time I'd seen you away from your work, I was in the back bar watching Dennis Alcapone and you were in the front. What was it – some birthday do wasn't it?'

'Yep, my nephew's eighteenth. All that fucking gangsta rap rubbish – did my head in.'

'That's right, it was "Leon Campbell what you doing here?" and "Steve Allen what you doing here?" I don't know who was more surprised…'

'Me man, you were the last person I thought I'd see in the Swan. Then you come out with all the stuff about reggae and ska – stuff that I had forgotten. I didn't even realise Dennis Alcapone was still alive.'

'He's a top man, he'll go on forever.' Steve replied.

'Go on then Steve, now you've started, embarrass me once more why don't you?'

'So there I was, seeing one of my all time favourites. Dressed up suited and booted and you giving me the double take. You couldn't believe I was an old skinhead into my ska and reggae, but worse, I couldn't believe you were one either. A genuine first generation rude boy – except you weren't into God's favourite music. What's all that about, a Jamaican not into reggae?'

'That's not quite true Mr A and you know it,' they were now joshing with each other – relaxed in each other's company, Leon punched Steve's arm, he didn't let on but it hurt.

'You, you just reminded me that's all. I'd forgotten it, forgotten just how uplifting it could be – you banging on about The Maytals, Derrick Morgan and the like, just reminded me of me yoot. Reminded me of what great music it was – still is. Okay man, you made me rediscover me culture – ha! White bwoy teaches Jamaican to be black, classic!'

They both laughed out loud. 'Classic indeed Leon, classic indeed.'

'Hey, talking of classics – look what I got!' said Leon as he walked over to his impressive record collection.

'You certainly made up for lost time,' said Steve, 'before you got to know me you just had a couple of Harry Belafontes and some UB40 if I'm not mistaken?'

'Alright don't push it,' said Leon. The joke was beginning to wear a bit thin. He thumbed through the shelves, past the Abyssinians, past Baba Brookes, past the Cimmarons, 'ah – here we go, Don Drummond's Memorial album, the original on Treasure Isle – look at this beauty.' He spoke in revered tones, a holy grail of an album recorded shortly after the great man's death in 1969.

Steve let out a low whistle. 'Shit – where'd you get that from?'

'Good ole eBay, cost me a fortune so not a word to Maggs eh?'

'Not a word mate, not a word.'

Leon switched on his Denon hi-fi – it was his one extravagance, the turntable alone cost nearly a grand, just so Leon could play his culture out loud. *'Sounds like dat one's recorded inna chip shop!'* Maggs would laugh – she wouldn't laugh if she knew the prices Leon paid for it all.

Drummond's unmistakable trombone playing filled the room – even with the sound of chips frying in the background it was still magical – a true gem from Duke Reid's recording studio. *What a flawed genius* – Drummond was an original member of the Skatalites, he died in prison four years after he'd been convicted for murdering his girlfriend. Some say he died of a heart attack after suffering from malnutrition, others thought he'd been murdered. There was also a lesser known sad fact about Drummond – he was a self-proclaimed racist with a genuine hatred of white people. *Even musical god's have feet of clay*, thought Steve.

They sat in silence for a while just nodding gently to the beat. Steve forgot his troubles while the ska washed over him and the rum warmed his insides – but not for long.

Leon rummaged around in a drawer and pulled out a bag of weed. He deftly rolled up a spliff and lit up, filling the room with the sweet smell of sensi – Steve let out an exaggerated cough.

'Sorry mate, forgot.' Leon got up and opened the window – then exhaled clouds of smoke into the night air, he let out a larger cough of his own.

'Missus wouldn't be 'appy anyway.'

Leon coughed again and then giggled – it didn't take long for him to get mellow. He offered the spliff to Steve knowing full well he wouldn't take it – Steve had never smoked in his life.

'Sorry mate, but I got nuttin' stronger.'

Leon knew, but didn't fully accept that Steve did a bit of gear. Not surprising really seeing as how they first met.

'I just don't get it Steve.'

'Don't get what mate?'

'You try to be a Jamaican more than some black folk I know. You love our women, our music and our rum,' he held up his glass in a toasting motion, 'but you don' like da ganja – man, you make one bad Jamaican!' He screeched with laughter. Steve joined in, raised his glass in appreciation.

'So w'happen, looks like you seen a duppy?' Leon finally asked.

'Shit happens mate, shit happens.'

'So tell me about it. That's what you're here for huh?'

'There's just so much shit going on mate. I don't know where to start.'

'The beginning sounds good to Leon, go on.'

As well as the Appleton's rum, Steve still had the remnants of the cocaine swirling through his brain – it made him agitated and lucid. He started by telling Leon about the Friday afternoon when he came home early to find Debbie in bed with Brad the Blindman.

He then deviated off on to a tirade of abuse against everyone and everything but no-one in particular – from *Loose Woman* and their regular attacks on men, to the state of British football. His worries over his health, his job, his kids – he was a white, middle-aged male with no voice and no-one fighting his corner in his own country. He held back from telling Leon of Kirsty coming back into his life and of the violence of the previous Saturday and of that evening. Leon motioned to Steve to calm down.

'Man, that's one big mid-life crises you goin' through. You gettin' a bit excited – chill, you don' wanna heart attack – and you sounding angry Steve. I never heard you sounding so angry and I tell you another ting. I don't know how to put this, but you sounding a bit racist man – that ain't good.'

'Me racist, how can you say that? I haven't said a word against, against you or anyone black – fuck me I donated £500 to the Haitian earthquake appeal. Does that sound like someone racist – how much did you donate Leon?'

'Fuck all mate. I know how corrupt that fucking island is – wouldn't give them voodoo worshippers a penny – think I been proved right eh? Anyway if that eases your conscience you go ahead and do it but I was on about you, you was going on about Pakis and Somalians. I ain't comfortable with that and I'm saying that as a friend.'

Steve counter attacked...

'C'mon Leon, I've heard you many a time, going on about Somalians and how they've taken over Easton, taken over your patch, your turf – this ain't no one way street Leon. Black people can be racist too you know – us whiteys haven't got a monopoly on racism.'

'I ain't denying that man that's for sure. I hated you white folks when I was a kid...' Leon abruptly stopped, he realised he was going the same way as Steve – they both burst out laughing. Leon continued.

'Look Steve – I've known you for what ten years? An' I got to say you haven't got a racist bone in your body. I know you was troubled in your yoot, you tol' me that, we all were. Hey remember the St Pauls' riots in 1980? I was there man – a robbin' an' a lootin'. I wanted to burn down Babylon, I loved it. But we all moved on, I thought you had too?'

'Mate I have, believe me – but, I guess I'm still guilty of being a selective racist if that's possible?'

'I'm sure it ain't. What you saying? You're still a little bit racist? It's like being a little bit pregnant – it just ain't possible.'

Steve gathered his thoughts – getting friendly with Leon was one of the best things that happened to him in his life. Steve considered Leon as his 'soul brother' – he felt good about that and of the relationship with him. Maybe it did ease his conscience – he kept telling himself he was forgiven for his past. He told himself so often he almost believed it.

'Steve, if you're thinking your friendship with me proves you ain't a racist then you're wrong man. Like you said it ain't a one way street – I lot of my breddren say they got white friends, but I know they calls them 'honky' behind their backs. You tellin' me that ain't the same for you and your mates?'

'I don't want to fall out over this Leon.'

'Hey man, we ain't fallen out. We're soul brothers – we're the good guys!' Leon erupted in another fit of laughter.

It immediately made Steve feel better, they touched fists – awkwardly. Leon fell about laughing even more, Steve felt embarrassed – again.

'I'll tell you one thing Steve,' Leon said with an air of gravity about him, 'wanting to bangarang with those young brown fucking machines down the gym, does not make you a brother or qualify you to being a bona fide, card-carrying member of the Anti Nazi League. Neither does wanting to jump the bones of Beyonce or Halle Berry.' He roared and clapped his hands once again.

'Hey man! How about Rihanna?' pleaded Steve.

'Man that's even worse, that just makes you a dirty ole man, she just a pickney gal!' he squealed.

'And how about you Leon?'

'Me? That Pixie Lott does it for me my man, she's gurt lush.'

Steve loved the way Leon slipped from patois to Bristolian at the drop of a hat. The two old friends gave each other high fives, laughing like drains as the second hand smoke permeated Steve's body – Margaret Campbell suddenly entered with her patties and two huge dumplings, causing the two men to rapidly sober up.

'Looks like you boys having a good time.' She stopped abruptly and sniffed the air.

'Leon Campbell you bin smoking in here again?'

She didn't really need to ask – their grins said it all. Maggs kissed her teeth, shook her head and left the two laughing in their world of ska and smoke. Steve felt like a weight had been removed from his shoulders, he felt absolved – for now.

'I ain't talking about Pixie Lott mate – that's not what I meant Leon. How about you – how's life treating you?'

The atmosphere abruptly changed. Leon gazed at the ceiling and slowly shook his head.

'Not good man, not good at all. I feel fucked all the time – got no energy, can't shake off this cough. Yeah I know...'

Leon stared at his spliff ruefully.

'Work, it's getting me down. I, I, started this job all those years ago to do something more worthwhile. Man, this ain't worthwhile, it's purgatory. I wanted to put something back, back into the community – but I'm telling you, this would try the patience of Martin Luther King. I feel like I'm drowning, drowning in a sea of red tape and bullshit.'

Steve could see Leon was upset, distraught even. 'How come, I thought you loved your job?'

'Hmmm, so did I. But things have changed Steve – I thought I was doing something noble, but from what I see there's some people out there beyond redemption, some of these kids and their parents... they just, I don't know. There's no hope – the lunatics have taken over the asylum. For every one decent kid out there who's lost his way and gone off the rails a bit, there's a dozen who are going to be career criminals. There's no reasoning with them, no rationale about what they do – they've fallen so low man, they ain't getting back up again.'

'And what's that down to?'

'I don't know bro. I sometimes do wonder if Britain really is broken. It's too simplistic to say it's all down to drugs, but when we were kids – hey man, we weren't no angels – I still ain't.' He paused and relit his spliff – then studied it hard.

'I remember carrying a ratchet but that was for show. I got in bother when I was hanging around in the Blues clubs – not to mention hanging around with the skinheads and fighting with the greasers – but these days, they've no self respect and no morals. When they get into their turf wars and the blades and the shooters come out it's all *"he dissed me man"* – they're pathetic. They're so off their heads on crack and heroin they don't know what they're doing – it's a fucking war out there, and I feel like the good guys are losing.'

'You one of them good guys Leon?'

'Hmmm, I'd like to think so.'

Dun Drummond and the rest of the Skatalites came to a scratchy halt – *sk-dunk, sk-dunk, sk-dunk, sk-dunk*. Leon rose and picked up the arm off the turntable. He flipped the LP over, repositioned the arm and dropped it with a thud...

'Leon, do you know someone with the street name of Venom?'

'Shit man, everyone knows Venom – he behind nearly all the drug deals on the streets of Bristol. That man has caused more misery, more pain and more death than anyone else I know.'

'So you do know him then?'

'Well, when I say I know him, I know of him – everyone know of Venom, he a bad yardie. His tag is everywhere – remember when the Council got arsey cos he'd sprayed on one of Banksy's pieces. Fuck me – a few years ago the Council couldn't get rid of Banksy's graffiti quick enough. Now, now – they're a matter of civic pride!' Leon shook his head.

'Yeah, yeah I remember,' responded Steve, 'so who is he?'

Leon deliberated for a moment and toyed with his goatee.

'You know, I don't honestly know, he a bad bwoy alright. He goin a bloodfire – I got my ear close to the ground in St Pauls and Easton but whenever Venom's name is mentioned everyone just clams up – bit like when the Aggi crew were around a few years back.'

Steve waited to play his trump card. He had done his homework, read through Kirsty's folder – Steve knew exactly who Venom was...

'Leon, have you ever heard of someone called Vernon Lewis?'

'Vernon Lewis? Leon mulled over the name – somewhere in his dark, distant past, the name rang a bell.

'Vernon – I know, I *knew* a 'Big Vern' Vernon Lewis – way back. Yes, I know of him – he was a bad motherfucker. Why?'

'Because Vernon "Big Vern" Lewis is Venom.'

'No fucking way man. Vernon Lewis has got to be at least my age. He, he a big ole biker boy, he a big ole *white* biker boy – he ain't no Venom.'

'Believe me, he is – he's 62, a granddad and lives in a big house in Sneyd Park. He's a successful property developer, owner of a racehorse and of a yacht he keeps in Poole harbour, not to mention the villa in Marbella – Vernon Lewis aka "Venom".'

Leon shook his head, got up out of his chair and walked over to his photo gallery on the wall. He took one down, an old black and white but gloriously nostalgic photograph of a gathering of young skinheads and greasers taken in 1970, it had appeared in the *Evening Post* over forty years previously.

'See that man.' He tapped the photo. 'See the big guy at the back with the beard, that's Vernon Lewis.'

Leon had shown the photo to Steve before. It was an iconic photo, taken on the day that the skinheads and greasers of Bristol declared a truce in their gang war that had been terrorising the city during that long hot summer – a gang war that had culminated in the death of a young biker. The two warring gangs met on College Green in front of the cathedral, shook hands and smiled for the cameras for posterity.

The smiles like the truce didn't last – within a week they were at each other's throats again. Also in the photo, right next to Lewis, was a good-looking black lad with short hair and a neat side parting – he was wearing a crisp, white Ben Sherman and braces. He smiled broadly, maybe nervously for the camera – it was a young Leon Campbell.

'No way mate – that's Vernon Lewis? That's Venom? Fuck me, you two do go way back don't you?'

'Man, that was a lifetime ago, good days – bad days as well mind. One of the biker kids got killed in the underpass.'

'Yeah, I remember – I was still at school at the time, the whole of Bristol youth were at each other's throats back then, wild times eh?'

'Probably the start of it all – wonder where all the boot boys and greasers have gone eh?'

'Well some of us have turned out to be respectable citizens eh Leon? While others, others like Vernon Lewis have gone on to be career criminals, serious career criminals – criminals who have spread hurt and misery... Don't you think it's about time blokes like Lewis got their comeuppance?'

'Comeuppance? How do you mean? Blokes like – Venom, Lewis whatever aren't playground bullies Steve. They've got where they are by playing dirty – we're talking about shooters here my man. This ain't "my ole man's bigger than your old man", and anyway, how come you know all this, what's all this about?'

'Look mate, I can't give you the full story, but I know things. Know things about people – the bad guys, the bad guys who have been getting away with it – the bad guys who are fucking up all the people you see Leon. All the youngsters, all their parents, all the fucked up people in this city – they're all victims. Victims of filth like Vernon Lewis, we need to take out people like him.'

'Whoah. Now hold on Stevie boy – who's talking about taking people out? If you know "things" about these people then you need to go to the law. Let them handle it mate, let them sort it out – that's what they're there for.'

'And you fucking believe that, you of all people?'

'Yes I do, well – I dunno, maybe no. I come across good cops and bad cops all the time – they're all just trying to do a job, just like us – they ain't all Babylon bwoys.'

'Well that's just it isn't it? The law's hands are tied, they know who Venom is – he's been picked up more times than a Stapleton Road hooker but he's got some well paid legals on his side. He takes the piss, always gets away with it, he's laughing at the law, laughing at us – the law have fucking had enough themselves. That's why I've got the info on him – the law have passed it on to me. They've giving the nod to blokes like me – and you, to do something about it.'

'Leon was stunned into silence, as was Don Drummond... *sk-dunk, sk-dunk, sk-dunk.* Leon slumped back into his old armchair.

'Man, you know what you saying? You saying, at least I think you saying, you want to take the law into your own hands, you wanna be a Johnny Gunman, is that it?'

'Johnny Gunman, Johnny Too Bad, Judge Dread, whatever – better than Barrister Pardon that's for sure.'

Leon paused, taken in the enormity of what Steve had told him.

'So what's brought this on, you say someone in the law has given you these details – how come?'

'Like I said I can't give you the full story, but someone, someone very close to me has passed me details of among others, Vernon Lewis – these are official police files. They haven't been stolen, they've been given to me on good authority, they, the law themselves want these people – sorted.'

'Sorted? In what way sorted?'

'In whatever way we see fit.'

'What's with the "we"? Is that what you come round here for? Trying to recruit me in to your little street army? Sounds like some kind of state execution policy to me. Some sort of final solution – can't say I'm too keen on that.'

'Not even for the likes of Vernon Lewis? You've seen the damage a bloke like that has done. Here you are – look at what he's involved in, go on read it...'

Steve handed the folder to Leon. He took it reluctantly and scanned Lewis's criminal CV. It read like something from *Crimewatch* – suspected involvement in handling stolen Brinks Matt gold, suspected kidnapping and demanding monies with menaces, suspected murder, suspected heroin and cocaine smuggling and dealing, suspected armed robbery, the list went on...

'*Suspected* Steve, suspected. All fucking suspected – apart from a few misdemeanours, couple of sessions in Borstal and DC as a kid, fuck all. You expecting us to be judge, jury and executioner 'cos of this?'

He flung the folder back at Steve.

'In a word – yes.'

'Is this personal Steve? Is this what it's about?'

'How do you mean?'

'Your Harry. S'pose you think the problems you got with Harry is all Vernon Lewis's fault eh?'

'Mate I *know* it's Vernon Lewis's fault and anyway if it's not him, it's vermin like him. Yes, is that a problem? And...' Steve trailed off.

Leon wondered how Steve knew it was Lewis's fault but didn't pursue it. 'And what?'

'And there's others. I got a couple of scumbags up in London who need sorting as well – and yes I admit it. That's fucking personal as well.'

'Fucking hell Steve, what's going on here? You trying to start a war? You definitely on a mission man – a fucking one man suicide mission!'

'Yeah well it ain't quite like that. I owe someone some big favours and so do my mates – you know JB and the others, they're on board, they're involved as well. We might just give some people a few slaps that's all...'

'Looks like you started already.' Leon looked down at Steve's ripped jacket.

'Oh, oh that. Yeah well, just a little warm up I guess.'

'But Steve, you said earlier "taking people out" – that don't sound like a few slaps to me. Look I know where you're coming from, don't think I haven't thought about this kinda stuff myself. Believe me I have, every fucking day I have to pick up the pieces, sort out the shit that these bastards leave behind, man I could ki..'

'Kill someone?'

'Figure of speech my man, figure of speech.'

'Sure?'

Leon hesitated for a second... 'I think it's about time you left Steve.'

CHAPTER TEN

CONTRARY to what she'd told Steve, Kirsty knew all along about the connection between Toby Ashurst and Ewart Samson. Not only was she party to it, she was also responsible for it – not through choice though. Samson had progressed from petty crime and street corner drug deals in the seventies to full blown yardie gangsta of the noughties – and all thanks to Kirsty Clifton.

Ewart 'Shiny' Samson had always been useful with his fists – Kirsty's body was testament to that fact. He was a young and feisty terrace bruiser, his lack of height compensated by his sturdy, muscular frame – he was a member of the Oak Road Boot Boys back in his home town of Luton in the early seventies. He reluctantly moved with his parents to Bristol in 1974 *'I ain't going momma, they all sound like farmers!'* he'd protested, but his dad got a job offer he couldn't refuse and besides it would be a new start for him – his parents were concerned about the company the young Ewart was beginning to keep in Luton.

He latched on to Bristol City and enjoyed watching them get promotion to the First Division in 1976, he even went to Highbury and watched them win at Arsenal on their first game of the season, but just two years later he was moving back east with Kirsty. He'd had enough of Bristol and Bristol had had enough of Ewart Samson. The two of them moved into a cheap dingy, damp flat on the edge of Notting Hill – as yet the yuppies and celebs hadn't moved in.

But it didn't work out – he packed his bags and moved out, no way was he going to bring up another man's kid, especially not a white man's kid – he was Ewart Samson, he had plans, big plans. No more working on the Underground for Ewart Samson, if the streets of London weren't paved with gold then they soon would be, Acapulco Gold – not to mention acid, amphetamines, Black Russian, Charlie and whatever the needle-freaked, wired, junkies of the capital so desired.

Like Kirsty he progressed through the ranks and like Kirsty he changed his name, he wanted now to be known as 'Earl' – Earl Samson, yes he liked the sound of that... Earl, it suited his new position in life. From a foot soldier to a corporal, corporal to trusted lieutenant, lieutenant to captain – by the start of the new Millennium he was a full blown general, a general of the streets, a general with an army at his disposal

He was now part of the elite, his face fitted on the now gentrified and trendy streets of Notting Hill. He rubbed shoulders and shared cocktails with the affluent upwardly mobile dahlings and fashionistas of Westbourne Grove – not to mention supplying them with whatever drugs they wanted and his success was all done to Kirsty. *Thank you Kirsty Donohue or Clifton – whatever your name is. Thank you Kirsty Donohue for making Earl Samson what I am today...*

The newly monikered Earl had first found out about Kirsty's fledgling career with the Met when he met some of their old neighbours at a Blues party in Ladbroke Grove. His initial dismay gave way to more malevolent thoughts… it didn't take long for him to contact Kirsty. He made it quite clear what he wanted of her – her wanted favours, wanted her to turn a blind eye to his crimes, give him a tip off if the law were after him – if not, well he had something on Kirsty Donohue. He was sure the Met would be interested in her past life in Bristol – her past life of council care homes, drug taking and shoplifting – not to mention her relationship with a low life drug dealer like him and her life as an upmarket call girl… *Oh yes Kirsty, what would the Met make of all that?*

She obliged, she had no choice. It wouldn't do any harm – just the once he promised. Just the one little case he had against him coming up, bit of possession, bit of dealing – nothing serious, no-one would even notice. But it escalated, it was blackmail, either she complied with Earl or he would spill the beans – did she want to take that risk? Did she want to lose everything, lose her job, lose her flat, maybe even lose her daughter? It was a risk she wasn't prepared to take, thirty years on and Earl Samson was at the top of a very tall criminal ladder and Kirsty Donohue had helped him climb up it.

There wasn't a day that went by that Kirsty didn't regret her decision to do as she was told by Earl Samson. She'd done something similar for Steve and his mates but that was her own volition and that wasn't something that was going to come back and haunt her. Samson didn't just haunt her, he owned her, she was in his pocket – until now.

It might have taken over three decades but she was now free of his clutches. It was now her turn to plot his downfall, it didn't matter what he threatened to do now she was out of it – her daughter was dead, her career was over. Now was the time, now was the time Kirsty would get her retribution – Samson's day of reckoning was coming.

Steve and Kirsty met for lunch in the River Station restaurant on the city docks. It was an old river police station – they both thought it somehow appropriate, if not ironic. Kirsty had the wild sea bass with dukka, while Steve opted for the twenty-eight day dry-aged Scotch sirloin steak – at twenty-two quid he thought it was a bit steep – they could at least have got him something fresh.

They wanted the day to be a good one – they agreed not to talk about the fuck up over Mike Cribb, anyhow he was making a good recovery according to Kirsty. He hadn't said anything about the attack on him, he refused to.

Karen had been to visit him, she'd told the police interviewing her husband that she had no idea what he had in the lock up, just thought he did a few jobs on the side. In twenty-four hours Avon and Somerset police would be charging him for his involvement in the supply and distribution of child pornography. He was a major player in a European paedophile ring – Mike Cribb would be going to prison for a very long time.

For the first time Kirsty spoke about some of the relationships she'd had over the last three decades. There had been plenty of marriage offers, but she always backed out at the last minute, she never seemed able to commit – there was always Cherry to consider.

She told Steve how the Met had been good for her, she loved working on the beat which led to a few undercover jobs, but they quickly realised she had a real talent for gathering intelligence and information. She had worked for the National Criminal Intelligence Service and the National Hi-Tech Crime Unit before being transferred to the fledgling Serious Organised Crime Agency when it was formed in 2006. Over the years she'd worked on some of the highest profile crime cases that Britain had seen including major drug and human trafficking rackets, illegal arms dealing as well as computer and high tech crimes.

When she joined SOCA they used her expertise to help them set up their Athena and HOLMES IT systems – she eventually 'retired' at the end of last year having reached the rank of Grade Two in SOCA, the equivalent of a super-intendent.

Steve exhaled deeply. 'And I thought *The Sweeney* was all made up,' he finally said.

'Oh it was,' replied Kirsty, 'but there were plenty of Regans and Carters in the early days – but times have changed, not always for the better though,' she added ruefully.

'How do you mean?' asked Steve.

'Well let's just say that the Regans and Carters of the world weren't averse to doing a spot of rule bending – planting evidence, falsifying statements, that kind of thing. Don't get me wrong, there wasn't anybody who went inside that didn't deserve to, so in a way it was accepted. We knew who the wrong 'uns were, sometimes we just didn't have enough evidence to lock them up that's all.

'Of course after all the high profile "bent cop" cases of the seventies and eighties they had to really clean up their acts, but it went too far – that's why so many get away with it these days. Prosecution has got to have every 'i' dotted and every 't' crossed, if there's one tiny little slip up then the bastard's will get away with it – and thanks to all these flash suited defence lawyers that's precisely what's happening. It's gone totally the other way.'

'So that's why you contacted me?'

'No, not really – well I guess in some way, yes, but not entirely. Although I was based in London I came back to Bristol regularly, SOCA has got a covert office in Bristol, up by the shopping mall at Cribbs Causeway. I guess coming back here just reminded me, pricked my conscience if you like, just made me remember you that's all – guess it planted a seed. So yes when all this blew up, Cherry's death, me getting kicked out, Bristol seemed the obvious place to come back to and yes, you seemed the obvious person to contact.'

'Why?'

Kirsty closed her eyes and raised her head, a memory of their past came to her…

'Oh I dunno… I remember being out with you in town one night, just the two of us. Think we were in Dunlops on the Centre, there were some City lads in there dogging you up. I said "come on let's go, anybody else would just leave" and you said "Yeah, well I'm not anybody else." You just held their gaze, stared back at them. They eventually bottled it and left – I always remember that night, I was so scared, but with you I, I just felt safe. Just felt you were so, defiant, brave if you like – I think I realised then just how much I loved you.'

Steve gave out a sly laugh.

'What? Was that, is that so funny?

'No it's not, but you haven't been back in Bristol five minutes and you're already slipping back into the dialect – "dogging you up". Sorry it just made me laugh that's all.'

Kirsty gave him a playful flick across the arm.

'You know what they say, you can take the girl out of Bristol, but you can't take Bristol out of the girl.' She gave out a laugh herself – it was the first time Steve had heard her laugh in over thirty years. They looked at each other and smiled, neither of them quite believing the situation they were now in.

'C'mon,' she said, 'hurry up and finish, I've got something to show you.'

They finished their meal and walked back to Kirsty's apartment – the steel and chrome of the apartments glistened in the unseasonal sun. She took Steve's hand as they entered her apartment.

'Close your eyes,' she said as she led him through the lounge. She made him stop.

'Okay you can open them now.'

In front of him stood a magnificent ROCK OLA 1484 jukebox, he was speechless – he let out a low whistle then finally spoke.

'Wow, that's incredible. How – when did you get it?'

'Just yesterday, that was why I couldn't meet you. It's beautiful isn't it?'

'Unbelievable. I've always wanted a jukebox – had my eye on a Seeburg myself but well... Debbie was never too keen, said it wouldn't look right in the house. You know, it's all brown and beige, leather and cushions – not quite fifties retro like this beast... does it work?'

'Sure does. I was up all night loading up the records – go on, try it.'

Steve studied the list of classics, he had to laugh – there wasn't one record on there that he didn't recognise – it was hardly an eclectic mix, more a collection of iconic soulful sounds of British and American youth from the sixties and seventies. Not only had Kirsty typed out the record title and artiste, every label had been carefully added – *Stax, Gordy, Atlantic, Motown, Capitol, Okeh, Chess, Sue* and then of course there were the ska, rocksteady and reggae sounds which the young skinheads of Britain had made their own – *Bluebeat, Studio One, Coxsone, Duke Reid* and the essential *Island, Pama* and *Trojan* labels. He was like a young boy in a sweet shop, no wonder he recognised them all – he'd bought most of them for Kirsty. He then panicked, he couldn't find the obvious – he turned and looked at her.

'Is it on here?'

'Of course,' she replied 'A-one.'

He couldn't believe how he'd missed it. His eyes had glazed over – there it was of course, right at the start. He pressed the two buttons simultaneously, the 1958 masterpiece burst into life, the record cradle started to spin, stopped with a jolt and the pickup arm collected the 45 and swivelled in one beautiful move. The needle descended, the crackling started, the strings came in, soaring and floating, *Guilty* by Tiger on the Camel label. Steve's heart lifted, he looked over at Kirsty as she smiled nervously.

'I can't believe you've still got these records after all these years,' he said letting the tune flow over him.

'Ah well, I've a little confession to make,' she answered. 'I don't know how to say this, but I actually got rid of a lot of them...'

'But not this one?'

'No, not "Guilty Tiger", I just, I just couldn't.' She still referred to it by its incorrect title.

'So this is our actual record, the very one I bought you?'

'Er no, not quite.'

'So how come?' He nodded back at the jukebox. She could hear the disappointment in his voice.

'Oh right. Yes, taken me years – and cost a bloody fortune. I destroyed a lot of the records you bought me just after we split. Smashed them up, burnt some – sorry.'

Steve looked distraught.

'I quickly regretted it – luckily when I moved to Notting Hill I discovered a shop in Shepherd's Bush...'

'Peckings on Askwith Road?' He interrupted.

'Yes, do you know it?'

'Anyone who's got the slightest interest in West Indian music knows Peckings – it's an institution,' he said, 'I've been there several times myself.'

'Yes well, over the years I've managed to track down most of the records, still got an odd few to hunt down but nearly all there – impressive eh?'

'Sure is,' he said, 'but you said you didn't destroy our record – but this isn't it?' Steve was baffled.

'No, that's not our actual record.' She took his hand again, led him over to the opposite wall. She had been busy since he visited the apartment the previous week.

'But this is...'

There amongst the photos of Cherry and the grand-children was their record, their *Guilty Tiger* beautifully framed. He looked closely at the label – there it was in blue biro *'Kirsty Donohue loves Steve Allen – 4 ever'*.

'I could never get rid of that Steve – ever.'

He walked back to the jukebox, *'Guilty'* was coming to an end, he searched for *'Cherry oh baby'* by Eric Donaldson, the next obvious choice – A-two of course.

'Our teenage years in music eh Steve?' she said over his shoulder.

She wasn't wrong – those troubled, angst-ridden but in-credibly happy days were all there encapsulated in the old Rock-ola... *Skinhead moonstomp, Heaven must have sent you, Please don't make me cry, I'm so tired of being alone,* he even found *Wet dream,* which probably summed up his teenage years more than Kirsty realised. Steve made a futile search for *Ever fallen in love with someone you shouldn't have?* but he knew it wouldn't be on there – Kirsty was not into punk the way that Steve was.

'C'mon,' she said taking his hand once again, 'we've got some real catching up to do.'

She guided him into her magnificent bedroom – the huge bed beckoned them. Tuesday afternoon illicit sex when he should've been at work – he had to admit it had a certain appeal. He forgot all his problems and immersed himself in Britain in the early seventies – all he needed was the fragrant smell of Brut crossed with Kiku and he would be in heaven.

Their lovemaking was less frenzied than the previous week – maybe the 28 day old steak had something to do with it. He explored her body, she did the same to him, they run their fingers over each other's tattoos, kissed more, hard

156

and heavy, she had no hang ups over her body unlike Debbie – the years of keeping fit for her job obviously paid off. She kicked off the duvet as they writhed, entwined in each other's bodies, he felt disconcerted that the floor to ceiling windows had no curtains – she assured him the glass was one way. The sun warmed their bare bodies, he explored every facet of her body with his tongue – he remembered how much she liked it.

Unlike in the films they didn't climax together – she came first. In their youth it was always the other way round, the two of them were thankful things had changed. She moaned and gasped, he grunted and started sweating – he thought his heart was going to leap out of his chest.

Even with Kirsty looking as magnificent as she did he had to resort to the 'wank bank'. He closed his eyes and thought of making love to Laura, then the young girls at the gym. A vision of Chantelle/Gill frigging herself off in the back of his Audi entered his mind. He then thought of screwing all of Girls Aloud – well maybe not the ginger on. He quickly focused on Cheryl and Kimberly in a threesome with him – he finally came and moaned, more in a sigh of relief than ecstasy. He rolled off her body, *thank fuck for that* – he'd survived.

They fell asleep in each other's arms, a light gentle content sleep, until he started snoring loudly and dribbling – must have been that overpriced Shiraz. She shook him awake.

'Steve, Steve – wake up, it's six o'clock – what time have you got to be home?'

'Eh? Oh right, sorry – did I fall asleep? Sorry.'

'Don't worry, it's not a problem.' Kirsty was just thankful he hadn't died on her. She was grateful to have a man in her bed again.

'It's okay, I usually work late or have a couple of beers after work – no hurry,' he leant over and kissed her, she responded and wrapped her legs around him. *Fuck, not again* – he broke away.

'Tell you what, how about a shower – together?'

'Mmmmm, sounds good.' She stood up and walked across the room past the windows towards the en-suite bathroom.

'Are you sure those windows are one way?' he queried, 'otherwise someone's going to get a right eyeful.'

'Oh yes – try it!'

She was as playful as ever. She pulled him out of the bed and pushed him towards the glass – the two of them stood there in all their naked glory. She banged on the window to a passing family of tourists – they looked up, squinted, looked at each other and shook their heads.

'Ha brilliant!' said Steve.

'Yep, just don't try it at night with the lights on that's all.'

He smiled, felt relieved she was talking as if they were a couple. It was so matter-of-factly, the assumption that he would one day be staying the night, living in her apartment even. She entered the en-suite and turned on the shower full power. Like the rest of the apartment the en-suite was impressive – god knows what the master bathroom was like, he wondered.

She entered the shower first. He followed – she plunged her head under the shower, it was easy big enough for the two of them. The sight of her lathering her body excited Steve again – she motioned him to turn around, her hands came around the front of his body, she lowered them and began rubbing the soap onto his now erect again penis.

'That's more like it.'

She pulled him around to face her, wrapped her right leg around him and straddled him forcing his penis into her – she groaned again, as did Steve – his back was fucking killing him.

His mind went back to their courting days. His parents had caught the two of them making love in the shower at their home, his mother was mortified – yet another reason she disliked Kirsty, corrupting her son like that. He wondered if Kirsty could recall that event also, she started laughing out loud, he guessed she had – he slowed.

'No, no, come on – fuck me, fuck me hard,' she begged.

This time he needed no visions of Cheryl and Kimberly – he climaxed just as she did, this was more like the films he thought – well at least the films he watched. Kirsty eased herself off of Steve's body, she held him close, the hot water drained over them. He felt both deliciously clean and dirty at the same time, but he felt no guilt – not after what he'd witnessed the other week. They kissed again, she turned off the shower and switched on the dryer, the warm air blew over their bodies – *fuck's sake can it get any better*.

They dressed – Steve back into his clothes while Kirsty slipped into a towelling robe. She poured out two large glasses of Merlot and they moved out on to the balcony and watched the world go by – pleasure craft pottered around the docks while cormorants dived for fish between the discarded kebab boxes and dog ends. She spoke again of Cherry – how beautiful she was and how beautiful the twins, Oscar and Olivia were. She told him of how they were now living with Ashurst's parents – Lord and Lady Ashurst.

Kirsty had fought for custody of them and lost – hardly surprising considering the events leading up to her exit from SOCA. If nothing else she desperately wanted to see the twins again, if they could somehow get to Ashurst, legally or illegally, discredit him – and his parents – then maybe she could get the twins. If nothing else came out of this sorry mess, they could at least get their grandchildren, the grandchildren that Steve had never met.

'You say the police had evidence against him, what sort of evidence, what's happened to it?' He asked.

'Who knows? There were statements made by his so-called friends and there was the evidence of the cocaine in their apartment, but I guess it's all filed in a shredder now.'

'You mentioned photographs – how did you get them?'

'Surveillance. There isn't much that happens on the streets of London, or Britain for that matter, that isn't videoed these days – it's just piecing it all together to make the complete story that's the problem.'

'Hmmm – and how about the Samson connection? You've said there is something?'

'Yes – but again I've got no proof of it. No hard evidence.'

'So how do you know – it's an amazing coincidence isn't it? You, Cherry, Ashurst, Samson – what's the tie up?'

'It's no coincidence. Like I said, Cherry and Ashurst met at work. She fell for him and they married within a couple of years. It was a huge society wedding – well it would be wouldn't it? Him being the heir to the Ashurst estate – of course the wedding appeared in the glossies, *OK*, *Hello* magazine – even made *Country Life* – can you believe it, Kirsty Donohue mixing it with the upper crust? Anyway Samson spotted it, spotted me in the photos – so of course he contacted me again.'

'More blackmail?'

'Well no, not quite – he, Ewart – had now rebranded himself. Like me he had changed his name, he was now known as Earl Samson and rubbing shoulders with the establishment, he was the establishment. Christ knows how, but he had become a football agent.'

Steve's eyes widened as a sudden realisation entered his head, he nodded knowingly.

Kirsty continued. 'He appeared in the glossies as well – but he was more *FHM*, *Loaded* that sort of thing, his street hustling days were long behind him. He now craved respectability – craved for something money couldn't buy –

class. He might have been established but what he wanted more than anything was to be part of the establishment.

'He got me to introduce him to Toby Ashurst. He was desperate to join one of the Gentlemen's clubs – Ashurst had all the connections, MCC, regularly dined at the Ivy, member of Fitches in St James'. He also has a box at Chelsea but that's another story. It would be Samson's last request of me – do this and he would be out of my life, no more favours, no more tip offs, no more blackmail. I agreed, reluctantly, but I thought if I did this one last thing, that would be it. I guess in a way it was, this was just over five years ago, just after Ashurst and Cherry had married – and thankfully I haven't heard a word from him since.

'Funny thing is, when I first mentioned Earl Samson, Ashurst thought I was referring to an Earl of Samson – perhaps that's why he agreed to put his name forward in the first place.'

Steve let out a snort of a laugh. 'You know, I've seen his photos in the papers, seen the name but dismissed it, thought it couldn't be the same "Shiny" that we knew all those years ago. Fucking hell, how low can football get to allow scumbugs like him to be involved in it?'

He shook his head in bewilderment.

'So what happened then – after the introduction?'

'Well we heard this story from several of Ashurst's so-called friends – they were all keen to grass him up just to save their own lily-livered skins... Samson stumped up the money and Ashurst supplied the references and somehow he managed to get invited to join the club – Fitches. He was their first black member, perhaps there had been pressure put on them from the CRE, who knows. Anyway he's in – he ditches his Tonic suit for something more Savile Row, hand-made shirts, hand-made shoes – he's arrived, big time.

'No more Red Stripe and spliffs, now it was all Cognac and Havana cigars. Ashurst may have vouched for Samson but he had no intention of becoming a friend of his – after all what would his parents say. No, he got him in after I'd put pressure on him but that would be it – until, until Samson visited the toilets there one evening and what did he hear coming out from behind the oak panelled toilet door? Yep the unmistakable sound of someone snorting a line – he was intrigued, he thought that would be the last thing he would hear in a Gentleman's club, he was even more surprised when who comes out of the cubicle but Ashurst himself.

'Well of course they got talking – turns out they had more in common than at first thought. Ashurst was finding it more and more difficult to find decent coke on the streets he said, what with all the crackdowns and the recent busts. His usual dealer had been banged up, he was fed up shoving benzocaine and god knows what else up his aristrocratic hooter. *"Any chance ole boy you can help out?"* he asked Samson – course Samson obliged, what better way than getting in with the toffs than supplying them with gear, and not just any gear...'

'Merck?'

'You got it. Merck cocaine – fresh from the laboratories of Eastern Germany. Samson had made a connection in Moscow where Merck is now the drug of choice with the nouveau rich oligarchs. Turns out he first visited when Chelsea played there in some pre-season friendly tournament – he saw the opportunities. Like I said, God knows how but he'd become a football agent – he's constantly in Russia, making out he's on scouting missions and now every time one of the Premiership club plays in Eastern Europe he's over there, doing his deals, arranging shipment – he's using football as a front for his drug dealing activities.'

'Hold on, you heard all this from one of Ashurst's tooting lackeys?'

'No – not quite. They gave us the background, this is what we've found out so far – this is the word on the street.

We've got the evidence that Samson goes to Eastern Europe for the football but that's it – it's not like he brings the stuff back hidden under his bobble hat is it?'

'No of course – football fans don't wear bobble hats anymore,' said Steve facetiously.

Kirsty shook her head.

'Tell you what was funny though – apparently this first time Ashurst and Samson met in the toilet of the club, some old duffer came in, did his business, washed his hands and then put 50p in Samson's hand – he thought he was the toilet attendant!'

Steve let out a snort of laughter, resulting in a derisory scowl from Kirsty.

'Sorry, just struck me as funny.'

'Well it would be if it wasn't so serious and if someone hadn't died because of all this.'

'Yeah, you're right – sorry. You mentioned Samson went to Moscow to see Chelsea play – always remember him as a Luton fan before he latched on to City?'

'Oh that was way back. Yeah I got to hear about him still running with Luton in the eighties. He was one of their top boys in their firm until he moved on to bigger things.'

'MiGs – Men in Gear.'

'Yeah that was them – I was involved in investigations into the football firms for a while. It was quite scary to be honest, some of them were grown men, educated and well organised – a bit different from your old Tote End boot boys that's for sure.'

Steve couldn't disagree. He was thankful he'd left those days behind him – although at times he craved for those adrenaline filled weekends he wasn't going to get into a debate with Kirsty about the rights and wrongs of football hooliganism.

'You're not wrong. Rise of the foot soldiers and all that, loads of 'em got into working the doors, protection, major players on the drug scene – course their penchant for violence didn't do their reputations any harm either. Guess Samson used a lot of his football connections to progress up the ladder.'

'Exactly – and now, now he's taken it to another level.'

'How do you mean?'

'Well this is where it gets really interesting. It's this that's still being investigated – and not by me obviously, but I've still got my ear to the ground,' she hesitated, 'look, I'm not sure if I should be telling you this.'

'For Chrissakes you keep doing this! Either tell me the full story or don't – this is still all to do with your little "proposal" to me, so I need, I want to know as much as possible. If you think I'm going to stop because of what happened to Mike Cribb you're wrong – I want Ashurst and Samson as much as you do – not to mention Vernon Lewis and any other dirtbag who happens to cross my path.'

'Hmmm, yes I heard about the incident with the "masked man and the baseball bat" in Southmead last night.' She gave him an accusatory look.

He shrugged sheepishly. 'Don't know what you're talking about.'

'No, okay. Let me top up your drink – think you're going to need it.'

She poured the remainder of the Merlot into their glasses and they both took large sips.

'This cocaine I keep going on about. It was originally made by the Merck Pharmaceutical company in Germany in the 1800s. Sigmund Freud was a user of it – he thought it was bloody wonderful apparently...'

She raised her chin as if she was contemplating her response... 'It can't be compared in any way to cocaine produced in Central or South America. It's pure, does not bring on depression or lethargy. It's a totally different type of euphoria, one of creativity. There are absolutely no withdrawal symptoms.'

Fuck me, sounds brilliant – thought Steve, wondering where he could get his hands on some.

'Sounds like you're promoting the stuff.'

'Not me. I was quoting Keith Richards – we had those words pinned up in our office at SOCA. He reckoned their 1975 tour was fuelled by Merck cocaine – shows what we're up against.'

'So what happened to this stuff? How come no one's heard of it – is it still around?'

'Why Steve, fancy trying some – is that it?'

He felt himself redden.

'No, no course not. Just interested that's all – never heard of it. If it's as wonderful as Richards says, how come it hasn't flooded the streets?'

'Not sure really, it's bloody expensive – it has an exclusivity about it so perhaps that's why Samson loves it so much. It was certainly popular with the rock stars and the glitterati back in the day, but it never found its way down to the masses, just as well really. Perhaps the Columbian drug barons wanted it all their own way and somehow suppressed it. But anyway this stuff that Samson got hold of in Russia – it's not actually cocaine made by Merck Pharmaceuticals, they're legit and one of the biggest drug companies in the world – but the generic name has stuck. In fact loads of people just assume it's Merc as in the car, they're not aware that it's a company name. Anyway this gear, this *Uber Coca* as some people are calling it, is a newer derivative of the old Merck – and there's one very big difference from the stuff Keith Richards used to hoover up his nose on tour.'

'Go on.'

'It can't be detected in the bloodstream, no matter what test is carried out, it can't be detected. It's foolproof.'

A furrow crossed Steve's brow, he was thinking back to what Kirsty had told him about Cherry's death.

'I'm confused, you said Cherry died from taking it. How do you know if it's undetectable in the bloodstream?'

'Good question. Well it was Cherry's death that made us become aware of the drug. Up until then we didn't really know about its reemergence, or rather the emergence of this new version.' She hesitated as a tear fell down her cheek. 'Sorry this is difficult for me...'

'I know, sorry if you'd rather not...' He lightly put his hand on her shoulder to console her.

'No, you need to know.' She took in a deep breath and continued.

'The autopsy didn't show any trace of drugs in her bloodstream whatsoever, but there was clear evidence she had been ingesting white powder of sorts... there were traces of powder in her nasal cavities and...' She trailed off once more, the pain clearly etched on her face. '...And in her vagina and rectum. There were also signs of sexual assault, but... Ashurst explained it away, just saying they enjoyed "boisterous sex" shortly before she died. It was only when the samples of powder were examined that it showed up in the toxicology tests as Merck cocaine, but it couldn't be proved that the Merck caused her death, only that she'd had a heart attack, hence Ashurst getting off.'

Steve felt sick in the pit of his stomach, he could only imagine the pain and torment that Kirsty had gone through.

No wonder she wanted revenge, he silently vowed to do all he could to help her get it. He shook his head, perhaps feeling her pain for the first time. Not wanting to dwell on Cherry's death for any longer his thoughts turned to the insidious drug once more.

'Okay, so it can't be detected in the bloodstream, so what's the big deal?'

'What's the big deal? Don't you fucking get it?' She replied loudly and bluntly.

Steve cringed, he could feel Kirsty's anger, perhaps he should've given her more time – before he had a chance to apologise she continued.

'This means that drug tests are a waste of time. No one can be caught out, no one can be sacked from their jobs – and no sportsmen or women can be found out – the repercussions are huge. You might as well scrap the Olympics and any other major sporting events for starters and...'

'And what?'

'And Premiership footballers can shovel as much up their noses as they want with impunity.'

'Can or do?'

'You're ahead of me.' She hesitated once more before continuing.

'We think – we know, that many, many professional sportsmen are taking this cocaine.'

'And footballers?'

'Football, at least Premiership football, is rife with it.'

'Fucking hell...'

'Fucking hell indeed. If all this gets out, this might, just might, bring down the entire Premiership.'

CHAPTER ELEVEN

A T last things started making sense in Steve's head. The latest revelations from Kirsty had answered his remaining questions regarding Ashurst's and Samson's connections and their involvement with Cherry's death. It might have been a tenuous link and there was no evidence that would stand up in court, as far as he knew no-one had forced Cherry to take the cocaine, sadly it was of her own volition. He was also sure no-one knew she had congenital heart problems – but it didn't make it any easier for him to accept.

He knew there was a history of heart trouble in his family. Just maybe if he'd known Cherry, he could have warned her. He suddenly reflected on his own reckless life-style, his own state of health – his own mortality. His father had battled against heart problems since his forties, finally succumbing to a massive heart attack when he was seventy. He had come through El Alemein, survived Monte Cassino and fought in Palestine after the war – but his heart finally gave out just five years after he retired from work. Steve knew that with the pressures and stress of his job and his use of recreational drugs he too could go the same way.

Steve was always seen as a pragmatist – he hated procrastination. It was why he was so good at his job, he was a problem solver – he never saw anything through a cloudy mist of indecision, nothing was ever grey to him. *JFDI – Just Fucking Do It*, was his motto. It was either black or white, here's the problem – solve it. He was however troubled with the meeting with his old friend Leon Campbell – he wasn't even sure why he'd visited him, he needed some reassurance and yes maybe even some sort of absolution but he came away with as many questions as when he went to see him.

At the back of his mind had been a futile attempt to 'recruit' him to his cause – maybe even a replacement for Mike Cribb. He knew Leon shared the same frustrations, the same sense of injustice that Steve and his mates shared but he'd been wrong to assume that he would want any part of it – he felt ashamed and embarrassed for his presumptions.

His thoughts turned back to Ashurst and Samson – the revelations from Kirsty about their involvement with the importation of Merck and its widespread use by known Premiership footballers was both bewildering and cataclysmic in its far reaching repercussions – it was yet another reason for him to despise the overblown juggernaut that the Premiership had become. It had gorged on the feast of TV money and had become a play thing for foreign billionaires, it had lost its heart and soul, turned its back on its roots, turned its back on its lifeblood – the working classes who had put it there in the first place. He would like to see it wither and die, to be reclaimed by the fans, prized from the prawn sandwich brigade – maybe, just maybe he had the knowledge and the power to do just that.

Steve was no stranger to violence. He realised how much he'd relished the attack on the chav family who had been making his mother's life a misery – in fact he'd enjoyed it. He knew this event was just a warm up but in the last week he'd participated in two attacks on people he'd deemed warranted it.

He felt uncomfortable about the beating of Mike Cribb – he hadn't participated but he knew if he was in Pete McNulty's shoes he would've done the same. Inked-up tracksuit man and his two loathsome offspring certainly deserved it, if not more – judging by the report in the *Evening Post* it sounded like the respectable residents of Southmead felt the same. There was little sympathy for the family who had made their neighbours' lives hell – the unknown masked man armed with the baseball bat was already re-ceiving plaudits and praise and the delay by the police and ambulance crews in attending the scene of the attack likewise received little criticism, although even Steve thought an hour wait for an ambulance was perhaps a little too excessive – especially when your legs were broken in several places and the hospital being located not half a mile away.

His Big Society with baseball bats wouldn't work for Ashurst and Samson – maybe even not for Vernon Lewis. Judging by Kirsty's file on Lewis he too was a man with a violent background and a proclivity for inflicting pain. Steve was baffled as to why he hadn't been prosecuted for his crimes – the evidence seemed overwhelming but whenever he came to trial, witnesses would suddenly disappear or suffer from acute memory loss. He was running rings around the law, there was only one law he would respect – the law of the street.

Steve would have to uphold the law – it was time to give JB and the others a call, time to call in the debt they owed Kirsty.

He decided to stay off work the entire week but he left home at the same time each morning in order to hood wink

Debbie. Driving his usual route into work, not exactly sure where he was heading up, he called JB on his hands free...

'Alright John, how's it going?'

'Steve Allen – where the fuck have you been? I've been phoning you since Saturday.'

'Yeah, sorry – things happened. Have you heard anything about Mike Cribb – did Karen get hold of you?'

'Yeah, yeah, she's phoned me a few times... she knows it was us.'

'Thought as much – what's she said?'

'Not a lot. To be honest don't think she gives two fucks – sounds like their marriage has been up shit creek for years and what with George slinging one up her, don't think she gives a monkeys to be honest.'

'Has she said anything to the law?'

'Well, yeah – she said they asked her questions. Whether she had any idea who might have done it to him but they were also asking her a load of questions about his lock up – what he had there, that sort of stuff. Seems like they're on to him all right.'

'Yeah, that's what I heard...' Steve trailed off, suddenly aware he'd said too much – again.

'Oh yeah – from who?'

'Who do you think – Kirsty. She knows what's going on. How come you think we haven't been pulled in for it?'

'You reckon?'

'I know so – told you, she knows what's going on alright, 'ere tell you what, I even got those toerags who've been doing our muh's house in. Took me baseball bat round and gave 'em all a hiding Monday night – it was Kirsty who told me where they live.'

'Fuck me – you telling me that SOCA's got details on your muh's house – that's scary mate.'

'No, no she didn't need SOCA for that, but she knows local plod as well – they tipped her the wink. Took 'em an hour to turn up.'

'Ha ha, fucking brilliant – nice one Stevie... who's next for a trip to the dentist?'

'Vernon Lewis. Only I think we'll need more than a baseball bat to deal with him – know of him?'

'Yeah, we've crossed swords a few times. He's into property amongst other things – heard stories about him being a hard nut, heard how he's done a few blokes over who've owed him but that's about it. You saying he's involved in bigger things?'

'You could say that – amongst other things he's the Mr Big of the drug world in the West Country. You ever seen the tag "Venom" sprayed around?'

'Can't fucking miss it. But what's that got to do with Vernon Lewis – I heard he was an old biker, can't imagine him spraying up the place like some wannabe Banksy.'

'Well no, I'm sure he hasn't been doing it, I guess he just uses his lackeys. He's just making sure his reputation is enhanced on the streets that's all – but yep he's one and the same.'

Steve was aware he'd had the same conversation with Leon a few days ago – he was hoping the outcome wouldn't be the same.

'So what are we going to do about him?'

Steve liked the word we.

'*We*, we're going to take the bastard out...' Before he could continue his hands free showed he had an incoming call from Kirsty.

'Sorry JB, got to go mate. We'll talk again later.' He abruptly hung up on JB and took the call.

'Kirsty, hi, how's things?'

'Okay Steve, okay.' She hesitated before continuing, 'I've been thinking. This *sort of* marriage you're in.'

'With Debbie? What about it?'

'How about it *sort of* finishing and you moving in with me?'

Steve hadn't expected this – he was about to call her and ask about how they could get to Vernon Lewis. How she could help them out, at the very least he was going to ask about more balaclava masks for his mates – when push came to shove he was going to ask her about getting a gun. He was now having his brain messed with – she was asking him to leave his wife, his wife of twenty seven years, the mother of his two sons. The woman he thought he would spend the rest of his life with, the woman who he came home to the other week to find her fucking Brad the Blindman...

'Okay,' he said.

He turned the big Audi around and headed back to his house. He would do it now – tell Debbie he was leaving her, tell her it was his fault and not hers, he still wouldn't mention Kirsty, he would just tell her he needed a bit of space, a bit of time – needed time to get his head sorted, he just needed... the white van was the same as the one that had been parked on his driveway the previous week.

Brad the Blindman didn't stand a chance as the baseball bat crashed down on his back, the sickening thud made Brad scream in pain and Debbie scream in terror – she thought she would be next. Steve raised it again and smashed it across the bare thighs of Brad – his howl of pain set the dogs barking downstairs.

Debbie's eyes met his as he raised the bat once more – she pleaded with him...

'Please Steve, please – no. No more, please!'

'No more? No fucking more? I ain't fucking started yet!'

'Steve, please. It's not his fault, leave him – he's nothing!'

Steve looked at Brad – he pitifully pulled the duvet around him in a vain attempt to offer himself protection. He whimpered like a scolded puppy. Steve looked at him in disgust – he could see his wife's wet juices on his now flaccid penis.

'It's not his fault,' she repeated, 'it's ours, yours... it's all your fucking fault!'

'Mine? How the fuck do you...'

'Yes yours. You're never fucking here! Always at fucking work! Always too fucking tired! Too tired to, too tired to look after me, too tired to do any fucking jobs around the house. That's why we've always had to get someone in to do the job, and yes I've had fucking loads in doing the job!' she screamed.

'You're fucking useless! Always have been, always will be. You've never been able to satisfy me – you can't even get it up these days, so just fuck off – and take those fucking dogs with you!'

She sat up – her large voluptuous bosom juddering as she shook with rage. He looked at them, momentarily compared them to Kirsty's perkier, still pert breasts. Shaking his head he turned and walked out, he heard her starting to cry as he walked down the stairs.

'C'mon boys,' he motioned to the dogs. They followed their master and jumped into the boot of his Audi, it reminded him of one of Pete's jokes... '*Lock your wife and your dog in the boot of the car and leave them for an hour, who do you think is the most pleased to see you?*'

Not knowing whether to laugh or cry he drove to Kirsty's apartment. Ten minutes earlier he was wondering how he would tell Debbie their marriage was over – now he was driving to see his first and perhaps his only love in the knowledge that Debbie had written her own obituary to their marriage.

He hadn't had the time or the inclination to pick up any of his clothes or belongings – that would have to wait. He had his dogs and his memories of what was in the main a good marriage, but that was all, a good marriage – they had ended up as friends, as he'd told Kirsty. They were like brother and sister, but even siblings fall out. It was now time for a new life – at the age of 56 Steve was starting a new life – what that new life had in store for him he could only guess.

His mother was delighted to see him – and the dogs. She doted on them, more than her two grandsons. For Sam it was inevitable what with him living the other side of the world, for Harry – well she knew what he was up to, knew what he'd done – it was a good job his granddad wasn't still alive, all that worry would've killed him she thought in her weird wonderful, illogical way.

It had been bad enough bringing up Steven – they thought he would be the only black sheep of the family, the amount of grief he gave them when he was a youngster, right tearaway, but well – now look at him, nice wife, nice house, nice car, nice important job – she was proud of her Steven, proud he'd made it in life, turned his life around, pillar of society was Steven. She told her friends at the bingo, he was a good son, never been in trouble since he was a youngster – there weren't many around her neighbourhood who could say that about their offspring that was for sure.

'Muh, are you okay to have the dogs for a bit? I'll drop off their beds and some food later. Just had to leave in a bit of a hurry that's all.'

'Course it's okay isn't it boys?' They were already being fussed over. Steve knew they would get more walks and more treats than at home – they thought they were on holiday every time they stayed with her.

'Why what's up?' His mother suddenly asked.

He knew he couldn't tell her – she wasn't that fond of Debbie, but compared to some of his previous girlfriends, especially Kirsty, she was a woman any mother-in-law could be proud of.

'No, nothing. Just me, uh me and Deborah going away for a few days. Bit sudden I know but got a last minute deal.

Anyway, how's things – quietened down a bit?' He was keen to change the subject.

'Oooo, I didn't say did I? Bit of trouble in the next road the other night, a right ol' ding dong. That nasty family with the dog, you know the ones, none of them work, always down the pub – the whole family's wrong 'uns, they're always causing trouble round here. Anyway they got beaten up quite bad, legs broken and all that. Good I says, bloomin' good job – funny thing is, the police and ambulance takes ages to turn up, they was in agony for hours, made me laugh that did!'

'Sounds like someone did you all a favour then eh muh?'

'I should say, don't know who did it though. Coppers haven't got a clue either – but then again they never have, waste of bloody time around here, never see 'em on the beat. Just a couple of those community bobbies that's all for what good they do. You know what I think Steven?'

He did actually, but he wouldn't ruin her little speech.

'No mum, what's that?' Here she goes...

'I think they ought to bring back conscription that's what I think, teach 'em a bit of discipline, bit of respect – that's what they need, bit of square bashing would do 'em good – capital punishment as well, buggers would soon learn then wouldn't then? I remember when you could leave your doors unlocked around here, twenty years ago we never had this trouble – country's going to the dogs I tell you.'

He didn't want to spoil her illusion, her illusion of a mythical rosier, sunnier world of yesteryear. Sorry mum he thought, but twenty years ago it was just as bad. Forty years ago when he was causing havoc she was right, people did leave their doors unlocked – but only because there was fuck all to nick and anyway the kids were too busy fighting each other then. But at least they had respect – both for themselves and for their elders, that was something that had changed – no respect, no standards and no pride.

'Yeah well, talking of dogs, you're okay then muh, just a few days eh? I'll pop their stuff over later if that's okay?'

'Don't worry about that, I've got some dog food from last time and well, they can sleep up in my bedroom, can't you boys – keep me company eh?'

Prince and Buster barked in agreement. Steve thought it an appropriate time to leave.

'Okay, bye mum,' he kissed her on the cheek, 'see you in about a week, alright?'

'Yes love, any time, no hurry – come on boys, think I've got some choc drops somewhere.'

He shut the door behind him, it was the happiest he'd seen his mother for a long time. Perhaps he would leave the dogs with her for good – he didn't want to, they were his dogs, he loved them, he loved his mother too but perhaps it was for the best – his dogs and his mother together. They would be good together – like him and Kirsty.

There was no parking outside her apartment so the illegally parked dark blue Volvo had already gained its first ticket of the day. He looked through the windscreen, there was no clue to the owner's identity – just a full, overflowing ashtray, a bag of mints and a blue folder on the passenger seat. It might just as well have had blue flashing lights on the roof – it had Old Bill written all over it.

He momentarily hesitated and thought about going to Brunel's Buttery for a bacon sandwich and a mug of tea, but the door opened before he could make a move. A thickset forty-something old male with close cropped hair stood before him wearing a cheap, crumpled Topman suit.

A large bull neck protruded from a frayed collar of a pale blue shirt. A loosened dark green tie with a small un-recognisable crest of some nondescript rugby club hung from it. On his feet he wore a scuffed pair of Doc Marten shoes. *'Oink fucking oink'*, said Steve to himself.

Steve begrudgingly accepted he was fairly good looking, even if he had deplorable dress sense. The copper pushed past Steve and made sure the door shut before he could enter. Steve could smell in no particular order Benson and Hedges, cheap aftershave and Mint Imperials. The copper studied Steve for a second – eyed him up and down as much as Steve had done to him. Steve had won on the sartorial stakes at least – one nil to Steve Allen.

The copper tugged at the ticket on his windscreen and thrust it into his jacket pocket. He eyeballed Steve once more and finally spoke...

'Be careful squire.'

Before Steve could ask him what he meant, he got in the Volvo and pulled away. *Careful you don't crash into the docks you fat fuck.* He turned and pressed the button – Kirsty viewed him on her entryphone screen and let him in.

Steve kissed her on her cheek – she returned the kiss, but on his lips. She tasted good with not a hint of Bensons or Mint Imperials – maybe just a whiff of the cheap aftershave. He felt relieved but she noticed there were questions in his eyes.

'What, what you think...? Oh for Chrissakes Steve, you always were the jealous sort. I thought you had got over that, he is, sorry *was*, a colleague, a friend. Yes I'm still in touch, he's on our side Steve – he's one of the guys helping me out, helping us out if you must know.'

He couldn't hide his embarrassment. 'Sorry, just thought – you know...'

'No I don't actually know. Look Steve just a few hours ago I was asking you to move in with me. I'm making a bloody commitment here, we've got a lot of time to make up, I've made a decision – I want to spend the rest of my life with you, I hoped you were feeling the same. But if you think I've been waiting for you all this time you're mistaken right? Yes I've had blokes over the years, what do you think

I was going to do, have my twat hermetically sealed up? Jesus Christ Steve we're in our fifties and you're still acting like a bloody lovesick teenager.'

The thought of Kirsty's hermetically sealed twat filled him with dread.

'Sorry, sorry – you're right, look I um, I've left Debbie. I'm here. This is it, just you and me – for now.'

'Steve that's great,' she put her arms around him, kissed him again, 'what do you mean, for now?'

Don't mention the fucking dogs.

'Our grandchildren – I want our grandchildren here with us. Don't you?'

'Yes of course. Maybe we can get them sooner than you think... C'mon I've got something to show you, courtesy of Simon Edwards, who I presume you've just met.'

'Er hardly met – but I guess he knew who I was?'

'Sort of, but he doesn't know that you are moving in with me. He's a good cop Steve, I worked with him in SOCA – treat him with respect, please?'

'Okay, okay – so what have you got to show me?'

'Not sure yet, he just dropped something off – he had to shoot off, something cropped up. As you know I've been trying to keep tabs on Ashurst and Samson, I've asked Simon just to keep me in the loop. If anything crops up I've asked him to let me know...

'We know the two have connections but we can't exactly prove it – sure there's the membership of Fitches but they're never seen entering or leaving together. They never socialise, eat or drink together, or go to Chelsea games together. They're very clever – we haven't even got any phone conversations going on between them. They obviously somehow get messages to each other – probably through Samson's dealers and Ashurst's city boys and their mutual interests, but if we could just get some evidence of them together it would all fall into place – hopefully this is that evidence. C'mon it's in my office.'

She walked across the lounge and opened a door to a room he hadn't been in before – he assumed it was another bedroom. It was of sorts but it had been converted into Kirsty's office, her den. Unlike the rest of the apartment it wasn't so lavishly furnished – it had a large desk with a Dell monitor and keyboard on it, printer, scanner – the usual office accoutrements. There was also a swivel chair, bin, filing cabinets, shelves crammed with books – typical home office – it even had a boasting wall of photos, certificates and framed press cuttings. Steve had similar himself, but his press cuttings were from a different era... *'Lore of the Tote End mob'*, Western Daily Press, 1971; *'Terror on Paddington station'*, Daily Mirror, 1982 – that kind of thing.

Kirsty's were of successful police operations against gang related criminal acts – headlines of murder, kidnap, robberies, drug busts – her life in headlines, he was impressed. There was a signed and framed photograph of Kirsty with Lynda LaPlante, Kirsty noticed Steve studying it.

'I advised Lynda on a couple of projects,' she shrugged modestly. Another photograph caught Steve's eye – it was of Kirsty and some big wig in the police force, dated August 1989. The big wig was shaking Kirsty's hand and presenting her with some sort of award. Steve looked to the left of the photo – the very same award was mounted next to it. He recognised the top brass as some ex-commissioner of the Met who'd hit the headlines back then for making commendable speeches against corruption and bribery in the Met and how he was going to stamp it out – the irony of the situation struck Steve. But not as much as the sight of a young Kirsty in a uniform, he pointed at the photo...

He let out a low cough. 'Still got the uniform?'

'Well yes, I still have a uniform, but not that one – and before you ask, yes I still have some handcuffs.'

A slow, languid smile spread across Steve's face.

'And if you're a very naughty – or perhaps a very good boy, you may get to see me in it.'

'How about a truncheon?'

'Don't push it Steve Allen – now where were we?'

She picked up a manila envelope from the desk, fumbled with the flap.

'This is what Simon dropped off – let's see what we got.'

She opened the envelope and took out a memory stick as well as some colour ten by eights featuring Ashurst and Samson entering and exiting their club, Fitches. There were others of them parking their Porsche and Bentley respectively at Stamford Bridge and of them being in adjacent corporate boxes. Of more interest were the grainy photos of both of them snorting a white powder – though not together unfortunately.

'Where's this?' asked Steve.

'Apparently it's a party at Samson's apartment in Notting Hill.'

'Who took them?'

Kirsty looked at him and winked. 'That's a need to know situation and believe me, you don't need to know.'

'So the two were at a party together, you've got photos of them both snorting a line,' Steve shook his head, 'surely that's enough isn't it?'

'Enough for what – a conviction? Christ, doing a bit of chisel at a party in Notting Hill is hardly a hanging offence is it? In fact it's probably bloody compulsory these days.'

Kirsty let out a long low sigh.

'I dunno Steve, this is just going nowhere – to be honest I've virtually given up on getting them convicted of any-thing, I'm never going to get my own back on them, never get any sort of justice, never going to get my grand-children...' She trailed off.

'Okay, okay, there's more than one way to skin a cat. Look, we need to reassess where we're going with all this – we need a bit of blue sky thinking.' He suddenly cringed at his use of one of the business clichés he abhorred so much.

She looked at him quizzically. 'You getting all business-speak on me Steve?'

'No not really, but you're the cop, I've got used to fire fighting over the years, we can solve all of this but I think we need to review what we've got and where we're going – let's get back to the start.'

'Go on.'

'Right – well you gave me that folder, amongst the low lifes in there were the scrote family who've been making my mother's life a misery – that's sorted so I can cross them off the list.'

'You sure?'

'Oh yeah, don't think our muh will have any trouble from them in the future – then there's Vernon Lewis, he's next on the list.'

'So this is a hit list?'

'What else would you call it? It was you who gave it to me – yes it's a hit list, maybe even a death list. But if we go that far it won't be any good for any of us, Vernon Lewis needs sorting as much as the scrote family did, as do Ashurst and Samson – but they won't be scared off by a few acts of random violence or a bit of a kicking from The Big Five.'

She raised her eyebrows again.

'Okay,' said Steve, 'the Big Four, but I'm working on a new recruit.'

She shook her head again, he continued.

'I need to take out Vernon Lewis. I didn't realise until I read your file but our paths have crossed in the past. No ifs or buts, he's got to go. What's more he's got his grubby fingers in so many rancid pies in this city that if we take him out the rest of the lowlifes will follow.'

'Sorry Steve but I don't think it's as simple as that. If anything he's kept a lot of wannabe gangsters down in Bristol, him and his gang in a way have kept order where there should be disorder. His death will probably just unleash all the second rate thugs – they'll all be fighting for a piece of the action.'

'Then let 'em fight – with each other. Kill two birds with one stone – Bristol isn't London or even Manchester, I've read your file, I remember what you said about the 3,000 organised criminal gangs in the country – Bristol hasn't got the history of street gangs that other cities have. Okay it had the Aggi crew from a few years back but that's been it – thank god. Cut the head off the snake and the body will die. Fuck it I'm not asking you to help me but you're the one who got me started on all this – and now I intend to finish it.'

She stared at him in amazement – and shock.

'Nice speech Steve, but unfortunately I don't think it's as simple as that, this snake's head you're going to cut off – more like a bloody hydra, cut one off and another two more will grow.'

'So why did you tell me about Lewis? Why didn't you just give me the nod on Ashurst and Samson, let me sort them out for your own personal reasons and leave Lewis to spread his misery down here and be done with it.'

'Oh I think you know why Steve – your boy Harry and the mess he's in, one stint in Horfield already eh? How many more do you think he'll have over the years eh? It's odds on that the crack he's smoking and the smack he's injecting in his veins has come via Vernon Lewis – and you know that. So who's getting personal now eh?'

There was something else about Lewis that made Steve want to get even with him, but now was not the time to discuss it with Kirsty.

'Okay Miss Marple – so let's stop trying to outscore each other shall we? Cards on the table – you've lost your daughter...'

'*Our* daughter Steve.'

'So you keep reminding me, but...' he hesitated, 'but, Kirsty – I never knew my daughter. If you hadn't come back into my life, I probably would never have known I had a daughter. That's hard for me, really hard – I'm not sure if I can ever forgive you for that, sorry but that's the way it is. But okay I've lost a daughter and – and the way it's going I'm going to lose a son as well. I might as well get my revenge in first.'

Apart from the hum of the PC there was silence in the small room. They looked at each other with a harsh realisation of the situation they were in – he was advocating murdering someone and she wasn't exactly condemning him.

'You might need this then.'

She opened a drawer and took out a heavy object wrapped in a yellowing oily rag. He knew what it was before she passed it to him – he took it and carefully took the rag off. A dark grey pistol revealed itself, not exactly shining in the light, more glaring.

'Fucking hell – what is it?'

'A gun.'

'No shit Sherlock – where did you get it?'

'D'uh. I'm an ex-cop, where do you think I got it?'

Steve's hands physically shook, his mouth was dry. He'd never handled a gun before – he didn't think the GAT air pistol he'd had as a twelve year old counted.

'It's an HS95 – Croatian made.'

'Was it your gun – what you used?'

184

'Me? No chance – uh, don't get me wrong, yes I handled guns, but no it's not my old gun. Christ there's no way that a gun from the Met or any other police force could go walkabout – that would be like trying to smuggle out the crown jewels from the tower. No, let's just say some weapons fall into the hands of the police, slip under the radar. I got my hands on this one when we raided a Turkish gang's hangout in Green Lanes a few years back. There's a shitload of these on the streets – they're copies of the Swiss made Sig P226. A whole batch, some 2,000 disappeared on their way to the States – most of them ended up in the UK. One of them was used to kill a PC in Leeds a few years ago.'

He remembered the case, the PC was shot on Boxing Day. Steve got the message, she knew her guns, he wouldn't ask again. This was a villain's gun – it made sense to use it exacting revenge on another villain, *quid pro quo* he thought.

'Here you are. You might want these as well.'

She handed over a box of what he took were bullets and some sort of hand held electronic device.

'It's a taser, careful it's live.'

'Fucking hell – and to think I was getting worked up thinking of the truncheon. You've got yourself an arsenal here.'

'Hardly, you want to see some of the weapons I've handled over the years.'

They both caught each other's eye, he smirked again – she shook her head in mock disgust.

'So now what?' he asked.

'Dunno Steve, it's up to you. Like you said, you're the fire fighter – go and put out some fires. I've given you the ammunition, literally – now it's up to you and your mates to use it.'

With the weapons in his hands Steve suddenly felt apprehensive. The enormity and gravity of the situation now dawned on him. This was no beer-fuelled boasting and bravado of a Friday night – this was real, scary shit killing she was advocating – he was going along with it, for what? There was no money involved, he wasn't going to do this for profit, he wouldn't benefit. He was doing it for Kirsty – for the love of Kirsty.

She read his mind. 'Cold feet?'

'No, not really – just, apprehensive I guess.'

'And so you should be. Vernon Lewis has got his minders and his heavies – it's going to be a battle just to get to him. Any ideas of how you might do it?'

'Not really. Just thought I'd turn up on his doorstep and let him have it.'

'I hope you're joking – his place is like Fort Knox. You'll have to do better than that – how about his work routine? Where he socialises, where he walks his dogs – that sort of thing. It might be better trying to get him when he's off his guard?'

'Hmmm, sounds like you've been thinking about this more than I have?'

'Perhaps I have ...'

She reached up to a shelf, thumbed along the row of folders, stopped and took one out.

'Here you go – it's a surveillance report on Lewis. Known associates, known whereabouts, cars, properties – all sorts of info you might find useful. Read it and let me know what you think. But be careful – he might be in his sixties but he's lost none of his wiliness, he's still a nasty piece of work.'

'Okay – and what then?'

'You know what then Steve. I'll give you as much help as I can. You go cut off that snake's head, and then – and then you go and get me Ashurst and Samson.'

CHAPTER TWELVE

H E was surprised at how many clothes he owned – not to mention shoes. Then there were the CDs, the vinyl, the photos, the general bric-a-brac of a fifty quid man. He had to make three journeys in the Audi, each time Debbie gave him the cold shoulder. He caught her looking at him a couple of times, he thought she might say something but she never did. Her eyes were puffy – she'd obviously been crying and her hair was unkempt for once.

He had been wronged, she the wrong doer – or so she thought. He actually felt guilty about taking the moral high ground, he thought about owning up to Debbie about her and Kirsty. But he would wait, she would find out soon enough anyway.

'Right, I think that's just about everything – are you sure about the records?'

'Yeah, whatever... Steve I, I'm sorry.' She finally said.

'No, it's okay. I'm the one who should be saying sorry. You were right, everything you said, everything about me –

work and all that. I must be an arsehole to live with – I'm the one who should be saying sorry.'

'Is there any chance you could...'

'No I don't think so. It wasn't a bad innings was it? We had some good times. But, but I don't know – what with the boys gone, it was just inevitable eh? Look, the house is paid for – do what you want with it, it's yours...'

'But where are you going to live?'

The question caught him unawares...

'I'm going to stay with one of the lads for a bit, then get something sorted. Don't know, might travel for a bit – perhaps get that Harley that I've always promised myself.'

She sensed his joviality was false, thought he might have other plans but she decided not to question him further. She knew he could lie like Hitler with a migraine when it suited him. She knew all about his cocaine habit but she kept quiet about it – anything for an easy life with Steve Allen. Still that would be someone else's problem now.

'Okay,' she finally managed to murmur. The two looked at each other, both thinking about giving each other a final hug – but neither of them made the move to do so.

'Bye,' he said as he turned and walked out of his front door for what he thought would be the last time.

'Oh Steve.'

'What?'

'Um... there was something I had to tell you,' she paused suddenly thinking it trivial, 'the dogs – Prince and Buster.'

'What about them?' He couldn't believe she was going to ask if she could have them – she knew they were his dogs.

'They um, they finally caught a squirrel the other morning, I was meaning to tell you, they tore it apart, it was horrible.'

'Right – is that it?'

'Yes. Sorry just thought you ought to know,' Debbie could feel herself squirming, 'they actually ate part of it, so just in case they go down with something, you know, in case they're sick – could be the squirrel.'

'Uh-huh, thanks for letting me know. Bye.'

'Bye,' she said. She turned, walked back into the kitchen and cried.

'The moon friday night, 7pm c u there' – John Burston, Pete McNulty and George Smolinksi read the text message on their phones simultaneously. They had been summoned – they knew they would.

JB, Pete and George were subdued when they met. The old Friday night banter routine was absent – JB bought a round of drinks which they supped in unison. For once George indulged – he had a pint of Stella. They looked around the pub, there was the usual assembly – nothing unusual just people winding down from the working week with alcohol uppermost on their mind. Pete finally spoke.

'Anyone heard from the law?'

The other two responded with slow shakes of the head.

'Nothing – had a few calls from Karen but that's been about it,' replied George.

'What did she want?' asked JB.

'Fucked if I know. Could barely make her out she was so pissed – think she wanted to see me, but I ain't going there – gonna give her a wide berth.'

'Yeah good shout mate. Steer well clear, bad move in the first place, shagging your mate's missus – that's just asking for trouble,' said Pete, 'stick to prossies mate, less grief.'

All three made a murmur of a laugh and wry smiles etched their faces – they were not in the mood for big time jokes. It was less than two weeks since the incident that saw their ex friend betray them – he was still in hospital, still seriously ill, still awaiting trial on serious sex offences – they felt no guilt.

'Jesus H fucking Christ,' JB looked up from his pint across the bar, the other two followed his gaze. They caught

189

sight of Steve entering with Kirsty on his arm. Steve acknowledged them with a slight wave, they pushed through the crowd, both men and women took in Kirsty, admiring men nudged each other while jealous women sneered, she may have been in her mid fifties but she could have passed for a decade or two younger.

'You remember Kirsty?'

She immediately made eye contact with John Burston – there was a definite frisson between them, Steve had often wondered if there had been something more. JB held out his right hand to shake hers – she took it and leant into him in one well practised move and kissed him on the cheek. JB felt awkward, mumbled something along the lines of nice to see you and quickly let her hand drop.

'You haven't changed a bit John,' she lied. JB was probably two stone heavier since she'd last seen him – the hair had also gone as had the moustache.

'Chrissakes Kirsty, you fucking have. I mean... sorry, not in a bad way. You look fucking brilliant.'

'Same old JB, always had a way with words,' she giggled. She already had JB eating out of the palm of her hand.

'George?' She eyed up Gerwazy Smolinski.

'Hi Kirsty – nice to see you again,' his eyes inadvertently wandered down to her cleavage.

'Blimey George, you've filled out. You used to be a scrawny little git – looking good for it.'

She repeated her greeting on George, leaning into him exposing even more of her décolletage. He made the most of it, sniffed at her perfume and returned the kiss on her cheek.

'Hello Kirsty. Still as fit as a butcher's dog – like me!' Pete patted his rotund stomach...

'Go on say it. I have changed a bit either have I?'

'Pete, look at you!' She put both arms around him and gave him a big hug. He returned it – almost squeezing the life out of her. He offered his lips to hers – she deftly moved

190

her head to the side. His lips clashed with the side of her nose and they both laughed.

The meeting had gone better than Steve had envisaged. He was wary of his mates meeting up with Kirsty again after all these years – especially in these circumstances. He got a round of drinks in – London Pride for him while Kirsty plumped for a house white and quickly regretted it.

'Should have stuck to snake bites Kirsty,' said JB, remembering her tipple from her teens.

'Hmmm, let's just say some things have changed about me since those days John – and mostly for the better.'

JB wasn't sure what Kirsty meant about that but he thought it best not to pursue it.

'How about we all find a seat eh?' She motioned towards the back of the pub.

Kirsty took the lead and found an empty banquette. She put her drink on the table and removed her jacket. George pulled out a chair for her – his eyes were on stalks...

'Thanks George, ever the gentleman. Did you ever find yourself a wife?' she queried.

Kirsty knew he had. There was little she didn't know about all of them – but she carried on with the charade.

'Um, yeah. Married Julie Bennett – remember her from school?'

Again Kirsty feigned surprise.

'Julie Bennett? Yes I remember her – she was in the same year as me, nice girl.'

She lied again. She did remember Julie, but she was not a friend of hers. In fact she was not a friend of many of the girls from her school days – her friendship with the male pupils saw to that.

They all sat down – before they had a chance to exchange any more pleasantries Kirsty spoke up.

'Okay boys you know what this is about. I know Steve has filled you in with some of the details and you know that

I was in the police force and that I saved all you lot from going down in 1982. If it hadn't been for me you would have gone to prison and your lives would have changed forever – and not for the better I hasten to add.'

Steve was taken aback. She'd always been forthright but he guessed her career in the police force had given her balls of steel. She'd become a leader, she was a professional, she was not going to take any shit from anyone – she was about to give her orders...

'So the bottom line is I want you to return that favour. I want you, The Big Five as you called yourselves, to get me and Steve even with someone – Ewart Samson. I know you all remember him.'

They looked at each other and shifted uncomfortably. JB wondered why Steve also had to get even with Samson. He knew he'd stolen Kirsty all those years back but it couldn't just be that. He interrupted Kirsty...

'How come Steve's got to get even with him Kirsty? We're not talking about the colour of Samson's skin here are we? What's this about exactly?'

Steve and Kirsty exchanged glances, seeking assurance from each other. Steve nodded for her to continue.

'Steve and I had a child – a girl called Cherry. Steve knew nothing of this, I kept it from him. He only found out a couple of weeks ago when I moved back to Bristol.' She hesitated for a second...

'Cherry is now dead, courtesy of Earl Samson and an-other shit – someone called Toby Ashurst. He was married to Cherry, he was my son-in-law. Samson supplied the drugs to Ashurst who gave them to Cherry. It was the first time she'd ever taken anything in her life – she died from a heart attack.'

Steve knew this wasn't strictly true, but he realised she'd put it this way for dramatic effect. It was near enough, near enough to describe the death of his daughter, the daughter he had never known.

'You said *Earl* Samson, Kirsty?' asked JB, 'that's the football agent, is it…'

'The very same John, your old adversary Ewart Samson is now the well-known football agent Earl Samson.'

JB and the others had already heard the basis of this story from Steve, hearing it from Kirsty now made it more real.

'Fuck.'

'Fuck indeed JB, fuck indeed.'

'So what do you want us to do about it?' asked Pete.

'I want you to avenge the death of our daughter – in whatever way you see fit.'

'Any ideas of how?' asked George.

'Plenty – but none of them legal. We, sorry the police have already investigated. Ashurst even appeared in court a few times, but, but let's just say it got uncomfortable for me, I can't take this any further. I can give help but it's up to you how you take this forward.'

JB looked at Steve. 'What's your thoughts on this?'

Steve glanced at Kirsty. 'I've got some ideas, I'm working on it – I'm working at killing two birds with one stone. If we can get Samson down here, set him up to meet Vernon Lewis then we can hit the two together.'

'Vernon Lewis – the local property magnate, what's he got to do with it?' asked Pete.

Steve had forgotten that he'd only mentioned Vernon Lewis and his involvement with the local criminal scene to JB.

'He's not who he seems Pete, for Vernon 'property magnate' Lewis read Venom the drug dealer – not to mention, pimp, pornographer and kidnapper. Isn't that right Kirsty?'

'Sure is – and you might want to add neo Nazi financier to the list as well.'

This was a new one for Steve to digest, she'd not mentioned this before – there was nothing in the file she'd given to him regarding Lewis's politics.

'Scuse me?' said Steve, 'what's that all about?'

'He donates a small fortune to the League of St George – a neo Nazi party with links to various European fascist organisations – they make the BNP look like a bunch of limp-wristed liberals.'

Steve wondered why Kirsty hadn't mentioned this to him previously. Was there still doubt in her mind about him and his politics? He gave her a querying look.

'Only just found out about this Steve. We knew he had right wing views – thought he was funding the EDL at first but they're just a bunch of corner street rabble rousers. The League of St George are, er... in another league, pardon the pun.'

Kirsty and Steve spent the rest of the evening telling the others of the history of Merck cocaine and of the involvement of Ashurst and Samson in its importation into Britain. Kirsty surprised Steve with even more revelations, the tie up between Ashurst and Samson was irrefutable – Samson was sourcing and arranging shipment in Russia while Ashurst was putting up the money, money that he'd obtained through his legitimate dealings in the City – the City that had almost bankrupted the country several years previously.

There were also strong suspicions in the force that Ashurst had been using his parent's private Jetstream and landing strip at their house in the country to fly the drugs in. Unfortunately they were suspicions only, the old school network and funny handshake brigade had been working overtime – it would take a miracle to make any of this stick, especially when there wasn't any evidence of Ashurst and Samson even knowing each other.

'So it sounds like all three of them are all round pieces of shit then,' said Pete – not as a question, more as a statement.

'They sure are. Not only that, but greedy pieces of shit – and that's what we can play on,' said Steve.

Kirsty looked at him quizzically... 'Go on,' she said.

'Vernon Lewis is like Samson – one greedy fucker. He's got where he has through being totally ruthless. Other cities have several crime lords divvying up the manor. Okay Bristol's a lot smaller than London, Manchester, whatever but nevertheless he's got a monopoly on the place, there's a few other street gangs but nothing in his league. He's not going to rest on his laurels just dealing in crack and smack – if something new comes along he'll want a piece of the action, otherwise he'll be terrified that someone else will step in. Like I said he's greedy – if we offer him something, something different he'll bite our hand off.'

Kirsty knew where this was going. 'I think I can guess what you're planning to offer him – Merck cocaine.'

'You got it in one.'

CHAPTER THIRTEEN

STEVE moved what he could into Kirsty's apartment – the rest he put into storage. His most valued possession apart from his vinyl collection and the photos of his boys, both human and canine variety, was his Apple laptop. Steve inserted the memory stick into the USB port, imported the images, clicked on the icon and opened the photos. They were of decent quality, the light wasn't good but that was understandable as they were taken sur-reptitiously, but the resolution was high enough for what he had in mind.

Apart from the folder named 'A_and_S_pics' there was another containing a video, intriguingly titled 'Si_and_kirsty _sorry'. He hovered over the icon for a second, double clicked then quickly regretted it. A video of the naked bodies of Kirsty and Simon Edwards filled the screen. At one stage Edwards looked directly into the camera and smiled – Kirsty had her back to the camera, Steve noticed there was no tattoo on her bare shoulder – *at least this sordid, squalid incident happened a good few years in the past.*

Kirsty was performing fellatio on the kneeling Edwards. He was looking directly at the camera, grinning inanely. Both of his hands were giving the thumbs up signal. It was evident that the video was filmed with a hidden camera and without Kirsty's consent as she was oblivious to the prying lens – it was not enough but it gave Steve a momentary respite from the horror and disgust.

Clasping his hands behind his head he stared at the ceiling in thought. *What the fuck was going on? What was she playing at – were she and that scruffy bastard an item?*

JB had warned him to be wary – was this one big scam after all? Was it just Kirsty using him or were they all in on it? Some sick stunt by the Old Bill, using him and his mates to carry out their nefarious corrupt deeds? This gave a whole new meaning to bent cops.

He wondered if after they had carried out their 'mission' as Kirsty had put it, they would all then get nicked. He even wondered if she was still in SOCA? *For fuck's sake they were the British equivalent of the FBI, they could do what they fucking wanted*, but – what was the meaning of the 'sorry' suffix on the file name – that meant something, he knew that meant something.

Kirsty was out visiting Cabot Circus – she'd told Steve she wanted to get some more bits and pieces for the apartment, maybe pop in Harvey Nicks for some new outfits. She couldn't believe how much Bristol had been transformed in the last few decades, that was an understatement if he'd ever heard one – C&A was the height of fashion when she'd left.

He'd asked her for the stick, she had an inkling of what he was up to and willingly handed it over, it was evident she didn't know what was on it, obviously just the photos of Ashurst and Samson she'd thought – not of her *in flagrante* with that bastard Edwards. He got up and headed for the kitchen, rummaged through the cupboards and found an opened bottle of Glennfiddich, poured himself a large glass and downed it in one, he felt nauseous – not just at the sudden consumption of the 18 year old malt but at the sickening situation he found himself in.

He wandered around the apartment and thought about having a real look around. Not sure of what he would find or what he wanted to find, he half-heartedly opened a few drawers and cupboards but quickly shut them again. He went through Kirsty's wardrobe, there were expensive designer labels – she must have been on some serious money, or... taking some serious backhanders for 'drinks' as they liked to call it.

He found her uniform with three pips on the collar – presumably her dress uniform before she joined SOCA. Going through her bedside chest of drawers he found tissues, Martina Cole paperbacks, iPod headphones and a vibrator – nothing unusual in that – there probably weren't many bedside drawers in the country that didn't contain the same objects. He was impressed with the size of the vibrator though – one of Ann Summers finest. *So, she liked sex?* He could himself vouch for that – it was hardly surprising knowing her past, perhaps that's all it was with Edwards, just a bit of down and dirty sex – some sort of young fuck buddy for her? If he hadn't seen the video then would it have made any difference to what he thought of her – did he really think that she hadn't had sex for the last thirty years? He thought of her reference to her hermetically sealed twat once again.

He went back to the kitchen and poured himself another malt. Walking through the lounge he momentarily stopped at the Rockola and pressed a couple of buttons. *'Just my imagination'* by the Temptations started up, pure class by Detroit's finest. He walked out on to the balcony – it was a beautiful spring day, the cold and the rain of the winter had quickly dissipated – it was warm and sunny and the docks had scrubbed up well. He could see the Cabot Tower on the horizon shrouded in scaffolding – it would be good to see the iconic monument back to its full glory again.

Pero's Bridge caught his eye. It had been built by the city fathers and named after one of the many unfortunate slaves that had made the city wealthy – it served not just as a foot-bridge linking one side of the docks to the other but as a memorial, an apology for Bristol's insidious past. To Steve it really didn't seem enough, it was merely a token apology – it barely measured on the *'We're sorry scale'*. Sometimes Steve felt the same – would he, like his city ever apologise enough for his dark past?

He sat down and contemplated his future, looking to his right he could just make out the concrete and glass office block of Pinnacle over at Temple Quay – his place of em-ployment for the last decade or so. He was planning to go back to work on Monday morning and hand in his notice – no matter what happened between him and Kirsty he'd had enough. He was like a square peg in a round hole there anyway, let the Lauras and Teflon Toms of the world take over. He was from a different era, cut from a different cloth – it was time to move on, mid-life crisis or not.

Movement below caught his eye. Kirsty was waving like a pubescent schoolgirl at her first teen idol concert. She was laden with bags – she glowed, she beamed, she looked beautiful. He half-heartedly waved back – decision time he thought to himself.

She spilt in over the threshold as he opened the door for her. Dropping the bags on the floor she spied the whisky glass in his hand...

'Starting early – whisky as well? Didn't think that was your poison?'

She put her arms around him and attempted to kiss him on the lips – he pulled away.

'Steve? What's wrong – something happened?'

For a moment he thought about telling her about the memory stick and the horror that he'd discovered on it. He decided not to, it was nothing to do with her – or him for that matter. It was in the past – he had to put it at the back of his mind no matter how painful it was.

'Nothing, nothing – sorry just a few things on my mind that's all.' He was eager to change the mood.

'So what did you get – anything for me?'

Kirsty was not convinced by his sudden change of mood. She sensed there was more to it than he made out, but now was not the time to pursue it.

'Yes I have actually... shut your eyes.'

He did as he was told. He could hear the rustling of bags and he could smell the distinct aroma of new clothes. Not far in front him something was being unfolded.

'Okay you can open them now... *Ta-dah!*'

She held up a new Baracuta Harrington jacket – his eyes lit up.

'I, I know it'll fit you 'cos I looked at your old one – you know the one with the rip on the arm that you haven't told me about?'

'Oh that, yeah been meaning to say – caught it on something. Bummer eh?'

'Well? Do you like it? Bought it in that John Anthony's – they got some nice stuff in there... for Bristol.' She couldn't resist the little dig.

'Yeah, it's great. It's just...'

'Just what?'

'It's just so...red.'

He screwed up his face and continued. 'Admittedly not bright red, but it's red... I don't...' He stopped mid sentence.

'You don't what?'

'You know... red. Not really my colour, don't usually wear red.'

'What because of football? Bloody hell Steve, didn't think you still had a hang up about that. Go on, try it on.'

She held it out to him. He put the glass down, turned around and put his arms through the sleeves – it fitted like a glove and could have been made for him. He turned to face her, her eyes lit up.

'Oh Steve, it looks really nice, the colour suits you – honest, I'm not just saying that.'

He strode over to a mirror and pulled the bottom of the jacket down then played around and adjusted the zip. He then held out his arms stiffly – he didn't know why, just a thing he did...

'Sweet.' He looked at Kirsty and smiled. 'Sweet,' he repeated.

'Good. Glad you like it – it was the only colour they had, so tough.' She poked out her tongue like a naughty school-girl. He reciprocated with the banter.

'I mean – it's bad enough you got me living south of the river – I've only been here five minutes and now you got me wearing City red!'

'South of the river? Christ Steve, you're about fifty feet south of the river, it's hardly bloody Hartcliffe!'

'Thank God, otherwise you would never have got me to move in.' *It was still fifty feet too far.*

She snorted a laugh as she bent down to show off her purchases. He spotted a couple of Harvey Nichols bags but of more interest was the La Senza bag – *happy days.*

He felt his iPhone vibrate in his pocket. *Pressure Drop* clashed with the last few bars of *Just my imagination.* Looking at the screen he read the text message from Leon Campbell – just four short words *'Steve, count me in'.*

* * *

'Leon – it's Steve, give me a call back mate, we need to talk.'

Steve had been trying to get hold of Leon since he'd received the text message the previous evening. He had phoned back straight away but Leon had switched to voice-mail. Steve's next move would be to pay him a visit – it was the last thing he'd expected, Leon saying he wanted to be part of his 'mission'. He wondered what had bought on the change of mind, especially after their last meeting when it was quite evident that Leon didn't want any part of it.

The text message had nearly ruined his evening, only nearly. As soon as soon as Kirsty had shown Steve what she'd bought in La Senza the mood changed – for the better.

Their love making was pretty near perfect but sadly for Steve the handcuffs and uniform were still to make an appearance. At least the Rampant Rabbit got out of his hutch, the only thing that spoiled the evening was the flashbacks of that bastard Edwards fucking Kirsty. In fairness Edwards had named the files *'sorry'*, presumably he didn't think Steve would see them, perhaps it was just that – an apology to Kirsty. Steve wondered if he now knew of their relationship, either way the bastard was taking the piss.

* * *

Leon answered the door to Steve – there was no hug, no smile, not even a touching of clumsy fists. Steve knew there was something up, he presumed the worst – Margaret had left him.

'Leon? What's up mate?'

'You'd better come in,' replied Leon.

Margaret Campbell appeared from the kitchen. She looked as bad as Leon, she'd obviously been crying. Well at least she hadn't gone so that was that theory out of the window.

'Maggs, Leon – what's happening? What's wrong?'

Maggs came up behind Leon, put her arm around him and kissed him on the cheek. She looked over his shoulder straight at Steve. Steve had never seen them looking this way, the grief was palpable.

'It's Leon,' whispered Maggs, 'he's got cancer.'

* * *

Driving south down the Gloucester Road towards the City Centre, Steve spotted the police helicopter hovering above, its intense light drilling down through the night sky. There was a glow to the city, not the normal peachy sodium street light that every city gave off – this was more vivid, more living, this was of the streets not from the streets.

He could smell the burning. Bristol with its history of riots was hitting the headlines again – not the dis-enfranchised black youth of St Pauls this time, but the crusty, soap-dodging, hedge monkeys of the 'People's Republic of Stokes Croft' – protesting against the opening of yet another all-consuming Tesco store. The protestors saw themselves as urban freedom fighters – anti-establishment anarchists intent on smashing the system – in reality they were in the main white, middle-class privileged, weed-smoking, dreadlocked Trustafarians trying to make out that they were down with the 'black yoot' and fighting a right-eous class war. He and Leon both despised them.

'Fucking hippy wankers,' muttered Steve.

The traffic ground to a halt around him, sirens wailed from every direction. He pulled to the kerb to let the riot vans past, not being able to pull out again he switched off the engine, put the hand brake on, got out and searched for the nearest pub.

He found it – it had hand-written posters in the window proclaiming *'Royal wedding free zone'* – that alone appealed to him. Thankfully it was a small independent and not a countrywide chain behemoth – at least Steve agreed with the hedge monkeys on something.

He ordered a pint of Old Bob and sat down on a stool at the bar. Looking around he took in the clientele – students mostly, both male and female enjoying each other's company, straggly roll-ups hanging from their mouths, about to be lit and enjoyed in the shabby back yard. An old boy nursing a half of cider sat in a corner with his ageing, but faithful Jack Russell at his feet – Steve looked at them both and smiled knowingly. Over in the far corner a couple of would-be, or even had-been rioters nervously watched the door.

The Old Bob slipped down well. Steve had asked Leon if he wanted to go out for a drink, thought he might need it, but his gaze at Margaret told the story – she didn't want him out of her sight. Steve understood – he wouldn't pursue it. He departed with a hug and a promise to give him a call in the next few days.

It was evident Leon didn't want to talk about his *'Count me in'* text message – not in front of Maggs anyway. Steve would leave it, perhaps for good – he didn't want to put any more pressure on Leon. In fact he now regretted even mentioning it in the first place – he could be such a selfish prick at times.

Steve tried to gather his thoughts – thoughts of what was happening to Leon, thoughts of riots on the streets of Bristol... again. He thought of the mess his football club was in. He thought of how he was fucking up his wife, fucking up his mates and fucking up his own head with his coke habit. He thought about his job, his health, his sons, his future – his mid-life crisis was real, it was to him. Debbie had laughed about it – Kirsty had virtually done the same. He thought about what was happening between him and Kirsty – thought about the video of her and Edwards.

'What a cunt' he said, louder than he'd intended.

'What's that?' said the barman.

'Sorry mate. Just slipped out – talking to myself.'

He felt embarrassed – as a means of atonement he ordered another drink. He got out his wallet and took out a fiver.

'Another pint please mate and um... one for yourself.'

'Cheers mate. I'll have a brandy.'

He muttered 'cunt' again – this time he meant it.

Reopening his wallet he took out another fiver then spotted the small poly bag nestling between the notes. He handed over the two fivers and got a couple of pieces of shrapnel in change – *so much for patronising the independent pubs – thieving bastards*. He finished off the last dregs of his first pint and took a sip from his second, got up from the stool and headed for the toilets. He found an empty cubicle and locked the door behind him – the cistern had been boxed in so he lowered the seat – it was black, which was always a bonus.

After sprinkling out the powder he deftly rolled up a crisp twenty pound note. Two long sniffs sent the cocaine swiftly to his brain. Rolling his head back he inhaled deeply and let the chemicals go to work on synapses, dopamine and neurotransmitters or whatever shit he'd read somewhere. The cocaine would also dilate his pupils, constrict his blood vessels, fuck up his heart, fuck up his liver and fuck up his nose – but he didn't care, it excited him, made him feel good, made him feel better than good. He felt invincible – he acted like a prick but he felt like a king.

After lifting the seat, he took a piss then exited and looked at himself in the mirror as he washed his hands. He felt an out of the body experience, found himself looking at his face but not taking it in. He stared deep in to his own eyes, his pupils were enlarging already.

'Like rocket fuel Stevie, like rocket fuel,' Bulldog Rattigan at least had got that right.

He studied his nose and his eyebrows – he opened his mouth wide, ran his tongue over his teeth then over his gums. He arched his tongue up to the roof of his mouth then closed his eyes and shook his head. Finally he took a couple of deep breaths and re-entered the bar.

'Cheers', said the barman raising his glass.

'Yeah. Yeah cheers mate,' replied Steve. He picked up his pint and downed it in one. 'Better be going.'

He raised the empty glass to the barman in a theatrical flourish – then dropped it on to the oak bar. The noise as it smashed drew the attention of the frightened neo rioters and woke the dozing Jack Russell.

'Cunt indeed,' said Steve as he left the bar.

The traffic had eased – he got into his Audi and headed back down the Gloucester Road towards the People's Republic of Stokes Croft and the maelstrom of the Tesco riot. He knew he could have avoided it, he could have taken a right at Zetland Road then headed through Cotham and its elegant Edwardian homes, down St Michael's Hill and back on to the Centre – he could have done that but he didn't want to, the devil in him made him head for the riot. At the back of his mind he was hoping to see Harry. But he knew it would be like searching for piece of snot in a bowl of porridge – they all looked the same, dressed the same, walked the same. He had no chance.

The blue and white police tape signified the no go zone, the PCSO who stopped him was immature but forceful.

'Back up mate and go home, there's nothing to see.' On another night he might have smelt the alcohol on Steve's breath and noticed the dilated pupils – but the plastic cop's thoughts were elsewhere.

'Honest mate just bugger off. They'll smash up a motor like this no sweat. This ain't anti-Tesco, it's anti-capitalism, anti-rich, anti-Monarchy – trust me you don't want to go there.'

He did as he was told, did a u-turn and headed up the Zetland Road – the helicopter made an appearance again, it came over the horizon, its searchlight panning across the warren of streets of Kingsdown and St Pauls. The coke was wearing off already, twenty minutes of euphoria, twenty minutes of despair. He thought about stopping and finishing off the remainder of the powder but instead he rummaged through his CD collection – he needed a dose of Al Green, he needed to mellow, take his mind of his problems. He found the Reverend's Greatest Hits – *I'm so tired of being alone* filled his head.... for a while.

He could hear it coming before he saw it – a low slung, moody hatchback, Corsa or Nova or some other nondescript marque ending with a vowel. They pulled up beside him at the lights, the boom boom of some sketchy drum and bass record made his windows vibrate and drowned out the Reverend – pissing Steve off big time.

They wanted him to eyeball them – he didn't want to disappoint. He pressed the button on the armrest and the window eased down – he looked at the four baseball-capped ferrets with disdain. At first sight he thought the one in the passenger seat nearest to him was wearing a neck scarf – on closer inspection it turned out to be a mass of tattoos, arching around his neck and up to his studded ear. The smell of high strength cannabis wafted into Steve's Audi, overwhelming its own natural smell of leather. The ferret in the passenger seat raised a can of Natch to his lips, took a swig then deliberately spat it at the Audi.

'Got a problem bruv?' he sneered.

The rest of the feral ferrets howled with laughter and slapped the seats and dashboard in appreciation of their mate's bravado.

'Nope – and you're not my "bruv". If you were I would disown you, you lowlife piece of shit.'

'Wha you sayin' bruv, you dissin' me?'

'Too right I'm "dissin" you – and why are you trying to sound like some black American rapper from the 'hood? You're as white as I am – *bruv*.'

The lights changed and Steve pulled away – not quickly. He was not trying to run or hide, he was just making a point. The ferrets in their hatchback roared ahead and got in front of Steve, they then hit the brakes forcing Steve to do the same. Both doors of the hatchback flew open spewing the inked-up chavs out onto the tarmac – they were a whirl of hoods, caps, baggy jeans and oversized trainers. Steve reached for the glove box and took out the Sig pistol that Kirsty had given him. He had loaded it earlier, just out of curiosity. He didn't have a clue how to use it – just thought he would.

He opened his door and held the gun in front of him – pointing at each of the baggy-arsed ferrets in turn.

'Come on then bruvs. Let's see how tough you are now!'

'Whoah! Whoah! Cool it mate, just cool it!' said one. The others screamed in fear as one.

'So who's got the problem now eh? Eh?'

Steve motioned them to the side of the road. The traffic was light – most people were behind locked doors, shutting themselves off from the trouble of the streets.

'You lot are just a bunch of wankers. What are you?'

They didn't respond. Steve repeated... 'I said what are you?'

'Um ... wankers. Look mate, sorry, just a bit of a laugh okay? Didn't mean it – just put the shooter away eh?'

'Yeah, you're right, just a bit of a laugh eh?'

Steve pointed the gun at each of them in turn. They cowered with their hands in the air – for dramatic effect he turned the gun on its side, like he'd seen in the movies. They flinched in unison – he guessed it meant something to the 'bruvs' – sort of Pavlov's dogs. He walked around to their car, never taken his eye off them. He glanced down through the open door of the hatch and looked back up to them.

'What's this row?' He nodded his head towards the CD player in the dash.

No-one answered. He motioned with the Sig again.

'It's Netsky,' answered the driver.

'Call that music – it's fucking shit,' said Steve. 'What is it?' he queried again.

'It's ... fucking shit,' they all answered.

'Correct. It's fucking shit.'

He pointed the gun at the CD player and pulled the trigger. The noise reverberated around the street and silenced Netsky forever.

'FUCK MAN WHAT YOU DOING?!'

He didn't answer. He was as shocked as they were – his ears were ringing from the explosion, the cordite stung his nostrils and his eyes watered. He strolled back to his car, got in and put the Sig back in the glove compartment and drove off. Al Green continued with the sweet sound of *Call me*.

* * *

'So what was it with your friend Leon?' asked Kirsty as he entered the apartment.

He didn't like the way she said 'your friend' – he wasn't sure why but there was just some sort of intonation in her voice that irritated him.

'Cancer. He's got lung cancer.'

'Poor bloke – how is he?'

'How is he? How is he? He's fucking dying – how do you think he is?'

'Alright, alright – sorry, were you um, were you close?'

He lightened up. It was time for him to apologise.

'Yeah, sorry – been a tough day. Yeah we were, sorry, are good pals. He really helped out Harry in the early days, bit late I guess now but... I dunno we just got on really well ever since we first met. He's been good for me as well – helped me in a way.'

'How's that?'

'Not sure really. Guess him being a black guy helped. We're very similar – well apart from the obvious. I helped him with his record collection.' Kirsty furrowed her brow.

'He's a nice bloke – and his missus, lovely lady. Just a really nice couple – you'd like them.'

She nodded her head, making out she understood.

'Yeah, yeah. How bad is he? Is he up to going out – perhaps we could go out for a meal or something?'

'Maybe,' said Steve, but he knew it wouldn't happen.

'One thing though...' he hesitated.

'Go on?' She suddenly sounded like the cop she was.

'He said he wants in. Wants to help me, us out – on our little... mission.'

'You told him?' She sounded even more like a cop.

'Well not directly. But we had a chat a week or so back – we got talking about the usual, the woes of the world – he's a social worker, worked on some real shit over the years. He's come across abusers, child prostitutes, drug users – and dealers. Unbelievably he knows Vernon Lewis.'

'How come?'

'Oh not directly – their paths crossed years ago – Leon was one of the old Never on a Sunday crowd, remember them?'

'The old skinhead gang from the late sixties? Yeah, just a bunch of spotty faced boot boys weren't they – nothing serious?'

'No, well most of them turned out alright. Had a few wrong 'uns amongst their number but yeah they were okay. Lot of them have gone on to be big shots, you know success-ful businessmen. Couple of 'em ended up in nick but then again so did a lot of us from back then.'

He caught Kirsty raising her eyebrow again. 'Yeah okay,' he said before she had a chance to comment.

'Anyway they got into a few scraps with the greasers back then. It got a bit out of hand – one greaser lad got killed.'

'I remember it – they had a truce after that didn't they?'

'That's right, they had a truce – which didn't last but anyway, like I said Leon was one of the skinheads, Lewis was one of the leaders of the greaser gang. He was known as "Big Vern" then, not Venom though.'

'What "Big Vern" as in *Viz*?'

'Eh? Oh yeah, guess he was the original though.'

'Whatever. So that was the only way Leon knew him – he hasn't been involved with him since those days?'

'No, no chance – Leon's on the level. He's sound as a pound. Like me he didn't have a Scooby Doo that Lewis was 'Venom' or the Mr Big of the Bristol underworld.'

'But he's willing to get involved with you lot – willing to go on a mission to... well whatever you've got planned for Lewis – his murder perhaps?'

'Perhaps,' muttered Steve, 'but let's not forget it was you who started all this. You who kicked all this off – and after Lewis it's Ashurst and Samson you want us to deal with.'

'Oh don't worry, I haven't forgot. In fact I can't wait to hear what your plans are for them – all of them.'

'Hmmm, well you can start by getting me something.'

'Sure, got a nice Chateauneuf du Pape in Sainsbury's today – it was on offer, I'll go get you a glass.'

She turned and walked towards the kitchen.

'That's not what I meant,' shouted Steve as Kirsty disappeared out of sight, 'I meant...'

Kirsty reappeared holding a glass of red wine in one hand and a package wrapped up in brown tape in the next.

'...Merck cocaine,' said Steve, in a barely audible whisper.

CHAPTER FOURTEEN

'WHERE the fuck did she get hold of that stuff?' asked JB as they took in the latest revelation from Steve.

'Ask me no questions, I'll tell no lies,' replied Steve.

'Meaning?'

Steve shrugged. 'Fucked if I knows, just something Leon always says. Talking of which, I caught up with Leon last night, the poor bastard's got cancer, thinks he's only got a year or so left. He's not bothering with chemo, says he can't stand the thought of losing his dreads – he's going to join us later.'

'Fucking hell – what a bummer. He's a top bloke is Leon, they say the good die young,' said JB.

'Amen to that,' agreed Pete, 'you say he's meeting us later – in here?'

The rest of the lads had met Leon previously, he'd been to a few barbeques at Steve's house over the last few years and they'd also been to a number of Soultrain events with him. They all liked him – it was impossible not to like Leon, but drinking with him in the 'Moon under water' was something else. They all looked around – there wasn't exactly an abundance of black faces at this end of Bristol, let alone in the Moon.

'Yes, what of it?'

'No, nothing, just saying that's all,' replied JB.

'Talk of the devil...' Pete nodded towards the door. Leon entered warily, he looked as cool as ever – black full length leather coat, *'Studio one'* logo'd pale yellow T-shirt beneath, distressed denim jeans, Puma trainers and wraparound shades. If he was trying to blend in with the locals he was failing miserably. Steve stood up and motioned his pal over.

'Alright mate?' Steve held out his hand and Leon shook it firmly, no Jamaican touch just a good firm shake – the others did the same.

'Sorry to hear about the, yunno....' stumbled Pete, awkwardly.

'Cancer Mac. It's called cancer – and you're not as sorry as I am believe me.'

'Yeah well, like I said, sorry – we're all sorry, life can be a right shitter eh?'

'Sure can mate – now who's getting ole Leon a nice cool Red Stripe?'

Steve got the beers in and they grabbed a booth at the back of the pub, there were a few nudges and comments as they made their way through the crowds which were met by dismissive scowls from the boys – Steve spotted the scaffolder and his mates, he reserved a special scowl for him. His time would come but there were bigger turds than him to flush down the pan at the moment.

'So this Vernon Lewis, he's going to get a visit from us is that right?' asked JB, as blunt as ever.

'Pretty much, we've now got the route in to see him. We'll dangle the bait and he'll come running, then we'll see what develops.'

'And Samson?' asked George. 'Last time we spoke you said you was going to kill two birds with one stone, well not literally. But you were going to get Samson here at the same time – is that still on?'

Steve paused for a moment, he actually did mean literally but he thought best not to mention it – just yet.

'Yep that's still the plan. Kirsty can get an invite to Samson to come down here, any whiff of some dodgy deal and he'll come running, he's got his fingers in pies in London and up north but fuck all down here – he probably thinks it's a backwater, but I think any chance he can get to put two fingers up to some of his old adversaries he'll come running. He's always on the lookout for more sources of Merck, it's still as rare as rocking horse shit – that's what makes it so expensive. If he thinks there's a new source, he'll come running.'

'And what about Lewis?'

'Likewise, he's bound to have heard of the stuff. There's only a limit to what he can make from coke and smack, he'll be like a bitch on heat if he hears these goodies are for sale.'

'But how do we get hold of him? It's not like we can phone him and say fancy meeting up for a beer and by the way do you want to buy some really rare designer coke?' said Pete.

There was a moment's silence.

'Ain't that right you know him Leon?' asked George.

'Only from way back. Hardly a good friend, more like a bad enemy – somehow I don't think he'll answer to a request on friends reunited.'

'How about Facebook?' suggested Pete.

They all looked at each other and rare smiles broke out, 'perhaps just google him, you know "drug dealers in Bristol"?' said George jokingly.

'JB. What about you? You've come across him haven't you?'

'Yeah, once or twice – he's developed a lot of properties in the West Country, I've been involved with some of the building projects he's run, mostly just the snagging though. I'm a bit out of his league to be honest, but yeah we've had contact – and I've met him at some Masonic do's.'

'Didn't know you was in the Masons?' queried Pete.

'I ain't now, couldn't afford the subs. Got some decent deals out of it a few years back but it all dried up, could do with one or two now.'

'So he knows who you are?' asked Steve.

'Sort of, I guess – yeah.'

'Well there you go, give him a call, say you've got some business with him, drop in some reference to the BNP, that'll prick his ears up.'

Leon's eyes widened, 'What's this got to do with the BNP?'

'Nothing – well not directly. Forgot to say Leon, not only is he the main man on the streets selling the gear and peddling the misery, he's also helps fund the League of St George, a paramilitary, neo Nazi organisation.'

'Fucking hell, I thought being a Mason was bad enough,' said Leon, 'so he's flogging that shit down St Pauls then the money he makes from those poor saps he ploughs into an organisation that wants to get rid of 'em. They're funding their own nemesis – what a sly fucker.'

'Venom by name, Venom by nature,' said JB.

'Talking of which,' said Steve, 'this "Venom" alias – one of the other stunts he pulls is out and out fraud. Now this is really clever... he gets his foot soldiers, his street dealers to get in with let's say normal smart lads, they befriend them. These targets they're mostly middle class, got jobs, got a bit of money themselves. They get chatting to them in the bars, at gigs, even at the gym – they're real hotspots for drug dealing. So these foot soldiers, mostly flash, well-dressed upwardly mobile black kids – they impress the targets and

215

get matey with them, they flash the money, tell them they can get them any gear if they're interested. Well, kids these days they're all at it aren't they? Especially coke – they can't get enough of it. So course, they're reeled in, they buy a little bit at first, just a gram here, gram there, then they start buying for their mates, they're right in with their new mate ain't they? I mean most white kids love having black mates, gives 'em some sort of kudos doesn't it?'

Leon nodded in agreement. Steve continued...

'So yep, they start dealing themselves. Only they don't see it as dealing, just getting money off their own mates and buying a bit of Charlie for the weekend – don't do anyone any harm does it? Good laugh ain't it?'

'If you say so Steve,' said JB which just a hint of sarcasm.

'But then the ante gets upped. The new mate says "c'mon you can start earning good money doing this, like me". Drug dealing all depends on knowing a lot of people, it's like pyramid selling – the more people you know, the more you'll make from it.

'So the middle-class mug boy buys in doesn't he? Instead of forty quid a gram, he buys half an ounce for a few hundred. He then sells it to his mates and makes a few bob – he's working, he's got a decent job of his own, so this is all profit. The dealer then pushes him to buy more off him, so next thing he's handing over a grand for a bigger bundle – then the sting hits.'

'The sting?'

'Yep, it's a sting. The next big deal is going to be five grand. The dealer tells the mug he can have 250 grams for that, that's only twenty quid a gram – he can double his money easy. So the punter goes for it, he's got five thousand in savings, his parents gave him a bit of money when he passed his exams – he'd put it aside for a car but he would then have ten grand in a matter of weeks – easy money.

'So he stumps up the cash and hands it over to his new mate – his new mate is sound, he knows it'll be okay but of course he never delivers. Mug boy phones him up and a different voice answers doesn't it – it's not his usual cool mate is it? It's one very scary, very black, very Yardie voice, *'Man you get your ickle white ass back 'ome to your mum and dad and don't come boddering me again, geddit? Cos if you do I'll come round and shank you – know what I mean? An don' you go a runnin' to Babylon cos Venom know where you live. Hear me bwoy, Venom know where you live, I'll shank you.'*

Steve trembled as he delivered it – the Jamaican accent was near perfect. Even Leon was impressed.

'So when did this happen Steve?' asked Leon.

'What?'

'That was no third party scenario was it? When did this happen... to *Harry* and to you?'

Steve hesitated before replying.

'About five years ago. That cunt Lewis eventually rinsed over six grand from my boy.' He fumbled for his iPhone and played with a couple of buttons, he turned up the volume – the same chilling message came out, word for word, the same distinctive Jamaican patois made their hair stand on end.

'If that's Vernon Lewis, he's does a better Jamaican accent than Lenny Henry,' said Pete.

'That wasn't even remotely funny mate,' said Steve.

'No, sorry you're right.'

'I've spoken to Kirsty about it. Apparently it's a common scam –it's happening all around the country, mostly though it is Yardies behind it. They just live off their reputation, live off the fear. Of course the muggy punter isn't going to run to the law is he? Or even tell his parents. We knew something was up with Harry but we didn't know what. Then he comes clean, told us all about it... of course I wanted to tell the police, but tell them what? Tell them our drug dealing son had been ripped off by another drug dealer? They wouldn't give me the time of the day, or even worse they would have arrested Harry. It's a perfect crime, win-win for the Venoms, the Vernon Lewis's of the world – the fuckers, they can't lose.'

'The clever bastard – so that's why you're so keen to get him.'

'Well yeah. But until I read the file that Kirsty gave me I didn't know this Venom character was Vernon Lewis, I just thought he was another black...'

He looked at Leon and grimaced in apology. 'Sorry mate –thought he was just another drug dealer from St Pauls.'

Leon shrugged. 'Well it just proves that not all drug dealers are black doesn't it? Lewis is making the most of the black stereotype isn't it? I just can't believe he's managed to rope in so many black kids as his foot soldiers – and him being a racist to boot – he is one sly fucker.'

They all nodded in agreement.

'Course it's not just about the money though is it? Since then Harry has just gone downhill. Well you all know the rest, heroin, crack, mugging that old lady – prison. Last we heard he's living in that squat down Stokes Croft. Fuck knows what he's up to now.'

'Well he ain't working on the checkout down Tescos that's for sure,' said Pete with a grin.

Steve shook his head in a way that barely registered with the others. He closed his eyes for a couple of seconds, he was lost in his thoughts of the last few weeks – the unexpected contact and subsequent meeting with Kirsty, the revelations of his unknown and now dead daughter, the grandchildren he longed to meet, his split with Debbie – and the violence, the violence that was never far away from him. Mostly he kept a lid on it – he liked to think he could keep a lid on his drug taking as well, but he'd already lied to the others in that respect. The brutality that was always there with him – the dark side of Steve Allen was beginning to resurface.

'Will you shut the fuck up Pete? If all you want to do is fucking laugh and joke about all this then just fuck off now.'

JB looked at the two of them. 'Alright, alright leave it out. You're bang out of order Steve, we've been through all this before – we've told you we're all in on this ain't we boys?'

The others – including Leon, nodded.

'But I've had enough of this fannying around. Okay we're doing this cos we owe Kirsty a favour, a big favour, but we're also doing this cos we've had enough with the shit on the streets – right?'

'Right,' they answered as one.

'Right,' repeated Steve.

'Right,' Pete said with real emphasis.

'Right... now what?' asked JB.

'Beers?' suggested George.

'Go on then,' said Steve.

The evening degenerated into an inebriated tirade against all of the worlds ills – like so many before them, but they at least managed to agree on one thing – Rhianna was hotter than Beyonce and Shakira was fitter than both of them put together.

CHAPTER FIFTEEN

VERNON Lewis sat in his oak panelled office on the twelfth floor of Brunel Heights, behind him on the wall hung a print of his favourite painting by Hieronymus Bosch. When he had a quiet moment to himself he would study the print in detail, take in the *minituae*, there was always some hidden delight that he would find – some beautiful little serendipity that would make his day. His office was at odds with the rest of the building – there was no chrome and glass for Vernon Lewis and no executive toys, Vernon Lewis was old school through and through and he liked it that way.

From his office he could see the vast council estates and tower blocks of Hartcliffe and Withywood to the south of the city. Just before them were the neat rows of terraced houses of Southville and Bedminster where he was brought up – the bomb sites and craters where he'd played as a boy had long gone and swathes of the two districts had been gentrified, but he still laughed at the 'Lower Clifton' tag that some of the newcomers liked to call it. To the West beyond the

Durdham Downs he could not see his mock Georgian mansion, but it was there, hidden behind the trees and the ten feet high security fence – he knew where he preferred to live, he'd been poor once and he didn't like it, didn't like it one bit.

Over to the east lay the badlands of St Pauls, Easton and Eastville – *ghetto shitpits every one of them*, shitpits that contributed to his wealth, but then again the whole rancid, putrid city contributed to his wealth. Whoever the northern monkey was who said where there's muck there's brass never said a truer word, and Vernon Lewis had a lot of brass – it spoke volumes for the muck he dealt with, north, south, east and west he had it sewn up. Crack for the black trash of the ghetto, smack for the white trash of the sprawling council estates on the city's periphery, coke for the vacuous upwardly mobile middle class of Clifton. But it was even better than that, cocaine was all consuming and respected no geographic, no fiscal and no ethnic boundaries, no wonder it was known as the champagne of the drug world – well it was for Vernon Lewis.

No one came close to threatening his stranglehold of the drug scene in Bristol, this big village suited him nicely thank you, there may have been bigger rewards to be made in London but at what cost? Turkish, Russian, Albanians – not to mention the home grown East End gangsters and Jamaican Yardies, Vernon Lewis liked dealing with people he knew from way back – old Satan's Slaves and Devon Road Rats, that'll do for him, good ole boys, good ole white boys, he wanted to keep it that way.

His phone rang and brought his contemplation to an abrupt end.

'Mr Lewis, I've got a John Burston on the phone for you – says he knows you? Apparently he's got a business proposition for you?'

John Burston? Where do I know that name from? He pondered for a moment... *John Burston, big JB, ex Marine, served in the Falklands – a good lad, think I met him at the Masonic Lodge. Bit gobby, bit rough around the edges but yes, John Burston...*

'Yes Nikki, put him through.'

'John – how are you?'

JB hesitated – surprised that Vernon Lewis had even remembered him.

'Mr Lewis, hello, it's John Burston.' He immediately felt stupid – Lewis knew who he was.

'Yes John, what can I do for you – and please call me Vernon.'

This wasn't going to plan. JB thought he must have the wrong Vernon Lewis, he sounded the consummate professional, the perfect gentleman. He certainly didn't sound like Venom the gangster.

'Um, um, I, I and a few business associates have a proposition for you Mr Lewis – Vernon.' JB referred to the notes that Steve had prepared for him. 'But um, it's perhaps not something you would like to discuss on the phone, I, we were wondering if we could meet you somewhere, perhaps for a drink – it might be easier to explain then?'

'Hmmm, I'm intrigued John but I'm far too busy just to agree to some random meeting with some ... associates of yours who I don't know. Can you be a bit more explicit – you're a builder aren't you John? Can I presume it's some sort of development you've got planned?'

'Uh, not quite Vernon – I'm not sure how to put this, but it's to do with your other business interests – if you get my drift.'

There was a moment's silence, JB thought Lewis was going to hang up – he was just about to ask if he was still there.

'I'm sure I don't know what you're referring to John?'

Now it was JB's turn to be silent – time for him to consider his response.

'I think you do Vernon, like I said perhaps we can discuss this over a drink – or a coffee perhaps?' JB said it with deliberation, a firm intent in his voice.

Lewis was both irritated and intrigued, he hadn't had a knock on the door from Avon and Somerset's finest for a while, perhaps this was their latest ploy – for all that, he sensed that John Burston was telling the truth, it sounded like he did have a genuine business proposition and Lewis was always up for new business.

'Okay. Do you know my club? Well one of my clubs, the Garden on Park Row – it's discrete, well actually it's not, it's fun but we won't be bothered by anyone. Come along with your business associates, tomorrow night – nine o'clock?'

'Yes Vernon, I know it – I didn't realise you owned it though, but yes we'll see you there – many thanks.'

* * *

And that was another thing about living with Kirsty – from her apartment Steve could walk to work, no more rat runs, no more thirty pound fines for driving in bus lanes, no more fucking gridlock – but it was now of no relevance, he was going to hand in his notice. No matter what, today would be the day he would walk away from the job he'd hated for the last decade or so.

He swiped his card and entered through the security door. It was more of a prison than an office – walkways, endless corridors, pods and silos, meeting rooms, one-to-one rooms, rooms to lecture in, rooms to be lectured in – he didn't know then but he was about to be lectured.

Fiona Mason was already in the office – power dressed as usual. She was a corporate animal, a decent corporate animal, but a corporate animal all the same. She'd bought in, she worked for the Man. Although she towed the company line, Steve had a lot of time for Fiona – mostly, but even more for her husband Barry, ex QPR hooligan, C Mob hard man, now sports editor of a Fleet Street, or what was left of Fleet Street, tabloid.

Barry and Steve were two of a kind – kindred spirits. They were unconventional, intelligent and belligerent – university of life educated who didn't suffer fools gladly, both from white working-class stock and in their youth disconnected, disenchanted and disaffected. They were still exactly the same, nothing had changed – except their age.

'Morning Fiona, didn't realise you were visiting us today – some poor sap getting a bollocking?'

There was an uncomfortable silence. Fiona eventually spoke.

'Steve. Sorry but there's no easy way to put this – can you report to HR please?'

'Morning to you to Fiona. Yes I had a nice break, thanks for asking. Um...what do HR want with me?'

'A random drugs test.' Her bluntness floored him.

'You what?' He felt the colour drain from his face.

'You need to report to Claire Price – she's a qualified nurse. I believe all you've got to do is piss in a pot, is that too much to ask?'

'I don't care what her name is, she's not taking the piss out of me – no-one takes the piss out of me.'

'Very funny. But like I said Steve it's a random test. It's in your contract if you remember – all staff must be aware that they are liable to random drug tests.'

'But why? How come? How come now?'

'Steve, have you got something to hide? It's random – just your turn now that's all.'

'Bollocks it is.'

The uncomfortable silence returned. Fiona pulled out Steve's chair and motioned for him to sit down. She looked around the office. It was still early – not too many of the battery hens had turned up for their daily shift yet.

'Steve, listen – how do I put this? There have been tongues wagging, not accusations just comments – look, for fuck's sake, we've all done a bit of gear in our time, me included – back in my Uni days. But let's just say some of us are more discrete – if you've got nothing to hide then...'

'Then you're fucked,' Steve interrupted.

'I beg your pardon?'

'I said you're fucked, not you personally Fiona, this fucking company – you're fucked.'

'How... how do you work that out? Pardon my ignorance but I think you'll find you're the one who's fucked.' Fiona raised her voice – several chicken's heads appeared above their screens.

'You said this was a random drug test. Believe it or not I've been waiting for this day, expecting it even, but you just said tongues have been wagging, comments have been made – that doesn't sound very *random* to me. I think you'll find that you're the one who's fucked – tell you what, give HR a call and see what they've got to say about it, then I think I'll give my union a call.'

It was now Fiona's time to feel ill at ease, she pondered for a moment, rubbed her forehead with her fingers – this was the last thing she wanted on a Monday morning.

'Steve can you give me a few minutes, perhaps get yourself a coffee, I, I um need to make a phone call.'

'Sure, no problem – tell you what, I need to take a leak if you know what I mean.' He rubbed his nose, sniffed loudly and gave her a wink.

* * *

Even he didn't know how he pulled that one off. By mid day Steve was leaving the office with a cardboard box under his arm containing his worldly possessions – well his crappy office possessions at least – a couple of photos of him and Debbie, others of him and his sons and the dogs, a Rovers' mousemat, a dog-earred *FHM* that he'd forgotten about and a chipped mug that Harry had bought him one Father's day, emblazoned with *'World's best dad'*.

Pinnacle had right royally fucked up – he knew it, they knew it. *A random drugs test my arse.* He had been fingered and with Fiona admitting it there was only one outcome, him walking away like a dog with two cocks and a big fat cheque in his wallet, well not quite, it would take a while for that to get sorted but he couldn't believe his luck, he was going to hand in his notice and they had given him redundancy – not all of what he was entitled to, but it was a decent compromise, he wasn't going to argue.

He thought the reference to contacting his union was a master stroke. The pricks didn't even realise he hadn't been in a union for the last twenty years – *what a bunch of dozy fucking wankers*. He shoved the photos in his pocket, the rest he dumped in a skip and he headed for the Shakespeare – for once Steve Allen was feeling very comfortable.

He was so comfortable that within a few hours he'd drunk himself into a stupor helped by the last remnants of Rattigan's rocket fuel. He'd drunk alone, a Monday lunch time session that turned into a Monday evening session – he unsuccessfully chatted up the Polish barmaid, she giggled as he flirted but eventually her boss, and partner, threw him out. He staggered back to Kirsty's apartment, embarrassed and apprehensive – thankfully for him she was out. He let himself in and haphazardly punched random numbers on the jukebox... *Love's gone bad* the Motown masterpiece by Chris Clark echoed around the empty apartment. He stripped off his clothes – falling as he did so. He showered then staggered into bed – the last working day of his life had ended with a monstrous hangover.

Steve woke in the morning with his head hammering and his mouth as dry as a nun's gusset. He rolled over to see Kirsty lying next to him – she was snoring lightly, more of a murmur. He leant over and smelt her hair, pulled up the sheets and looked down at her still, naked body. He lightly touched the 'Cherry' tattoo on her shoulder – she didn't stir.

The smell of the coffee woke Kirsty from her slumber. She gratefully took the mug from Steve, sipped it then queried why he wasn't in work and why he was in such a state the night before.

'I've left work – let's just say it was by mutual consent.'

She nodded in approval – there was nothing else to say. She was happy for him, they spent the rest of the day making love and watching day time TV. She cooked him a light lunch – cheese omelette and a tomato salad, they opened a bottle of Crozes Hermitage, hair of the dog for Steve. If this was retirement then it felt good, very good, they even watched *Loose women* – Kirsty smirked and smiled at Steve, Steve remained silent and falsely laughed at their anti male jokes – inside he seethed with resentment.

* * *

JB was waiting for Steve in The Ship on Park Row, a pub just a hundred yards or so away from Lewis' club – a pint of Doom was waiting invitingly for Steve on the bar. They had agreed they would dress smart but casual, a description that covered all ills and generally meant for middle-aged white blokes, leather bomber jacket, Fred Perry shirt, jeans and loafers – they could have passed for brothers. JB had a smile as wide as the Bristol Channel.

'What you grinning at? You look like you're on summat?' asked Steve.

'Just got a bit of a result today that's all. A mate of mine in the council tipped me the wink about a nice little job coming up – demolition at first then all the groundwork. With a bit of luck I'll get the development as well – and you'll never guess where it is?'

'Go on.'

'Only the row of lock ups where we caught Cribby.'

'You're kidding?'

'Nope – turns out the fire did more damage than we thought, spread through the arches, they're council owned. They say it'll cost too much to do 'em up so they're going to pull 'em down – and that's where I come in, result!'

'Nice one John – every cloud eh? Didn't know you were in to demolition?'

'Me? I can turn my hand to anything, you know that.'

'Too fucking right. Hopefully it'll be the start of some decent business eh mate?'

'Fucking hope so,' JB paused, took a sip of Stella... 'anyway you got the gear?'

Steve patted his jacket breast pocket. 'Yep, Kirsty cut it down for me mind. Bit tricky walking the streets with half a kilo of Charlie. Should be enough to convince him we mean business though.'

'Good man, how we going to play it?'

'Just wing it JB, just wing it – like we always do.' He winked giving his old mate assurance he didn't really need. 'Why – worried?'

'Sweating like a paedo in a playground to be honest, but yeah, we'll be okay.'

'C'mon then – drink up.'

The apes in their suits gave the two of them the once over, JB and Steve sneered back.

'We got a meeting with Mr Lewis.'

The bouncers nodded. 'E's expecting you,' one managed to grunt. He turned and tapped on the door, a hatch opened and small talk was exchanged. The door opened and the first ape ushered them in and directed them to the bar.

'The drinks are on Mr Lewis, wait here and he'll be with you shortly.'

Steve had never been in a lap dancing club before. He looked around uneasily, taking care not to make eye contact – especially with the girls. There was no ale so he ordered a Guinness, at least he knew what he was getting with a Guinness, Euro fizz lager gave him flatulence. JB had no such misgivings – either on the lager front or the girls...

'Look at the fucking thre'penny bits on that!' Exclaimed JB as he tugged at his crotch.

Steve kept staring at his Guinness. 'Alright John keep it quiet, anybody would think you haven't seen a naked woman before.'

'I ain't – well not one like that. Jeez, look at her fucking mate!' He pulled at his crotch again.

Steve eyed JB with disdain and shook his head.

'For fuck's sake will you stop playing with yourself?'

JB grinned and nudged Steve. 'Can't help it,' he said in a near whisper, 'I got a Johnny on.'

'You what?'

'Got a Johnny on me knob haven't I? That way I can come in me pants and no-one will know.'

'I don't fucking believe you. I'm here with a couple of ounces of high grade cocaine in my pocket and you've got a fucking rubber on. We're meeting the biggest villain in Bristol, on his patch, risking our fucking necks and all you're thinking about is shooting your load.'

'Pretty much yeah. Clever eh?... for fuck's sake, she's only coming over. Steady boy, hold your horses.'

'Hello boys, care for a private dance?' She purred in a well rehearsed line.

Steve stayed rooted to the bar, his back turned against the dancer. There was something about her voice, something that sounded familiar – he turned more out of curiosity.

'No, I think we're... fuck's sake Laura!'

'Oh bollocks, what are you doing here?' asked Marketing Manager Laura Essex from Pinnacle, who until yesterday was a work colleague of Steve's. She made no attempt to cover herself up – much to the delight of JB.

Not surprisingly Steve's eyes were drawn to Laura's pert breasts. He had dreamt about seeing Laura naked for years, she'd always been one for the wank bank. Now she stood not two foot away from him, naked as the day she was born apart from a piece of dental floss and a three inch slip of satin that barely covered her neatly manicured beaver.

'Jesus, Laura – I, um, well – fucking hell, you, you look... For fuck's sake, what am I doing here? What about you?'

She grabbed a satin wrap from a chair behind her and hurriedly put it on. She pulled it tight to her body, causing JB to sigh in disappointment.

'I, I uh, I've worked here for a few years, started when I was at Uni, decided to carry on after I got the job at Pinnacle. Fuck it why not? To be honest I enjoy it, it keeps me fit and it's easy money... but how about you? Didn't think this was your sort of place?'

'Uh, no – got a business meeting with the owner, Vernon Lewis – nothing else, just business, not here for um, the um, girls if you know what I mean.'

Laura took that as a signal to relax, she giggled saucily.

'That's okay Steve you haven't got to make excuses. I suppose you're out spending all that redundo eh?' She winked. 'Tell you what, I'll do you and your friend here a special turn later if you like.'

She gave a little tug on her wrap, making sure it came undone – her left breast made a brief but welcome appearance, JB thought his rubber might be needed sooner than he thought. She leant into Steve and purred in his ear.

'Admit it Steve, you've always wanted to fuck me senseless haven't you?'

He whispered back... 'In your dreams Laura, in your dreams.' He returned her wink and they both laughed. She pulled open her wrap again and eased her fingers down into her g-string and pulled it aside, giving the two of them a long lingering view of her neatly trimmed bearded clam – JB very nearly came in his condom.

'Ah, you've met Lola – one of my favourite girls.'

The man who'd haunted Steve and his family for so long stood not a foot from him. Vernon Lewis was resplendent in a charcoal grey Paul Smith suit and black Ralph Lauren polo shirt. He looked fit, tanned and a good decade younger than his sixty two years. His eyes were steely ice blue, partly hidden by expensive designer glasses. He oozed confidence and smelt of money – and a whiff of Jean Paul Gautier aftershave.

His hair was long but neat, once obviously jet black, now distinctively salt and pepper – it was swept back and banded into a pony tail. Apart from the hair there was no indication of the rebel in him – no indication of his old biker days, however if you looked closely at his ear lobes you could possibly make out a couple of small pin prick holes where once crucifix earrings hung from. Likewise if you studied his large gnarled hands you could spot scar tissue and just make out that there had once been 'ACAB' tattooed across his knuckles – but like a lot of things about Vernon Lewis's past they had been erased for eternity. *'All Coppers Are Bastards'* – the thought was still there with him though, some things would never change. He held out one of those large hands to JB.

'John. Nice to meet you – again.' His huge hand was matched by JB's equally large appendage. JB remembered his Masonic handshake, Lewis responded with equal vigour.

'Yeah likewise... Vernon, this is my business partner – Steve Allen.'

'Pleased to meet you Steve. I see you've been enjoying the company of Lola.' He nodded towards Laura.

'Yes, yes, I was just saying she reminded me of someone.' Steve replied, suppressing the urge to punch him in the mouth.

'Hmmm, lucky you. Now then Lola, how about you leave us gentlemen to discuss business? No doubt we'll see more of you later.' He motioned to her to move, slapping her perfect derriere as she left.

Laura let out a small girlish giggle, winked at Steve and slinked away. Steve could barely believe this was the same hard-nosed, sharp as a razor, ball-busting Laura from Pinnacle – he knew she would be cursing Lewis under her breath.

'Gentleman, shall we go into my office?'

They followed Lewis past the bar and the leering punters. Semi naked girls gyrated all around them, Steve tried his hardest not to make eye contact while JB tried even harder not to prematurely shoot his load. They entered Lewis's office through a door marked 'Private'. The door shut behind them muffling the sounds of some trashy R&B that accompanied the girls' movements.

There was a large oak desk, several comfortable chairs, a mini bar, filing cabinets and surprisingly not much else. The walls were adorned with framed photos showing Lewis in the company of dignatories and celebrities from around the world – Mick Jagger, Eric Clapton, John Major – pride of place on one wall was a signed photo from Margaret Thatcher. Next to it was an old, large black and white photo of Enoch Powell – *no surprise there*, thought Steve.

On the far wall there were old photos, some in black and white and some in that strange dull red that all colour photos of several decades ago seemed to turn to. They featured Lewis in his younger days, showing the big power-ful biker dressed in leather and denim and usually posing in

232

front of, or astride Nortons, Triumphs or Harleys. There was one of him and Sonny Barger shaking hands – Lewis towered over the diminutive founder of the Hells Angels movement. It had obviously been taken somewhere on the West Coast of the USA and by the look of the two of them, bedecked in their full biker regalia and easy rider shades, sometime in the seventies.

'Is that a 1970 Super Glide?' asked Steve – anxious to impress Lewis.

'Sure is Steve – I wouldn't put you down as a Harley enthusiast?' replied Lewis.

'Just been looking that's all – my wife says I'm having a mid-life...' he tailed off, not wishing to labour the point.

Lewis made a snorting noise – clearly not impressed by all the middle-aged wannabe bikers that had appeared over the last decade or so.

'Yeah well I was an original one-percenter,' he replied curtly.

Still are, thought Steve, but considered it wise not to mention it.

Next to the picture of Lewis and Barger was the same photo from the *Evening Post* that Leon Campbell had in his den, the same forced smiles, the same false handshakes – of the truce that never lasted.

All the photos however were overshadowed by a huge print that covered one wall, Steve had seen it before, it unnerved him. As a youngster he had seen it in an encyclopaedia and it had given him recurring nightmares. He remembered reading in Kirsty's files about his love of Northern European Renaissance artists. Lewis caught Steve looking at it.

'You're familiar with the works of Hieronymus Bosch?'

'Not really, I've seen it before – it's quite, I don't know, quite...'

'Beautiful?' suggested Lewis.

233

'I was thinking more of interesting. But yes I suppose beautiful in a way.'

'I thought he played for West Ham a couple of years back?' interrupted JB.

The other two turned and looked at him in bewilderment.

'That Erroneous Bosch – centre half for the 'ammers wasn't he?'

Steve wasn't sure if JB was being serious or not. Perhaps he was trying to lighten the mood – either way it didn't go down too well with Lewis.

'Football fan eh John? Might have guessed – the opiate of the masses.'

Steve was certain it was religion that Karl Marx had referred to and not football, but he could see Lewis's point. He thought it best not to challenge him.

'We um, we follow the Rovers a bit. You Vernon – football not your thing?'

'Used to go down Ashton Gate when I was a kid. Brought up in Bemmy so no option really. But no, not now. Footballers are gutless, pampered, overpaid and overrated – and there are too many *fucking foreigners*. Art is my passion, especially Northern European Renaissance paintings.'

It was the first time Steve had heard Lewis swear. He emphasised, almost spat the word out, said it with real – *venom*.

Steve remembered the name of the painting... 'The garden of earthly delights,' he said. 'The garden' he repeated – with the sudden realisation of the name of the club.

'Indeed, indeed – and there was me thinking you two were a couple of Philistines.' Lewis falsely laughed out loud.

Lewis wandered over to the painting and studied it as if he'd never seen it before in his life.

'It's near perfection isn't it? The only thing that spoils it is the *fucking negroes*.' He tapped the central panel.

'Still we all know where they're going don't we – straight to hell, isn't that right gentlemen?'

Steve and JB exchanged glances – they both nodded in false agreement.

'Yeah, yeah – too right.' Replied JB uneasily.

'Anyway, enough of this culture – let's get down to business, I understand you have some proposition for me? So what can I do for you?'

Steve took the initiative, he didn't want JB putting his foot in it again.

'That's right, um, we have something that we think you might be interested in, it's...'

'Let me stop you right there.'

Lewis removed a mobile phone from his inside pocket and turned his back on them as he spoke – it sounded like he was giving an instruction to someone. The door to the office opened as soon as he put his phone away, the ape they saw earlier entered – the trashy music filled the room once again.

'Gentleman,' said Lewis, 'please don't take this personally but I have to take ... precautions as it were.' He nodded to his minder.

'Sorry lads, but if you could just raise your arms in the air like, I need to frisk you – like Mr Lewis says, don't take it personally.'

The two complied, they raised their arms.

'Spread your legs as well please gents.'

For a big man he was surprisingly gentle. He ran his hands up and down their legs then patted down their arms, next he felt their chests and arms – he'd obviously done this before.

'They're clean boss.'

'Thank you Darren. That will be all.'

Darren the ape left the room. Another blast of trash filled the room as he opened the door.

'Sorry gents but I can't be too careful. I know you're not the filth but you could be someone trying to muscle in on my patch. You could have been wired or tooled up – forgive me for the intrusion.'

The two of them straightened their clothing.

'That's okay Vernon, we understand,' answered Steve in a mock apology of his own, mindful to stay on the right side of Lewis – for now.

'So where were we, you mentioned you have something that might be of interest to me?'

'Maybe – let's talk in analogies Vernon. Let's say you're in the motor trade – over the years you've made good money from selling second hand motors, you get a lorry load of them delivered – Astras, Fiestas, pretty run of the mill stuff. You patch them up and add a few extras – dress them up a bit then sell them to the first eager punter who comes along. You make a nice wedge out of them, but you could be making more – a lot more.

'You want to get away from Mondeo man though. You'd rather be selling Ferraris if truth be told, new Ferraris – you can still add your little extras, that way you get more bang for your buck, only now you haven't got to deal with Mondeo man – you get to deal with Champagne Charlie and his missus.'

Steve reached inside his jacket pocket and took out a small package. He placed it on the desk in front of them, Lewis carefully studied it – mulling over his response.

'Hmmm, I appreciate the analogy Steve. I presume we're talking about cocaine here ... so what makes this,' he tapped the bag lightly, 'what makes this a top of the range Italian supercar as opposed to a bottom of the range rust bucket from South America?'

'Because this isn't low grade shit Vernon – and it's not even from South America.'

Lewis raised his eyebrows and squinted through his designer glasses. 'What is it?' He said in a curious whisper.

'It's from Germany – it's called Merck. Do you know of it?'

Lewis leant back in his chair and nodded.

'Merck – the holy grail of cocaine, yes of course I know of it. Never come across it before, I was beginning to think it was a bit of an urban myth to be honest. How the fuck did you two come across it?'

Steve resented the way he said *'you two'* as if they weren't worthy to be associated with him.

'We obviously can't reveal our sources at this time but let's just say we have a reliable supplier in London who is keen to expand his distribution network. He doesn't want to muscle in or tread on your toes but he is willing to do business with you. Let's just say he's an acquaintance of ours from way back, he asked us if we might be interested in helping him – so here we are.'

Lewis stroked his chin, perplexed about how they had known to make contact with him, but he was too preoccupied with the small but significant package in front of him to let it concern him.

'Is it as good as they say it is?'

'Better. This makes the crap out there look like rocket salad not rocket fuel. And as an added bonus...' Steve hesitated, deliberately raising the tension and interest of Lewis, 'it's undetectable in the human body, no trace shows up in any test – so you can imagine the consequences of that.'

Vernon Lewis's eyebrows knotted.

'Being undetectable opens up a whole new market Vernon. You won't need to sell this on the sink estates to all the two bit scumbags, this is for the Dom Perignon set of Clifton and Bath – they'll be able to take it without fear of being caught, or of losing their jobs or getting nicked – this takes British drug culture to a whole new level.'

Lewis liked what he was hearing – Steve had lit the candle and like a moth Lewis was heading straight for it.

'How do I know this is what you say it is? It could be the same chopped up crap I'm flogging already?'

'Try it, you'll know straight away.'

'Oh I will but how about it being undetectable – how do I know that?'

Steve's mind raced, he was not prepared for the question and worse he didn't have an answer. There was an uneasy silence in the room – apart from the dull boom, boom from beyond the door.

'I'll take it,' said JB unexpectedly.

Steve threw him a 'what the fuck you playing at?' glance.

'I'll take it,' he repeated. 'I don't do drugs – I've never taken any gear in my life, I'll do a line right now in front of you. You arrange a test and if it comes back clean you'll know that we're not bullshitting.'

Steve had known JB for the best of his life and in that time the big fella had come up with some hare-brained schemes, but even he had to admit it was a brilliant proposition – but he couldn't believe what his best mate was offering to do.

'Hmmm, gallant offer John but actually I've got a simpler alternative. Let's just say I was testing you.'

Lewis took out his mobile again and made a quick phone call – within a minute the large frame of Darren re-entered the room.

'Darren, I need you to do something for me. You trust me right?'

'Er ... yes boss.'

'You know my policy on drugs don't you – zero tolerance, correct?'

Darren hesitated. 'Um yes boss, you said if we ever take any drugs we'll lose our jobs – if not worse. Honest boss I ain't taken so much as a paracetamol.'

Steve and JB could only guess what he meant by '*if not worse*'.

'It's okay Darren I trust you... You see gentleman all my staff are very loyal to me, I have a very strict drugs policy and all of my staff regularly take drugs tests, if any show up positive, well – let's just say they won't work for me ever again. Darren I'm asking you to break those rules, I'm asking you to take a small sample of this powder for me please, I will take it with you so you can trust me that it is not dangerous. You will then give me a urine sample and no more will be said, do you understand?'

'I guess so boss – whatever you say.'

Lewis opened a drawer of the desk and took out a small mirror and a razor blade-shaped item of jewellery. He opened the polybag and emptied a small pile onto the mirror – he then chopped and spread it into two equal length lines and a third smaller length. Reaching inside his suit jacket he opened his wallet and took out a clean unused £50 note, he then deftly rolled it into a tube which he offered to Steve.

'Steven, after you – I presume you partake?'

'I uh, yes, I suppose. Just thought you might want to go first?'

'What and risk being poisoned? I don't think so.'

Lewis laughed but Steve didn't think he was joking. Steve nervously took the note and tapped it on the desk in front of him – leaning over he inserted it into his left nostril and sniffed his first line of Merck cocaine.

Steve sat back down and handed the note back to Lewis who promptly unravelled it and put it back in his wallet. Steve wondered what he was playing at – he was about to object when first the Merck hit him hard and secondly Lewis spoke – spotting the concern in Steve's eyes.

'Relax. I just always like to use a clean note – no offence meant.'

'None taken, none taken at all Vernon ... shit, shit, I don't think you'll um... fucking hell, shit, hey, hey – you'll fucking love it, top stuff, top stuff.' He reached out for his Guinness and took a long hard gulp.

Lewis laughed out loud again. Taking a fresh note out, he snorted the second line of Merck then dabbed the remnants on his gums with his finger. He blinked repetitively and handed the note to Darren. Darren took the note gingerly – his large hand visibly shook.

'Are you sure about this Mr Lewis – only I'm not too happy.'

'Darren, please do as you are told.' Lewis said with a firmness that was palpable.

Darren moved uncomfortably around the desk and nervously inserted the rolled up note into his nostril, he bent down and sniffed the remaining small line of powder on the mirror. He returned the note to Lewis and walked back to the other side of the desk – his hands were already sweating as the blood rushed around his body. His face flushed red, he loosened his tie, slumped down into a chair in the corner and put his head in his hands.

By now Steve was conscious of the effect the drug was having on his body. He had never experienced a feeling like this before – his heart started pounding, euphoria swept through him, the lights in the office became brighter, the music from the club became louder, he wanted to go out and start dancing – he started tapping his left foot. Nodding his head he drummed out a tune on the desk with both hands

'I like this tune John, like it, like it, brilliant eh? Eh?'

'I'll, um... I'll leave you guys to it okay? I'll be in the bar,' said JB. He could stand the situation no more – he made for the door.

'JB, JB, where you going mate? We got business to discuss, John come back mate!'

Lewis, Steve and Darren all looked at each other – then burst out laughing simultaneously.

'Fucking hell, where the fuck have you been all my life?' shouted Darren. He started tapping the desk in rhythm with Steve's own drum machine racing in his head. Lewis rolled his head back and laughed uproariously.

'Mr Allen. I think we can do business.'

* * *

Steve woke to the sound of Ben Gunstone... *'The flowers are dead and gone behind the Eastville goals. The traffic's a little quieter on the Stapleton Road...'* He looked at the display, it was Debbie.

'Hello Debs, what's up?'

'Steve, I need you to come home... please. It's Harry.'

Kirsty rolled over to face him – he made an apologetic face and shrugged. He got up, power showered and dressed and within thirty minutes he was in his car heading back to his old house. Debbie hadn't said any more, she didn't need to, as soon as she'd mentioned Harry he knew he had to be there, be there for his boy – and his wife.

On the way he reflected on the events of the evening before. It had gone better than he'd expected, JB was pissed off but that was understandable, his spirits quickly lifted though as soon as he spotted Laura making out with a pole. Steve and Lewis had joined him once the Merck had worn off. Lewis was the consummate host, champagne was on the house and Laura put on a private show for the three of them – JB's surreptitious Johnny served its purpose.

The plan was coming together. They had reeled in Lewis and all that was left was for Kirsty to deliver Samson – she'd told Steve she was working on it, having made contact with one of her old snouts in the capital. Steve thought it all a bit of a long shot but she'd assured him her informant was kosher – he was close to Earl Samson, even trusted by him, it was in his interest to get shot of Samson. Kirsty had supplied the contact with the same sample of Merck that they had used for Lewis, she knew Samson wouldn't leave it at that – he would either be interested in meeting up with a new supplier or eager to dispense with the threat, curiosity would get the better of him either way.

Steve asked no more, he would leave the delivery of Samson to Kirsty – but Toby Ashurst was another matter. The downfall of Toby Ashurst was in Steve's capable hands, if it all went to plan within a short time he would be exacting revenge on the killers of their daughter.

Parking his car on the driveway he felt apprehensive, even nervous about entering the family home. Neither of his sons knew that their parents had split up. For the time being he would go along with the partial lie that he'd left their mother because of her infidelities. He wouldn't go into detail, he didn't need to, for now he would make out he was living with one of his mates – perhaps JB, certainly no mention of Kirsty – the mother of their deceased half sister.

Before he had a chance of putting the key in the lock Debbie opened the door. Judging by her rheumy eyes she'd been crying, he both feared and expected the worse, he knew it would only be a matter of time before he had to identify his youngest son's body on the morgue slab – he prayed to God it wasn't to be now.

'What's up? Where is he?'

'He's in bed asleep, Steve he's been arrested again.'

'Fuck's sake, what for now?'

'He was involved in those riots down Stokes Croft – protesting against Tescos, he was one of the squatters in that Telepathic Heights.'

'I might have guessed, and?'

'And what – isn't that bad enough?'

'Yeah, yeah of course, sorry – I uh, I don't know. Guess I feared the worse. I suppose I'm thankful for small mercies... has he been charged?'

'Yes, yes – think it's violent misconduct or something, he chucked masonry at the police – they got him on video. They've bailed him, course he didn't have an address to give them, so he gave them ours. That's what he's doing back here.'

It could have been worse, a lot worse. He let out a small sigh and knew he would have to ask Kirsty to pull those strings again.

'Did, um... did you tell him about us?'

'No, I guess I thought...Yunno, I guess I thought we might be able to patch things up – perhaps with Harry back it would be different?'

'What the fuck do you mean *different*? How fucking different does this make it? I caught you giving a blow job to some fucking dipshit and you think I'm going to come back because our drug-addled waste of space of a son gets nicked again! For fuck's sake, I don't fucking believe you, and...' He trailed off and bit his lip as he toyed with telling Debbie about Kirsty.

'And what?'

'Nothing – fucking nothing.' He pushed past Debbie and walked out into the garden – 'his manor' as he liked to call it. The grass needed cutting and the hedges needing pruning, he thought about telling Debbie to get some gardener in but she would only end up get shagged senseless. *What a fucking mess* – and he didn't mean the garden. He tried to calm down.

'I'll go up and see him – I'll have a word.'

'I'll make a cup of tea. You can take it up, he would like that.'

He thought back to when his boys were young and the light of his life – two boys to mould, build and shape into better men than he would ever be. He would spend time with them, read to them, play football with them and take them to watch the famous quarters. Whatever they wanted they would get, nothing would be too good for his boys, he would get it right for his boys. He had fuck all growing up in Southmead – the only contact he got from his dad was when the old man gave him a whack with a boiler stick. His dad had been too busy working to spend any time with the young Steven. No he would be the perfect dad, he would get it all so right...

Gently opening the door to Harry's bedroom he looked in. Harry was dead to the world, where once an angelic face of a boy child lay on the pillow smiling, a fully grown, bruised, spikey-haired, pierced-up adult head now lay. He put the mug of tea down on the bedside cabinet – Harry stirred and murmured, shifted position and caught his father's eye.

'Um, alright dad,' Harry coughed. 'How's things?' he coughed again, then rubbed his eyes.

'Alright son – I'm okay, okay. How about you – been in the wars again?'

Harry exhaled loudly. 'You know how it is dad, fucking law – they got it in for me.'

'Heard you were chucking bricks at them? Perhaps that's the reason they have it in for you?'

The boy picked up his mug of tea and took a sip, knowing full well where this conversation was going, same as every other one he'd had with his father in the last ten years. He shook his head and thought better of getting into an argument at this time in the morning.

'Whatever,' he eventually grunted.

Steve thought the same – he didn't want to pursue it. He held out an olive branch.

244

'Look son, you're welcome to stay here as long as you want, tidy yourself up a bit, get a bit of home cooking inside you eh?'

'Yeah okay, like I said whatever. Uh dad?'

'Yes son, what is it?'

'Um, don't suppose you could lend me fifty quid could you?'

Whatever his boys wanted, his boys got. Steve knew what it was for so it was pointless refusing him and getting into another argument. If he didn't give it to him then Debbie would, or he would nick out of her purse as he'd done many times in the past. He took out his wallet, counted out the notes and gave them to his son like he'd done so many times before. He didn't say a word – he just handed it over.

Harry took the notes and spotted how one of them was curled – realising it had been rolled up recently he looked at his father and winked.

'Thanks dad, I owe you.'

Too right you do – more than you'll ever realise.

* * *

He drove back towards the city centre down the Stapleton Road, past the Dur Dur delicatessen, past the Mogadishu Express take out and past the Horn of Africa Halal butchers. Each one full of war weary Ethiopians, displaced Somalians and downtrodden Eritreans – a north east Africa diaspora finding a home on the streets of the city that made its wealth from the slave trade. For a moment, just a brief moment he thought of Vernon Lewis and his garden of earthly delights. Steve needed to go to confessional – he phoned Leon.

'Leon, how's things – how you feeling?'

'Yeah alright mate. Well, not brilliant but considering the circumstances alright. How's tings with you?'

'Not great,' he said, quickly feeling guilty – his problems paled into insignificance compared to Leon's, 'okay I suppose, but I... we've got Harry back home.'

'Well that's good innit mate – thought that's what you wanted?'

'Yeah, but he hasn't come home of his own accord. He was one of them living in that Telepathic Heights, he got nicked for those Tesco riots – chucking rocks at the coppers. Fuck knows what's going to happen to him.'

'Sorry to hear that Steve, but...'

'But what?'

'Well I'm not trying to trivialise it man but I got nicked thirty years ago doing the same ting, not a half a mile away from Stokes Croft and let's just say it didn't do me any harm.'

'Leon – you can't compare you and Harry and you can't compare the St Pauls riots with the Tesco riots – you lot,' he hesitated, he was always careful with his choice of words when he spoke to Leon, 'sorry you guys had a genuine grievance, you know suss laws and all that. These kids are just a bunch of middle-class wasters spoiling for a fight, anti-capitalists and anarchists my arse. Soon as they get in trouble they go running off to mummy and daddy.' He realised he was digging himself a hole.

'Like Harry then.'

'I suppose I asked for that, but I'm not middle class.'

'Okay Steve, keep saying that long enough and eventually you'll believe it... like you keeping telling everyone you're not racist.'

Steve was in shock, his first reaction was to shout down the phone, his second reaction was to deny it – but he wouldn't play Leon's games.

'Just joking mate, just joking – Steve, stop seeking reassurance from me. You're a sound bloke, if you weren't I wouldn't give you the time of day and I certainly wouldn't be getting involved in your death wish adventure that's for sure, okay?'

'Okay, okay.'

'And I tell you something else, the St Pauls riots...'

'Yeah. What about them?'

'Well, the reason they started was because the law raided the Black and White cafe and we all know what that was like don't we? The biggest drug den in the South West, we knew that, you knew that and the law knew it. So was it legit for them to raid it? Yes course it was, and look how we reacted. And of course that riot was the catalyst for all the other riots in the black ghettos that hit the cities in the early eighties. Brixton, Toxteth, Broadwater Farm – all kicked off following St Pauls and now... Steve, you still there?'

'Yes mate still here.'

'Well they now call the Brixton riots an uprising – the local council forked out for celebrations of it recently. For sure tings have got better for us since then. It was a bad time not just for us but the whole of the country, that Thatcher woman had a lot to answer for.'

'You know I agree with you there Leon but what's this got to do with Harry and the Tesco riots – surely you can't compare the two?'

'Maybe, maybe not, but sometimes the means justify the ends. Sometime you just feel you have to fight back, take the law into your own hands – d'you know what I'm saying bro?'

Steve nodded on the end of the phone. 'Yes bro, I know what you're saying.'

CHAPTER SIXTEEN

T HROUGH her connections with the London underworld, Kirsty managed to get an anonymous
message to Earl Samson – there was someone in the
West Country who wanted to meet him, said he knew of
Earl and thought they could be mutually beneficial to each
other. A small package also found its way to him, on the
front of the package was a neat handwritten message in
capital letters... *'YOU MIGHT WANT TO TRY THIS'.*

Earl knew what was in the package, he knew one day
someone would contact him regarding Merck. He was intrigued however – he mulled it over. Why not? He'd only
visited Bristol sporadically over the last thirty odd years –
the last time was to attend his mother's funeral. He had
some good memories of the place – The Bamboo Club, The
Dugout, The Guildhall – he remembered them all with
affection. Good sounds, good gear back in the seventies, not
to mention the football at Ashton Gate – promotion in 1976,
the First Division for a year or so. *Yeah why not?* He could

look up some old mates, avoid old enemies and perhaps do some business as well.

'Okay, you tell them I'm prepared to meet this Vernon Lewis – I can make it next week. You tell them Earl Samson is heading back to Bristol.'

He'd checked out Lewis – he had impeccable credentials. To the outside world he was monied and a legitimate businessman, but for those in the know his money came from entirely different sources. Earl liked the look of Lewis – yes they could definitely do business together, but one thing baffled and intrigued him as he toyed with the package – *where the fuck did he get this consignment of Merck from?*

* * *

The Big Five had the meet arranged and Lewis and Samson in their sights. Lewis suggested a warehouse he'd recently purchased in St Philips which overlooked the Feeder Canal, he was eventually going to convert it into apartments – it would be the latest in a long line of 'up and coming areas' of Bristol that Lewis had helped to develop with the help of the local council. He was sure he could put some of the business John Burston's way, *'could be the start of some big things John,'* he'd promised.

Steve brought Kirsty up to speed with the latest developments. He'd told her about the meeting that had been arranged and of how he and the others, including Leon, also planned to be there. Although what the 'final solution' was going to be he wasn't quite sure just yet, he was still working on that 'minor detail'.

'But what about Toby Ashurst – you seem to have forgotten him?' queried Kirsty as the two of them lay in bed, she was lying across Steve, casually running her fingers through his chest hair.

'Far from it. But like I said there is more than one way to skin a cat – he's cut from a different cloth than Lewis and Samson. He needs a good hiding in a different sense.'

'And is that what you're going to do – just give them all a good hiding?'

'I dunno, just got to play it by ear.'

'Steve you can't just play these people "by ear" – they've got where they are through intimidation and brutality. This isn't going to be resolved by a bit of a kicking like you used to dish out on the terraces.'

'I know, I know – if you recall it was me who said this to you a while back. So what is it – you getting cold feet now?'

'Maybe. I'm just worried about you and your mates that's all. Perhaps all this is one big, bad mistake – perhaps we should pull the plug on it. I, I don't think I thought this through. Steve... you know I love you don't you? Always have done, always will.'

Steve was troubled by Kirsty's *volte-face*. 'Of course I do. What's this all about?'

'Nothing, nothing.' She put her arms around him and pressed her face into his shoulder. 'I lost you before Steve, I don't want to lose you again, that's all.'

He kissed the top of her head. 'You won't. Trust me you won't.' He was keen to lighten the mood...

'Tell you what, how about we have a big night out with the boys – and the girls, forget all this for a bit. There's a soul and ska night at Tricky Dickies in Denmark Street, the Sole Room are putting a show on again. They're brilliant, they play some great music – and it's all on vinyl. Friday night eh? We can put on our old gear and have a bit of a sesh. Fancy it?'

Kirsty looked up at him, moved up the bed and kissed him on the lips.

'Sounds like a plan to me Mr Allen, but I'm not sure about the old gear – I don't think my uniform would go down too well with the clientele… talking of which…' She rolled over and off of him, opened the bedside cabinet drawer and took out the handcuffs, 'let's play cops and robbers' she cooed.

* * *

What was left of The Big Five and their partners – and the new recruit Leon Campbell and his wife Margaret, met in The Elephant in St Nicholas Street, yet another one of their old haunts from back in the day, but unlike The Shakespeare the pub had changed beyond recognition. The Elephant had had more changes than Katie Price had had boob jobs. At one time it was one of Bristol's few gay pubs, then when the lads frequented it in the early seventies it was notorious and even celebrated for being a both red of City and blue of Rovers pub.

The jukebox had long gone – as had the rough and ready clientele. The fights that blighted it on a Friday and Saturday night were thankfully no more, neither were the light splits and rum and blacks, it was now all Pinot Grigio and designer beers – at designer prices.

'Fucking 'ell Allen, do you know how much that round cost me?' bemoaned George studying the handful of coins in his palm. 'Fuck's sake – nice pub, shame about the prices.'

The women were already seated, there was a wary acceptance of Kirsty – only George's wife Julie and Pete's partner Sue knew Kirsty from way back. None of the women particularly liked Debbie, she always thought she was better than the rest of them and always revelled in telling them of their wonderful holidays and how well off they were. They of course all knew about Harry's troubles, but it was the elephant in the room that no-one dared discuss. In secret they were all pleased that Steve had left Debbie – *fucking stuck up cow.* Then of course there was Margaret Campbell, *poor, poor Margaret Campbell...*

'Maggs, don't know what to say. How is he, Leon. How is he – in himself?' asked Sue McNulty.

Margaret had met the girls before, they weren't a bad bunch – bitchy and judgmental but then that was women for you when they got together she thought. She accepted their sympathies knowing Sue had enough problems of her own – the question still baffled her though, *'in himself'?*

'Good days, bad days Sue – he's accepted it. He keeps saying he's had a good life, but, well he's only in his sixties. No age is it? ... No age.'

'No, they say the good die young,' said Julie – it was an inane platitude, but it had to be said.

Maggs started sobbing. 'I'm going to miss him so much...' she trailed off and reached for a tissue.

Kirsty caringly put her arm around her, 'Shhhhh, shhhh – it's okay, okay – let it out.'

They all looked up at the boys stood at the bar – carefully nursing their pints they bemoaned the price of beer and Rovers' relegation. Leon put his pint on the table and tenderly touched his wife on her shoulder.

'Come on, come on – I said none of that, not tonight anyway. We're going to enjoy ourselves, eh? Have a good time yeah? That's what we said Maggs, didn't we?'

She put her hand on his, then held and kissed it. 'Yes honey,' she whispered.

'Anyway, tell the others what we've just done – go on, tell them.'

They all looked at Maggs in anticipation of the announcement.

'It's nothing, nothing – we just booked a holiday that's all. A Caribbean cruise, we go next Saturday – it'll be nice.'

'Nice? Wow, that'll be fantastic,' said Sue, 'sort of a holiday of a lifetime...' she trailed off, aware of what she was saying, 'sorry, sorry I didn't think,' she went silent and stared into the bottom of her glass.

'Yeah well, apart from Jamaica we've seen nothing of the little islands, thought it was about time we did it – can't wait,' said Leon, beaming from ear to ear.

'Saturday?' queried Steve. It was news to him, but he decided not to pursue it.

'Sounds sweet – right who's for another beer?' asked JB, his Stella long gone. He put his hand on Leon's shoulder, the awkwardness was over – they quickly went back to their conversations.

They had another round in The Elephant – courtesy of Steve, his redundancy cheque now being common knowledge. Kirsty faced awkward questions from the girls, wanting to know what she was doing back in Bristol? What had she'd been doing for the last thirty odd years? How many kids did she have? Had she had botox? She took it in her stride and deflected the flak – eventually she told them about Cherry, bringing on yet another awkward silence.

On leaving the pub they strode across the City Centre and headed towards Tricky Dickies – the boys in front, the girls behind. Sue McNulty nodded towards the boys who were walking in perfect alignment.

'Look at 'em – aven't changed a bit have they? Still strutting around like they own the town – Chrissakes they think it's 1971 not 2011. And as for your Steve, Kirsty – he's always fancied himself hasn't he?'

Kirsty liked the way she'd said *'your Steve'* – it sounded good, sounded right.

Sharon feeling the young outsider chirped in. 'How about my Johnny boy, always was the cock of the roost wasn't he? Got to say though, they do look pretty good don't they? And there's something about that old skinhead gear, making me proper horny seeing all that testosterone running through their hard bodies.'

'Shaz. What you like?' chortled Sue.

'What I like? What I like? Big JB inside me that's what I like!'

They arrived at Tricky Dickies with the women still giggling and the blokes still posing. The small bar was already heaving with other like-minded sixties and seventies revivalists as they entered – a cheer went up, the boys were well known and respected. Half a dozen or so vintage Lambrettas and Vespas belonging to the local Scooter Club were parked up outside, earning admiring looks from passing Friday night revellers.

Steve wore his black and gold-trimmed Fred Perry, his new red Harrington jacket and a pair of black Bass Weejuns. He'd also just managed to squeeze into his Levi 501s, but he drew the line at the braces or boots – there was nostalgia and there was full blown living in the past. He thought of his look as vintage classic rather than 'Spirit of 69' hard man. The look suited him well he thought, it was both effortless and timeless, more Steve McQueen than Joe Hawkins, more New England Ivy League than East London boot boy. Some of the rest of the clientele tried too hard, too many Doc Martens, too many shortened jeans, too many tattoos – *still their heart and their heads were in the right place.*

Knowing nods greeted them, hands pumped theirs – there were back slaps all round. They wallowed in the adoration while the girls looked on and shook their heads – secretly proud of their boys and their reputation. Kirsty smiled and winked at Steve, he looked so fine and it reminded her of when she first saw him all those years ago – he was as fit and as good looking now as he was then, she really loved him. She was beginning to hate herself for what she was putting him through.

'Well, what do you think?' shouted Steve above *How long?* by Pat Kelly.

She nodded. 'It's great, really great, I'm loving it – could do with a bit of Motown though!'

'Oh they'll be plenty of that don't you worry,' he kissed her cheek – 'it's like Monday nights at the Locarno all over again. All we need is our picture taken in the photo booth and a knee trembler in the car park!'

Kirsty elbowed him in the ribs. 'Well I can't see a photo booth and I'm way past knee tremblers thank you Mr Allen!'

JB sauntered over and gave Steve a bear hug, 'cracking mate, fucking cracking – they're going to play our song next!'

On cue Prince Buster's ribald lyrics rang out...

'Come over, get me brush up.

Going to rub a pussy here tonight.

Heavy rain's falling,

I can feel my cock getting stiff in her hand.'

Tricky Dickies was only a stone's throw from the old Locarno but it could have been a whole world away, for all that it served a purpose and the assembled mods, skinheads and suedeheads both young and old were grateful for it. To them it was a cultural oasis in a desert of musical dross – no migraine inducing strobes, no chrome, no leather, just a bar with beer. It had no musical heritage and no class, in a year or two it would probably be gone, the same way as a multitude of other drinking holes in the centre of the city but for now it did for the boys and they made the most of it. Prince Buster faded and Max Romeo carried on with more incomprehensible lyrics with his *Wet Dream*.

Melodic Motown pleased the girls and got them dancing, soulful Stax and Atlantic pulled at heart strings and reduced grown men to tears, Trojan, Pama and Studio One filled in the gaps and got the whole place stomping. The Sole Room boys made JBs night when they played the dance floor filler *Sock it to 'em JB* by Rex Garvin and the Mighty Cravers – it was his song. *'Sock it to 'em JB!'* the place sung as one.

Six olive green MA1 flying jackets appeared at the door. Shaved heads on tattooed necks protruded from their collars, six pairs of identical cherry red DMs strode across the floor and headed for the bar. Lagers ordered they drank in unison, swore in unison and leered in unison. Steve noted their arrival but thought nothing of it, *c'est la vie*. The skinhead world was a broad church and all were welcome – *just obey the rules lads and enjoy the ambience, no-one wants any trouble.*

George stood at the urinal and aimed at the toilet cake sending it on a spiral journey – he whistled along to Gloria Jones Northern Soul masterpiece *Tainted love*. A pair of pristine cherry reds appeared at the side of his ink black brogues.

'Alright mate?' Asked the owner of the cherry reds. But as a greeting – not a question.

'Yeah, not bad mate. Not bad at all.'

'Could do with a bit of Oi though eh? Had enough of this fucking *wog* music don't you reckon?'

George hesitated, gathered his thoughts and studied the crude British Movement sun wheel tattoo on the skinhead's neck.

'Uh, no. Never got into Oi to be honest.'

He'd experienced similar situations many times in his past. Thoughts flooded through his head – he weighed up the skinhead and come to a simple decision, *I could have him – have him no sweat.*

'And less of the "wog music" if you don't mind.'

'You what? You some kind of nigger lover? Thought you was one of us?'

George knew the situation was about to turn nasty – for him, the nastier the better.

'And what's "one of us" when it's at home?'

George fumbled with the buttons on his 501s – as he always did.

'Us, us – white English. Under threat Anglo-Saxons mate, that's what. Good fucking white English stock, there ain't many of us left, we got to stick together. Fuck's sake, been bad enough in the past with all the niggers and pakis, now, now you got every fucking nationality under the sun here – Somalians, Ethi-*fucking*-opians, *fucking* heads on sticks. Now... now we get all them sponging fuckers from Eastern Europe – Albanians, Bulgarians, Latvians, the fucking lot...'

He paused to catch his breath – given George a momentary respite from his tirade...

'You been up Gloucester Road lately? It's all fucking jam rolls up there now. Fuck me there's nearly as many of them here as coons – talking of which, you seen that one out there and his black bitch of a partner? What's he doing here anyway? Trying to make out he's some sort of skinhead with his Ben Sherman on and his Monkey boots, huh? Fucking appropriate if you ask me – *fucking monkey*.'

The skinhead had barely finished his diatribe before George's forehead smashed into his nose with a crack that resembled a rifle shot. The force of the headbutt made him stagger and slump into the urinal, he tried to recover by grabbing the sides but he couldn't get a grip – he slid into the pan slowly and pathetically. George motioned for the skinhead to pull himself up – unexpectedly for George he managed to do so and he threw a heavy punch which caught George on the side of his head. George retaliated quickly and savagely with a flurry of punches to the skinhead's face – the blood from his battered mouth now mingled with that from his broken nose, he slumped back into the urinal – the blood and piss mixed as one and trickled away in a claret stream.

'Learn your fucking history. You're the sort who give skinheads a bad name – and what's wrong with us jam rolls? *Spierdalaj ty glupia pizda* – mate!' George quickly washed his hands and headed back to the bar.

'JB, Steve – get the girls out, I think it's going to kick...' Now it was George's turn to leave his sentence hanging mid air. A bottle crashed down onto the back of his head sending shattered glass around the bar – the battered skinhead stood in front of them, arms outstretched like some bloodied scarecrow.

'Fucking come on them, come on you old cunts let's 'ave it!' His cohorts stood behind him, a phalanx of hate, the same 'come on' pose, the same wide eyed look of menace and violence – there was no turning back.

There was no hesitancy from The Big Five – they sprang into action as they had done many times before. The girls made for the door while the DJs cut the music – futile pleas for calm fell on deaf ears. The boys were seasoned bar room fighters as were the skinheads – Steve's adversary swayed and crumpled as his ferocious fists hit home. Quick punches to the face, body and back of his neck made him fall – Steve followed up the punches with a couple of kicks from his Weejuns for good measure.

The skinheads fought back just as ferociously – Pete still had his strength but he had lost his speed and his agility. He collapsed under a barrage of punches and kicks from two assailants – as he hit the floor he received yet more savage kicks to the body and head courtesy of the lethal Doc Martens.

The poor sap who was unfortunate to be paired with JB was shown no mercy and was quickly despatched in yelps of pain and terror. He made for the door as JB turned his attention to the two who were mercilessly kicking Pete as he lay prostrate on the floor – a punch to the ribs of one sent him cartwheeling backwards while the other grabbed a bottle and smashed it across JB's face causing his nose to explode and send a spray of blood towards the bar. JB momentarily stopped to wipe the blood away with the back of his hand – his retribution was swift and brutal, he needed no weapon – he lunged at his assailant without mercy and jabbed swift punches into his face – the boxing lessons he learnt in the Marines serving him well.

Leon's anger raised his adrenaline levels enabling him to overcome his fear. Although he was still agile and nimble his rapid punches lacked strength and failed to sting his opponent, he took a few punches and the two fell to the floor as they grappled with each other. A stiletto heel wielded by Maggs made her husband's adversary squeal out in pain, release his grip and clutch his bloodied forehead. Maggs helped Leon to his feet and gave the skinhead another stab with the heel as she did so.

The screams of the women were relentless, cries of *'leave it out lads, c'mon break it up'* from Stan the landlord echoed around the bar, the DJs had seen it all before and pulled the plug on the music and desperately tried to protect their precious collection.

'Steve! Steve! Come on, leave it, the law are coming, leg it!' JB shouted above the noise and chaos, they helped Pete to his feet and they managed to stagger outside and regroup with their bewildered partners. The sounds of sirens in the distance hurried their steps – they quickened their pace and doubled back along Denmark Street and headed for Unity Street.

Steve tried to bring some order to the chaos...

'Girls, we need to split up – get in The Hatchet. We'll go find another pub and get cleaned up. I'll phone later okay?' he said breathlessly.

As the battered skinheads fled back towards the Centre the boys went under the bridge and headed for the Horse and Groom. In front of them two PCs headed straight for them – one stopped and took a call on his radio.

'Fuck it. In here – come on.'

Steve pushed open the door of the Queen's Shilling, they filed in one after the other.

'Steve you know this is a gay...'

'Well hello boys, looks like someone's been in the wars.'

'Er, yeah alright – no problem is there?'

'Not at all. Nice to see some new faces, especially handsome ones like you lot – come on in.'

The boys were careful not to make eye contact, Steve went to the bar with Pete and Leon, JB and George headed to the toilets to patch up their wounds. Steve nodded to his new found mate. 'What you drinking?' he asked, still struggling with his breathing.

'Voddy Red Bull gorgeous – seeing as you're asking.'

'Four Vodka Red Bulls – quick.'

They took their drinks. Steve sipped his and grimaced, he hated Vodka Red Bulls – just the smell made him want to heave.

'So what's your name?'

'It's Roger, but you can call me anything you want.'

'Okay Roger, let's just make out we know each other.' He motioned Pete and Leon. 'You two do the same.'

'You what? What the fuck you on about?'

'You fucking heard. Make out you know each other – or just fucking make out.'

Pete and Leon looked at each awkwardly. The door opened and one of the PCs entered – his radio crackling with static. Steve looked Roger in the eye, giggled and whispered in his ear...

'Roger, you might just be saving my life tonight.'

Roger cooed back. 'That's original – usually it's a DJ.'

Steve falsely giggled again, looked at the other two and then towards the copper at the door. Leon leant forward and touched Pete's hand as it rested on the bar. They both coquettishly laughed – the PC gazed around the bar, there was nothing in there of interest to him.

'Alright gents, have a good evening.'

The copper exited just as JB and George came back into the bar. They had washed and patched up their wounds as best they could – JB had a cut across the bridge of his nose and a bruise was beginning to appear around his left eye, but nothing he hadn't had before, George had a large lump on the back of his head and a smaller one on his forehead where his headbutt had made contact with the skinhead – but apart from that not a scratch. Pete had a discernible imprint of a Doc Marten sole on the right hand side of his face – the rest of the boys had bruised knuckles and not much else – no broken bones, no dislodged teeth, no serious cuts, more importantly their egos were fully intact.

'So who's your new bezzie mate?' asked JB, casting his eye over Roger.

'Roger meet JB, he's harmless. JB meet Rog – think he just saved our – arses.'

'You should be so lucky,' replied Roger.

JB spotted Leon's hand still on top of Pete's on the bar, he thought they made a nice couple.

'A couple of weeks back we all made confessions, came clean if you like, got a few things off our chest.' He gave a casual, lazy wink to Steve and his new mate Roger before continuing... 'Leon, Pete – is there something you want to tell us?'

* * *

The next morning Steve sat on the balcony of Kirsty's apartment in a pair of G-Star Raw shorts and a T-shirt that Sam had given him for his last birthday emblazoned with *'Intellectual hooligan'* across the chest. He nursed a strong black coffee and an even stronger headache. His body ached and his fists were bruised and sore – he smiled to himself and thought of the old cliché *'you should see the other guy'*.

The unseasonal warm spring continued. The early morning sun reflected off the water and a slight mist hovered a foot or so above it – the Floating Harbour looked relaxed and at ease with itself, it was hard to envisage it as the working docks it once was, let alone as a safe haven for pirate and slave ships from its even murkier past – the past that had made the city so wealthy.

A slow, wry smile creased his face as he reflected on the events of the previous evening – they had done well. Of course they had to live with the consequences from their partners, but he knew even they were quietly proud of their boys. Apart from a few cuts and bruises, mainly to George and JB, who sustained a broken nose – again, they were all okay. In fact they were better than okay.

He would drop in to see Stan the Man a bit later – Stan was an old mod who knew the game and played the game. Steve would give him a brown envelope with a wad of cash to cover the damages and to make sure he hadn't seen or said anything. He knew Stan would be okay, knew he would have said to the law the CCTV was broken, knew he would get rid of the tape – knew he would say it was a bunch of skinheads causing the trouble. It wasn't the usual lads who frequented Tricky Dickie's – just some outsiders, no one knew who they were. The law wouldn't pursue it – they would just log it as a Friday night pub fight, same as Friday night pub fights for the last century. No change of government, no change of laws, no change of drinking culture would change what was deeply ingrained into the British male's psyche.

The Rockola clicked and whirred behind him, he heard the familiar clunk and crackle as the needle settled onto the vinyl, a moment of anticipation swept through him…

'Walking down the road
With your pistol in your waist,
Johnny you're too bad.

Walking down the road
With your ratchet in your waist,
Johnny you're too bad.'

Kirsty appeared behind him and slipped her hands inside his T-shirt onto his muscular but aching shoulders.

'Oooo someone needs a massage.' She bent down and kissed the top of his head, then remembered she should actually be chiding him.

'What are you like? You lot never learn do you?'

It was the same sort of mock admonishment he used to get from his father – in front of his mother his dad would be severe, threaten him with the dreaded boiler stick or worse still, threaten to take him to the law. But away from his mother's gaze and out of earshot he would ask how the boys did, how many of them were there – did anyone run? His dad didn't like that, running. Walking was fine – *takes a man to walk away from a fight son*, that was his motto. But Steve knew his dad didn't always practice what he preached – he remembered him nursing bruised knuckles on a Saturday or a Sunday morning after many a tear up down the Pegasus.

'They started it.'

She shook her head. 'Yes and you lot bloody finished it – as usual.'

The night before they had all managed to regroup and catch separate taxis back to Kirsty's apartment – everyone had been suitably impressed.

'Landed on your feet here Stevie boy – very nice, and the apartment ain't bad either.' Lisped Pete through bruised and battered lips.

The girls had the grand tour, the boys huddled around the Rockola, drank cold beer and recounted the evening's events and recalled many similar ones over the years. Leon no longer felt like an outsider looking in, he had stories of his own to be told, this was just another to add to the list.

They partied on until the early hours, the Rockola whirred, clunked and played on through the night, they danced, skanked, monkey shined, twisted and bumped until the sun poked its head up over the cranes and the city came to life.

'For all that it was a good night eh?' What Steve really meant was that it was an even better night because of it.

'Yes, yes it was. Good to see the boys – and the girls, think they all enjoyed it. They're all a good bunch, always have been, and Leon, he's a nice bloke – such a shame.'

'Yeah, it is – I'm going to miss him.'

Kirsty needed to talk – Steve knew there was something on her mind. She wandered back to the kitchen and poured herself a coffee. He heard her putting some bread in the toaster.

He picked up his iPad and went to the BBC news site. The conflicts were escalating in the Middle East – the press now dubbing it 'the Arab spring', FIFA was embroiled in some bribe and corruption scandal and there were stories of married Premiership footballers, page three models and super injunctions – he shook his head, there wasn't much good news around these days.

At least it looked like QPR weren't going to be docked any points – they were now heading for the promised land of the Premiership, it reminded him he had to contact Barry Mason and send him his congratulations – or commiserations. More importantly he had to contact him about Earl Samson and Toby Ashurst – Steve needed Barry's help, he would phone him in the next couple of days, let the euphoria over Rangers' promotion and the disappointment over Rovers' relegation settle down.

A few years back they were facing each other in the same league, now Rovers were in the basement and QPR in the penthouse – who the fuck said football was a funny old game obviously hadn't watched Bristol Rovers. There was fuck all to make you smile about them – tears maybe, but no smiles.

'So what are you – a hooligan with intellect or intellectually a hooligan?' She nodded at his T-shirt.

'Oh this? Yeah nice play on words eh? Dunno, depends what kind of mood I'm in, last night a hooligan with intellect I guess.'

Kirsty nodded like she understood his logic.

'Steve…'

'Kirsty.'

'Steve – all this. All this revenge thing, all this retribution – for Cherry…'

'Not only Cherry,' interrupted Steve.

'Well okay, not only Cherry. But I guess for me it is – I know other events have taken over, especially for you and Harry and this Vernon Lewis, but…'

'But what?'

'I dunno, maybe it's all got a bit out of hand. Maybe I didn't think this through. Maybe, maybe we should just call it off.'

Steve exhaled deeply. 'What's brought all this about – last night's escapade? Suddenly remembered that violence can be a bit … nasty?'

'No, not last night. Well I guess in a way, it was nice seeing all you guys together and I don't want to see anyone get hurt.'

'Apart from Samson and Ashurst?'

'Well I suppose, but apart from them two. Maybe I've been a bit hasty, perhaps I should just draw a line under it, move on. Just accept that Cherry's … dead. Just start that new life, me and you, move to our big house with a garden in Clifton that I always wanted. Perhaps just fight for the rights to see the grandchildren and leave it at that.'

Steve inwardly cringed at the thought of the big house in Clifton. 'I think it's a bit late now don't you? Besides I don't think Vernon Lewis would take too kindly to be fucked around like this – he's got my number, literally. I'm sure he would smell a rat if I just said it was all off, he thinks he's going to be doing the deal of the century. He's not going to be a happy bunny if he thinks we've been fucking him about. He smells money – lots of money and he wants in.'

'But you still don't know how you're going to deal with him. Have you thought this through?'

'Have I thought this through? It was all your idea, remember? You're the one who hasn't thought this through, I mean you gave me the gun, what do you think I'm going to do with it – shoot tin ducks at the fair to win a cuddly toy?'

'Then don't take it, don't take it to the meet.'

'Are you mad? I bet a pound to a pinch of shit he'll be there with his thugs armed to the teeth – and you just know Samson will be the same. You're the cop, I bet you've seen this sort of thing loads of times before, you know how it works.'

'And that's precisely the reason I don't want you to go ahead with it, just finish it now. I don't want you to take this any further.'

'Tough, it's happening – I sorted it with the boys last night. We're all up for it, including Leon. We've all been whingeing for years about the scum on the streets and now we've got a chance to do something about it. You put us up to this – you were the one who said we owed you so we're now paying our debt to you – and to Cherry.'

'But Steve…' she trailed off again.

'But Steve what?'

'Nothing, nothing – just be careful.'

Steve looked at her questioningly. Someone else had said that to him recently – for the life of him he couldn't remember who.

* * *

Steve had first met Barry Mason at a Marketing Awards ceremony at some swanky London hotel, hosted by a B-list celebrity comedian who now worked the lucrative circuit. It was the usual banal, tired jokes, the usual false back-slapping and the usual overpriced bar. Barry had gone along to represent his newspaper and to give his wife, Fiona some support. Fiona introduced Barry to Steve, before she'd even said their names they had the measure of each other – just the way they looked, dressed and their mannerisms. They both knew they were two of a kind.

'Steve, meet my other half Barry. Barry, meet Steve Allen, my other half in work. I've got a feeling you two might have a lot in common, starting with football.'

'Brizzle boy eh? City fan I guess?'

'No fucking chance, Gashead through and through – don't tell me, Arsenal or Chelsea?'

'Cheeky fecker. Nope, born and bred on the White City Estate. Rangers fan to the core.'

Fiona was right, they did have a lot in common, starting with Gerry Francis and Ian Holloway and finishing with Gil Scott-Heron and The Jam. Barry was ten years younger than Steve and consequently a second generation skinhead, he was more Specials than Skatalites, more Madness than the Maytals but Steve soon got on his musical soapbox and educated Barry in the same way he had Leon Campbell. They had been forced to sit down at the table and listen to the ceremony by Fiona, neither of them wanted to – they preferred each other's company and that of a cold Guinness at the bar. They applauded politely on cue, observing the niceties of the evening until some overpaid, overblown suit from the famous West End advertising agency of *'Bollocks, Bullshit and Fuckwits'* referred to 'soccer' as a super brand with fans who were a commodity who had yet to be fully exploited.

To this day Steve and Barry believe they were the first people to be ejected from an Awards ceremony for trying to storm the stage...

'Barry you fucking Cockney cunt.'

'Steve? Steve you fucking dozy Bristolian worzel. What's this you've taken a golden handshake? You lucky fucking bastard. How the fuck are you?'

'Not as good as you – least you got a decent team to support.'

'Hey hey, too fucking right up the R's!' Barry suddenly felt guilty about his elation, 'oh and sorry to hear about the Gas – back in division two eh?'

'Yeah, where we belong – fucking joke, us and The Shit now two divisions apart, that's never happened in the past. Wish my old man had never taken me down Eastville now.'

'You don't mean it mate, they're in your blood, always will be – they'll be straight back no worries.'

'I wouldn't bank on it. No money, no ground, no support – and one less next year, I won't be going. You never know I might make a few trips to Shepherd's Bush next season instead.'

'Yeah? Well you better bring your wallet cos the fuckers have only increased the cost of tickets by forty per cent – thieving gits.'

'Welcome to the Premiership Baz.'

'Fucking tell me about it. Course I'm now in a club that I never wanted to be a member of in the first place. That rant by the Rangers fan against the Premiership, fuck, now we're part of it – it's a poison chalice, we all dream about promotion to the promised land, now we've got it I'm not so sure. Now we'll just be the latest in a long line of cannon fodder for the big guns.'

'Still at least those Chardonnay and prawn sandwiches will taste good.'

'Prawn sandwiches my arse. Give me a pie and a pint anytime mate. And another thing…' said Barry in a near whisper, 'fucking law got the Premiership all sewn up – all the action's in the Championship these days mate, especially with the 'ammers down. Fucking hell, it'll be kicking off every week! Still at least you got… Accrington Stanley to look forward to, huh, huh!!'

'Alright, alright – don't rub it in.'

'So, what's my old Gashead mate phoning me up for? Not just to bemoan the state of modern football again and tell me how much he's got in his sky rocket – Fi told me all about it, she's gutted, can't believe you've gone.' Barry hesitated for a second then lowered his voice again.

'Steve – there's rumours about you doing a Patsy Cline in work mate – what's all that about?'

'Like you said, rumours mate, just rumours. Anyway I haven't phoned you up to talk about my, or your, come to mention it, Bob Marley habit. So yeah well, I walked before I was pushed – couldn't have worked out better to be honest.'

'Shhhh, okay, okay – so what have you phoned me for then, not just to impress me with your knowledge of Cockney rhyming slang surely?'

'Nah, leave it ahht me old china… tell me have you heard of a geezer called Earl Samson?'

'Oh yes, I sure know of Earl Samson. He's so sharp he could cut himself, bit of a known face in West London years back, dodgy fucker, can't believe he's a football agent now – and to top it all a Chelski cunt.'

'Hmmm, I hear he speaks highly of you as well. So it goes without saying you're not a fan of his?'

'Let's see – a football agent and a Chelski fan? No, can't say he's at the top of my Christmas card list, why?'

'Okay, so apart from Chelsea, who do QPR fans hate the most?'

'You don't really have to ask do you? Luton – everyone hates Luton.'

Steve knew that would be Barry's response. A lot of football fans hated Luton with a real passion, going back to the eighties and nineties when they were seen as Thatcher's club, her scheme to make all football fans carry membership cards hardly endeared the Iron Lady to them, well apart from John Burston. She wanted to rid football of the scum who had ruined the beautiful game – scum like Steve Allen and Barry Mason. She wanted to ruin their Saturday afternoon escapades, ruin their thuggery, make football stadiums a safe place for the family to watch the game. Luton went along with her scheme, fucking Tory voting arseholes thought Steve – on reflection though he thought maybe she was right after all.

With QPR though it was different, QPR and Luton had long been at each other's throats, back in the eighties when Lacoste and Sergio Tachinni ruled the terraces, Barry had been a member of C-Mob – QPRs casual firm. The battles with Luton began at a cup match at Kenilworth Road in the late eighties. The MiGs were out in force and tooled up, eager to exact revenge on any visiting Cockneys following the riot in 1985 when Millwall took the place over – several QPR fans were badly beaten and stabbed.

Just a week or two later C-Mob turned the tables and attacked Luton fans at St Pancras station – what followed was a bitter rivalry that lasted to this day, over twenty five years of bad blood. Barry had been stabbed at Luton that night – he could taste that bad blood in his mouth again.

'Okay so add Luton fan to the list of reasons of why Barry Mason should hate Earl Samson.'

'You're kidding?'

'Nope, back in the day Earl Samson nailed his colours to many a football mast. He's Luton born and bred, ex Oak Road boot boy, then he moved to Bristol – that's when I got to know him. He latched on to City for a bit and ran with the East End boys for a couple of years before moving to London. He made his name on the streets, worked the doors, petty drug dealer, then full time drug baron, still is – all covered up with a mask of respectability. He went back to watching Luton and became one of the original Men in Gear but then well, little homely Luton weren't good or big enough for him, he moved on to Chelsea – as well as any other Premiership club that qualified for Europe, he's a proper glory hunter. Now, well he's one of the parasites that blight our game, a fucking football agent – and not just any football agent, a football agent who deals in drugs.'

'That's some dodgy CV he's got there. So how come he's got away with all this? How come he's now on the cover of *GQ* and not on *Crimewatch*?'

'Well let's just say he's got friends in high places – he's had more strings pulled for him than Pinnochio, but now it's time for Earl Samson to get his comeuppance, along with someone else you might have heard of – does the name Toby Ashurst ring any bells?'

'Toby Ashurst? Sure, he's some big noise in the City, son of Lord and Lady Ashurst, tipped to get into politics one day, no guessing which side he bats for. He's always in the gossip columns of the red tops – including mine – usually photographed falling out of a West End club with some bit of posh totty on his arm, hardly playing the grieving widower.'

Barry paused for a second – realising his mouth was running away with him.

'Grieving widower?' queried Steve, feigning surprise.

'Yeah, his wife died last year, the rumour was she was doing a bit of Charlie during a party at their gaffe. The Old Bill sniffed around for a bit – pardon the pun, and at one time it looked liked Ashurst might get charged with something, but it just all fizzled out.'

271

Steve felt like he'd been punched in the solar plexus, he momentarily thought of telling Barry about Cherry and his connection with her.

'Steve – you still there?'

'Yeah, yeah, still here. Go on.'

'Nothing much else to say about the bloke – a right Hooray Henry and a Merchant Banker to boot – what is there to like about him? Why, what's he got to do with Earl Samson?'

'Plenty as it happens – the boys from Stamford Bridge for starters.'

'I'd heard Ashurst was trying to get in with that lot. Surprising really – old Etonian, not exactly known for their love of the beautiful game, thought he'd be more of a funny shaped balls man.'

'Yeah well both he and Samson are using football as a front – a front for their clandestine and very illegal business.'

'You mentioned drugs – no surprise with Samson but apart from his missus snuffing it, what's Ashurst got to do with the seedy world of Britain's drug culture.'

'Quite a lot as it happens, and that's why I need your help. Help to get a bit of revenge.'

'Revenge? Revenge for what? What is this – Deathwish part five? What you got in mind anyway, me and a few of my old C-mob mates to pay the two of them a visit? Sorry Steve but I've left all that behind me – thought you had too?'

Steve would be lying if he said the thought hadn't crossed his mind, but he had other plans.

'I have, well of sorts, but someone once said the pen is mightier than the sword, so let's see if they're talking bollocks or not...'

* * *

'Ya fucking raz clat man, you tryin' to stitch I and me breddrin up?'

The voice sent a chill down Steve's spine – he'd heard it before several years ago and still had a recording of it on his phone. It terrified him then and it terrified him just as much now. Could he and the police be totally wrong about Venom and Vernon Lewis being one and the same, was this the *real* Venom coming back to haunt him.

'Who, who the fuck is this?' he asked nervously.

'Ha ha! Got you Mr Allen!'

'Vernon... Vernon Lewis?'

'Of course. Who did you think it is, Barack Obama?'

'No, I mean yeah, sorry you just threw me – what's that all about?' Steve's relief was palpable.

'One of my many talents Steven, you'll be surprised at what I can turn my hand to – it's made me a lot of money over the years.'

I bet it has you fucking bastard.

'To what do I owe this pleasure Vernon?' said Steve through gritted teeth, wishing he could tell Lewis exactly what he thought of him.

'Yes, pleasure eh? Did you enjoy yourselves at my club the other night – I certainly think John did. Was it also to your liking?'

Steve thought for a moment of JB embarrassing himself when he shot his load in his surreptitious condom, then thought he best not mention it.

'Um yes, yes – very good night, good company... um lovely girls.'

'Hmmm, you mean Lola? Think she took a shine to you, beautiful girl, truly beautiful – play your cards right Steven and I think you might be in there.'

Steve could feel himself reddening.

'I'll uh, I'll bear that in mind. Sorry Vernon what was it you wanted, presume we're still okay for our meeting next Friday?'

'Oh yes, definitely – that was why I was phoning, I hope you don't mind me calling you and not John, let's just say I find your company more – stimulating. John's a lovely fellow but somehow I don't think he's the brains behind all this hmmm? Anyway I just wanted to say the um, merchandise, excellent quality, had some of my people check it out if you know what I mean. We carried out some tests on it – excellent and as you said some impressive results.'

Lewis was acting the perfect gent again, almost avuncular in his manner. It was hard to imagine him as the gangland hard man, the drug baron, the long time biker from way back. Steve was not fooled – he continued with the conversation.

'And Darren?'

'Darren is fine and AS you promised no adverse effects and a negative test result, most impressive. However I do have one question?'

'Yes?'

'This Earl Samson fellow, the one who has the merchandise – do I take it he's a negro?'

'Er yes, he's black. Why is that a problem?'

'Could be. Let's just say I'm not a fan of our colonial cousins. Not too enamoured with doing business with them. Can't trust them – they're dangerous Steven, dangerous people.'

Not as fucking dangerous as I can be.

'He's very well respected Vernon. Like yourself he's a successful businessman and he's a member of Fitches of St James.'

'Really. Fitches eh?'

Steve hoped this would placate Lewis, it was evident he also craved respectability, craved to be part of the same establishment that Samson yearned for. They had both come from the wrong side of the tracks and both been successful for very similar reasons, Lewis and Samson had more in common than the two of them realised.

'Not to mention a business associate and good friend of Toby Ashurst, heir to the Ashurst Estate in Buckinghamshire.'

'Well that is good news. Perhaps he's not such a bad fellow after all – even so, it's best to come prepared.'

'Prepared?'

Lewis hung up without answering.

CHAPTER SEVENTEEN

'AT the very least this could expose the Premiership for what it is – full of bent, corrupt cheats who don't give a toss about the very people who pay their wages – the long-suffering fans. Come on Suzi we got to go with it.'

Barry Mason's editor-in-chief, Suzanne Viljoen wasn't so sure. She was a petite, spiky and blunt South African who like Barry was none too enamoured with Premiership football and its excessiveness – either on or off the pitch. She'd arrived in London from Cape Town in 1994 and after taking a work colleague's advice to take up the national sport to get into the psyche of the English she decided to see what all the fuss was about.

She had a small flat in Hackney and went along to her local club, Leyton Orient. It was not quite what her colleague had in mind and her first introduction to the beautiful game ended in a 0-1 defeat to Orient by Stockport County – hardly an auspicious start, but surprisingly she fell in love with the homely O's and still followed them to this day – much to the chagrin of her Arsenal season ticket holding husband and their children.

She had to admit though that it was one incredible story, but she was naturally wary of taking on the establishment and of having to explain it to her board of directors – not if, but when the brown stuff hit the fan. And then of course there would be the inevitable illegal phone tapping and surreptitious email hacking which she'd have to authorise...

'You're sure these photos are legit? Sure this whole story is legit for that matter? I mean how well do you know this... Steve Allen – can you trust him?'

'With my life. I got to know him over the years and yes he's legit – and anyway why would he make up something like this? It's a hell of a story, could be the story of the decade – for this paper anyway. It's just what we need and what's more if we play this right we won't have to name any names – we'll just let Twitter do all the work.'

Viljoen sat at her desk and leant back in her chair to study a stain on the tiled ceiling. She looked around her office and her gaze fell on the photo of herself and Nelson Mandela. 'What would you do Nelson? You're the real hero of these times, not these jumped up, overpaid Premiership prima donnas.'

She stood up, walked around the office and pointed at a photo of the Springboks 2007 rugby world cup holders. 'At least *bleddy* rugby still got some morals.' Barry knew her passion for the O's was surpassed by her love of the Springboks, but rugby supporters shouldn't be so quick to take the high ground when it come to morals thought Barry – *give it another twenty years of professionalism and it'll be as corrupt as 'bleddy' football.*

She turned her gaze back to Barry who was eagerly awaiting her decision.

'Twitter you say? No names, hmmm – this could be big. Or it could be bad – real *fucking* bad.'

* * *

Kirsty had pulled yet more strings. Harry was let off with a caution on the proviso he returned home to his parents' house – a house that was now devoid of his father.

Harry knew something was not right in the Allen household, he was used to his father's absences as a youngster, used to him coming home late from work, used to him being away from home – some meeting or conference in the capital which always seemed to take preference over his sons. He would often come back with a small present for Harry and Sam, thinking it would appease the boys for a bit – Harry still had his collection of London snow globes somewhere in the attic. Harry could handle it as a youngster but when he hit his teens and adolescent pains and anger started to trouble him, he needed his dad around – needed him to help him out. By the time his dad realised, it was too late.

It had been easier for Sam – he was always the favoured son. He took an interest in football and loved watching the Rovers with his dad but Harry never really got football, never got any sort of sport. Harry was more cerebral and deeper – he loved his Marvel comics, loved reading in general, especially Roald Dahl and J K Rowling. While Sam enjoyed a kickabout with his dad, Harry would watch from the sidelines or better still for him, stay in his bedroom reading about Willy Wonka and Hogwarts or getting lost in the world of Warhammer or Battlelore.

'What's happened between you and dad?'

'Um, nothing – just got a lot on his mind at the moment, said he needed a bit of space.'

'Needed a bit of space? Think you'll find that's a euphemism for he's shagging someone else muh. And as for him moving in with John Burston – don't make me laugh,

278

he's got more fucking kids living in his house than old mother Hubbard.'

'Language Harry.'

'Sorry muh and another thing – where's the dogs? He doesn't go anywhere without the dogs these days. He thinks more of them than he does of me and Sam.'

'That's not true, he thinks the world of you two – and anyway your nan's looking after them for a bit.'

Debbie could hardly admit to her son that his father had caught her with Brad's cock stuffed in her mouth. She still hoped that Steve would come back, especially with Harry back under their roof. Perhaps Steve would give him and her for that matter, one last chance.

'No, if you ask me muh, he's gone off with some bit of stuff – he always was a ladies' man. Even I could see that, sure you could too.' Harry said it so matter-of-factly, so non-chalantly. *Was it that blindingly obvious?* Was she ignoring what everyone else could see? Her husband had left her for another woman.

Harry grabbed a piece of toast off his mother's plate, mumbled something about needing some money for lunch and took some notes from her purse. He wandered into the hall way and put his jacket on, zipped it up and pulled up the hood, even though it was warm and sunny outside.

'Bye muh. See you later.' She heard the front door slam behind him, leaving her to wallow in her own self pity.

Debbie would be lying if she said the thought hadn't crossed her mind. Perhaps Harry was right – perhaps Steve had gone off with one of those young girls from work that he always teased her about. She'd noticed it when they'd been to firm's dos together – he always had a little posse of pretty young things hanging on his every word. He always denied it of course but she knew if he wanted to he could have any one of them – especially that Laura,

*fucking whore that she was with her pert arse and her long legs –
the fucking bitch.*

Or... or one of those fit young black girls from the gym. *What was her name?* Steve always dropped it into conversations... *Shaneice – that was the cow.* He always said he fancied a bit of black – Beyonce, Halle Berry, Rihanna – he was always going on about them, she always thought he was trying to make up for his past.

She remembered him in his early twenties when she first met him – he was so angry, he fucking hated immigrants he told her, wanted them all out of his country, wouldn't piss on one if he saw them on fire in the street, in fact he would pour more petrol on them. Fucking ruining his country, taking their jobs, taking their women – he hated, hated every one of them. *There ain't no black in the Union Jack,* he'd said, *send the bastards back.*

She shook her head and told him she didn't like him talking like that, said he was talking rubbish and anyway had he ever looked at his record collection?

'There's your proof you're not a racist Steve Allen, Motown, Stax, Trojan – not a white label amongst them, Christ you even got Young, gifted and black'.

Until Johnny Rotten came pogoing along every record he owned was by a black artist – how did he square that circle? How did Steve Allen explain that to his neo-Nazi mates?

'Anyway it's not true – I got "Ghost in my house" by R. Dean Taylor', he'd replied facetiously.

'A token white guy on a black music label does not count Steve and you know it.' She'd chided him, playfully. Typical Steve – even when he was being serious he was joking.

And then, and then he suddenly changed – he didn't like talking about it but she remembered he'd been on some sort of march in London – some meeting of the 'master race': neo-Nazis, crypto fascists and Aryan nation warriors from across Europe. He came back altered and troubled – said he didn't like the behaviour of some of the attendees, there were some serious head cases, people who really did want to see immigrants dead, really did want to see them hanging from lampposts – he might have said it in jest but he didn't really mean it. The day had disturbed him.

Then there were the ones who didn't go on the rally, the ones who stayed behind in the pub, the ones who didn't want to be seen – the teachers, the doctors, the accountants, even the politicians. No they didn't want to get their hands dirty, it wouldn't do their profile any good. Okay for the terrace warriors and the street fighters – the unemployed dross of Thatcher's Britain to go out and do their dirty work, okay for them to get spat at, okay for them to get bricks thrown at them, okay for them to get arrested by the law. And that was another thing – the police, he was no respecter of the law, he'd seen enough of them dishing out hidings at football or in Bridewell, been on the end of too many of their kickings himself, heard enough of their lies not to respect them. Yet there they were, on the march, showing the marchers their NF badges pinned on the inside of their lapels, laughing and joking with them – at first he thought it was amusing.

Then... well the older he got, the wiser he got. He realised what an idiot he was, realised what an ignorant fool he'd been. It wasn't the fault of the black youth who were fighting for their rights in England's inner city ghettoes, it wasn't the fault of the Asian shopkeepers who worked all hours to give their children a better life than they had. It was Thatcher's fault, Thatcher's fault he was one of three million unemployed, Thatcher's fault he had a mortgage he couldn't afford and Thatcher's fault his house was worth less than what he paid for it just a couple of years previously.

He regretted those days. He often wished he could turn the clock back, he wished he'd never got involved, but most of all he wished that that overweight, lecherous, neo-Nazi thug of a 'leader' had never molested him in the toilet. Steve had fought back – he wasn't going to let some fat faggot abuse him like some Soho rent boy... but he did wonder – just momentarily, wondered what it would be like to have another man inside him, just wondered for a while what another man's cock would be like in his mouth.

He had only touched him for a second or so but that was enough for Steve. He fought back, fought like he'd never fought before – he probably would have killed him if he hadn't been dragged off. He kept telling everyone, *I would have killed him, honest* – Steve Allen would have killed him – *the fucking fat faggot.*

CHAPTER EIGHTEEN

STEVE barely slept. He awoke in the early hours, poured himself a large glass of Glennfiddich and sat on the balcony watching the city first wind down, then wind up again – slowly. It was that sort of city, so laid back it was almost horizontal. Not really a twenty-four hour party city, more of a *'come around our house for a couple of beers – if you've got nothing better to do'* sort of city. He liked it that way – he wondered, hoped even, that it would never change.

Kirsty got up and poured a malt for herself, wandered over to the jukebox and studied it as if she'd never seen it before. Her fingers hovered over the buttons, maybe '*Dark end of the street*' by John Carr, deep, meaningful and full of soul, like her man – she thought better of it, sometimes silence spoke volumes. She joined him on the balcony and kissed the back of his neck before sitting down. They looked at each other and smiled – a loving smile that put the two of them at ease – for a while.

They ended up back in bed and made love as if their life depended on it – perhaps they would never make love again, they both knew it, but neither of them dared mention it. When Kirsty reached orgasm she cried out his name and cried real tears. She held him so tight and dug her nails in so hard she drew blood from his back, he winced but he felt good about it, it felt good to be loved, to be wanted – he'd missed that.

She cooked him breakfast but he barely touched it, he sipped a strong coffee then went to the bathroom and threw up, he thought about not taking his medications – what was the point? But then he reconsidered, it might be tempting fate. He washed them down with the dregs of the coffee.

Over the scrambled egg and bacon Kirsty had again pleaded for Steve not to go ahead with it – but it was too late, the express train was pulling out of the station. No stops, just one fucking long tunnel to go through – one long tunnel with revenge and retribution at the end of it. Steve was still haunted by events that occurred over thirty years ago, perhaps the next few hours would at last lay those ghosts to rest.

He wondered why she had such a change of heart. When they first met after all those years it was her who said he and his mates owed her – with or without Mike Cribb. It was Kirsty who wanted the revenge, Kirsty who provided the information – the dossier, the taser, the gun, everything about this was down to her. Get revenge on Earl Samson and Toby Ashurst, get them out of the way and it would be happy ever after – big house in Clifton with roses around the porch, two beautiful grandchildren to dote over and spoil – it would be perfect. They would have holidays by the sea together, grow old together, make up for the years they had lost and make up for all the times that they should have had. They would be like teenage lovers all over again. He would be Marvin Gaye and she would be Kim Weston, *It takes two baby – me and you*.

The law would help them – *they were the good guys* she kept saying, they would be on their side. They too had had enough of scum like this and they needed them out of the way as much as she did. Those strings would get tugged again and they would be on their way – and anyway no jury in the land would convict them, not for ridding the country of scum like Lewis and Samson. That's what the outraged moral majority of the country wanted anyway, this would be David Cameron's Big Society in practice – the little man hitting back. There would be online petitions to free them, the *Daily Mail* would love it and make heroes of them – he could see the headlines now – '*Revenge of The Big Five*'.

Then of course there was Leon, if it all kicked off he would do the business, he would pull the trigger, he had nothing to lose – well apart from his holiday of a lifetime with his wife. She would forgive him – she would know why he did it, why he got involved. All the shit he'd seen in his life, all the shit he had to put up with in work, all the scum, the druggies, the child-molesters, the low-lifes, the underclass of society – they would raise a statue to Leon Campbell in St Pauls, they would set up a charity in his name – he would be a hero, a proper working-class hero.

Friday nights would never be the same again. No more empty promises, no more hollow threats, no more bullshitting and bluffing, no more beer doing the talking. They were doing something about it, something about this shit life they all lived, something about the scum on the streets – this was their time, it was payback time for The Big Five... then of course it could all go tits up. If they got caught and convicted they could be looking at spending a large part of the rest of their lives inside or... or they could end up dead. They were out of their comfort zone and mixing it with the big boys – this was no Saturday afternoon toe-to-toe on the terraces. Who knows what Samson had up his sleeve? He had cut his teeth and earned his reputation wheeling and dealing in West London – he would be no pushover. Likewise Lewis was an unknown quantity – to Steve at times he still seemed like a jovial uncle, albeit one who dealt in Smack and Charlie, his mellifluous tones were at odds with his physique and his history. He had hinted at his hatred, hinted at his violence, Leon had warned him that back in his greaser days he was known for his casual violence, *'beware dat man'*, he said *'dat Leopard ain't gonna change his spots'*.

* * *

The taser felt heavy and awkward as he put it into the rear waistband of his jeans, he no longer had the pistol – he'd somewhat reluctantly given that to Leon. He kissed Kirsty and she told him she loved him *'no matter what – I'll always love you'* were her exact words. He wasn't sure what she meant by the *'no matter what'* – he dismissed it with a shrug as he unlocked his car and got in. He picked up Pete McNulty and George Smolinski from JB's house where they all waited uneasily for him.

Their partners knew they were up to something as they weren't behaving like they normally did when they were off on some jolly. This was no day out at the races or the football, when they would usually stagger back home in the early hours, drunk and sheepish and giggling like naughty schoolboys. They were unusually quiet, sullen even – the girls were worried, they didn't like the sound of this *'business that needs sorting'*.

They'd already discussed the weapons and agreed that what Kirsty had given Steve was the least they needed, George had previously said something about getting a gun – *'five hundred quid from a geezer down the gym, some eastern European make, meant to be shit hot – only got six bullets though, that gonna be enough?'* The others had nodded – depended, thought Steve to himself. Depended on what kind of arsenal Lewis would turn up with – and Samson for that matter.

Christ I could murder a line. Steve might have been desperate but he wasn't that stupid, but the marching powder would help, help him think he could do it, help him think he could pull this mad, bad stupid, suicidal plan off.

* * *

Earl Samson's Bentley left the M4 and headed down the M32. He was familiar with the motorway and the way it started with countryside and ramshackle allotments then finished abruptly in the centre of the city, after piercing its way through the bustling cosmopolitan neighbourhoods of his old stamping grounds of St Pauls and Easton.

'You want me to phone him now boss?' asked Tyrrel L'estrange, long-time trusted lieutenant of Earl Samson, a man so large he carried his own postcode. It was impossible to tell where L'estrange's body finished and his head begun, he had no neck to speak of, just a head the size of a medicine ball growing out of a body that was as wide as it was high – he was a Spanish Town behemoth and Samson trusted him with his life.

'No not yet Tyrrell, think we'll drive round for a bit. I haven't been down here for a few years – we'll take in some sights, let them sweat for a bit.'

L'estrange nodded, knowing full well not to query his boss any further.

L'estrange filled, rather uncomfortably, the front passenger seat. Driving the sleek black limousine was Trevor 'Teet' Thomas – half the size of L'estrange but just as fearsome. Thomas was the proud possessor of numerous gold teeth and a Cockney accent that should've belonged to a Pearly King doing the Lambeth Walk. He was black, English and proud, born in Broadwater Farm and a big-time Tottenham

Hotspur fan. He looked around at the green fields and the grazing cattle, just feet away from the tarmac of the motorway.

'Shouldn't take long,' said Thomas.

'What shouldn't take long Trevor?' asked his boss.

'Taking in some sights – this ain't no city, it's a fucking village. You sure you used to live 'ere boss? What a fucking backwater.'

'It has a certain charm Trevor. I had some good times down here – perhaps I'm going to have some more.'

'Christ boss – look at that tower block over there, it's got a thatched roof!' chortled Thomas, pleased at himself for cracking a joke.

'Very funny Trevor – don't give up your day job.'

Samson looked to his right and took in the huge Tesco and Ikea stores as the motorway elevated and rose above the shabby terraced houses on entering the city.

'That's where Rovers used to have their ground, fucking shitpit it was – scary, but a fucking shitpit all the same.'

'Who?' asked Thomas.

'Rovers, Bristol Rovers – you remember Gary Mabbutt?'

'Sure do boss, Spurs legend – one of the best.'

'Started here Trevor. Started his career playing at Rovers.'

'Shut the fu...' Thomas quickly remembered who he was talking to, 'sorry boss – you're kidding right?'

'No, little ole Bristol Rovers, that's where he started – back in the Seventies.'

Samson instructed Thomas to turn off into St Pauls, some things had changed thought Samson, but not St Pauls. Still the same – scruffy around the edges but vibrant and edgy – he liked the place. They drove down onto Ashley Place then left onto Grosvenor Road.

'Black and White café down here boys, where it all kicked off years back. I used to hang around in here a bit, it's just here on the…'

The old café was no more. It had been shut down by the police after too many altercations and drug raids – its clientele now fragmented and dispersed around the city.

'Oh well, pull over here Trevor, we'll pay the Inkerman a visit instead – at least that's open.'

Large, red brick, weathered and ugly, the Inkerman pub, built in Victorian times and named after the Crimean War battle, stood forlornly at the end of the road. Like a lot of Bristol since Samson has last visited, it too had changed – it had been renamed The Jamaican Inn, but the grimness was still there and on entering Samson could see that despite the name change, the pub was exactly as he remembered it. The same stained grey tiles on the floor, the same old boys playing Dominos, TV on but no sound and gentle rhythmic reggae playing in the background – like its clientele The Jamaican Inn had seen better days.

The locals weren't impressed by the sharp suited inter-lopers and the shiny black Bentley Continental Flying Spur parked outside. In fact nothing much impressed them – they had seen far too many outsiders over the years trying to muscle in on St Pauls. They would give them short shrift – if they wanted trouble they would get it, if not fine – *no trouble man, no trouble.*

'Two straight Appleton Specials an' a orange juice – please.'

Thomas cursed under his breath – put out for having to have the OJ. Three plastic cups were served up, no ice, the minimum drink measure. Samson looked around and saw the others drinking out of glass tumblers topped with ice – he got the message.

'You boys a stayin?' asked the landlord.

'No just passing through.'

'A weh ya baan?'

Samson was not taken aback by the landlord's bluntless. He remembered how straight talking Bristolians could be, they didn't stand on ceremony – even less Jamaican born ones.

'I'm originally from Luton but I used to live in Bristol. My friend here...' he nodded in the direction of Trevor Thomas, 'he from Broadwater Farm in London, my other friend...' he motioned towards Tyrell L'estrange, 'he from Spanish Town – J.A.'

'Ah know where Spanish Town is bwoy.' The landlord kissed his teeth and nodded, clearly not impressed by the origins of two of them. He leant forward and said something in L'estrange's ear – they both roared with laughter, L'estrange's hulking body visibly shook.

Samson fired his employee a look that only he could. L'estrange remembered his position and his place – he quickly snuffed out the laugh and gazed at the floor.

'Sorry boss,' he mumbled in apology.

'You know a brother called Venom?' asked Samson.

'Who askin?'

Samson took out a crisp fifty pound note from his wallet and placed it on the bar with an exaggerated flourish. Realising the clientele were listening in the landlord eyed the note up warily.

'He a bad man, that's all I know.' He took the note, rung up the cost of the drinks and gave Samson his full change – he was taking no risks.

Samson mulled this over. The landlord's response was enough to make him think Vernon 'Venom' Lewis was legit, someone to be feared even. His sources had given him the background – what they didn't know they made up. What Samson had found out both shocked and surprised him, Vernon 'Venom' Lewis was not what he seemed. He was in his sixties, white and racist – hardly a 'brother'. He had a penchant for Renaissance paintings and for inflicting pain. Samson had heard tales of bolt cutters being used on victims' fingers and toes, *very 1960s* he thought, *very Richardsons – very old school.*

What he hadn't been able to find out was where the hell Lewis got the Merck cocaine from. Samson thought he was the only importer into the country – he and Ashurst had a monopoly on it, or at least he thought they had. How the fuck did some West Country bumpkin of a drug baron get pharmaceuticals from Eastern Europe? He knew Lewis owned a yacht and that he had a place in Marbella, that may have been his route into Europe for heroin from Afghanistan and cocaine from South America, but that didn't explain the Merck from Eastern Germany? Samson was sure of one thing, he didn't want to do business with Lewis – he wanted to eliminate him.

Samson drunk his rum in one and indicated the others to do the same – he nodded towards the door, an instruction for them to leave. As was customary Thomas exited first, looked around then unlocked the Bentley, leaving L'estrange to escort his boss out and open the car door for him. Samson turned to the landlord, nodded and thanked him for his hospitality.

'No problem man – come again.'

The laughter and sniggers from the locals stung his ears as he got into his Bentley – it was not an experience he was used to.

'Hey boss – you askin' about Venom?'

Samson and L'estrange turned in unison. In front of them stood a tall, rangy youth – all bloodshot eyes and bad teeth. Below his left eye a two inch scar did nothing for his looks. He wore a polyester Adidas tracksuit trimmed with red, gold and green stripes which ran along the sleeves of the jacket and the seam of his torn trousers.

'I might be – and who are you?'

'The name's Augustus Lee – my friends call me Ugly Man.' He laughed nervously and offered his clenched fist in a greeting. Samson studied his fist, dismissed it with disdain and wondered what his enemies called him.

'Jump in Mr Lee. Perhaps we can do business.'

Ugly Man didn't need to be asked twice. He got in between Samson on his right and L'estrange on his left, his body odour and the distinct smell of crack cocaine followed him in like a heavy fog.

'Man dis a sweet car, I got a Legsus meself.'

'Do you mean a Lexus?' asked Samson, surprised that such a character could afford such a prestigious car.

'No man a Leg-sus, as in me legs – dey take me hany-where I want.' He repeated the same nervous laugh.

Samson allowed himself a smile of his own. *A joker eh? As well as a smelly bumclot in the back of my motor, that's all I need.* He signalled to Thomas to drive on, as he did so Samson caught his first sight of the tag 'Venom' sprayed on a wall in front of them. He glanced to his right and spotted another – he couldn't help but wonder if the information he'd received about this mysterious Venom was incorrect. Perhaps he was just some teenage wannabe Yardie, there were enough of them about. He had to remind himself that if his information was correct, Lewis was nothing of the sort.

'Trevor – just follow the signs for Clifton. I'm sure this business won't take long.'

Thomas caught his boss's eye in the rear view mirror – Samson gave a very slight but imperceptible nod. Thomas made sure the doors of the Bentley were unlocked.

'So you know Venom?' queried Samson.

'Do I know Venom? Man does Dolly Parton sleep on her back – course I know Venom.'

Samson smiled yet again – at least this guy had all the lines he thought.

'Okay, what do you know of him.' Samson reached for his wallet and took out another fifty pound note. He held it temptingly in front of Ugly Man.

292

'He a bad man, you don wanna mess with 'im boss, he runs everyting in dis town. All the blow, all the sniff, all de nice ladies – he run dis fuckin' town man. He a bad motherfucker.'

Samson nodded knowingly. 'So I've heard my friend, so I've heard – and tell me what colour is this Venom character?'

Ugly Man pulled a face like he'd just been asked the most ridiculous question in the world. For a moment he took his eye off the note Samson waved temptingly in front of him, he would tell this man anything he wanted to hear – the lure of his next crack hit was proving just too much.

'Dat a trick question man? He black like you, black like me. Venom – he a black man.'

Samson nodded again. Ugly Man thought it was a sign to take the note, L'estrange knew differently, he grabbed Ugly Man around the neck and pulled him across his own body, momentarily disgusted that his own hand-made Hugo Boss suit had been soiled. With his left arm he opened the door of the Bentley just as they rounded the Bear Pit, they heard Ugly Man squeal like a pig having his throat cut. Thomas looked in the rear mirror, not quite sure if the bus that was behind them had hit him or not. He watched as the pathetic bundle rolled to the kerb before coming to an abrupt stop against the railings.

'Trevor wind the windows down there's a good chap – there's an awful smell in here.'

'Der was boss, der was,' giggled L'estrange, 'but I fink it gone now.'

They allowed themselves another laugh – this time nothing was forced.

'Where too now boss?' asked Thomas once again.

'Follow the signs for the Clifton Suspension Bridge – even you can't miss it Trevor. I feel the need for some fresh air and a bit of class – and a spot of lunch.'

It was quite possible that the Avon Gorge Hotel had never seen three such characters before – it had seen rock stars, politicians, celebrities – real celebrities, before the word had become so overused and sullied. It was a grand old hotel, built in the shadow of Brunel's masterpiece – the Clifton Suspension Bridge, the ultimate folly. A beautiful bridge that neither served a purpose nor went anywhere, it just spanned the Avon Gorge – magnificently.

Thomas let out a long low whistle. 'Man, now that's what I call a bridge.'

Samson thought he couldn't have put it better himself, it needed no further embellishments – Thomas was right, it was some bridge. Their moment of wonder was brought to a sudden halt by an eager, fresh faced youth.

'Table for three gentlemen? On the terrace for the best view?'

Samson turned to the boy, spotted his name badge and politely smiled.

'Yes *Ryan* that would be nice.'

Ryan Calloway beamed. He always liked it when someone called him by his name – it generally meant they would be easy going and with a bit of luck they would leave him a decent tip. Fuck knows he needed it to pay off his horrendous student loan.

There was something about the man's face, he thought for a moment he recognised him – maybe from the TV? He wondered if he perhaps was a musician or a big name DJ about to play a gig in the city. Ryan showed the three of them to the best table – it was now two o'clock and most of the lunch time guests had departed back to their offices for their final snoozy hours in front of their PC or for some, the last illicit work time shag of the week. In a few hours the cider monsters would be appearing – no matter what the grand old hotel tried to do to stop them, on a warm spring evening the loonies would invade Clifton and cause havoc –

as they had done for the past forty or so years. It was nice to have such pleasant and cultured clientele for a change thought Ryan as he took their orders.

He quickly passed the order to the chef then remembered where he'd seen the handsome, suave face before. He ran to his locker and took out last month's *FHM*. Flicking through the pages he momentarily stopped on the double page spread of The Saturdays, sighed at Frankie then delicately pulled the next page apart where he'd spunked all over it the night before. He stopped once more and looked longingly at Una then found the page he was looking for. It was definitely him, staring at him in the same cool way he'd looked not five minutes before... *'Earl Samson – the most powerful man in football?'* read the headline.

He'd read the article and looked at the photos of Earl Samson leaving some club in Soho called The Box with a young leggy blonde fixed to his arm. Ryan admired his clothes, his build, his attitude, his wealth – what was there not to like about him? *Play your cards right Ryan and you'll get a tip – hopefully a very big tip.*

'So boss, when do you want me to call this Campbell guy? They wanted to meet at two.'

'Let them wait Trevor, let them sweat, we're in no hurry – I don't know who he is anyway... Campbell that's all I know, perhaps he's another honky like this Vernon Lewis. All I know is they reckon they've got their hands on a shitload of Merck to flood the market with. More than we've seen in our lives – so let's keep an open mind.'

'Didn't you mention this could be worth ten million boss?'

Samson raised his hand to Thomas, motioning for him to be quiet. Ryan appeared with a bottle of Chateaneuf du Pape and two glasses, plus some bottled water for Thomas who sighed deeply. Ryan expertly opened the bottle, poured a small amount for Samson to sample who then nodded in appreciation. Ryan poured out two glasses and gave a small sycophantic bow as he left the table.

The boy quickened his step, opened his locker again, took out his BlackBerry and quickly logged on to Facebook... *'OMG, got Earl Samson at my table, wots he in town for ne1 know?'*

He went back to the kitchen and collected their plates, he felt his BlackBerry vibrate in his pocket.

'Enjoy your meals gentlemen. If there's anything else you want please let me know.'

'Thank you Ryan,' answered Samson – not sure if the youth had heard anything of their previous conversation.

'Keep it quiet boys. I don't want anyone hearing what's going on. If you open your big mouth again Trevor, you'll end up taking a walk off that bridge – *kapeesh*?'

'Yes boss,' replied Thomas, suitably admonished – yet again.

Ryan checked the message he had received on his Black-Berry, it was from his mate James... *'Rumour is he's lookin at rafael newton, he's at the gate l8r'*

Ryan nodded, he had definitely heard ten million being mentioned – his fingers flew across the keys: *'Heard him mensh 10 mill, sounds like its deffo newton.'*

He eagerly waited... *'reckun goin to chelsea, thats samsons club neway, makes sense??'*

'Fink your right jimbo, rafael newton is signing for Chelsea for 10 mills – you heard it here first!!!!'

* * *

By the time Chris Pomphrey, chief sports editor of the *Evening Post* got to hear about it was too late for the day's edition. He hurriedly updated the paper's web page then set about writing the story for the next day's paper little knowing that other events would overtake the 'exclusive' he was so looking forward to writing.

Rafael Newton was a talented if headstrong lad – aged only eighteen he'd just scored twenty-one goals in his first season for the Robins. He already had all the accoutrements of a modern day footballer – corn row hairstyle, full sleeve tattoos, flash motor, a pretty if somewhat vacuous blonde WAG and most importantly of all – his own agent.

There had been a lot of speculation about him moving away in the close season, mostly conjured up by himself and his agent – a Jersey-based parasite by the name of Danny Wall. Danny had assured Rafael that he would make a fortune when the time was right, but for now he just had to bide his time and get his hometown club to give him a rise while he would tout his name around to the Premiership clubs. All he had to do was to keep City guessing and dangling, then when the big boys came running he could fuck off and the two of them could pocket the dosh. Never mind all the time, money and effort they had sacrificed in nurturing him since he was a twelve year old – *fuck 'em*, said Danny.

Rafael had been brought up in Eastville. His father was none too happy that he signed schoolboy terms for City rather than Rovers, but Delroy Newton understood his lad's thinking. It pained him but he had to admit that City were now light years ahead of Rovers in developing the schoolkids – but being from Rovers' own backyard, it riled Delroy big time.

Like many other Afro Caribbean lads from East Bristol, Delroy had followed Rovers since back in the seventies, but by the end of that decade it seemed the club was in terminal decline. And as for the terraces... Delroy and his mates weren't made too welcome by the reborn skinheads on the Tote End.

He finally called it a day in the early eighties when they started abusing Errington Kelly – their very own black player, admittedly he wasn't a Pele or a Eusebio, he wasn't even a Clyde Best, but he was one of their own. He also remembered one unsavoury incident in particular when one of the leaders of the Tote End, a fearsome fighter he only knew as 'Steve' screamed in his face: *'There aren't no black in the Union Jack, send the bastards back!'* – Delroy felt the spittle running down his cheek and could see the hatred in the white boy's eyes – he and his mates knew then it was time to leave football to the Neanderthals and the bigots that had infested it.

Fortunately, the last two decades had seen the racists move on, due in no small part to the success of players like Barry Hayles and Jason Roberts gracing the famous shirts. Delroy returned to watch his team – he knew the racists were still around but he often wondered where all the old boot boys like 'Steve' had gone – he hoped that they'd crawled back under the rocks that they had first emerged from.

It wasn't quite the same watching the blue and white quarters from a terrace a fraction of the size of the Tote End and at a painfully ramshackle ground that was clearly built for rugby, but nevertheless he enjoyed watching the Pirates at Wembley – perhaps the good days were heading back after all. As ever though the football gods conspired that Rovers' moment of glory wouldn't last and as the 2010-11 season came to an end they were once again facing basement football.

Delroy picked up his mobile and phoned his son. 'Rafael – at least you joining a club who play in blue, never did look right you playing in red. Big money too – well done son, well done.'

'What you talking about pops? I ain't going nowhere.'

'Really? Well it says online you're going to be joining Chelsea for a cool ten million, so don't forget your dear old mum and dad eh son?'

Rafael scratched his head and pondered just for a moment. He knew it was just paper talk or Danny talking up his price yet again – he wasn't overly concerned.

'Dad I'm telling you now, if I'm going to Chelsea you'll be the first to hear. Oh and tell mum I'll be over on Sunday with Jade for dinner. We can have a catch up then okay? Bye dad.'

Delroy looked at his phone and shook his head, baffled by his son's ignorance. *If it says on that worldwideweb surely it got to be right* he thought. 'Me, I'm just all confuseddotcom,' he finally said to himself.

* * *

The meal over, Samson indicated for the bill. He paid in cash and left a twenty pound tip for Ryan.

'Thanks Mr Samson, greatly appreciated. Have a nice day – hope the deal goes well.'

Fuck the student loan, I could do with a bit of a session, bit of MDMA would go down very well tonight – thank you Earl Samson.

Samson did not like being recognised – not while he was on clandestine business. He was incandescent with rage – he instructed L'estrange to attend to business as he eased himself onto the plush leather seat of the Bentley.

Eager to spend his little bonus Ryan was already on his phone when L'estrange's huge frame appeared in the doorway of the cramped staff room. There was no one else around – Ryan looked up as L'estrange's head cast a shadow over the screen of his BlackBerry.

'Oh hello sir – have you forgotten something?'

* * *

The deal was for Samson to phone at one o'clock, they would arrange the meet for two and Leon was to give him the exact address of Lewis's warehouse. It was already way past two – Leon was getting impatient.

Pins and needles ran the lengths of his legs as he crouched in one of the side rooms of the old Victorian building – it was rundown and decrepit with buddleia growing through the broken windows and the gaping holes in the roof. It stunk of shit and piss of indistinguishable origin but in a year or two's time it would be a tastefully decorated apartment block bringing in a small fortune for Lewis, but this would pale into insignificance compared to what his more illegitimate business operations contributed to his wealth.

Leon's mobile rang in his hand as he studied it once again causing him to twitch in surprise. He straightened himself up, giving momentary respite from the near paralysis in his legs.

'Mr Campbell, this is Mr Thomas – Mr Samson' associate. We are ready to make the appointment now.'

Leon half smiled at the formality of Mr Thomas's tone. He replied in a similar manner.

'Thank you Mr Thomas. I'll text you the postcode, presumably you have SatNav?'

'Indeed we have, we'll see you shortly – goodbye.'

'Goodbye.'

Steve Allen, John Burston, George Smolinski and Pete McNulty – four fifths of The Big Five anxiously waited for Leon's call. They'd arrived at the warehouse at just before two but there was no sign of either Lewis or Samson. They sat in Steve's Audi hardly speaking but they all thought the same – *this ain't gonna happen – it'll be a no show.*

300

Pete shifted uncomfortably in his seat, 'I need a fucking piss,' he said.

'I need a fucking shit,' responded George.

JB needed neither. Instead he sought reassurance from Steve.

'Can you remind me again of what the fuck we're doing here?'

Steve had anticipated the question. He had a speech of sorts prepared.

'Retribution, revenge, gratitude – because we owe someone, owe someone big time.' He decided to say no more – if they didn't get it by now they never would.

'What Kirsty Donohue? I know you're back shagging her but it's hardly grounds for us to risk our fucking lives and liberty just to please her is it?' George whined.

Steve gave George a dark look – if there was anyone who was going to jump ship it would be him. He tried to remain calm.

'You know it's not about me pleasing or shagging her. It's about March 1982 and what she did to save us from going inside if you recall. Without her intervention who knows how our lives would have turned out. Probably career criminals – no nice houses, no nice cars and no nice holidays. Fuck me, you might not have ever got married and had kids – think about that.'

There was silence again, eventually broken by Pete. 'The fucking bitch, wait till I see her next.'

The others gave out stifled laughs, JB piped up again.

'Seriously Steve, what if it all goes tits up? What if it all kicks off, we'll be stuck between two gangland bosses and their cronies – what if the two of them set about us? This could get really nasty.'

'Well that's why we got our fighting gear on ain't it – and besides you've never been one to duck out of a good scrap.'

'Good scrap? Good fucking scrap? This ain't no Saturday afternoon punch up down the Tote End. These boys are gonna have shooters and fuck knows what else, we got one gun between us and a taser – and the gun you've given to Leon. At least I should've had the shooter, seeing as I'm the only one who's every fired one in anger before.'

'We got two.' George interrupted – almost sheepishly. They rounded on him, 'I, um bought that gun down the gym that I was on about – thought it might come in handy.'

Pete didn't want to feel left out. 'An' I've got me boots on – an' a knuckle duster.'

'Oh that's alright then ain't it? We got a regular little fucking arsenal here haven't we?' bellowed JB.

'What you gonna do then Mac when some Cockney villain aims a Uzi at you from fifty yards? Run up and kick him in the bollocks with your Doc Martens, then whack him on the napper with your brass knuckles – and as for you George, give me the fucking gun you tart, you haven't got a clue how to use it – gimme!' He lunged at George, rifling through his jacket.

'Just leave it, fucking leave it John,' interjected Steve, 'I told you to bring what you could, you should have got something. Like the boy scouts – be prepared.'

'Just as well I got this then.' JB nonchalantly pulled out a meat cleaver from his waistband with his right hand. With his left hand he reached inside his jacket pocket and pulled out a can of CS gas.

'You fucker, thought you was having us on there,' said Steve.

'Like you said Stevie boy be prepared – dib dib, fucking dib.'

Steve shook his head in despair.

'Anyway, I've told you, if this goes to plan none of this will be needed.'

'Plan, plan? What fucking plan? Oh yeah, run this by me again why don't you Steve? Let's see, we got the West Country's biggest gang boss, who happens to be an ex Hells Angel and raving Nazi, meeting a black crime lord and ex football hoolie from the smoke. The Nazi is thinking he's going to be getting a shitload of this new wonder cocaine from the black hoolie, a drug which he then thinks will make him a fortune – course, the black hoolie also happens to think that the Nazi is going to be a new source for the drug, which of course is nonexistent...

'Hmmm, and, and, this is the best bit, we're the fuckers who'll be in the middle of this little war when they both discover they've been set up – so sorry Steve, what's the fucking plan again?' JB finished with a flourish. He was not merely questioning his old time mate, more like questioning his sanity.

'Yeah Steve, what is this fucking plan you keeping going on about? Only it's getting near slap o-fucking-clock, 'bout time you told us eh?' asked George.

Steve gave out a small but discernible cough.

'The plan is, the plan is we introduce the two of them to each other and exit. You know, light the blue touch paper and retire, they'll be so wound up we won't be needed. We just let the two gangs fight it out.'

George had a vision of tumbleweed blowing across the horizon, magic-like as in the cartoons – an old ragged shit-streaked piece of newspaper sufficed and cartwheeled over the bonnet of the Audi. He looked wistfully at Pete sat next to him, not saying a word he took the pistol out of his pocket and placed it on the seat, opened the car door and walked off.

Steve stared at Pete, a slight nod of the head was the signal for Pete to get out his knuckle duster from his jeans pocket – he too placed his weapon on the seat, opened the door and exited.

'Oi, where you two going?' shouted JB half-heartedly, knowing full well it was in vain.

'John, John leave 'em – it's just you and me then matey, like it always has been, carrying the banner of Cameron's Big Society.'

'You're a mad fucker Stevie Allen, always have been, always will be – so tell me, how does Leon fit into this?'

Steve had almost forgotten Leon Campbell's role in the plan.

'Leon...' he hesitated, not sure how his best friend would take it, 'Leon, is going to pull the trigger – he's going to fire the first shot in the battle of the Big Society fighting back.'

JB knew of Leon's cancer – they all did, he didn't know how long he had to live but it was safe to assume not long. Knowing Leon it would have been him who volunteered, Steve would never have put him up to it. JB could only admire Leon at that moment. He would go out of this world with a bang – literally.

Steve's iPhone jumped into life, *'The flowers are dead and gone behind the Eastville goals...'*

'Leon, what's happening?'

'At last the bastards have made contact. I've given them the details. They should be with you soon – any sign of Lewis yet?'

'No, fuck all.'

He considered telling Leon about the departure of George and Pete, but then realised it wouldn't serve any purpose – in a way it was probably better. They would be more in control of their actions, who knows what George was capable of with a gun anyway – he was bad enough with his fists. Steve didn't blame him or Pete for leaving for that matter, it was his battle and his alone, having JB and Leon on board was a bonus. He wouldn't forget them, The Big Five – now the one true Big Three.

'Hold on Leon, something's happening.'

304

Steve nudged JB. 'End of the road, battered old Transit. Can't imagine it's Samson's somehow.'

The Transit pulled up in front of the Audi, both front doors opened simultaneously, Lewis got out of the passenger side while Darren, the overblown skinhead from Lewis's club got out from the driver's side. Lewis walked towards the Audi while Darren disappeared around the back of the van and opened the rear doors – three meatheads got out, all similar build, all similar bloated faces. The faces of white, street fighting bully boys, one in particular caught Steve's eye – it was Garry 'Bulldog' Rattigan – ugly as ever, scowling as ever.

'It's Lewis and his cronies Leon. Just waiting for Samson now, better hang up. Good luck mate, take care.'

'You too my man.' The phone went dead.

Steve looked at JB. 'Get rid of the weapons John. Just sling 'em in the back. We'll do it our way – the right way.'

Steve put his hand in the pocket of his Harrington, removed the taser and discovered a small folded up piece of paper. He put the taser on the back seat next to the discarded gun and set of knuckles. JB shook his head but complied, he pulled the machete out from his waistband and placed it on the seat alongside the rest of the weapons.

'I'm keeping the CS gas, just in case.'

Steve nodded. 'Dib dib dib.'

A furrow crossed Steve's brow as he unfolded the piece of paper. He studied it then chuckled – it was a mobile number with *'Phone me big boy – Rog X'* written on it.

They opened the doors and walked towards Lewis, he held out his hand and greeted them warmly.

'Gentlemen, what a pleasure to see you again, keeping well I hope?'

Lewis was dressed in a dark blue woollen suit – probably Armani thought Steve. A pale yellow shirt and a matching silk handkerchief in his breast pocket completed the sartorial

305

ensemble. In the daylight he looked bronzed and his capped teeth shone pearl white, he was far removed from the street brawling Hells Angel of old. The avuncular well manicured raconteur was still there, Steve had to remind himself of what the man was capable of, think bolt cutters and toes, not fine clothes and expensive cologne...

'Vernon. Very well thanks. Looking forward to doing business?'

'Oh yes, I always look forward to business, especially business which makes me a lot of money. Talking of which – your friends from London not turned up yet?' He looked at his Rolex. 'I so dislike tardiness don't you?'

Steve nodded, he wasn't in the mood for small talk. He motioned over Lewis's shoulder. 'I see you've brought some friends?'

Lewis followed his stare. 'Oh them? Not really friends, just precautionary. You know how it is – better safe than sorry.'

Rattigan spotted Steve and JB and lowered his gaze, suddenly finding something of interest under his fingernails. He quickly disappeared into the building.

'How about you two? On your own?'

'Us, yeah, yeah – just us, like we said Vernon, we're just the middle men. Earl Samson is an old friend of ours, once we get the introductions over and done with it's up to you guys – I'm sure you'll be able to come up with some mutual agreement.'

Lewis nodded. 'So what's in it for you?'

The question caught Steve unawares. 'Us, um – well we'll take our commission naturally. But we, well let's just say we owe Earl – owe him big time.'

'Honesty amongst thieves eh? Admirable qualities – oh, it looks like they're here, nice British motor, looks like Mr Samson has good taste.'

Steve's heart lurched into his throat. The old memories, the old thoughts and the old hatred of Samson ran through his body. He hadn't met his old adversary for over thirty years but nothing had changed – he still loathed the man with a passion. Samson had taken his Kirsty all those years ago and now he had taken his daughter – he wanted him dead.

'Come on,' he said to JB, 'we need to get inside.'

Samson caught a glimpse of two powerfully built men hurrying into the building. There was something about one of them, the one wearing the red Harrington, the way he carried himself, something about his manner and his gait that reminded him of someone he once knew. He also vaguely recognised the building – he was pretty certain he'd organised a rave here back in the early nineties, he remembered doing well that night, E's and Acid were going down well, easy money, easy women, good music – good times.

Thomas eased the Bentley to a halt in front of the building, L'estrange exited the car which rose at least three inches once he got out, he waddled around the back and opened the other passenger door allowing his boss to step out. As Samson exited the car he trod onto a fresh turd as he did so, he at least hoped it was of canine origin but he doubted it.

'Fucking disgusting bastards.' He grimaced as he wiped his Church's brogues on the remnants of a patch of shabby grass.

'That's meant to be good luck boss,' said Thomas, 'or is that a seagull shitting on your head?'

Samson was tiring of Thomas's banalities. 'Shut the fuck up Trevor. Let's get this over and done with,' he snapped.

L'estrange and Thomas stood side by side behind their boss as they entered the building, all three gingerly watching their steps. Shafts of light entered through the broken windows, their entrance disturbed two pigeons from their courtship – causing them to flap and depart abruptly. Thomas kept a wary eye on them, hoping they wouldn't shit on his boss and make him even more pissed off than he already was.

The building seemed a lot smaller on the inside, it had rooms leading off the main open area that once echoed to the sounds of lathes, grinders and metal presses. At the far end of the building stood five men, the one at the front was immaculately dressed but a little tasteless thought Samson, behind him stood four meatheads, four white meatheads. Cheap leather jackets, jeans, boots – unshaven, unclean – Samson had no opinion of them, they were insignificant animal lowlifes with not an ounce of sophistication or style. The brute in front however was a totally different beast – Samson presumed he was Vernon Lewis – the enigmatic and elusive 'Venom'.

Over to Samson's left stood the two men whom he'd seen hurry into the warehouse as they pulled up, the garish red Harrington at odds with the dreary background. Next to him stood an ox of a man, upright and muscular, a touch of the military about him thought Samson, it was too gloomy to make out their faces, either side of them were shafts of light, Samson wondered if they had deliberately positioned themselves there. The silence was broken by Lewis.

'Well Steven, John – aren't you going to introduce me to our guests?'

Steven, John – Samson repeated the names in his mind, *Steven, John – Steve Allen, John Burston?*

'Vernon Lewis meet Earl Samson. Earl Samson meet Vernon Lewis.' The familiar Bristolian accent echoed around the warehouse.

It had changed somewhat, not so harsh, not so juvenile, but still distinct thought Samson, still Steve *fucking* Allen...

'And who might you be?' asked Samson, even though he knew exactly what the answer would be.

'Oh I think you know who I am Earl or should I say Ewart. It's Steve, Steve Allen – and you probably remember JB here, John Burston?'

'Of course, I'd like to say what a pleasant surprise but I'd be lying. It's got to be what... thirty odd years?'

'Something like that.'

'Still living in little ol' Bristol then? Still living in your big village that you were always so proud of? You two were always so, so parochial, so ... small time. I bet you're still having fisticuffs with the City boys at weekends aren't you? You know you really ought to move on – like me...' Samson was relishing his position, relishing showing them how he had made it to the big time.

'So what makes two narrow-minded, bigoted boot boys like you want to mix it with the criminal elite of the world?'

He was a little unsure of the situation though, he thought there was still a deal to be made, he could smell a rat of sorts but more importantly he could still smell cash, lots of cash in his nostrils. It was possible that these two were behind the deal, perhaps at last they had moved out of their small time villainy, their petty prejudiced violence and moved on to bigger things.

Samson glanced at Lewis who was uncharacteristically quiet. Lewis's henchmen, including Rattigan, surreptitiously fingered the assortment of knives and guns they carried, Rattigan was nervous, he was only along for the ride – he owed Lewis but he didn't fucking owe him this much.

'So what's this all about then Allen? I hope you haven't dragged me down here on some wild goose chase, the message I got was there's some business to be had here, big business. Somehow I can't see that it's with you or Burston so I take it it's with you Mr Lewis?'

Lewis shifted his weight from one foot to the next – he too was confused by the situation. Steve Allen had told him that Samson had been an old friend of his – but from the last couple of minutes it didn't seem that way, even so he was still eager to progress with the transaction.

'Correct. So now we've got the introductions out of the way shall we get down to business? Mr Samson... Bristol's the gateway to the West Country, I've been running the drug scene from here down to Land's End since you were in short trousers, you might think this is some sort of hick town but there's more old hippies and old bikers down here than the rest of the country put together, they alone contribute a great deal to my wealth.

'On top of that many of your relatives and colonial cousins have settled in Bristol as you well know, and well, we all know how partial people *like you* are to, shall we say, recreational drugs – some of my best customers are of, well, *your persuasion*. And of course now, just when *you people* were getting established, we get the Asians, the Somalians and the Eastern Europeans beginning to make a name for themselves, not that I can say any of these endear themselves to me, nor you dare I say. But business is business, so please Mr Samson, give me the respect I deserve and I'm sure we can have a long and fruitful relationship.'

If it was meant to be a speech to impress Samson it failed miserably. He was neither impressed nor intimidated, he did not like Lewis nor did he like his mannerisms or his cheap efforts at looking stylish – and he certainly didn't like his tone. If he was going to do business with him it would be on his terms.

'Okay Mr Lewis, you've made your little speech and I'm aware of your credentials but with all due respect, the West Country is not London.' *It's not even West Ealing*, he thought. 'We've got more dealers and users in London than the rest of the country put together, so I'm not getting involved in a game of top trumps to see who's the biggest dealer her. I'm dealing in the sort of shit and the sort of money that you can only dream of, which brings me to the point of this meeting, or so I'm led to believe. I'm always looking for different sources, different outlets, even I'll admit that London is getting a little… crowded, and yes there's so much crap out there, so little quality cocaine coming in from Columbia these days that yes, I'm looking for new suppliers, and if that means doing business with your Mr Lewis so be it – if the price is right, but tell me, there's one thing that's baffling me. Where the fuck did you get your Merck from – I thought I was the sole importer in the country, I wasn't aware you did business in Eastern Europe?'

Steve knew this was the seminal moment, the moment when the penny would finally drop, the vinegar stroke, the big kahuna, the whole enchilada, all wrapped up in one. He didn't have time to think of what his reaction would be, Lewis spoke – surprisingly there was no anger in his voice.

'Sorry, did you say where did I get *my* Merck from?'

Samson gave him a quizzical look, he was becoming agitated.

'Yes, *your* fucking Merck. The Merck you kindly gave my contact a sample of. I had it tested, very good it was too – if I didn't know better I'd say it was of the same quality and origin as mine. That was why I was so interested, so I'll repeat – where the fuck did you get your Merck from?'

Lewis looked at Steve Allen and John Burston, the two of them could smell the shit as it headed towards them.

'I was led to believe that we were brought together to discuss me obtaining this drug from you, I thought it was you who was going to be offering it to me – not the other way round,' he fired a look at Steve. 'Allen, can you explain – do you care to enlighten us?'

It was not so much a penny dropping, more of a manhole cover. Samson took a step towards Steve, he stood not six feet from him.

'So this rat I can smell, it goes by the name of Steve Allen – this is some set up, even by your standards. So you get me to come all the way down to Bristol to meet up with this, this old has-been Nazi here for what – a bit of light entertainment? Do you know what? What's the betting that bitter and twisted fucking bitch of a whore Kirsty Donohue and her dead druggy slag of a daughter are wrapped up in this somehow? After all these fucking years she's still got you believing all the crap, she's still got you right where she wants you, under her fucking thumb – am I right?'

Thirty plus years of regret and hatred spewed out from Steve, he didn't want to argue, he just wanted to lash out. He aimed a 'Bristol Kiss' at Samson's head, it was the same as a 'Glasgow Kiss' but fuelled with years of cider consumption. Samson had lost none of his street fighting skills, if Steve had thought Samson had got flabby with all the good living over the years he was mistaken, Samson deftly moved to one side, Steve's flying head butt only grazing his cheek, Steve lost his footing and tumbled to the floor at the feet of Tyrrel L'estrange who deftly let a telescopic baton fall from his jacket sleeve, he effortlessly extended it with one flick and within a second it was smashing down on the back of Steve's neck.

JB leapt forward and pulled the gas canister from inside his jacket pocket. He squirted it at L'estrange who immediately dropped the baton and clutched his face. He sank to his knees screaming – only to be dealt a kick to the head from JB's boot.

'Fucking leave it Burston – this is between me and Allen. I've been waiting for this moment for a very long time.'

At the far end of the warehouse stood a very perplexed and slightly amused Vernon Lewis together with his henchmen. Steve pulled himself up and glanced around, trying to get his whereabouts. He could see Darren had his hand inside his jacket pocket, Rattigan was ahead of him, he had a pistol of some sort already drawn, darting from figure to figure with it – even from this distance Steve could see he was shaking.

To Samson's right stood Thomas, he too had a pistol drawn, a sleek shiny silver one, it made Rattigan's look positively antique. He had it aimed at JB's head.

'C'mon Allen get up, have a go at ole 'Shiny' eh? That's what you used to call me wasn't it, 'Shiny Samson', and I don't think you were referring to my teeth were you? You racist fucker. Let's fight it out man to man, if you can call yourself a man that is.'

Steve rested on his knees, Samson stood over him gesturing him to get up, he'd casually removed his jacket and taken off his tie, this was to be a proper street fight, a bar room brawl – Steve had been in many over the years, Samson probably more.

Steve used his strong legs to propel himself upward, his head smashed into Samson's midriff, they both tumbled to the floor, rolled over several times and traded punches to the head, each time Steve connected he thought of Samson's words *'dead druggy slag of a daughter'* – that was his daughter he was talking about, he would make him pay.

The punches from both men were getting slower, less forceful, they both may had been stronger than in their youth but their stamina had gone.

Steve felt himself wheezing, at one point their faces were within inches of each other, he could feel Samson's heavy breath against his face – it smelt of garlic, expensive cigars and French wine, Steve had to end it just to get away from the odour, he sank his teeth into Samson's cheek, causing him to yelp in pain, his blood gushed and spurted over the both of them, it seeped into Steve's eyes and the two fell apart. Samson put his hand to his face – he was not impressed.

'You always were a dirty fighter Allen. What happened to your sense of fair play – your Queensbury rules?' He

313

wiped the blood from his face with the back of his hand, causing a diagonal smear of claret to form from his cheek down to his chin.

His hand disappeared behind his back, Steve could see he was reaching for something in his back trouser pocket, his hand appeared again, this time holding a knife. He heard the click as the switchblade came to life.

'Okay, two can play at that game,' he snarled. He took up the pose – legs apart and bent at the knee, his low slung body and low centre of gravity emphasised the street fighter that he was. The blood seeped down and stained his hand-made shirt, he menacingly motioned with the knife…

'C'mon then, let's see how dirty you can really get. C'mon Steve Allen, do this for Kirsty – that's what this is about ain't it? You never have forgiven me for fucking her and taking her away from you have you? You never liked the thought of my black cock inside of her have you? And boy did she like that black cock, couldn't get enough of it, better than that skinny ickle white man's dick that you got, eh? Well that's what she told me anyhow – and all me breddrin, oh yeah, you didn't know about that did you? She couldn't get enough of black meat inside her, if it wasn't me she was shagging it was my mates – and that reminds me, it wasn't just my mates she was shagging was it? Eh Burston?' He momentarily took his eyes off of Steve and focussed on JB.

Steve followed his gaze and stared at JB with as much hatred as he had at Samson. At the far end of the hall he could hear Lewis laughing out loud, it echoed around the building – he and his cohorts were actually enjoying the spectacle.

'Steve, mate – you know how it was back in those days, fucking hell we used to shag anything with a pulse. Mate, you was going through a bad time with her. She told me, she just needed someone, it didn't mean anything you know

314

she always loved you... fuck's sake Samson, I'd forgotten what a cunt you are!'

'Bigger than you two will ever realise!'

Samson roared with distinct glee in his voice, his head rolled back to laugh again and Steve took the opportunity to lunge at him. He made a grab for his right wrist to keep the knife at arm's length at the same time bringing his right knee up into Samson's groin, it winded him temporarily but he recovered and somehow managed to transfer the knife to his left hand – he slashed at Steve, cutting his face, an arc of blood spurted out forcing him to scream in agony. Samson transferred the knife back to his right hand and stabbed at Steve but he shifted position again and landed a couple of powerful punches to Samson's face, the knife dropped to the ground and Steve made a grab for it.

Samson was staggering from the powerful punches, Steve held the knife firmly in his hand, his anger and adrenaline told him to do it, he could finish him off... *JFDI – Just Fucking Do It!*

He launched himself at Samson. He thought he could see pleading in his eyes but he wasn't going to let up – three decades of hate would be ended right here, right now...

A lone shot rang out, rapidly followed by another two, three, maybe four. Steve both heard and felt the first one, he wasn't sure about the others, he heard noises, people shouting, he felt the bullet tear through his flesh, he'd never know pain like it, his legs crumpled and he staggered around like a drunkard on a Friday night bender.

He sank to his knees and a heavy darkness came over him – was it really going to end like this? As he fell to the floor he was surprised that he didn't feel any pain to his face as it smashed into the concrete.

CHAPTER NINETEEN

'STEVE, Steve Allen – can you hear me?'

He'd been hearing voices for what seemed like hours, some he thought were familiar others he couldn't make out at all. He tried to open his eyes but something appeared to be stopping them – they felt like they were welded shut. He had recurring dreams, but they weren't really dreams – they were more visions, then there were the memories, he saw the body of the Petrel crumpled on the pavement, he'd heard it shriek momentarily as it broke its neck when it hit the window – it landed at his feet with a dull thud. He saw burning crosses, white masks, marching boots and stiff right arm salutes, he saw a mirror with lines of cocaine on it, more than he'd ever seen in his life.

He heard Mick Jagger singing *Sister Morphine,* he heard the roar of a football crowd, they were chanting, chanting his name – *'One Stevie Allen, there's only one Stevie Allen...'* the roar subsided, it was now just a lone voice, a lone gentle voice, low, deep and velvety – he felt like he could physically climb into the voice and disappear, it was reassuring and comforting…

'Steve, Steve Allen, can you hear me? It's Sister Ekwinsi. How are you feeling?'

His mouth was dryer than a Saharan sand dune, he desperately needed a drink, he spoke through cracked lips, 'Sister…*Morphine*?'

'No Mr Allen, no more morphine. I'm Sister Ekwinsi but you can call me Edna. You're in hospital Mr Allen, the BRI – I'm afraid you're in a bit of a bad way.'

You don't fucking say, thought Steve… 'Can I have a drink Edna?'

'Here you go, here's some water.' She held a plastic cup to his lips, he sipped it and felt every drop going down his parched throat – it felt good.

'You've got some visitors Mr Allen, I'm sorry but they want to ask you some questions.'

The only visitor he wanted to see was Kirsty, he looked around the room in anticipation. There was no Kirsty – apart from Edna there was a uniformed PC and a large, slightly dishevelled man who looked like he needed both a bath and a good night's sleep. Steve had seen him twice before – once outside of Kirsty's apartment in the flesh and once on screen when he was fucking the living daylights out of her.

'Hello Mr Allen, I'm Simon Edwards from the Serious Organised Crime Agency, SOCA – we've met before I believe?'

Steve played dumb. It wasn't difficult in his current state – he shook his head and gave an unconvincing frown 'I, I don't recall – what's this all about?'

'Hmmm… what this is all about Mr Allen, is your involvement in what can only be described as a gangland altercation. I'd like you to tell me what you can recall – up to the shooting?'

Up to the shooting? Until this point Steve wasn't so sure what had happened to him. He remembered the fight with Samson and the slashing of his cheek, he was also aware he had a bandage across his face – he could feel the tightness of the stitches. He recalled having a knife in his hand and lunging towards Samson – then the shot and the pain in his shoulder…

'I, I don't know what you're on about... I've no idea of how I got here.'

'Oh is that a fact? Well let me give you some details and perhaps you would be so good to fill in the blanks for me – how does that sound?'

Steve nodded and then thought of the obvious question... 'Am I under arrest? Do I need a solicitor?'

'No you're not under arrest – yet. You're merely helping us with our enquiries, and it's entirely up to you whether you want a solicitor or not. Perhaps after what I tell you, you might decide you do need one. Okay?'

'Okay,' nodded Steve.

'You and at least one accomplice of yours, a John Burston, set up a three way meeting between yourselves, local property magnate cum major drug dealer Vernon Lewis and football agent cum major drug importer Earl Samson. The purpose of this meeting was to discuss the illegal importation and distribution of an illicit substance, namely Merck cocaine. Its presence has been known to us for a while, we have been monitoring its usage in this country for some time and been aware of Samson's involvement, therefore it came as a bit of a shock to us to learn of your association with him, and with Lewis for that matter. We couldn't work out how you and Burston – and your other mates – were tied up in all this... Don't take this the wrong way squire but it's pretty evident you're not major players in the British underworld, in fact you're not even players at all.'

Steve did not take it the wrong way, he was not offended. He was probably more relieved to think they were thought of in that way. It was evident though that they had been trailing him and the others for some time, he wondered just how much Edwards knew – he must have known about the involvement of Kirsty.

'We know you've had a few tugs over the years Allen, you and your mates. But you've been pretty clean for the last few years, upstanding citizens even. So what brought about this – this mixing it with the big boys?'

Steve remained silent, mulling over his response. He took the obvious route. 'I still don't know what you're on about.'

Edwards was not a patient man, his anger and agitation was obvious.

'For fuck's sake Allen, you're in shit street. You're in it up to your neck so don't give me all this crap.' He pulled out a notebook from his inside jacket pocket and quickly referred to it.

'I've got a John Burston, a George Smolinski and a Pete McNulty banged up in the cells in Bridewell and as soon as you get up out of bed you'll be joining them, so stop all this bullshit about not knowing what went on... you arranged a deal, it went tits up, you and some Cockney gobshite get shot and some local toe rag ends up on the mortuary slab so stop fannying me around!'

'Who – who died?' Steve suddenly thought there had been no mention of Leon Campbell. *Please don't let it be Leon.*

'A little shit called Gary Rattigan. No great loss I admit but I'm sure his mother loved him.'

I wouldn't bank on it. 'How – what happened?'

'Are you forgetting Allen, it's me asking the questions not you. So you tell me how all this came about and then I'll tell you what happened.'

Steve knew he was only delaying the inevitable, he could no longer continue with the charade, he would tell Edwards what he wanted to hear – within reason.

'Came about? Pretty much like you said – I got wind of this Merck cocaine, Earl Samson was selling and Vernon Lewis was buying. I just acted as the middle man – none of the others were involved. John Burston...' he abruptly stopped at the thought of his best friend fucking Kirsty...

'John Burston had nothing to do with it. He just happened to be there – wrong place, wrong time. There was a disagreement, a disagreement over price and it just kicked off. I ended up having a scrap with Samson, the rest as they say, is history.'

Simon Edwards leant over the bed – his face within inches of Steve's. Steve could smell the fags and mint imperials again.

'Bull-*fucking*-shit,' Edwards said in a barely audible whisper – he continued in the same low tone, 'next you'll be telling me Leon Campbell's whiter than white and Kirsty Clifton is a reincarnation of the Virgin Mary.'

* * *

JB paced around the dingy cell, it wasn't the first time he'd seen these familiar spartan walls and he had a feeling it wouldn't be the last. He recounted the previous day's events, the desertion of Smolinski and McNulty – although he didn't entirely blame them – and the fuck up when it all kicked off. In a way they got off lightly, when Samson's sidekick fired his gun at Steve, JB thought he was a goner.

He'd heard '*Stop armed police!*' just as the shot had been fired, then he heard a crack from Rattigan's pistol as he shot at the sidekick – him with all the gold teeth. There quickly followed a double bang, bang from the police marksmen as they felled Rattigan, next thing the place was swarming with the Old Bill and he was being bundled into the back of a meat wagon. *Fucking coppers – never around when you want them, and always around when you don't.*

The police and JB had no idea why Rattigan shot Trevor Thomas, but the marksmen weren't going to take any chances as to whether he was going to shoot anyone else. There would be an inquiry by the Independent Police Complaints Commission but the outcome would be inevitable – lawful killing of an armed suspect.

JB wondered what had happened to Leon. The plan was for him to hide in the building, they knew he was there, he'd told them as much when he phoned to let them know the meet was on, but from then on there had been no contact from him, perhaps he'd bottled it like the other two. Either way it looked like he'd escaped, that copper – Edwards, he'd asked about him. JB denied all knowledge of Leon, Edwards didn't believe him but it was clear they had no idea where he was – they had raided his house but he wasn't there. No sign of him – he'd just vanished.

JB would keep schtum. He was good at that – it was drummed into him in the Royal Marines. He remembered meeting some US Marines when he was stationed in Germany, although meeting was hardly an appropriate word, it was a punch up in a bar on the Reeperbahn, but fair play to the Yanks, they stuck to their motto *Semper Fidelis* – 'Always faithful', they stayed faithful to their fellow Marines and remained silent when the Red Caps came knocking. He would do the same, he would always be faithful to his mates, well apart from shagging Steve Allen's girlfriend, but that was over thirty-five years ago. He wouldn't grass on his mates and neither would they – they would stick together, even if they hadn't the day before, they would say fuck all and with a bit of luck get off with a bit of time and a slap on the wrist. Anyway hadn't Kirsty said the law were the good guys, she could pull strings – she would get them off.

* * *

The large frame of Edna Ekwinsi reentered the room. She was having no more of this treatment of one of her patients.

'That's enough for now gentlemen. Mr Allen has to get some rest. He's lost a lot of blood and a whole part of his shoulder. Please, he needs to get some sleep.'

Edwards gave the nurse a look that said I haven't finished, Sister Ekwinsi gave him a look that said *'I'm in charge. This is my hospital.'* Edwards was determined to have the last word, he stared unblinkingly at Steve.

'At least we've got Vernon Lewis and Earl Samson in custody – and this time neither of them is going to weasel out of this one. So perhaps your plan worked out after all.' He turned and walked out of the room, leaving Steve to his thoughts – his thoughts of Kirsty and how the fuck he'd got into this mess.

He had a fitful sleep, the painkillers helped but his thoughts mixed with his dreams and his nightmares, the Petrel with the broken neck and the shitty arse, his Harry facing a life of drug addiction and no hope, his fucked up marriage, his fucked up relationship with Kirsty, his dead daughter. The grandchildren he'd hoped for and now, now he wondered if he would ever even see them – *fucking Facebook, fucking, fucking Facebook. Mark Zuckerberg you're a cunt.* He wished he'd never fucking logged on.

Sister Ekwinsi woke him with a cup of tea and a radiant smile.

'Good morning Steven. Did you sleep well?' She reminded Steve of his mum, apart from the obvious. She didn't wait for his answer. 'I'm sorry but you have a visitor again.'

Standing behind her in the doorway was a uniformed officer and Edwards. He had washed, shaved and was wearing a new suit, *not a good sign,* thought Steve – for once he looked smart, alert and pleased with himself, making Steve feel distinctly uneasy.

'Steven Allen I'm charging you with the attempted murder of Earl Samson – you do not have to say anything but it may harm your defence if you do not mention when questioned something you later rely on in court. Anything you do say may be given in evidence.'

'You have got to be fucking kidding.' It was the only response Steve could muster – the officer noted it down in a pad.

'Do I look like I'm fucking kidding squire? And what's more that's just for starters. Before the day's out you can expect to be looking at illegal importation of a controlled drug, possession of a firearm and importuning.'

Steve looked at him quizzically before Edwards replied rhetorically.

'The loaded pistol in your car? Not to mention the taser, the machete and the knuckle duster – very 1970s. I'll tell you one thing, it's a good job you didn't use that shooter – would have taken your hand clean off.'

'Okay, okay. But what's with the importuning?'

'An incident at Tog Hill a few weeks back?'

'For fuck's sake, that was a wind up by my mates. It was fucking joke.'

'Do you see me laughing squire – it was still logged and I'm going to throw every piece of shit I can at you, I'm sure some of it will stick.'

Steve shook his head. 'I'm not saying another word until I get a solicitor.'

'That sounds like an admission of guilt. Get dressed – I'll give you five minutes.'

Despite the protests from Sister Ekwinsi, Steve was forced to dress and handcuffed to the PC. Debbie and his worried mother had called in to hand over some clothes and toiletries for him, they had momentarily seen him but at that time he hadn't regained consciousness, they were shocked and stunned by his appearance, his mother sobbed uncontrollably. She'd seen him beaten and bruised in the past but not to this extent. Steven's father had been right *'You're a bad 'un young Steven, you'll end up in serious trouble one of these days.'* His mother knew that this was that day.

Edwards escorted him to the police car and they drove the short distance to Trinity Road police station, on arrival he was taken into an interview room and introduced to a Detective Sergeant Shandra Kapoor of the Avon and Somerset Constabulary. There was also a duty solicitor waiting for him – he looked tired and weary and although only in his mid forties, his thinning hair and sallow complexion made him look a good decade older. In front of him was a battered, ancient laptop and several Styrofoam cups half filled with stale coffee.

It was now Sunday morning, two days after the events in Lewis's warehouse. The solicitor had been working through the night – stabbings, robberies, attempted rapes – standard Saturday night drunken violence. Steve wasn't impressed. He wanted his own solicitor – someone who looked like they at least would take some interest in his predicament and hopefully remain awake.

The solicitor was introduced, his name was Johnson. Steve didn't take any notice. 'I understand I'm allowed one phone call?' He asked of no one in particular.

'If you're thinking of phoning your girlfriend I wouldn't bother,' replied Edwards, 'she's in the next room.'

Steve slumped into the seat and leant on the table with his one good arm. *This is just getting worse by the fucking minute,* he thought dejectedly.

Edwards sat in the chair opposite Steve. He took out some cassette tapes from a drawer, unwrapped them and starting fiddling with an antiquated tape recorder that was covered with hand scrawled, grimy, little messages stuck on with Sellotape. Steve wondered how many confessions, sob stories, lies, boasts and bullshit it had recorded over the years.

'Okay gentlemen, shall we begin. For the record my name is Simon Edwards, I work for the Serious Organised Crime Agency, my rank is Grade Two.' He broke off sensing that Steve was mystified by his comments.

'Just to explain, SOCA does not have ranks as the rest of the police force, my colleague here is Detective Sergeant Shandra Kapoor, she is an officer working for the Avon and Somerset Constabulary and we are both investigating this case. The date is Sunday...'

There was a heavy knock on the door. A tall, rangy male in his early fifties entered, he had an air of authority about him and judging by the fact he didn't wait for an answer he was probably Simon Edwards and Shandra Kapoor's superior.

'Can you stop the interview Simon? I need to have a word,' he demanded. It was definitely not a question.

Steve wasn't one hundred per cent sure but he thought he heard raised voices from outside of the room. He could definitely hear Edwards's shrill Welsh accent getting stronger, he couldn't make out what they were saying but it didn't sound like they were discussing the weather. Steve looked at Kapoor and Johnson, they both shrugged as the door opened revealing a very red faced, irate Welshman. Edwards whispered in Kapoor's ear – she promptly got up and left.

Edwards didn't bother to take a seat. He stood in front of Steve with his hands dejectedly in his trousers pockets, he coughed and cleared his throat... 'Mr Allen, you are free to go.'

'You what? What's going on?'

'Never mind, just go – we, I shall be contacting you and your mates again so don't get so fucking smug. Just fuck off before I have a change of mind.'

Steve stood up while Edwards stayed rooted to the spot, his hands still thrust deep in his pockets which forced Steve to walk around him. Edwards nudged Steve's bandaged arm as he brushed past, he winced but he wouldn't give Edwards the satisfaction of knowing that it had hurt him.

'I haven't finished with you yet squire – this isn't over by a long fucking shot.'

In the reception area Steve was met by a beaming JB and shamefaced-looking George Smolinski. They hugged each other causing Steve to let out a yelp in pain.

'John, George – alright? What's happening? Where's Pete? Where's Kirsty – you seen Kirsty?'

'No, dunno – fuck knows what's going on,' replied JB, still unsure of the situation with either the law or Steve.

The door beside the reception opened again, Pete McNulty appeared with a PC beside him who ushered him out.

'Get your possessions from the Desk Sergeant then you're free to go.'

They shook Pete's hand. 'Alright mate, what have they said to you?' asked George.

'Nothing – I was sat in the cell then that Welsh knobhead just came in and told me I was free to go – how about you lot?'

'Same,' they all replied in unison.

'How about you Steve – alright? Heard you been shot?'

Steve half-heartedly raised his sling. 'Too right, passed right through my shoulder, lost a lot of blood but they reckon I'll be alright, should make a full recovery.'

'And your face?'

'Samson slashed me with a knife, just a flesh wound.'

'Sweet – it'll make you even more irresistible to the women you handsome bastard,' replied Pete.

Steve gave a sheepish grin. The only woman he could think about right now was Kirsty – he looked at John Burston. JB knew he needed to say something but he wasn't sure what. Whatever he said would be a sham, an inappropriate platitude.

'Good to see you Steve. Uh, about, about me and Kirsty...'

Steve shook his head.

'Forget it. Fuck me how long ago are we talking about?'

'Last week,' joked Pete, 'banged her over the bar in the Moon when you weren't looking.'

'You bastard – must have been when I was shagging your Sharon,' replied Steve, trying to make light of the situation.

They quickly signed for and collected their possessions – the Desk Sergeant stared at Steve and finally spoke.

'Don't I know you from somewhere?'

Steve shook his head while the others chuckled.

'Nah, must be mistaking me for someone else.'

'Yeah, like *Wayne Kerr*,' giggled George.

Steve gave him a sideways look – *okay joke's over*.

'I understand you still have a Kirsty Clifton in your custody.' He said, eager to get back to more important matters.

The Sergeant picked up a clipboard from behind him and studied it momentarily. 'What if we have?'

'Just wanted to know what's happening with her, when will she be released?' Steve presumed she would be, just like them. Then perhaps it would all become clearer.

'I honestly can't say but it doesn't look like she'll be joining you. She is still in custody and by the looks of it she'll be staying there.'

The conversation was interrupted by a cacophony of digital bleeps, buzzes and musical notes as their mobile phones rang simultaneously – two days' worth of messages, voicemails and missed calls from distraught wives, partners and mothers heralded their release.

'Sorry, sorry.' Steve fumbled with his phone and switched it back off. 'Look I really need to find out about Kirsty Clifton, that SOCA bloke, Simon Edwards – I need to talk to him. Please, it's important.'

The Sergeant didn't reply, he just picked up the phone and made a quick call. Almost instantly the door opened and Edwards appeared.

'I thought I told you to fuck off.'

Steve could see he was still angry, still red-faced, more Welsh now than a gathering of leek fanciers at an Eisteddfod.

'Look, I need to know what's going on. Kirsty told me you were one of the good guys. She had a lot of time for you – she even said you were helping her out. I know you were close at one time, please, I'm begging you – I need to know what's happening to her – is she alright?'

Edwards shook his head and ushered him aside.

'Look squire, no she's not alright, but I guess I owe you an explanation.' He reached inside his jacket and took out a business card which he handed to Steve.

'I can't talk now but here's my card, give me a call later – we'll have a catch up okay? If I was you lot I'd get my sorry arses out of here and get down to the nearest pub to celebrate. You've had the narrowest escapes of your lives believe me, now…'

'Yeah we know, fuck off – *squire*.'

The nearest pub made the black hole of Calcutta look like a West End cocktail lounge – they gave it a miss and jumped in a taxi and headed for the Moon. They caught up on their phone messages and placated their loved ones. Steve had message after message from Kirsty – all through Friday evening and the early hours of Saturday morning, they then stopped abruptly – probably when she was arrested he thought. He half-heartedly texted her back knowing full well she wouldn't read them until she was released – if she was ever to get released. He phoned his mother then Debbie, told them he was okay. He was desperate for a shower and a change of clothes, but even more desperate for a pint.

Over their drinks they recounted Friday's events, pieced together what they knew and surmised on the rest.

Samson and Lewis were in custody together with their henchmen, including the man mountain who JB had gassed. Rattigan was dead courtesy of the Old Bill and one of Samson's minder's – the one with the gold teeth who had shot Steve – was in a critical condition in hospital under armed guard.

'So apart from us all getting released, the other real mystery is what the fuck happened to Leon?' asked George.

'Dunno. Perhaps he bottled it and legged it like you two,' replied JB scornfully.

Steve had also wondered what had happened to his friend. The friend who he thought he knew, the friend who said he would help him out. He felt guilty that he'd asked Leon to get involved in the first place – it was not his battle, he had battles of his own to fight. Come to think of it, it was not his friends either, not JB, not Pete, not George – it was Steve's and Steve's alone. Not for the first time in his life was Steve Allen filled with regret and remorse.

'Yeah well, it worked out okay-ish so let's not go over that again. The thing is, the law know about him but not his whereabouts, so with a bit of luck he's on that cruise ship right now drinking a nice cold rum and coke, and I get the feeling that matey boy Edwards hasn't got a Scooby Doo about that... here's to Leon – cheers.'

They raised their glasses as one and toasted their absent friend...

'To Leon.'

CHAPTER TWENTY

THINKING it pointless going to Kirsty's apartment Steve got a taxi back to the family house. He knew Kirsty wouldn't be at the penthouse and what's more he had no idea when, or if, she would be.

Debbie greeted him with a kiss on the cheek. Harry was in bed asleep, Steve decided not to wake him even though it was two in the afternoon. He realised a shower was out of the question so he took a rather awkward bath and some-how managed to shave using his one good hand. He finally relented and asked Debbie to dress him, he only had the dregs of his wardrobe left – scruffy underwear plus a few old T-shirts and a couple of ill-fitting washed out jeans. Debbie took her time and fussed over him, making sure she didn't upset him. She didn't dare question him about the events of the last couple of days – she was just pleased to have her man, her husband, back home.

They crashed out on the settee like a normal lazy Sunday, he flicked through the papers and read of the shootings in a warehouse in Bristol – no names, no real details, 'black on black crime' the papers presumed. He took some painkillers and dozed off in front of the *Antiques Roadshow* – like he always did.

He awoke with a start, his iPhone playing the familiar tune. It was Barry Mason. *Fuck, fuck* – he'd totally forgotten about Barry and the deal he had with him.

'Steve, what's happening mate? You were going to give me a call, we got the presses ready to run. Is this story going to bed or not?'

'Sorry mate, it all went a bit Pete Tong but yeah, go. Go with the photos and the story exactly as I told you, but link it with the shooting that's in the news.'

'You what?'

'You've heard of the shooting in Bristol – one dead, two others shot and suspects in custody?'

'Yeah, but what the fuck has that gone to do with your story of Merck and the Premiership? We've had a press release from the Old Bill but it's all a bit sketchy, hold on I've got it here...'. The phone went dead for a minute. Steve could heard a rustling of paper.

'Steve... still there?' Barry asked but continued without waiting for a reply. 'Right, it says here that there was a shooting in Bristol on Friday afternoon – probably drugs related, they've called in officers from The Met who've been involved in Operation Trident which infers it's black on black. Let's see what else does it say, oh yeah... one was shot and killed at the scene by police marksmen, two others were also shot and there's another seven in custody... uh four got released today and the police are still looking for one other suspect who fled the scene – so what's the connection with your story, sorry I don't get it?'

Steve did a quick calculation in his head and counted up the numbers. Of the seven in custody, one had to be Kirsty, the one who had fled the scene was obviously Leon.

'Well one of the bloke's who was shot was me, the four that got released was me and my mates, y'unno John Burston and the others – you've met them. There's a massive story here, but just go with what I've told you for now but I dunno, mention that it's linked to the shooting in Bristol, no other paper will know that. I got to be careful but I should be able to tell you more later – just get that story out there.'

'Fuck me mate, you've been shot? I don't know what to say? Just take it easy yeah, give me a shout when you got some more info, sounds like this could be a biggie?'

'You could say that – I'll phone you later.'

As soon as he hung up, his phone burst into life again.

'Steve Allen? It's Simon Edwards. Fancy a beer?'

Debbie dropped him off at The Phoenix, a recently refurbished pub behind Cabot Circus in St Judes, not far from Trinity Road police station. How it had escaped the bulldozer no one knew, but Steve was thankful that it had. Edwards was waiting outside, pint of Stella in one hand, a lit Bensons in the other.

'Alright squire, what you drinking?' he asked.

'Whatever – pint of bitter.'

They sat down in a seat that had once belonged in the back of a 1970s Jaguar, all 420G tanned leather and distress marks – witness to the hundreds of rear ends that had no doubt enjoyed its comfort over the years. They nodded an insincere 'Cheers' to each other.

'So what's going on?' asked Steve, 'how come we got released?'

'Well if it was down to me you wouldn't have been. But certain events have taken over. Let's just say it all got a bit messy.'

'You're telling me.' Steve made a weak effort to raise his injured arm.

'I don't know what you lot think you were playing at. What were you trying to do? Be some sort of vigilantes dishing out retribution and revenge? And what's all this 'Big Five' lark? What the fuck's that all about?'

Steve thought he would be guarded with his answers – mindful that this might be some sort of set up. At the back of his mind he even wondered if Kirsty was still involved, perhaps still a colleague of Edwards in SOCA, and rather than being in custody she was coordinating this whole operation. *Was this being recorded?* Edwards could sense his hesitation.

'Look mate, this is all off the record. I'm off duty – this ain't no stitch up... look I'm not wired or anything.'

He stood up, opened his jacket and patted himself down. 'Trust me, I'm a good guy.'

'So I've heard... Kirsty told me.'

'Ah Kirsty... nothing burns as hot as an old flame eh Mr Allen?'

'So you know about me and her, what else do you know?'

'Okay, I'll tell you what we know seeing as you're not so forthcoming – then perhaps you can fill in the gaps. Alright?'

Steve nodded, took a swig of Doom Bar and waited to hear what he'd wanted for a while now – the truth.

'We know everything about you ... well nearly every-thing, there's a few missing pieces in the jigsaw, but we know about you and Kirsty Clifton and how she set you and your mates up. How she spilled the beans on your old mate Mike Cribb and how you nearly murdered the poor bastard. We know about how she talked you into her hair-brained scheme to get even with Earl Samson and Toby Ashurst. What we didn't know was why and how she managed to talk you in to it – we couldn't work out what hold she had over you to make you do this?'

Steve delayed answering, aware that Edwards was fishing. He would not make it any easier for him and gave a slight shrug of the shoulders.

'So how come you know about it all?'

'Well for starters, mobile phones – you know what they call them in the States? *Cell*-phones. That's cos every dumb fuck of a criminal who uses one usually ends up in one. So when we knew she was up to something we tapped her phone which led on to you, then on to John Burston and so on and so on – so we had all your calls, all your arrangements, the lot... well most of it.'

Steve suddenly thought of his calls to Barry Mason and how his paper would be full of the shootings and the links with Earl Samson and Toby Ashurst, he remembered he had called him from his landline, hopefully they hadn't tapped that. It was too late anyway, the presses were rolling and in a few hours the papers would be hitting the newsstands.

'So you know all about Samson and Ashurst – what they're involved in, the drugs – Merck and how it got Kirsty's daughter,' he hesitated, 'how it got *my* daughter killed.'

Now it was Edwards turn to hesitate. He held back for a second before speaking.

'Yes Steve we know all about what those two are up to, we and the Met and the Drugs Squad, not to mention the choirboys in Customs – we all know what they're up to. We've been investigating for years, since before the death of Kirsty's daughter last year. But she – Kirsty – fucked it all up then and she's very nearly fucked it all up again this time.'

Steve was aware it was the first time Edwards had called him by his first name. He didn't read too much into it, he sure as hell wouldn't refer to him in the same manner.

'How come? She told me she was set up. She said Merck was planted in her house, implicating her in Cherry's death. She said she was forced out – politics and all that?'

'That's mostly true, she was set up – but it didn't stop us investigating, investigating what is one of the biggest drug deals this country has ever seen. Ashurst did use his

334

influence but because Kirsty was poking her nose in where she shouldn't she made it easy for them to stitch her up. If she had just let it go, let the proper procedures take their course we would've had them by now – we already would've had them banged up.'

'Okay, so what's happening now? How come me and my mates got let off? How come I'm here with you now, chatting like a couple of mates over a pint?'

'Yeah well, you've got Kirsty to thank for that.' He reached for his Stella and took a sip – Steve thought that at long last he was getting near to the truth.

'Look Kirsty was a brilliant cop, one of the best. All that she said about how she got into the force, how she worked all hours to bring up Cherry on her own, that's all true – she had, still has a real head for figures, information, names – you didn't need a computer when Kirsty was around, she recalled everything, every detail, it was just her way.'

Steve remembered how as a teenager she was bright at school, how clever she was, especially at maths. But her dark side always seemed to win out – she left school with no qualifications and what seemed no hope.

'But this brilliance, well it just made her even more demanding of her colleagues. She judged everyone else against herself, so this mission of hers, yours... whatever you want to call it, she's deemed it a failure. Never mind we got two drug barons and their cronies in custody, to her it's a failure. So she's owned up to everything, confessed to everything, told us all we wanted to know. Told us about how she forced you lot into this scheme and how it was all her idea.'

'So what? You caught us red handed, me with a knife in my hand about to stab Samson, you got all the evidence you need to get at least me as well as Kirsty banged up – so how come me and my mates are in the clear?'

'Look, you know about Kirsty and Samson, the relationship they had?'

Don't remind me, that was how all this shit started.

'Of course I do, when she had Cherry and it was evident she wasn't his, he gave her a hiding and fucked off and left here to fend for herself.'

'Steve, look there's something...' he trailed off.

'Something what? What aren't you telling me?'

'Nothing, nothing – yes but after he fucked off, when she'd made it into the Met.'

'Yeah. What about it?'

'Well, when he found out about her working for the Met he got back in touch with her and in effect started black-mailing her. He made sure she covered up his crimes, destroyed evidence – bit like what she did for you and your mates years back eh?'

So the bastard does know – 'You know about that?'

'Well not at first, that was one of the missing jigsaw pieces. But she confessed all this yesterday. So we guessed it explained why you were willing to help her.'

'Well that and the fact that Cherry was my daughter.'

'Yeah well back to Samson and the hold he had on her. Course she's confessed to all this now, told us all about the evidence she destroyed, how she covered it all up – all under threats from Samson of course. If she hadn't had done what he told her, he would've exposed her. She would've been thrown out of the Met, probably got banged up herself. It just all escalated, she couldn't bear to lose Cherry, not after what she'd been through herself as a kid.'

'Tell me something I don't know.'

'Okay, so we know why she did it, to be honest back in those days this wasn't a rare occurrence, backhanders, brown envelopes, destroying of evidence – par for the course for the Met back then. Operation Countryman was a success, but it missed a hell of a lot of bad apples, including some of Kirsty's old bosses.'

'I don't think I like the way this is going.'

'I'll shut up now if you want?'

Steve shook his head, motioned to Edwards to continue.

'Tongues began to wag about Kirsty. Accusations about what she was up to with Samson, her bosses got to hear about it... but well, she was a looker – still is. I mean fucking fabulous back then. Do you need me to paint the picture...?'

'She screwed her way to the top?'

'I wouldn't put it like that exactly. She had a lot to lose – her bosses were blackmailing her as much as Samson was. She had to sleep with them or they would hang her out to dry. She had no choice – and now, well yesterday anyhow, she spilled the beans and turned the tables. She threatened to name all the head honchos who she's slept with over the years. Some of them are now Chief Constables – one of them is a Government minister. It was her turn to blackmail them and yep, she pulled it off. A few phone calls and you and your mates were off the hook – scot free.'

Steve felt numb, sick and betrayed. He let the enormity of the story sink in. He shook his head in disbelief and stared into his glass.

'This is doing my fucking head in – I just can't believe all the lies she's told me.'

'Yeah well, all cops are liars in some shape or form – goes with the territory,' Edwards said, matter-of-factly.

Steve looked at him quizzically then threw him a curveball. 'Well that's an Epimenides paradox if I ever heard one.'

'Eh? What the fuck does that mean?'

'Epimenides was a Cretan philosopher – he said "All Cretans are liars".'

'You've lost me squire.'

'That statement uttered by a Cretan, or you, is true if and only if, it is false.'

Edwards rolled his eyes, now it was time for his head to spin.

'Whatever – all fucking Greek to me. Anyway thought we were here to discuss Kirsty Clifton?'

Steve could never resist proving his intellect, it was something to do with his upbringing – even at a time like this he had to score points. Oneupmanship confirmed he got back to the matter in hand.

'So where does that leave her? If she's threatening to name names presumably she'll also be walking soon?'

'Hmmm, not so sure.' Edwards rubbed his chin, 'I mean some of the stunts she's pulled are just too big to turn a blind eye to, and at the moment... well she's holding her cards closer to her chest than a thalidomide poker player. Apart from insisting you guys walked free in return for her not revealing her past... her past lovers, she's not saying a lot. But we can't just ignore all of her indiscretions, for starters there's the gun she handed over to you.'

Steve briefly thought Edwards could give Pete McNulty a run for his money in the non-PC joke department – then his thoughts turned to the Sig pistol she'd given him. The last time he saw it he was handing it over to Leon, on his insistence. He hadn't spoken to him since Friday and they were due to fly out for the cruise on Saturday – he presumed he would now be sunning himself somewhere in the Caribbean.

'You know about the gun?'

'Sure do, we found it in one of the side rooms of the warehouse, just dumped there on the floor – got a feeling you know more about it than you make out. Presumably it ties up with your missing mate Leon Campbell?'

It was now Steve's turn to pull a poker face. He shrugged and shook his head.

'No use denying squire. We know him and his missus are on the Azure Princess sailing around the Caribbean, we've also spoken to his doctor so we know about his cancer – only about six months to live apparently?'

'So?'

'So let's just say the Scottish authorities aren't the only ones who can be compassionate. Only we got it right and they got it wrong.'

Steve creased his forehead and gave him a quizzical look.

'al-Megrahi?'

Steve nodded, he got the picture.

'Keep up Mr Allen. Oh don't worry we'll nick him as soon as he gets off the plane, but for now, we'll let him enjoy his little sojourn in the sun with his missus eh? Holiday of a lifetime huh? He got that one right... so this gun – it went missing from a Kurdish drug baron's house in North London a few years back. We've already done some forensic tests on it, we're waiting on the results but we're pretty certain it can be linked to at least five murders since she took it, murders that haven't been solved – up until now that is.'

'I don't get it. Why? Why would she have taken the gun? What was in it for her?' He had a sudden chilling thought. 'Five murders with this gun? Are you saying Kirsty has been involved in them?'

'No, no, of course not. Well not directly.'

Steve suddenly wondered just how much she'd done for Samson.

'Samson?'

Edwards nodded. 'We think so – she stole it for him or at least for his cronies to use. So the ironic thing is, she wanted you to get rid of Earl Samson with the very shooter that has earned him his reputation in the underworld.'

'That was some hold he had on her.'

'Sure was, but it obviously just got deeper and deeper for her. She was desperate to keep her job and more importantly desperate to keep her daughter, he knew that. He kept going back and kept blackmailing her for years. Without Kirsty helping him out he would not be the powerful figure he is now – all those years of guilt came out and now, well now it

339

looks like she's facing up to her responsibilities. I think she's going to go down, go down for a long time.'

Steve bowed his head. He knew he couldn't take much more, the gun still baffled him. 'So how come the gun was back in her possession again?'

'Well we know she was also close to one of Samson's sidekicks, one of his trusted henchmen. She had him in her pocket – we can only guess as to why or how. Perhaps she was just biding her time, waiting for the moment when she could exact her revenge, waiting for the time to make contact with you.'

Illicit thoughts flooded through Steve's mind once more, he quickly tried to dismiss them. Edwards continued.

'She used him to keep an eye on Samson – you know, keep your friends close and your enemies even closer – think he had designs on taking over from him one day, he probably thinks that day has come, but it's only a matter of time before we nail him as well. She must have called in her favours with him and it seems like he got the gun back to her.'

That explains how Kirsty had got the message to Samson about the meet with Lewis thought Steve.

'This is just too much, you know what I think about Kirsty, she meant everything to me – when she came back into my life after all these years... well I couldn't believe my luck. We spoke about getting a house together, she said we would be able to get custody of the grandchildren, our grandchildren, it just all made sense – I can't believe it's all turned out like this.'

He shook his head once more...

'It's a fucking nightmare.'

'Steve, she was using you. Trust me I know, she's not what she seems – I don't know if you know about me and her...'

Steve knew alright, he couldn't get the images of Edwards and the woman he loved, who he thought he loved, out of his mind.

'Oh I fucking know alright, I... I saw the fucking video.'

'Bollocks. How? How the fuck did she let you see that?'

'She didn't, she doesn't know anything about it – I presume you filmed it without her consent?' Steve could barely contain his anger.

'Look mate, sorry, sorry – it was a few years back. We were an item for a while – until it got too hot, can't say relationships are encouraged in the force for obvious reasons and especially with her being my boss. But it wasn't a one night stand or anything, we, we had some good times Steve. I thought a lot of her, still do – that's why I'm as angry about all this as you are, that's why I'm here now, telling you all about it. I feel just as sick about all this as you do.'

'How can you? You can't possibly feel the same – it was much more than that for us.'

'I know. She often spoke about you. She told me you were her first love. I know how much she thought about you.' He said this hoping it would make Steve feel better.

'Steve, she loved you like no-one else. That's a fact mate.'

'Don't you fucking *mate* me, you're no mate of mine – and you never will be. I mean for fuck's sake why did you have to video yourself shagging her? And why did you give it to her? I bet it's really done the rounds eh? Showed all your fucking mates down the nick, what's the betting it's on Redtube eh?'

'Sorry, sorry – it's not, and no else has ever seen it, I promise – that was the only copy. That was why I sent it to her. I should have fucking destroyed it and you would never have known about. I feel sick now – I never thought you would see it.'

341

'Yeah well I did, she gave me the memory stick, she didn't ... she still hasn't got a clue about the video's existence.'

'Good, thank fuck for that,' Edwards hesitated for a second, 'so how come she gave *you* the memory stick?'

A thought crossed Steve's mind, he turned the tables. 'Never mind that, how come *you* gave *her* the photos? She gave me the impression you were in on this, that you were actually helping her to nail Ashurst and Samson... something's not quite adding up here is it? It sounds to me like you were in on her plan as well, you knew exactly what was going on. You knew full well she was going to recruit me and my mates. You wanted us to nail them two 'cos you lot were incapable of doing it yourselves – you were setting us up to do your dirty work...'

'Whoah, whoah, whoah – you pal, are talking a load of bollocks. I did it as a favour. Kirsty asked me to keep her updated that's all – and that's all I did, keep her updated. Fuck knows why I did it, fucking wish I hadn't now, perhaps all this shit would never have happened if I hadn't – and you still haven't answered me, how come she gave you the memory stick?'

Steve was placated for a while and realised the ridiculousness of his accusations. He then thought about the photos that would appear in the *Daily News* tomorrow morning and wondered what Edwards' reaction would be when he saw them. He was past caring – he couldn't give a rat's arse what Edwards would think about the retouched photos.

'I asked for them. I thought I could do a bit of work on them. You'll see, perhaps sooner than you think.'

'What do you mean "do a bit of work on them"? What have you been up to?'

Steve shrugged and changed the subject once more... 'I need to see her.'

'You can't. I mean she doesn't want to see you.'

'Why the fuck not?'

'Probably too ashamed – she realises she's dropped you and your mates in the shit, she just used you to carry out her dirty work, there's no more to be said. She's going to carry the can for it all, probably go inside for a few years. Basically she's fucked.'

'Look, like I said, she didn't exactly have to twist my arm – and what about me getting Vernon Lewis involved, that was nothing to do with her. It got personal between me and him. I ought to be taking the rap for him at least, that was nothing to do with her. And you keep forgetting that Cherry was my daughter as well – not just Kirsty's.'

There was an uncomfortable silence not for the first time that evening. Edwards had visibly squirmed when the subject of Cherry came up.

'Yeah well... Lewis was a bonus for us. The fact that he was boasting of his involvement in the drugs trade was even better, we got it all on tape...' He stopped abruptly, suddenly realising he'd said too much.

'You got his little speech in the warehouse on tape – how come?'

'Rattigan, we had him wired. Luckily when he got shot by our marksmen the recorder wasn't damaged. I told them to aim for his legs if it all kicked off.'

'So what happened?'

'Bad day at the office – took his head clean off.'

Steve made a vomiting motion. Edwards rolled his eyes and continued...

'We knew all about the meet thanks to your phone calls and Rattigan's been on A&S's radar for years. He was a known associate of Lewis so we offered him a deal.'

'Yeah a deal that cost him his life. Sounds like another fuck up to me. I'm baffled though, let's just say Rattigan and me, we weren't exactly the best of buddies, well we used to be. But the last time I saw him I punched his lights out. I

343

can't work out how or why he shot Samson's sidekick – if he hadn't done that I could well be lying on the mortuary slab and not him.'

'Dunno. Perhaps it was a final act of friendship – perhaps he was genuinely trying to help you out. Either way we managed to pick up some good stuff from the tape including Lewis clearly saying...'

Edwards stopped and surreptitiously looked around the pub before continuing. 'We got him saying "shoot the nigger", so that's something else we got against Lewis, incitement to murder – and what with the racist inference and his links to the far right that's him banged to rights. Of course the half a kilo of Merck we found in the transit will be the final nail in the coffin for him – so job's a good 'un.'

Steve was now more confused than ever. The furrows in his brow were deepening by the second.

'But he didn't have any Merck. That was the point of the set up – he thought he was going to be buying and Samson was going to be selling – Samson just wanted to know where Lewis supposedly got his Merck from, but it was non-existent.'

'Yeah well, let's just say some of the things Regan and Carter got up to in the seventies haven't entirely died out.'

'You mean you…'

'Means to an ends squire, means to an ends. And besides, it was some of Samson's, that we er, somehow acquired in the first place, so the intent was there.'

Steve shook his head, partly in admiration and partly in bewilderment. He brought the conversation back to the Merck that Kirsty had given him.

'Kirsty had a half a kilo in her apartment. I took a sample of it to Lewis, he had it checked. He told me it was the real deal. Kirsty also said she'd sent some to Samson, she said, no sorry, she intimated that her colleagues in SOCA – by that I take it you – had supplied her with it?'

344

'Like I said all this inference that SOCA were involved in her scheme is bullshit, total bullshit – just another ruse of hers to get you on her side, I told you she was devious. She obviously thought if she mentioned our involvement that it would seem all this operation was legit. Some sort of street justice sanctioned by SOCA. We might bend the rules a bit but there's no way we would get involved in a stunt like that. And another thing...'

By now Steve was used to these 'other things' that kept cropping up, all these truths and half truths of Kirsty's that turned out to be nothing but lies, he couldn't believe how much he'd been deceived by her.

'That was no half a kilo of Merck in her flat.'

'But I saw it. Saw it with my own eyes.'

'No you didn't. You saw a brown parcel taped up to look like illicit drugs. It was just a bag of Homepride. We found it when we searched her apartment yesterday, the only thing that was good for was baking a decent cake. The sample she gave to you and which she sent to Samson was her own, or at least Cherry's from a year or so back.'

'But I thought she never did gear, she gave me a right ear bashing about my...'

'About your habit? Course we know about that. How do you think we know about your connection with Rattigan? But no you're right Kirsty didn't do drugs, but Cherry shoved more stuff up her nose than a supermodel on her hen night. She was right into it thanks to Samson and Ashurst – they used to have parties at Ashurst's apartment in the City that had more drugs than a Boots warehouse – well they were more like orgies judging by the stories we've heard. Course that's how she ended up with those kids of hers...'

'The twins? How do you mean – are you saying they aren't Ashurst's?'

Edwards was at the point of no return – he stood at the edge of a gaping precipice, a precipice that both he and Steve

Allen were about to plunge into. He looked at Steve, then at his pint of bitter.

'Do you drink anything stronger than that old man's stuff?'

'Yeah, Appleton's rum. Why?'

'I'll get you a double.'

CHAPTER TWENTY ONE

S TEVE had a distinct sense of *deju vu* as he nursed his bruised right hand and inspected the damage to his face in the mirror – it was not a pretty sight, Edwards could sure pack a punch – and him with only one good hand made it a bit of an uneven contest. The fact that he'd landed at least two good punches on Edwards' chin before he'd responded was some cause of celebration – but not much.

It was Monday morning. He took his tablets again like he'd done for the last few years, plus the Tramadol that the hospital had given him and a couple of Dichlofenacs that he found in the back of the medicine cabinet. He washed them down with strong black coffee, he felt no better – in fact he felt like vomiting.

He took his coffee out to the garden which seemed strangely empty without the dogs, he would make a point of visiting his mother later and picking them up. They had probably ate her out of house and home anyway – as much as she loved them she would be glad to see the back of them.

The night before had gone from bad to worse. Kirsty had been a consummate liar, not only to him but to herself. The lies about her involvement with Samson, the lies over the gun and the drugs had floored him, but the revelations about Cherry and her children had kicked him when he was down and left him gasping for air.

'Cherry is not your daughter,' Edwards had said. The two angelic blond haired children Steve had seen in the photo frame at Kirsty's apartment were not his grandchildren – Edwards didn't know whose children they were, she'd probably cut the photo from a magazine.

'Kirsty had Cherry in October 1980. Do the maths squire.' Edwards almost taunted him with it. Shortly after he spoke Steve had thrown two quick punches to his jutting jaw.

Kirsty and Samson had left Bristol in 1978, Steve knew to the day the last time he and Kirsty had made love. They'd got back together *'just for a catch up, just as friends'* but they had fallen into each other's arms and made frantic, explosive passionate love to each other – well as frantic, explosive and passionate it could be in the back of his 1973 1600E Ford Cortina – the date was etched into his memory, 30 August 1978.

She left Bristol with Samson twenty-four hours later. The next time he was to see her was just three weeks ago, three weeks that had changed and totally wrecked his life. He now had to survey the damage, perhaps try and put his life back together again – perhaps there was nothing to put back together.

She had not lied about one thing. The child she had, the one she christened Cherry, was not Samson's – in fact she didn't know whose child it was. She had an idea, maybe a dream that it was that West German diplomat – the one she'd picked up in Belgravia. They had sex in a five star hotel in Mayfair on a huge bed with feather pillows and Egyptian cotton sheets. He was tall, handsome and very striking, he reminded her of Steve. He'd treated her really well – unlike some of her clients, she actually felt like she was making love – making love to her Steve.

What's more he gave her a huge tip for not using a condom – she really quite fancied him, but truth be told if it wasn't him it could have been any one of the punters who fucked and abused her up against a wall down some piss-stained, grubby alley in Shepherd's Market.

Of course her pimp Samson wasn't happy. Never mind the little blonde-haired bastard wasn't his, it took his prize asset, his income stream, his cash cow – Kirsty, off the streets. How could she have been so stupid? She hadn't lied about the beating though, he gave her a hiding she would never forget then left her on her own, on her own with her newly born bastard.

He went off in search of another young blonde girl to replace Kirsty. It didn't take him long, the early eighties were a time of recession and hardship – he found her wandering alone around Soho. She was called Tracey and was from Barnsley, she did well for him, made him money and it wasn't long before he'd forgotten all about Kirsty Donohue – until he heard about her job in the Met that is.

So the blackmail went on for a few years, long enough for Samson to climb up the criminal ladder, then he gave her a respite – until he saw the wedding photos of Cherry Clifton and Toby Ashurst, son of Lord and Lady Ashurst, in *Hello*. There in the photos to the right of the bride was Kirsty, smiling proudly alongside her daughter and her new son-in-law.

It was time to take their relationship to another level, the introduction to Ashurst, the membership of Fitches, the days out at Ascot, Henley and the box at Stamford Bridge. Ashurst and Samson got on surprisingly well considering their different backgrounds, of course they shared a commonality – drugs united them, drugs made them happy, but most importantly drugs made them wealthy.

Samson sourced the Merck while Ashurst collected and delivered it – courtesy of his parents' private jet. Footballers, actors, models, media men, politicians, City fat cats in the Square Mile and Canary Wharf – they were all clients of Ashurst and Samson enterprises.

But then Samson got greedy. Not over money or drugs – he wanted something Ashurst had, he wanted it badly, he needed it, it reminded him of his past. He wanted Cherry – he got Cherry.

Not that she knew much about it. She was off her face, comatosed courtesy of Cristal and Merck during one of their many drug fuelled parties. Samson forced himself upon her but she didn't know or care, in another room her husband was spit-roasting some pretty young brunette from Loughton in Essex who had just appeared in *Loaded*. Facing him was a pony-tailed and heavily tattooed Spanish foot-baller who had cost his new club in the region of twenty-five million pounds. Nine months later Cherry gave birth to twins – a girl she named Olivia and a boy named Oscar. They were healthy, beautiful and black – they were Earl Samson's babies.

Ashurst kicked her out and she and her children moved in with Kirsty. At the time of her death Cherry and Ashurst were in the throes of divorce, but because of her addiction they remained in contact and she still attended his depraved and immoral parties at his apartment, including the one which ultimately caused her death when Ashurst not only supplied her with drugs but also sodomised her with a Merck-coated dildo.

When Cherry died, just after the twins' second birthday, Kirsty's life fell apart. The rest Steve knew about, except the 'grandchildren' weren't in the custody of Lord and Lady Ashurst. Toby Ashurst and his parents couldn't disown them quick enough – they were now in the care of Notting Hill Social Services – and fostered out to a loving couple living in Pimlico by the name of Claudette and Brevitt Sutherland.

* * *

Steve finished his coffee and strolled around his 'manor'. 'I'm just going down the shops to get a paper love – anything you want?'

Debbie wondered why he was buying a newspaper, he usually read them online these days but she guessed he just fancied the walk. He bought a copy of the *Daily News* – Barry Mason had done his job, beneath the headline of '*Premier league drug shame*' ran the story as Steve had told him – and more. The involvement of a '*high profile football agent known as Mr X and a City financier known as Mr Y, who was heir to a country estate*' filled the front page as well as double page spreads on pages pages two, three, four and five.

The revelations of Merck cocaine and how it was undetectable in the human bloodstream was accompanied by graphics showing the route from Eastern Europe to a private airfield in Buckinghamshire. From there, arrows spread out across the country to the major cities of England.

There were also references and quotations attributed to Keith Richards and Sigmund Freud, who in 1884 waxed lyrical about his experience of Merck: '*...exhilaration and lasting which in no way differs from the normal euphoria of the healthy person...You perceive an increase of self-control and possess more vitality and capacity for work... In other words, you are simply normal, and it is soon hard to believe you are under the influence of any drug... Long intensive physical work* is *performed without any fatigue... This result is enjoyed without any of the unpleasant after-effects that follow exhilaration brought about by alcohol... Absolutely no craving for the further use of cocaine appears after the first, or even after repeated taking of the drug...*"

The front page featured Steve's retouched photo of Mr X and Mr Y together, wearing expensive suits and snorting white powder from a mirror at a party – their faces carefully blacked out.

The inside pages featured more of Steve's handiwork showing the same two men – in one it showed them coming out of Fitches gentlemen's club together, but the one Steve was most proud of was of the two men shaking hands in front of their cars at Stamford Bridge. The number plates and their faces were also blacked out, but Samson's Bentley Flying Spur and Ashurst's Porsche 911 Carrera were there to be seen and recognised by those in the know.

The paper claimed it had 'evidence' of systematic and prolonged Merck use in the Premiership and that it would go on to name the guilty players in forthcoming editions – they didn't but Steve knew the inference was enough. The most hard-hitting and damning indictment in the paper came from the editor-in-chief Suzanne Viljoen, her opinion piece pulled no punches and went for the jugular of the Premier League:

'Today, the Daily News breaks a story that will shock the high-octane, highly-paid world of top-flight professional football to its very core. It gives us no pleasure to tell honest, hard-working football fans how their heroes, managers and coaching staff have become involved in a deeply seedy underworld of hard drugs, bribes, prostitution, violence and intimidation. The talented multi-millionaires who thrill whole nations every Saturday have become nothing more than a gang of drug-addicted hooligans, no better than the very worst examples of those who claim to support them. In short, the Daily News today announces the violent, squalid and brutal death of the Premier League.

We do not make this statement lightly. This paper has provided the best in sporting coverage, especially of pro-fessional football, from the day it was founded in 1921. But at no other time in the past has the national game sunk so low. During our investigation we found that drug-taking and corruption was rife. Barely a club remains untouched by the antics and criminality of those who wear their shirts. There are many players who imported their appalling behaviour to previously trouble-free clubs during the transfer season. There are others who stayed at their preferred clubs, and took delight in corrupting young, highly-impressionable players new to the glittering, have-it-all world of the Premiership. There are managers who turned a blind eye, agents who accepted staggering bribes, WAGs who blatantly slept around to procure the insidious drug known as Merck, which is at the dark heart of the Premiership scandal.

No doubt there will be highly-paid lawyers sharpening their quills. Let them take all the legal action they like, for they will fail. The Daily News has left no stone unturned in its efforts to root out criminality from every corner of the dressing room. We have recorded evidence; phone conversations, video, photographs and emails. We have sworn and signed statements. We have enough evidence to rattle the gates of every mock-Tudor mansion from Ascot to Alderley Edge. For those now feeling the uncomfortable breeze of truth, make no mistake – in the coming weeks we will publish every last scrap.

This is not the end of professional football as we know it. There are many decent, honest players – particularly among the lower leagues – who will be as horrified as we were at the revelations. It is these players who will form the backbone of English football's new beginning, the re-emergence of a game that places fair play, on and off the field, as its cornerstone. We hope we will be supported by such players, their clubs and their managers and, most of all, by the fans. We know they will be devastated by today's news. We ask them to stand firm, hold their nerve and remain true to the founding values of their clubs – values that will rise once again from the ashes of the English Premier League.

The article finished with 'STOP PRESS: As the Daily News went to print last night we have learnt from a source within the Avon and Somerset police that the football agent known as Mr X is helping them with their inquiries into a gangland shooting in Bristol which left one man dead and one other with life threatening injuries. We are also led to believe a large amount of Merck cocaine was seized at the scene.'

Social networks went into meltdown as Ashurst and Samson's names flew across cyberspace and unnamed foot-ballers issued super injunctions through richer by the minute lawyers and solicitors. By the end of the day transfer requests and torn up contracts were as common as wasps in a baker's window on a summer's day.

A pretty brunette from Essex who went by the name of Amber O'Toole appeared on TV claiming she was gang raped at a party a few years ago by the man known as Mr Y and a well known Premiership footballer. She remembered 'the posh bloke' had a small tattoo on his hip – it was in Latin, he'd told her it was their family's motto. 'My dad's got a motto,' she'd told him, 'never wipe your arse with a broken bottle,' she giggled.

According to her newly appointed publicist Cliff Maxwell, 'this aristocrat known as Mr Y plied Amber with drink and drugs before assaulting her and we shall be cooperating fully with the authorities to bring this deviant to justice.' Of course what he really meant was '*I shall now get Amber into as many lads' mags as I can and hopefully on to a reality TV show, and if Toby Ashurst wishes to settle out of court I shall be more than willing to negotiate on Amber's behalf.*'

Steve phoned Barry Mason on his mobile, predictably he was busy. Steve left a voicemail: 'Mate, it's the worzel here, what can I say, brilliant mate, just brilliant – give me a call when you can.'

He switched on his TV – Sky News featured the story in full, they had live links outside Wembley Stadium, the House of Commons and the Professional Footballer's Association office in Manchester. According to the news reader Mr X and Mr Y had already been named on Twitter and rumours circulated on Facebook over what players and which clubs were involved. It would only be a matter of time, perhaps just days before players as well as Samson and Ashurst were named.

There were already uneasy mutterings coming from the Premiership's main sponsor and Sky itself was getting twitchier by the hour. Club sponsors were issuing statements declaring that they were reviewing their deals with their respective clubs, naming rights were put on hold and individual player's sponsorship deals were torn up and cancelled.

No player was above suspicion – the inference was clear, trophies had been won fraudulently by cheats who relied on drugs to enhance their performance. The Premiership had been the flagship of the Football Association, held up to the world as the finest league on earth – it was now sullied, tarnished and debased. The game had been abused by the very players who owed their living and existence to it – the players whose greed and selfish cravings had now brought the beautiful game to its knees.

Steve's mobile played his song again. It was Barry returning his call. 'You've done it mate, you've fucking done it!'

'Baz, calm down, calm down. I've done what?'

'The Premiership – you've fucked it. You've fucked up the Premiership. Believe me mate, it's gone, it's fucked. We've got it back, the fans have got it back – trust me. This is, this is like the Berlin Wall of football coming down, this is a great day – football's going back to its roots. Football really is coming home – we've won!'

'Feels like a bit of a hollow victory to me, should do for you too, what with Rangers just getting promoted?'

'So what? We'll be down next year anyway – but think of it. The game will be reclaimed by the fans, the real fans. With a bit of luck all the glory hunting, middle-class, replica shirt wearing Johnny-come-latelies will fuck off and find another past-time to spunk off over. No more prawn sandwiches and Chardonnay, it'll be back to pies and Bovril – and kick offs at three o'clock on a Saturday, wahoo!'

'Nice thoughts mate, but I wouldn't bank on it. One step at a time eh? Talking of which, what you planning for tomorrow's edition and where the fuck did you get all that other stuff – all that "bribes, prostitution, violence and intimidation" – I only told you about the use of Merck cocaine?'

'Yeah well – journalistic licence. We did some real digging, set up some meetings. I'll tell you Stevie, these modern day footballers, they ain't no Pat Nevins, they're as thick as shit and as greedy as buggery. They'll tell you any-thing if you shove a suitcase full of money under their noses... you've heard of all that fake sheik stuff? Well we went one better, we set up an "imitation nation" – told 'em we were representing a new oil rich Balkan state with an oligarch in charge who made Abramovich look like a pauper. Offered them big money if they come to play for his new plaything of a football club in Zhivistan.'

'So, I don't get it – how did you get them talking? How come they spilled the beans on the carryings on in the Premiership?'

'Simple. We told them that our oligarch wanted his team to be competing in the European championships within two years – and he would achieve that no matter what the cost. We dangled the carrot to them that certain "performance enhancing drugs" would be available, in other words we told them that we had Merck on tap. Well the muppets fell over themselves telling us that wouldn't be a problem as they were already on it! Course we laughed and joked about it, then they told us all the other sordid tales of the prostitutes and orgies. We got it all, clubs, names, agents, managers – the whole shooting match, they're fucked, totally fucked.'

Barry couldn't contain his delight, it was what he'd become a journalist for, Steve wasn't so sure.

'Baz, haven't you heard of injunctions? The lawyers will be going apeshit.'

'Fuck the injunctions, fuck the super injunctions. That's the beauty of social networking mate, we just need to *imply* we have the names and the stories and then let Facebook and Twitter do the rest, job done.

'You wouldn't believe the stories that are now coming out... We got other names, not just footballers. We got actors, politicians, not to mention financiers linked to Toby Ashurst – just think how the public will respond to this. It'll will make MPs fiddling their expenses look like kids being caught with their hands in the cookie jar – and as for those City fat cats spending their bonuses on drugs, those bastards in the Square Mile have only just recovered from causing the credit crunch – they'll get a right kicking believe me... Steve mate, sorry I got to go – I got the BBC on the other line. Laters.'

Steve allowed himself a wry smile but he wasn't so upbeat. Although his plan to expose Ashurst was coming together and the revelations of drug use in football were about to come to glorious fruition and perhaps deliver the game back to the fans, the plan to mete out a less subtle justice to Samson and Lewis hadn't quite gone to plan. They were in custody admittedly, facing charges that would put them away for a long time, but there was no taste of sweet victory for him, it was more of a sour, bitter taste of defeat.

Kirsty, his *Guilty Tiger* had lied and cheated on him. He couldn't believe how foolish he'd been. She'd warned him – at the last moment she'd pleaded with him not to carry on with the plan, he knew something was wrong, he knew she was warning him off but his ignorance, quest for revenge and love for her blinded him and deafened him to her pleas.

Despite what Edwards had said he knew he had to see Kirsty – he found Edwards' card and phoned him.

'Steve Allen, Steve *fucking* Allen – you sure are full of surprises aren't you? What else have you got lined up? What else have you got in store for us eh?'

Steve was taken aback by his questions, by his tone. He thought after the previous night's revelations there wasn't much more to be said – he thought he might even be in a conciliatory mood.

'Sorry, what are you on about?'

'The fucking paper. That story of yours in the Daily *fucking* News. Well done squire, just well done – this could blow the case wide open – you might just have fucked it all up. Samson, Lewis, Ashurst – all their cronies, they might just all walk free because of this. You've jeopardised this whole case, just like Kirsty *fucking* Clifton before you, for fuck's sake keep your trunk out and let us deal with this.'

At this stage Steve couldn't care less, he was just concerned about seeing Kirsty, weeks of anger and bile rose up in him.

'Shut the fuck up. I don't give a flying fuck, no names have been mentioned – if they do it's fuck all to do with me. Nothing's been compromised so just get on with your fucking job and get those bastards locked up. I've put my life on the line all because British justice is a fucking joke – if you, the police and the courts did their job properly, British people could safely walk the streets and sleep secure in their beds at night and none of this would have happened in the first place.' He said it all in one breath, he inhaled deeply.

'Finished?'

'For now.'

'Well that was probably one of the shittiest pieces of defence I've heard in my life – I won't even dignify it with a response, you're bang out of order and you know it.' Edwards hesitated, then calmed before continuing...

'Look I know you're wound up, we all are, but we've been building up a case against Samson for a number of years and I don't intend to lose it now, and the others – well like I said they're a bonus, so back off now okay?'

'Okay, okay point taken – just nail the bastards eh?'

'We will, we will – now then, what did you phone me for?'

Steve had momentarily forgotten that he'd phoned Edwards. 'Oh yeah, yeah – look I know you said she doesn't want to see me, but please get a message to her. I must see here, please – I'm desperate.'

'I'll see what I can do, but no promises and squire... no more revelations in the press okay?'

Steve didn't dare respond.

CHAPTER TWENTY TWO

L EON awoke early on the last day of the cruise, eager to see the outline of Jamaica, the island of his birth as soon as he could. It looked magnificent as the sun came up and broke through the clouds and the dawn mist. The Azure Princess took an age to dock in Montego Bay, the huge liner finally came to rest at the dockside where the customary, if somewhat tiresome, sound of local musicians once again played some lame calypso beat.

He still felt uneasy, still felt he'd let his mates down, but he just couldn't do it – couldn't go through with the plan. He'd lain there in wait, the gun was loaded – all he had to do was shoot Earl Samson, it was that easy, just had to do the one thing for his mate Steve Allen, shoot that scumbag Samson. *Anyone else would be a bonus* said Steve. Vernon Lewis was a piece of shit, he was responsible for so much misery on the streets of Bristol, so much misery and pain that Leon had to deal with and clean up – *do him as well Leon, do him*.

But worst of all, Leon had volunteered. He'd been the one who had suggested it to Steve, he had nothing to live for, six months time he would be dead so what would it matter... but he hesitated, he bottled it – something troubled him. The way that Steve was determined to get Samson, it seemed so personal with him. He made it quite clear – *I want that black bas...* but Steve had quickly apologised and corrected himself, *I want that man dead,* he'd said – forgetting for just a second who he was talking to. That had unnerved Leon.

Leon had watched as the horror unfolded in front of him, watched as Steve was shot, watched as that meathead accomplice of Lewis had his head blown clean off – at that point he dropped the gun and ran...

Leon and Maggs had enjoyed the cruise, they enjoyed the 'little islands' as Leon insisted on calling them almost as much as the food and drink on board. The entertainment was a little embarrassing, especially the 'Caribbean night' with its cod reggae band performing *Yellow bird* and *The Banana Boat song* which sent Leon scuttling back to his cabin in search of his iPod and some Don Drummond. The lush verdant forests, the pure white sands and the azure seas captivated the two of them. The happy, friendly faces of the locals made them smile and made them realise what they had missed over the years. The Caribbean sun and fresh air had worked wonders on Leon, he felt alive for the first time in a number of years although the persistent cough told him otherwise.

They had checked in their luggage ready for their flight back to England not knowing what the future would bring for the two of them. They had a few hours to kill on the island before the flight, most of the other cruisers stayed on board, soaking up the last few hours of Caribbean sun before heading back to the dreary weather and their dreary jobs. Others headed to the 'hip strip' of Gloucester Avenue to listen to Bob Marley and spend their last bit of their holiday money on faux rasta hats and T-shirts promoting the merits of Red Stripe and ganja. Leon and Maggs wanted to do neither, they had had no reason to spend any more time in the sun and they had heard enough of *Two little birds* to last them a lifetime – however long that may be.

They had packed some clothes and their valuables in two overnight bags, not that they had much of real value – a few bits of Maggs's best jewellery plus some photos of friends back in Bristol and of the kids they had fostered over the years. Reluctantly Leon had left his vinyl collection at home, including the Don Drummond Memorial Album which he'd already told his wife to leave to Steve. There was not much more they needed, not where they were going.

'My name's Dillinger, where ya goin' my friends?' asked the middle-aged, rotund taxi driver as he peered over his Foster Grants.

'Alpha Boys School.'

'Where's that mon?'

'South Camp Road... Trenchtown, Kingston.'

'You pullin me pipe? Dat's over eighty miles away.'

'No mon I'm not having a laugh, then on to Accompong – you know where dat is?'

'Dat's in the mountains, St Elizabeth Parish... mon this going to cost you some serious money.'

Leon reached for his wallet, took out a roll of Jamaican dollars. 'This gonna be enough?'

Dillinger thumbed out the dollars, counted out twenty thousand. 'That should do it mon – plus me tip.'

'As long as you don't tell anyone about this okay?'

'H'ask me no questions...'

'I tell no lies.' Leon finished his sentence for him.

'H'ask me no questions,' Dillinger continued, 'I play music...'

He turned on his radio, the cool rhythms of Jackie Mittoo filled the cab. Dillinger looked at his passengers in his rear mirror. He coughed and looked slightly embarrassed, then held out his hand to Leon. 'My real name's Dennis – pleased to meet you.'

'Hi Dennis – we're Leon and Margaret.'

Dennis smiled at Margaret, 'you folks just sit back an henjoy the scenery.'

It took a couple of hours to get to the school, Dennis gave them a running commentary on the way and pointed out places of interest – places where he'd been, girlfriends he'd known. He constantly beeped his horn at pedestrians and other drivers – in turn they would look and wave, Leon wondered if there was anyone on the island Dennis didn't know.

Of course Dennis went to school with Bob Marley – he and Bob were close friends, Bob would play his tunes to Dennis and get his opinion of them. It turned out Dennis partly wrote *No woman, no cry* – Maggs was transfixed and captivated by the sweet-talking Dennis, Leon didn't believe a word he said, but nodded and smiled all the same – it made the journey go quicker.

They arrived at the school and Leon sought out one of the sisters. He didn't want to make a big deal of it, he just shook her hand and handed over the envelope containing the cheque. They met some of the budding musicians and took a few photos, although Leon wasn't sure why. Once finished they got back into the taxi and told Dennis to head for the Maroon town of Accompong.

Dennis asked if they wanted to visit the centre of Kingston on the way. They just had to go to the Bob Marley museum or perhaps to Brentford Road – home of Studio One, or Prince Buster's record shack on Charles Street. Leon was tempted but he was feeling tired and reluctantly declined. They headed for the mountains and Leon fell asleep to the sounds of Alton Ellis – Maggs holding his hand all the way.

They arrived late afternoon in the rush hour – a couple of trucks laden with local vegetables and fruit gingerly eased its way past their taxi, a donkey eyed them suspiciously as did a couple of locals as they sipped on their Red Stripes. Dennis helped them with their bags and gave both of them large manly hugs – he slapped Leon's back and gave Maggs a small peck on the cheek as he put their bags on to the dusty road.

'Whatever you two doin, may Jah be with you – respect, live life irie and you will lead a happy life.'

He gave Leon a parting handshake and got back in his Toyota, driving off in a cloud of dust he gave a final beep of his horn, Leon noticed a sticker on his bumper *'Jah is my co-pilot'*, Leon grinned and thought knowing Dennis, he probably was.

'Mon you look like you need a drink,' Leon's cousin Dexter 'Flashy' Campbell greeted them with a cold beer and a hug.

Leon wasn't sure what he appreciated the most, the greeting or the Red Stripe. He took a swig and savoured it, it tasted different – better, fresher than what he drunk at home.

Dexter smiled broadly, flashing his teeth, 'welcome home cuz.'

Leon's extended family laid on a big party, he and Maggs were tired but stayed up late. They ate callaloo, goat curry, dasheen, jerk pork and oxtail, they drunk Red Stripe and Appleton's and listened to aleke and reggae. They stayed up until the small hours, caught up on family gossip and recounted African folklore and the story of the Maroons and their rebellious fight with their slave masters that earned them their freedom in the mountains.

The two of them went to sleep to the sound of chirping crickets and awoke to the chatter of parakeets and braying donkeys – the smell of freshly cooked ackee and saltfish wafted around the house. Leon woke up happy for the first time in a number of years. He leant over and kissed Maggs on the forehead, she hardly stirred – he swore she'd been sleeping with a smile on her face. He got up, washed in a bowl and entered the kitchen where his Dexter's wife, Lois chided him playfully for staying in bed, he responded with a sheepish grin and an apologetic look.

He wandered past her and drifted haphazardly into the yard where he gave their dog 'Blue' a gentle pat, Blue responded with the most laid back bark Leon had ever heard in his life. Leon chuckled and took in the view of the lush Appleton Valley spreading out before him, he then shielded his eyes as he looked up at the clear blue sky. He felt Margaret's arms come around him and her lips gently kiss him on the back of his neck – he told her the tear running down his cheek was because the sun made him squint – she nodded sympathetically but she didn't believe him.

* * *

'Steve? Hi, um it's Simon Edwards, you ain't gonna believe this but Kirsty has been released... There's no way we could have prosecuted her, let alone get a conviction, think about it... If this went to court it would make huge headline news, at the moment Samson, Lewis or Ashurst's lawyers don't know about her involvement in any of this. They might have an inkling but they've got no evidence. If she gets convicted, well, you can imagine the rest, they would all walk free, anyway, um ... give me a call sometime eh?... Oh and one other thing, your mate Leon Campbell wasn't on the plane when it touched down at Gatwick – looks like he jumped ship.'

Steve played the voicemail back again just in case he hadn't heard it right, but he had. His face broke into a wry smile as he thought of Leon and Margaret – he knew they had done the right thing. He phoned Kirsty once more but knew she wouldn't answer. He then phoned JB.

'John mate, I need a lift – quick.'

'I'm in work. Can't Debbie help you out?'

'Oh yeah, "sorry Debs, can you give me a lift to Kirsty's flat, you know, the woman I've been in love with since I was fifteen, yeah that's right, where I've been staying and shagging for the last few weeks and who talked me into trying to kill some drug barons because they were involved in the death of my daughter, who in fact turns out not to be my daughter".'

'Give me ten minutes.'

True to his word JB turned up, this time in a battered old Renault van, the Range Rover had gone as at last he faced up to his financial problems. As JB dropped him off at Kirsty's apartment, he asked his old friend if he needed any help. Steve shook his head, he wasn't sure what he was going to say or do but he knew he had to do it alone.

'No it's alright mate, thanks for the lift – see you in the Moon Friday eh?'

JB nodded and gave Steve a clumsy hug. 'But no more putting the world to right yeah?'

They exchanged wan smiles and JB drove off.

Steve keyed in the code, he was thankful she hadn't changed it. The door opened and he entered. He took the lift to her apartment and rung the bell.

'Who is it?' She asked, but she knew who it was.

'It's Steve – let me in Kirsty.'

She realised she had no choice, if she hadn't opened the door he would have kicked it in. She opened it and waited for the chaos to begin...

'Steve, please don't do anything you'll regret.'

'What like slap you around a bit? Cos you sure as fuck deserve it. Anyway it's a bit fucking late to have regrets now.'

'I know, I know. Please, don't be mad with me. It just all got out of hand, I tried to tell you, honest, but it just all spiralled – spiralled out of control.'

'Don't be mad with you? If you were a bloke I'd break your fucking neck. You're telling me it spiralled out of control. But how could you, how could you lie to me that I had a daughter, a daughter that had died. What the fuck were you thinking of? How fucking sick are you?'

'I'm sorry, so sorry, I, I don't know what came over me. I was desperate, desperate to avenge her death, desperate to get back at Samson, for everything he'd done to me over the years and, and for what he'd done to Cherry...' She broke off, unaware if Steve knew the full story. The two of them slumped into chairs.

'I know what happened to Cherry – Edwards told me. I know the full story, everything. He's told me all of what you got up to in the past and what you've been up to lately, everything – I can't believe the lies Kirsty... never mind Cherry not being my daughter or that she was really a junkie, but the kids, our so-say grandchildren...' He hesitated, thinking of the lie after lie she'd told him.

'Then there's the gun that's been used in murders and in a way you're responsible – you're as guilty as whoever pulled the trigger. Those drugs you said Edwards had gotten for you, they were Cherry's. You really thought this through didn't you? This wasn't something you just made up as you went along, everything that came out of your mouth was lies – lies, lies, fucking lies, you're nothing but a fucking liar!'

He put his head in his hands and began to weep.

'You know Kirsty...' he stopped and wiped his eyes before continuing, 'you were that good a liar you even had *me* feeling guilty... I, I actually felt guilty that I might have passed on some hereditary heart disease to Kirsty, I thought her death was all my fault.' He stopped abruptly, he had no more to say – the tears flowed uncontrollably.

Kirsty could take no more.

'I'm sorry, sorry,' she blubbed through the tears that flowed mercilessly down her face. 'I'm so sorry – but, but it wasn't all lies Steve, I love you Steve Allen, always have done, always will. You meant, you mean everything to me. Cherry could have been your daughter, *should* have been your daughter – we could have had our house in Clifton, it could have been so different.'

'Yes, but it wasn't was it? You strung me along, strung all my mates along, fucked up our lives, fucked my best mate on the way...' she momentarily stopped crying and looked up at Steve.

'Oh you think I didn't know about that?' Steve continued. 'I told you I know everything, you fucked my best mate all those years ago, you fucked your colleagues, literally – yep, you fucked Simon Edwards, I know that too. Not to mention all your bosses – you're what you've always been Kirsty – nothing but a cheap fucking lying whore!'

Kirsty had no answers for Steve. She had nothing to say to him, nothing that would placate him, nothing that would fool him – everything he'd accused her of she couldn't deny. She was guilty, guilty as charged. She had no more lies and even fewer truths. She knew then there was no way back into the heart of the only man she had loved.

She wandered over to the jukebox and pressed the inevitable buttons – A One, the soaring strings came in just after the chip shop scratches...

'Well hello baby
Come sit down, make yourself comfortable
Tell me something, how long have we known each other?'

Steve put his head in his hands once more, his tears returned as he listened to the words of the song – their song.

He was vaguely aware that she'd brushed past him, he smelt her perfume as she momentarily stopped by the side of him – he felt a slight touch of her fingers across his forehead, he felt her tears fall onto the top of his head, run down into his fingers then onto his cheek and mingle with his own.

He heard the balcony doors open. He guessed she was studying the large houses of Clifton on the horizon, for a moment he thought she might make one last plea, one final attempt for them to get together and to realise her dream. He couldn't bring himself to look up at her.

Even when he heard the dull thud and the screams of the passers-by above the song, he didn't look up. He kept his face buried in his hands – through the tears he found himself mouthing the words to their song...

'According to the code of love, if there is such a code.
See love is a thing well, you know?
It's a bit like quicksand.
The more you wriggle the deeper you sink.
And when it hits you you've just got to fall.
That's why I do believe that I am guilty,
Guilty of loving you.'

CHAPTER TWENTY THREE

FORTUNATELY for Steve there were numerous witnesses to Kirsty falling from the balcony – and of course there was the all-seeing CCTV. When he eventually looked down at the horrific scene below him, he noticed how much she resembled that wayward seabird he'd seen just a a month or so ago.

Kirsty's arms were outstretched like the wings of the Petrel and her head was twisted to the same acute angle – her eyes stared back at him, wide, cold and dead. She died instantly of a broken neck, at least that was what the post mortem concluded, it was not possible to tell if she had died of a broken heart, although Steve had his suspicions. He'd been questioned about her death but it was just a formality. In reality her death made it easier for the police – there would now be no loose ends, no embarrassing questions, no calls for resignations of chief constables or of government ministers.

Samson and Lewis were at last brought to account for their crimes. The evidence against them was overwhelming and despite counter allegations by their lawyers of set ups and planting of evidence they were found guilty on all counts of conspiracy to commit murder and of the illegal importatation and distribution of Merck cocaine, which had now been reclassified as a Class A drug. Scientists meanwhile were well on their way to making the drug identifiable in the bloodstream, ensuring its appeal to sportsmen would be on the wane, until the next *Uber coca* appeared that is.

The police were also looking into a multitude of illegal activities that the two were involved in, including murder and extortion cases going back many decades – it was unlikely that they would ever be free men again.

Tyrrel L'estrange received a life sentence for the attempted murder of Augustus Lee and the murder of nineteen-year old Ryan Calloway – the unfortunate waiter in the Avon Gorge hotel who just happened to be in the wrong place at the wrong time. The prosecution did not accept L'estrange's plea of manslaughter – *'I only gave him a slap'* he said. It fell on deaf ears, L'estrange giving someone a slap was akin to a normally built person hitting someone with a sledgehammer.

Trevor 'Teets' Thomas, after his release from hospital was charged with numerous offences including attempted murder and illegal possession of firearms and controlled drugs – he was sent to prison for fifteen years.

Toby Ashurst despite his protestations and threats of 'having friends in high places' was eventually charged and found guilty of conspiracy to import and supply Merck cocaine – he was jailed for ten years. His company crashed and burned as did his parents Lord and Lady Ashurst. Although they were acquitted of aiding and abetting their son in drug trafficking there was enough guilt by association to ensure the local hunt would black ball them for the foreseeable future.

Simon Edwards tried but ultimately failed to bring about any charges relating to the untimely death of Cherry Clifton – her death stayed on record as 'death by misadventure due to illicit drug use'.

As Barry Mason had predicted the Premiership went into meltdown as sponsors, backers and sugar daddies pulled out. The great pariahs of the beautiful game – the football agents were vilified, crucified and eventually made *persona non grata* with the players they used to represent faring no better – contracts were reviewed and cancelled while salaries were slashed and brought in line with everyone else's – *'We're all in this together'* became the new mantra.

Once again footballers played football with passion, loyalty and commitment and more importantly for the love of the game, not for the money.

The goose that laid the golden egg stopped laying as TV companies renegotiated and pulled out of deals. Foreign owners put their clubs up for sale and scuttled back across the Atlantic or to the Middle East. Season ticket prices subsequently tumbled and consequently sales soared. Replica shirts *without* sponsor's logos emblazed across them made records sales, stadiums reverted back to their original names and clubs put 'football' back onto their club badges.

Football dispensed with the prawn sandwiches, reinstated meat pies and eventually reclaimed its soul, it became the game of the working class once more. Football had well and truly come home.

* * *

Steve moved back in with Debbie, went back to the house he called home and back to the woman he called his wife. Prince and Buster went back to harrassing squirrels and Harry went back to being Harry – Steve at last spent more time with him, they talked, talked properly for the first time in their life. There was perhaps hope, hope that Harry would get his life on track and get off the drugs – but they had all thought that before.

He continued taken his Statins and his Angiotensin-Converting Enzyme inhibitors although he stopped take anti-depressants and refrained from snorting cocaine.

Mike Cribb was found guilty of being in possession of over two thousand pornographic images and videos of children as well as gross indecency and child molestation – he was sentenced to fifteen years in prison. The remaining members of The Big Five carried on meeting at the Moon under Water every Friday evening – they vowed never to try and put the world to right again.

* * *

Steve's was the only white face at Leon's funeral in the tiny parish church of St Elizabeth's. He was given a warm welcome by Leon's family and especially by Margaret who greeted him with a hug and a kiss to the cheek, the other mourners nodded respectfully and thanked Steve for making the long trip.

As the Nyabinghi drummers started their mournful beat Steve found it difficult to suppress the tears from flowing. By the time Bob Marley's *Redemption Song* started up there was no stopping him and the tears flowed relentlessly. He spilt tears not just for Leon but also for Kirsty – and not least for himself. He hoped and prayed that finally he too, had achieved redemption.

In the course of time Avon and Somerset police seized assets from the estate of Vernon Lewis while the Met did the same with Earl Samson's ill gotten gains. Some of the money from the sale of the assets, including the yacht in Poole Harbour and the villa in Spain found its way back into the public coffers under the 'community cashback scheme' and eventually funded the building of a new community and drug rehabilitation centre in St Pauls.

Margaret Campbell had a smile as wide as the brim of her hat when she unveiled the plaque with *'The Leon Campbell Centre'* engraved on it.

* * *

He spotted the flatbed lorry parked illegally on double yellow lines – the St George's cross flag with 'BCFC' emblazoned across it in the rear window first caught his eye. He then spotted the company logo on the doors – *Hook & Eye scaffolding*. He parked up just a little past the lorry and took his baseball bat out of the boot. The first blow did more harm to his still aching shoulder than it did to the scaffolding – it also brought cries of dismay from above.

'Oi, what the fuck you doing?'

Steve peered up and spotted the scaffolder – it was definitely him. He knew it was all along but it was reassuring for him to confirm it. Steve swung another blow at the corner piece – it moved some more, there was a creaking and a scraping noise above him.

'You! You fucking arsehole. Are you trying to fucking kill me?' The scaffolder screamed with a sound of terror in his voice.

Steve didn't need to reply. He always believed that actions spoke louder than words – at times in his past that had got him in trouble. The third blow skewed the scaffolding pole to an absurd angle, some of the planks started falling above him, the creaking became louder – almost animal like.

The fourth blow did more damage than the three preceding it – the pole scrapped across the pavement in a shower of sparks then eventually uprooted completely. The creaking became a thunderous crash – the scaffolding, planks and brackets tumbled to the pavement in one dusty, noisy heap. The lone scaffolder fell – bouncing and tumbling as one with the dislodged metalwork. Steve heard his screams of pain as he got back in his Audi and slowly drove off.

Steve read the report later in the *Evening Post* – it stated that the scaffolder had broken an arm as well as both legs and sustained severe internal injuries – he was lucky to be alive. Police were appealing for witnesses and following up leads that a well-built, middle-aged male wearing a red jacket and a broad smile had been spotted leaving the scene.

He turned the pages and studied the ads for Harley Davidsons, a wry smile creased his face for a second before he put the paper down and picked up the folder that Kirsty had given him – Steve Allen never did like to leave a job unfinished.

Lyrics to 'Tote End boys' – courtesy of Ben Gunstone:

The flowers are dead and gone behind the Eastville goals.
The traffic's a little quieter on the Stapleton Road.
Ghosts of Bamford and Barrett still, shadows on a drizzled field.
And can you hear the Tote End Boys sing?
I can hear everything.
When the north Bristol chorus rings,
I can hear everything.

The flowers are shopping malls on the Eastville goals.
I was blue and white quarters from the age of three years old.
The Francis golden age, we paid that player's wage.
And can you hear the Tote End Boys sing?
I can hear everything.
When the north Bristol chorus rings,
I can hear everything

Bradford, Meyer, Biggs. The seventh of January, 1956
And can you hear the Tote End Boys sing?
I can hear everything.
When the north Bristol chorus rings,
I can hear everything.
And can you hear the Tote End Boys sing?
Irene, I'll see you in my dreams.
And can you hear the Tote End Boys sing?
I can hear everything.

The flowers are dead and gone behind the Eastville goals.

www.youtube.com/watch?v=awmW-7GvTYo

Thanks to Karen Knott of *Midlife Matters* for permitting me to reproduce her Mid Life Crisis article in Chapter One.

Guilty Tiger is Chris Brown's first novel, his autobiography *Bovver* was published in 2001 and subsequently republished with new material and retitled as *Booted and Suited* in 2009.

He has been married to Carole for thirty years and they have two children – Daniel and Chloe. He is as fanatical about ska, reggae, soul, funk and punk as he is about football, or more correctly Bristol Rovers who he has followed since the sixties.

He detests the Premiership, not the clubs themselves just the Premiership and prays for the return of the soul of the beautiful game to its rightful owners – the fans.

Lightning Source UK Ltd.
Milton Keynes UK
UKOW030701231112

202659UK00001B/4/P